THE BODLEY HEAD

SCOTT FITZGERALD

VOLUME I

THE BODLEY HEAD

SCOTT FITZGERALD

WITH AN INTRODUCTION BY

J. B. PRIESTLEY

VOLUME I

THE GREAT GATSBY

THE LAST TYCOON

THE BODLEY HEAD

LONDON

Introduction © The Bodley Head 1958
Made and printed in Great Britain for
THE BODLEY HEAD LTD
10 Earlham Street, London, W C 2
by William Clowes and Sons Ltd, Beccles
Set in Monotype Plantin
First published 1958
Reprinted 1960
Revised edition 1963
Reprinted 1966

CONTENTS

Introduction

SCOTT FITZGERALD wrote in one of his notebooks: 'There never was a good biography of a good novelist. There couldn't be. He's too many people if he's any good.' (But he himself came out better than most. His biography by Arthur Mizener, called *The Far Side of Paradise*, is not only an excellent record of his life and work but also a book that can be enjoyed for its own sake.) Certainly Fitzgerald was anything but an integrated personality. His was a richly confused character, in which, as I shall try to show, at least two sharply contrasting and opposed strains can be discovered. Everything about his character and career, his name and fame, tends to be odd and unexpected, paradoxical, bizarre. He was thought to be the trumpeter of the Jazz Age and yet in fact never identified himself with it and was deeply hostile to many of its manifestations. At the very time when he was accepted as a symbol of youthful sophistication, he was essentially unsophisticated, naïve and romantic, a provincial newly arrived in New York. He was big hot news in his and the century's early 'twenties, and was largely forgotten, often thought to be dead, by the middle 'thirties. By the time he had been dismissed as a drunken playboy, the worst type of irresponsible expatriate, he was in fact bringing to his work an unusually pure and single-minded devotion and shouldering appalling burdens. He was considered an alcoholic hack by writers who never possessed and could hardly begin to understand his fine artistic conscience, his sense of obligation to his talent. He was a wild drunk who yet never ceased to regard himself and his doings with astonishing detachment and truthfulness. He never learnt to spell properly yet achieved what is perhaps the best prose style of any American novelist of his generation. When he died in 1940 all his books were out

7

of print and in many of the obituaries his life was hastily dismissed as a cautionary tale, yet within a few years his reputation and his sales had shot up like rockets, soon reaching a height they had never known in his lifetime. While he still drew breath, he had nothing: once in the grave he had everything. And if no rumour of his ultimate triumph has ever reached his spirit, if nothing could be known to him after his unhappy time ran out, then there is indeed no pretence of justice in this universe.

Francis Scott Key Fitzgerald was born in 1896 at St. Paul, Minnesota. His father, the pattern of 'a Southern gentleman' (a pattern that imposed itself to some extent on Fitzgerald), was an affectionate but ineffectual man, whose attempts to earn a living left his family feeling insecure in every sense of the term. His mother was a rather eccentric woman, of Irish extraction, who determinedly spoilt the handsome lively boy, possibly, as he believed, creating difficulties for him in later life. He was educated at a Catholic boarding school and then went to Princeton, where an illness, midway in his career there, robbed him, to his lasting regret, of some social triumphs. After America entered the war, he joined the army, took a commission, was aide de camp to a general but never went overseas, again to his lasting regret. He fell in love with Zelda Sayre, the daughter of a judge and very much the dashing young Southern belle, and married her after he had successfully published his first novel, *This Side of Paradise*. They were passionately devoted to each other but shared too many weaknesses to create a solidly rewarding relationship; she balanced him nowhere and was jealous of his work, which she constantly endangered by her restlessness, extravagance, and what appeared at first to be determined eccentricity. Later during the 'thirties, after a heartbreaking series of breakdowns and partial recoveries, she was found to be suffering from schizophrenia. Now far from being the advocate of sexual licence he was often supposed to be, Fitzgerald was in fact old-fashioned and almost prudish in his ideas about sex (his letters to his daughter are nearly those of a heavy Victorian father), and there can be no doubt that for his complete emotional commitment to Zelda he paid an appalling price. Another kind of woman, as he discovered when it was all too late, might from the first have given him the security and tranquillity that the artist in him, if not always the man, needed so desperately.

In the 'twenties the Fitzgeralds divided their time, hardly ever wisely, between New York or somewhere not too far away (see *The Great Gatsby* for some glimpses of this life) and Paris and the Riviera (see *Tender Is The Night*). It was a time of endless parties and heavy drinking, and unfortunately Fitzgerald at this time was anything but a quiet drunk and was always apt to do something senseless or ugly, too often first embarrassing and then losing his friends. This gave him the reputation of being on a permanent 'binge' when later, in the 'thirties, he often made heroic sacrifices to keep sober, live plainly and away from people, and try to pay his debts. He passed these years mostly in or near Baltimore, with Zelda spending more and more time in mental hospitals, and then in Hollywood (see *The Last Tycoon* and *Crazy Sunday*) where he died, of a heart attack, in 1940. *The Crack-Up* is a disturbing self-portrait of the writer in his fortieth year. A more elaborate portrait of him, a year or two later, may be found in a strongly-autobiographical novel, *The Disenchanted*, by Budd Schulberg, who had been sent on a script assignment from Hollywood to the Dartmouth Winter Carnival with Fitzgerald as his collaborator and travelling companion. Fitzgerald had been on the wagon and was in poor health; he drank some champagne on the plane going East and then there followed a huge nightmare binge when he was drunk and half delirious for days on end, disgracing himself at the college, getting himself and poor Schulberg fired from the film and sent back to New York, where they arrived looking so unkempt and desperate that no hotel would accept them, and Fitzgerald had to be taken to hospital. 'You know,' he said at this time to Schulberg, almost as if he were already the pale ghost his appearance suggested,

'I used to have a beautiful talent once, Baby. It used to be a wonderful feeling to know it was there. . . .'

That was no drunken boast. A beautiful talent is exactly what he had and what shines undimmed through all his best work. Nor was it ever ruined, in quality if not in quantity, as his life was. In a miraculous fashion, against frightening odds, the writer in him, as distinct from the self-destructive man, was preserved to the very end. Although it was left not only unfinished but never finally revised (Fitzgerald always revised his novels with unusual care), *The Last Tycoon* contains some of his finest writing and, if he had lived to finish it, would have been his masterpiece. But his unique talent is very difficult to describe, classify, assess. As so many good American critics have proved to us, Fitzgerald is an elusive subject for just criticism. Too many things, including his own legend, get in the way. So it is possible that our distance from that legend may help us here.

As I suggested earlier, there can be discovered in him at least two sharply contrasting and opposed strains, and it may well be that from the tension between them, ultimately destructive to him as a man, came the unique character and enduring creative force of the writer. The first strain, obvious and triumphant in his early work, belonged to a romantic adolescent who bounced through Princeton and the war (without ever really finding the war, to his regret) into the new freedom and the apparently limitless opportunities of the early 'twenties. This is the Fitzgerald, himself socially insecure, who was fascinated by the rich, by the New York of the Jazz Age, by the Paris and the Riviera of the rollicking expatriates, by a long dream of golden girls and heroes and wits and extravagant parties that went on for ever. This was the good-looking high-spirited boy suddenly let loose, into a dazzling world, from a narrow life in the Middle-West. His education was sketchy, his tastes often doubtful, his values frequently shoddy; what was vital in him was an immense innocent eagerness, a romantic desire and capacity for rich experience.

It led him to play the fool and at times, when he suddenly saw the bright surface cracking and all the drink in him turned sour, to seem worse than a fool, making his protest against sudden disenchantment by doing something violent and ugly. This explains the conduct that cost him so many friends; it is not uncommon among hard-drinking young Americans, who, having apparently burst their bonds, then expect too much too soon, cannot fall back on self-discipline at the moment of disillusion, and react too violently against their disappointment. It was this side of his nature that took charge of Fitzgerald's life during the 'twenties. Its final emotional bankruptcy is movingly described in *The Crack-Up*. Fitzgerald wrote and talked as if he believed that each of us has a given amount of *libido*, so much zest and capacity for feeling like capital in the bank, and that when we have spent it we are done for. But of course mature and reasonable integrated persons are not in this predicament; they have access to resources that renew their zest; they keep the gold of the psyche in brisk circulation; their feelings and mental energy are not being sucked down and drained away by some deep hidden conflict, some endless war in the dark of the mind.

It is this romantic adolescent in Fitzgerald who is responsible for his pursuit of 'glamour'. In his earliest work he is in full cry after it, and to the very last we can still catch faraway echoes of the hunting horns. This explains the initial fascination the very rich had for him. He felt they were free of all those pressures and limitations that are the enemies of glamour. He was intensely aware, as only the adolescent mind can be, of their strangeness, their mystery; and glamour is the bright aspect, the alluring promise, of the unknown. Of course we cannot live with it but can only follow the glimmer of its retreating edge; which is what Fitzgerald did in his essentially American and ironic Odyssey of the 'twenties, an Odyssey he finally completed ten years later, with the last flicker of irony, in the great dream factory of Hollywood. It is this side of his nature and work that is best known; indeed, too many critics have been content to interpret him almost entirely in terms of it. And this will not do. In spite of many setbacks, when the man might be in retreat, the artist in him advanced, matured, as we shall see. But this adolescent pursuit of the will o' the wisp of glamour, supported as it was by a superb literary talent, expressed in a manner and style marvellously flexible, graceful, appealing, gives his work to the end a curious and characteristic sheen and glitter, dazzling careless readers so that they fail to perceive its increasing depth.

This brings us to the second strain in him, to the man behind the beglamoured adolescent, the one who began, if unsteadily, to grow, to take command, while the romantic boy, facing emotional bankruptcy, unable to renew his early zest, dwindled and withered. This was the Fitzgerald who could write in his note book—and mean it, for all his antics —*I do not lie to myself*. The golden boy was everybody's fool; this man was nobody's. He was as detached and cool as the other was hot, messy, involved. It is he who endlessly observes and records, who has the wonderful sense of time and place, who gives to the action of his novels at their best a surprising depth, a rich and enduring symbolical value. (Again at their best, these novels might be said to have the speed and grace of lightweights and the punching power of heavyweights. When the punches don't 'connect' it is because the reader has not stayed still long enough to be hit.) He was, this hidden man, this secondary self below the dazzling but cracking surface, removed from all the drunken pranks and shifts and fresh starts and grotesque failures, not only a truly dedicated writer but one of the most deeply dedicated writers in the America of his time. When the explosions came—and they were always blowing up in somebody's face—it was because the tension could not be maintained, the tension between the large loose excitable adolescent and this small but compact and disciplined man behind him, the diminutive artist-priest at the back of his mind. The wonder is that he was there at all, this artist-priest, not that he was diminutive and found it hard to grow (though he did), for what was there in the uproarious and rootless life of the American 'twenties to nourish him? The wonder is that so horribly handicapped he did what he did, sold good short stories as well as bad ones to the popular magazines, and somehow at last wrote *Tender Is The Night* and what we have—and it is something to be thankful for—of *The Last Tycoon*. I do not include *The Great Gatsby* here, not because it lacks the merit, for in many respects it is Fitzgerald's finest achievement, succeeding better as a whole than anything else he wrote, but because it seems to me to represent the one point of balance between these two conflicting strains in him, the brief period when they were able to collaborate successfully. It is in the later work that the dedicated writer, the tiny but indestructible artist-priest, takes charge, slowly and painfully (so much energy having gone), with an obvious loss of quantity but a clear gain in quality.

There is a place here for a note on Fitzgerald and sex. It is one of the ironies, part of the paradox, of his legend that he should be assumed to be a novelist of passionate and even wild sexuality. He was nothing of the kind, neither in life nor in letters. And, remembering the two different strains in him, we can easily see why this should be so. The adolescent in pursuit of glamour has not yet arrived at sex, which is somewhere, as a reality, beyond the summer lightning, the rainbow, the moonlight, the lighted hall where the band is playing. The man behind, the dedicated writer, the artist-priest, might be said to be out on the other side of sex, not ignoring it nor denying it but refusing to stay engrossed by it, regarding it as one manifestation out of many, one bright or fading thread in the pattern. And again, in *The Great Gatsby*, these two attitudes are neatly balanced, so that the sexual life is there but never immediately, always in front of us or behind us; while *Tender Is The Night* begins with sex and then moves through it to something else; and *The Last Tycoon*, though it contains a kind of love story, is essentially a novel about something else. But in truth all his best writing is about something else, something a long way removed from his legend and popular reputation : it is about 'wanting better bread than can be made out of wheat' and then finding each loaf rotten with decay, about the corruption beneath the glittering surface, about the soul of man in a society bent on dissolution. In his own fashion this notorious playboy of the Jazz Age was one of our religious writers. And unlike most religious writers he happened to have 'a beautiful talent'.

It includes, this talent, an unusually sharp eye for a character and a scene, a marvellous ear for dialogue, one of the finest prose styles in contemporary fiction, an uncommonly acute sense of time and place, and an unforced and easy and very economical power of what I can only call symbolic effect. As an example of this last, take a tiny scene from *The Last Tycoon* when Stahr, the head of a great film studio, probably the most powerful man in Hollywood, a man who has formed the tastes and coloured the dreams of millions, is on the beach at night, idly watching the running of the fish, and has an apparently casual conversation with a negro. Learning that Stahr 'works for the pictures', the negro says that he never goes to the movies and does not allow his children to go, thereby later compelling Stahr to make huge and difficult changes in a whole elaborate programme of production. Over and over again, without forcing anything, never losing his ease of narrative, Fitzgerald produces this effect. And his notes and revisions, especially for *The Last Tycoon*, show how true and delicate his feeling was for a scene, a character, a situation, a moment, even right to the end, when he was so weary, so frail, that he seemed like a ghost. But of course although he had so much, he hadn't everything. He could plan a scene with exquisite care, but except in *The Great Gatsby*, when everything went right, his general construction, his architecture in narrative, was curiously faulty. Thus, even in *The Last Tycoon*, the novel of his final maturity, his device of using Cecilia Brady as a narrator seems to me quite wrong and would, I suspect, have had to be abandoned if he had lived to finish the work. Another weakness is a lack of thickness, solidity, in what might be called the middle distance of his panorama of narrative. Every surface detail is right, and the depths are wonderfully suggested, but there is an uneasy suggestion of emptiness between them, so that when we are not completely captivated or moved we begin to feel the story he is telling is too thin, too brittle. It is as if Fitzgerald, for all his sense of time and place, did not know quite enough about the world and the persons in it he is describing. Gatsby will pass, because he has to be mysterious, but I for one never quite believe in Dick Diver, in *Tender Is The Night*, either as a social charmer or as an earnest young psychiatrist; and even Stahr, though a triumph in so many ways, a real person and not merely a central figure in a fascinating scene, never quite imposes himself on me as a man still in his early thirties who has been able to fight his way to the top in Hollywood, even though we see him convincingly in action and are told that his vitality is now ebbing out. Sometimes we feel, for all the clean sharp detail, there is too much ghostly distance between that inner man, the enduring dedicated writer, and the crowded noisy world he is trying to re-create for us. All these are serious weaknesses but the beautiful talent shines through them. This is a very good novelist indeed.

I hope that this first volume of *The Bodley Head Scott Fitzgerald* will please his many admirers, and that it will attract a great many other readers not yet acquainted with him, for it contains the two works which I believe to be his finest and those most likely to endure. *The Great Gatsby*, his most perfectly planned and rounded piece of fiction, is one of the key novels of the 'twenties, and perhaps his masterpiece. *The Last Tycoon* contains his most mature writing and promised to be his supreme achievement. Its central character, Munroe Stahr, is undoubtedly Fitzgerald's finest individual creation, and the Hollywood of the middle 'thirties that the novel reveals to us, from the inside, is not the usual gaudy and unreal backcloth of film fiction but the real place as some of us remember it. And for my part I would rather have written this unfinished novel than the total works of some widely-admired American novelists.

J. B. PRIESTLEY

THE
GREAT GATSBY
[1925]

Then wear the gold hat, if that will move her;
If you can bounce high, bounce for her too,
Till she cry 'Lover, gold-hatted, high-bouncing lover,
I must have you!'

Thomas Parke D'Invilliers

THE
GREAT GATSBY

CHAPTER I

IN MY YOUNGER and more vulnerable years my father gave me some advice that I've been turning over in my mind ever since.

'Whenever you feel like criticizing anyone,' he told me, 'just remember that all the people in this world haven't had the advantages that you've had.'

He didn't say any more, but we've always been unusually communicative in a reserved way, and I understood that he meant a great deal more than that. In consequence, I'm inclined to reserve all judgments, a habit that has opened up many curious natures to me and also made me the victim of not a few veteran bores. The abnormal mind is quick to detect and attach itself to this quality when it appears in a normal person, and so it came about that in college I was unjustly accused of being a politician, because I was privy to the secret griefs of wild, unknown men. Most of the confidences were unsought—frequently I have feigned sleep, preoccupation, or a hostile levity when I realized by some unmistakable sign that an intimate revelation was quivering on the horizon; for the intimate revelations of young men, or at least the terms in which they express them, are usually plagiaristic and marred by obvious suppressions. Reserving judgments is a matter of infinite hope. I am still a little afraid of missing something if I forget that, as my father snobbishly suggested, and I snobbishly repeat, a sense of the fundamental decencies is parcelled out unequally at birth.

And, after boasting this way of my tolerance, I come to

the admission that it has a limit. Conduct may be founded
on the hard rock or the wet marshes, but after a certain
point I don't care what it's founded on. When I came back
from the East last autumn I felt that I wanted the world to
be in uniform and at a sort of moral attention for ever; I
wanted no more riotous excursions with privileged glimpses
into the human heart. Only Gatsby, the man who gives his
name to this book, was exempt from my reaction—Gatsby,
who represented everything for which I have an unaffected
scorn. If personality is an unbroken series of successful
gestures, then there was something gorgeous about him,
some heightened sensitivity to the promises of life, as if he
were related to one of those intricate machines that register
earthquakes ten thousand miles away. This responsiveness
had nothing to do with that flabby impressionability which
is dignified under the name of the 'creative temperament'—
it was an extraordinary gift for hope, a romantic readiness
such as I have never found in any other person and which it
is not likely I shall ever find again. No—Gatsby turned out
all right at the end; it is what preyed on Gatsby, what foul
dust floated in the wake of his dreams that temporarily
closed out my interest in the abortive sorrows and short-
winded elations of men.

My family have been prominent, well-to-do people in
this Middle Western city for three generations. The Carra-
ways are something of a clan, and we have a tradition that
we're descended from the Dukes of Buccleuch, but the
actual founder of my line was my grandfather's brother,
who came here in fifty-one, sent a substitute to the Civil
War, and started the wholesale hardware business that my
father carries on to-day.

I never saw this great-uncle, but I'm supposed to look
like him—with special reference to the rather hard-boiled
painting that hangs in father's office. I graduated from New
Haven in 1915, just a quarter of a century after my father,
and a little later I participated in that delayed Teutonic
migration known as the Great War. I enjoyed the counter-

raid so thoroughly that I came back restless. Instead of being the warm centre of the world, the Middle West now seemed like the ragged edge of the universe—so I decided to go East and learn the bond business. Everybody I knew was in the bond business, so I supposed it could support one more single man. All my aunts and uncles talked it over as if they were choosing a prep school for me, and finally said, 'Why—ye-es,' with very grave, hesitant faces. Father agreed to finance me for a year, and after various delays I came East, permanently, I thought, in the spring of twenty-two.

The practical thing was to find rooms in the city, but it was a warm season, and I had just left a country of wide lawns and friendly trees, so when a young man at the office suggested that we take a house together in a commuting town, it sounded like a great idea. He found the house, a weatherbeaten cardboard bungalow at eighty a month, but at the last minute the firm ordered him to Washington, and I went out to the country alone. I had a dog—at least I had him for a few days until he ran away—and an old Dodge and a Finnish woman, who made my bed and cooked breakfast and muttered Finnish wisdom to herself over the electric stove.

It was lonely for a day or so until one morning some man, more recently arrived than I, stopped me on the road.

'How do you get to West Egg village?' he asked helplessly.

I told him. And as I walked on I was lonely no longer. I was a guide, a pathfinder, an original settler. He had casually conferred on me the freedom of the neighbourhood.

And so with the sunshine and the great bursts of leaves growing on the trees, just as things grow in fast movies, I had that familiar conviction that life was beginning over again with the summer.

There was so much to read, for one thing, and so much fine health to be pulled down out of the young breath-giving air. I bought a dozen volumes on banking and credit and investment securities, and they stood on my shelf in red and gold like new money from the mint, promising to unfold the shining secrets that only Midas and Morgan and Mæcenas knew. And I had the high intention of reading many other books besides. I was rather literary in college— one year I wrote a series of very solemn and obvious editorials for the *Yale News*—and now I was going to bring back all such things into my life and become again that most limited of all specialists, the 'well-rounded man.' This isn't just an epigram—life is much more succesfully looked at from a single window, after all.

It was a matter of chance that I should have rented a house in one of the strangest communities in North America. It was on that slender riotous island which extends itself due east of New York—and where there are, among other natural curiosities, two unusual formations of land. Twenty miles from the city a pair of enormous eggs, identical in contour and separated only by a courtesy bay, jut out into the most domesticated body of salt water in the Western hemisphere, the great wet barnyard of Long Island Sound. They are not perfect ovals—like the egg in the Columbus story, they are both crushed flat at the contact end—but their physical resemblance must be a source of perpetual wonder to the gulls that fly overhead. To the wingless a more interesting phenomenon is their dissimilarity in every particular except shape and size.

I lived at West Egg, the—well, the less fashionable of the two, though this is a most superficial tag to express the bizarre and not a little sinister contrast between them. My house was at the very tip of the egg, only fifty yards from the Sound, and squeezed between two huge places that rented for twelve or fifteen thousand a season. The one on my right was a colossal affair by any standard—it was a factual imitation of some Hôtel de Ville in Normandy, with a tower on one side, spanking new under a thin beard of raw ivy, and a marble swimming pool, and more than forty acres of lawn and garden. It was Gatsby's mansion. Or, rather, as I didn't know Mr. Gatsby, it was a mansion, inhabited by a gentleman of that name. My own house was an eyesore, but

it was a small eyesore, and it had been overlooked, so I had
a view of the water, a partial view of my neighbour's lawn,
and the consoling proximity of millionaires—all for eighty
dollars a month.

Across the courtesy bay the white palaces of fashionable
East Egg glittered along the water, and the history of the
summer really begins on the evening I drove over there to
have dinner with the Tom Buchanans. Daisy was my second
cousin once removed, and I'd known Tom in college. And
just after the war I spent two days with them in Chicago.

Her husband, among various physical accomplishments,
had been one of the most powerful ends that ever played
football at New Haven—a national figure in a way, one of
those men who reach such an acute limited excellence at
twenty-one that everything afterwards savours of anti-
climax. His family were enormously wealthy—even in
college his freedom with money was a matter for reproach
—but now he'd left Chicago and come East in a fashion that
rather took your breath away; for instance, he'd brought
down a string of polo ponies from Lake Forest. It was hard to
realize that a man in my own generation was wealthy enough
to do that.

Why they came East I don't know. They had spent a year
in France for no particular reason, and then drifted here and
there unrestfully wherever people played polo and were
rich together. This was a permanent move, said Daisy over
the telephone, but I didn't believe it—I had no sight into
Daisy's heart, but I felt that Tom would drift on for ever
seeking, a little wistfully, for the dramatic turbulence of
some irrecoverable football game.

And so it happened that on a warm windy evening I drove
over to East Egg to see two old friends whom I scarcely
knew at all. Their house was even more elaborate than I
expected, a cheerful red-and-white Georgian Colonial
mansion, overlooking the bay. The lawn started at the
beach and ran towards the front door for a quarter of a mile,
jumping over sun-dials and brick walks and burning
gardens—finally when it reached the house drifting up the

side in bright vines as though from the momentum of its run. The front was broken by a line of French windows, glowing now with reflected gold and wide open to the warm windy afternoon, and Tom Buchanan in riding clothes was standing with his legs apart on the front porch.

He had changed since his New Haven years. Now he was a sturdy straw-haired man of thirty with a rather hard mouth and a supercilious manner. Two shining arrogant eyes had established dominance over his face and gave him the appearance of always leaning aggressively forward. Not even the effeminate swank of his riding clothes could hide the enormous power of that body—he seemed to fill those glistening boots until he strained the top lacing, and you could see a great pack of muscle shifting when his shoulder moved under his thin coat. It was a body capable of enormous leverage—a cruel body.

His speaking voice, a gruff husky tenor, added to the impression of fractiousness he conveyed. There was a touch of paternal contempt in it, even towards people he liked—and there were men at New Haven who had hated his guts.

'Now, don't think my opinion on these matters is final,' he seemed to say, 'just because I'm stronger and more of a man than you are.' We were in the same senior society, and while we were never intimate I always had the impression that he approved of me and wanted me to like him with some harsh, defiant wistfulness of his own.

We talked for a few minutes on the sunny porch.

'I've got a nice place here,' he said, his eyes flashing about restlessly.

Turning me around by one arm, he moved a broad flat hand along the front vista, including in its sweep a sunken Italian garden, a half acre of deep, pungent roses, and a snub-nosed motor-boat that bumped the tide offshore.

'It belonged to Demaine, the oil man.' He turned me around again, politely and abruptly. 'We'll go inside.'

We walked through a high hallway into a bright rose-coloured space, fragilely bound into the house by French windows at either end. The windows were ajar and gleaming

white against the fresh grass outside that seemed to grow a
little way into the house. A breeze blew through the room,
blew curtains in at one end and out the other like pale flags,
twisting them up towards the frosted wedding-cake of the
ceiling, and then rippled over the wine-coloured rug,
making a shadow on it as wind does on the sea.

The only completely stationary object in the room was an
enormous couch on which two young women were buoyed
up as though upon an anchored balloon. They were both in
white, and their dresses were rippling and fluttering as if
they had just been blown back in after a short flight around
the house. I must have stood for a few moments listening
to the whip and snap of the curtains and the groan of a
picture on the wall. Then there was a boom as Tom
Buchanan shut the rear windows and the caught wind died
out about the room, and the curtains and the rugs and the
two young women ballooned slowly to the floor.

The younger of the two was a stranger to me. She was
extended full length at her end of the divan, completely
motionless, and with her chin raised a little, as if she were
balancing something on it which was quite likely to fall. If
she saw me out of the corner of her eyes she gave no hint of
it—indeed, I was almost surprised into murmuring an
apology for having disturbed her by coming in.

The other girl, Daisy, made an attempt to rise—she
leaned slightly forward with a conscientious expression—
then she laughed, an absurd charming little laugh, and I
laughed too and came forward into the room.

'I'm p-paralyzed with happiness.'

She laughed again, as if she said something very witty,
and held my hand for a moment, looking up into my face,
promising that there was no one in the world she so much
wanted to see. That was a way she had. She hinted in a
murmur that the surname of the balancing girl was Baker.
(I've heard it said that Daisy's murmur was only to make
people lean towards her; an irrelevant criticism that made it
no less charming.)

At any rate, Miss Baker's lips fluttered, she nodded at me

almost imperceptibly, and then quickly tipped her head back again—the object she was balancing had obviously tottered a little and given her something of a fright. Again a sort of apology arose to my lips. Almost any exhibition of complete self-sufficiency draws a stunned tribute from me.

I looked back at my cousin, who began to ask me questions in her low, thrilling voice. It was the kind of voice that the ear follows up and down, as if each speech is an arrangement of notes that will never be played again. Her face was sad and lovely with bright things in it, bright eyes and a bright passionate mouth, but there was an excitement in her voice that men who had cared for her found difficult to forget; a singing compulsion, a whispered 'Listen', a promise that she had done gay, exciting things just a while since and that there were gay, exciting things hovering in the next hour.

I told her how I had stopped off in Chicago for a day on my way East, and how a dozen people had sent their love through me.

'Do they miss me?' she cried ecstatically.

'The whole town is desolate. All the cars have the left rear wheel painted black as a mourning wreath, and there's a persistent wail all night along the north shore.'

'How gorgeous! Let's go back, Tom. To-morrow!' Then she added irrelevantly: 'You ought to see the baby.'

'I'd like to.'

'She's asleep. She's three years old. Haven't you ever seen her?'

'Never.'

'Well, you ought to see her. She's——'

Tom Buchanan, who had been hovering restlessly about the room, stopped and rested his hand on my shoulder.

'What you doing, Nick?'

'I'm a bond man.'

'Who with?'

I told him.

'Never heard of them,' he remarked decisively.

This annoyed me.

'You will,' I answered shortly. 'You will if you stay in the East.'

'Oh, I'll stay in the East, don't you worry,' he said, glancing at Daisy and then back at me, as if he were alert for something more. 'I'd be a God damned fool to live anywhere else.'

At this point Miss Baker said: 'Absolutely!' with such suddenness that I started—it was the first word she had uttered since I came into the room. Evidently it surprised her as much as it did me, for she yawned and with a series of rapid, deft movements stood up into the room.

'I'm stiff,' she complained, 'I've been lying on that sofa for as long as I can remember.'

'Don't look at me,' Daisy retorted, 'I've been trying to get you to New York all afternoon.'

'No, thanks,' said Miss Baker to the four cocktails just in from the pantry, 'I'm absolutely in training.'

Her host looked at her incredulously.

'You are!' He took down his drink as if it were a drop in the bottom of a glass. 'How you ever get anything done is beyond me.'

I looked at Miss Baker, wondering what it was she 'got done.' I enjoyed looking at her. She was a slender, small-breasted girl, with an erect carriage, which she accentuated by throwing her body backward at the shoulders like a young cadet. Her grey sun-strained eyes looked back at me with polite reciprocal curiosity out of a wan, charming, discontented face. It occurred to me now that I had seen her, or a picture of her, somewhere before.

'You live in West Egg,' she remarked contemptuously. 'I know somebody there.'

'I don't know a single——'

'You must know Gatsby.'

'Gatsby?' demanded Daisy. 'What Gatsby?'

Before I could reply that he was my neighbour dinner was announced; wedging his tense arm imperatively under mine, Tom Buchanan compelled me from the room as though he were moving a checker to another square.

Slenderly, languidly, their hands set lightly on their hips, the two young women preceded us out onto a rosy-coloured porch, open towards the sunset, where four candles flickered on the table in the diminished wind.

'Why *candles*?' objected Daisy, frowning. She snapped them out with her fingers. 'In two weeks it'll be the longest day in the year.' She looked at us all radiantly. 'Do you always watch for the longest day of the year and then miss it? I always watch for the longest day in the year and then miss it.'

'We ought to plan something,' yawned Miss Baker, sitting down at the table as if she were getting into bed.

'All right,' said Daisy. 'What'll we plan?' She turned to me helplessly: 'What do people plan?'

Before I could answer her eyes fastened with an awed expression on her little finger.

'Look!' she complained; 'I hurt it.'

We all looked—the knuckle was black and blue.

'You did it, Tom,' she said accusingly. 'I know you didn't mean to, but you *did* do it. That's what I get for marrying a brute of a man, a great, big, hulking physical specimen of a——'

'I hate that word hulking,' objected Tom crossly, 'even in kidding.'

'Hulking,' insisted Daisy.

Sometimes she and Miss Baker talked at once, unobtrusively and with a bantering inconsequence that was never quite chatter, that was as cool as their white dresses and their impersonal eyes in the absence of all desire. They were here, and they accepted Tom and me, making only a polite pleasant effort to entertain or to be entertained. They knew that presently dinner would be over and a little later the evening, too, would be over and casually put away. It was sharply different from the West, where an evening was hurried from phase to phase towards its close, in a continually disappointed anticipation or else in sheer nervous dread of the moment itself.

'You make me feel uncivilized, Daisy,' I confessed on my

second glass of corky but rather impressive claret. 'Can't you talk about crops or something?'

I meant nothing in particular by this remark, but it was taken up in an unexpected way.

'Civilization's going to pieces,' broke out Tom violently. I've gotten to be a terrible pessimist about things. Have you read "The Rise of the Coloured Empires" by this man Goddard?'

'Why, no,' I answered, rather surprised by his tone.

'Well, it's a fine book, and everybody ought to read it. The idea is if we don't look out the white race will be—will be utterly submerged. It's all scientific stuff; it's been proved.'

'Tom's getting very profound,' said Daisy, with an expression of unthoughtful sadness. 'He reads deep books with long words in them. What was that word we——'

'Well, these books are all scientific,' insisted Tom, glancing at her impatiently. 'This fellow has worked out the whole thing. It's up to us, who are the dominant race, to watch out or these other races will have control of things.'

'We've got to beat them down,' whispered Daisy, winking ferociously towards the fervent sun.

'You ought to live in California—' began Miss Baker, but Tom interrupted her by shifting heavily in his chair.

'This idea is that we're Nordics. I am, and you are, and you are, and——' After an infinitesimal hesitation he included Daisy with a slight nod, and she winked at me again. '—And we've produced all the things that go to make civilization—oh, science and art, and all that. Do you see?'

There was something pathetic in his concentration, as if his complacency, more acute than of old, was not enough to him any more. When, almost immediately, the telephone rang inside and the butler left the porch Daisy seized upon the momentary interruption and leaned towards me.

'I'll tell you a family secret,' she whispered enthusiastically. 'It's about the butler's nose. Do you want to hear about the butler's nose?'

'That's why I came over to-night.'

'Well, he wasn't always a butler; he used to be the silver polisher for some people in New York that had a silver service for two hundred people. He had to polish it from morning till night, until finally it began to affect his nose——'

'Things went from bad to worse,' suggested Miss Baker.

'Yes. Things went from bad to worse, until finally he had to give up his position.'

For a moment the last sunshine fell with romantic affection upon her glowing face; her voice compelled me forward breathlessly as I listened—then the glow faded, each light deserting her with lingering regret, like children leaving a pleasant street at dusk.

The butler came back and murmured something close to Tom's ear, whereupon Tom frowned, pushed back his chair, and without a word went inside. As if his absence quickened something within her, Daisy leaned forward again, her voice glowing and singing.

'I love to see you at my table, Nick. You remind me of a —of a rose, an absolute rose. Doesn't he?' She turned to Miss Baker for confirmation: 'An absolute rose?'

This was untrue. I am not even faintly like a rose. She was only extemporizing, but a stirring warmth flowed from her, as if her heart was trying to come out to you concealed in one of those breathless, thrilling words. Then suddenly she threw her napkin on the table and excused herself and went into the house.

Miss Baker and I exchanged a short glance consciously devoid of meaning. I was about to speak when she sat up alertly and said 'Sh!' in a warning voice. A subdued, impassioned murmur was audible in the room beyond, and Miss Baker leaned forward unashamed, trying to hear. The murmur trembled on the verge of coherence, sank down, mounted excitedly, and then ceased altogether.

'This Mr. Gatsby you spoke of is my neighbour——' I began.

'Don't talk. I want to hear what happens.'

'Is something happening?' I inquired innocently.

'You mean to say you don't know?' said Miss Baker, honestly surprised. 'I thought everybody knew.'

'I don't.'

'Why—' she said hesitantly, 'Tom's got some woman in New York.'

'Got some woman?' I repeated blankly.

Miss Baker nodded.

'She might have the decency not to telephone him at dinner time. Don't you think?'

Almost before I had grasped her meaning there was the flutter of a dress and the crunch of leather boots, and Tom and Daisy were back at the table.

'It couldn't be helped!' cried Daisy with tense gaiety.

She sat down, glanced searchingly at Miss Baker and then at me, and continued: 'I looked outdoors for a minute, and it's very romantic outdoors. There's a bird on the lawn that I think must be a nightingale come over on the Cunard or White Star Line. He's singing away—' Her voice sang: 'It's romantic, isn't it, Tom?'

'Very romantic,' he said, and then miserably to me: 'If it's light enough after dinner, I want to take you down to the stables.'

The telephone rang inside, startlingly, and as Daisy shook her head decisively at Tom the subject of the stables, in fact all subjects, vanished into air. Among the broken fragments of the last five minutes at table I remember the candles being lit again, pointlessly, and I was conscious of wanting to look squarely at everyone, and yet to avoid all eyes. I couldn't guess what Daisy and Tom were thinking, but I doubt if even Miss Baker, who seemed to have mastered a certain hardy scepticism, was able utterly to put this fifth guest's shrill metallic urgency out of mind. To a certain temperament the situation might have seemed intriguing—my own instinct was to telephone immediately for the police.

The horses, needless to say, were not mentioned again. Tom and Miss Baker, with several feet of twilight between them, strolled back into the library, as if to a vigil beside a perfectly tangible body, while, trying to look pleasantly interested and a little deaf, I followed Daisy around a chain of connecting verandas to the porch in front. In its deep gloom we sat down side by side on a wicker settee.

Daisy took her face in her hands as if feeling its lovely shape, and her eyes moved gradually out into the velvet dusk. I saw that turbulent emotions possessed her, so I asked what I thought would be some sedative questions about her little girl.

'We don't know each other very well, Nick,' she said suddenly. 'Even if we are cousins. You didn't come to my wedding.'

'I wasn't back from the war.'

'That's true.' She hesitated. 'Well, I've had a very bad time, Nick, and I'm pretty cynical about everything.'

Evidently she had reason to be. I waited but she didn't say any more, and after a moment I returned rather feebly to the subject of her daughter.

'I suppose she talks, and—eats, and everything.'

'Oh, yes.' She looked at me absently. 'Listen, Nick; let me tell you what I said when she was born. Would you like to hear?'

'Very much.'

'It'll show you how I've gotten to feel about—things. Well, she was less than an hour old and Tom was God knows where. I woke up out of the ether with an utterly abandoned feeling, and asked the nurse right away if it was a boy or a girl. She told me it was a girl, and so I turned my head away and wept. "All right," I said, "I'm glad it's a girl. And I hope she'll be a fool—that's the best thing a girl can be in this world, a beautiful little fool."

'You see I think everything's terrible anyhow,' she went on in a convinced way. 'Everybody thinks so—the most advanced people. And I *know*. I've been everywhere and seen everything and done everything.' Her eyes flashed around her in a defiant way, rather like Tom's, and she laughed with thrilling scorn. 'Sophisticated—God, I'm sophisticated!'

The instant her voice broke off, ceasing to compel my
attention, my belief, I felt the basic insincerity of what she
had said. It made me uneasy, as though the whole evening
had been a trick of some sort to exact a contributory emotion
from me. I waited, and sure enough, in a moment she looked
at me with an absolute smirk on her lovely face, as if she had
asserted her membership in a rather distinguished secret
society to which she and Tom belonged.

Inside, the crimson room bloomed with light. Tom and
Miss Baker sat at either end of the long couch and she read
aloud to him from *The Saturday Evening Post*—the words,
murmurous and uninflected, running together in a soothing
tune. The lamp-light, bright on his boots and dull on the
autumn-leaf yellow of her hair, glinted along the paper as
she turned a page with a flutter of slender muscles in her
arms.

When we came in she held us silent for a moment with a
lifted hand.

'To be continued,' she said, tossing the magazine on the
table, 'in our very next issue.'

Her body asserted itself with a restless movement of her
knee, and she stood up.

'Ten o'clock,' she remarked, apparently finding the time
on the ceiling. 'Time for this good girl to go to bed.'

'Jordan's going to play in the tournament to-morrow,'
explained Daisy, 'over at Westchester.'

'Oh—you're *Jor*dan Baker.'

I knew now why her face was familiar—its pleasing
contemptuous expression had looked out at me from many
rotogravure pictures of the sporting life at Asheville and
Hot Springs and Palm Beach. I had heard some story of her
too, a critical, unpleasant story, but what it was I had
forgotten long ago.

'Good night,' she said softly. 'Wake me at eight, won't
you?'

'If you'll get up.'

'I will. Goodnight Mr. Carraway. See you anon.'

2 + S.F.

'Of course you will,' confirmed Daisy. 'In fact, I think I'll arrange a marriage. Come over often, Nick, and I'll sort of—oh—fling you together. You know—lock you up accidentally in linen closets and push you out to sea in a boat, and all that sort of thing——'

'Goodnight,' called Miss Baker from the stairs. 'I haven't heard a word.'

'She's a nice girl,' said Tom after a moment. 'They oughtn't to let her run around the country this way.'

'Who oughtn't to?' inquired Daisy coldly.

'Her family.'

'Her family is one aunt about a thousand years old. Besides, Nick's going to look after her, aren't you, Nick? She's going to spend lots of week-ends out here this summer. I think the home influence will be very good for her.'

Daisy and Tom looked at each other for a moment in silence.

'Is she from New York?' I asked quickly.

'From Louisville. Our white girlhood was passed together there. Our beautiful white——'

'Did you give Nick a little heart-to-heart talk on the veranda?' demanded Tom suddenly.

'Did I?' She looked at me. 'I can't seem to remember, but I think we talked about the Nordic race. Yes, I'm sure we did. It sort of crept up on us and first thing you know——'

'Don't believe everything you hear, Nick,' he advised me.

I said lightly that I had heard nothing at all, and a few minutes later I got up to go home. They came to the door with me and stood side by side in a cheerful square of light. As I started my motor Daisy peremptorily called: 'Wait!

'I forgot to ask you something, and it's important. We heard you were engaged to a girl out West.'

'That's right,' corroborated Tom kindly. 'We heard that you were engaged.'

'It's a libel. I'm too poor.'

'But we heard it,' insisted Daisy, surprising me by open-

ing up again in a flower-like way. 'We heard it from three
people, so it must be true.'

Of course I knew what they were referring to, but I
wasn't even vaguely engaged. The fact that gossip had
published the banns was one of the reasons I had come East.
You can't stop going with an old friend on account of
rumours, and on the other hand I had no intention of being
rumoured into marriage.

Their interest rather touched me and made them less
remotely rich—nevertheless, I was confused and a little
disgusted as I drove away. It seemed to me that the thing
for Daisy to do was to rush out of the house, child in arms
—but apparently there were no such intentions in her head.
As for Tom, the fact that he 'had some woman in New
York' was really less surprising than that he had been
depressed by a book. Something was making him nibble at
the edge of stale ideas as if his sturdy physical egotism no
longer nourished his peremptory heart.

Already it was deep summer on roadhouse roofs and in
front of wayside garages, where new red gas-pumps sat out
in pools of light, and when I reached my estate at West Egg
I ran the car under its shed and sat for a while on an
abandoned grass roller in the yard. The wind had blown
off, leaving a loud, bright night, with wings beating in the
trees and a persistent organ sound as the full bellows of the
earth blew the frogs full of life. The silhouette of a moving
cat wavered across the moonlight, and turning my head to
watch it, I saw that I was not alone—fifty feet away a figure
had emerged from the shadow of my neighbour's mansion
and was standing with his hands in his pockets regarding the
silver pepper of the stars. Something in his leisurely movements and the secure position of his feet upon the lawn
suggested that it was Mr. Gatsby himself, come out to
determine what share was his of our local heavens.

I decided to call to him. Miss Baker had mentioned him
at dinner, and that would do for an introduction. But I
didn't call to him, for he gave a sudden intimation that he
was content to be alone—he stretched out his arms towards

the dark water in a curious way, and, far as I was from him, I could have sworn he was trembling. Involuntarily I glanced seaward—and distinguished nothing except a single green light, minute and far away, that might have been the end of a dock. When I looked once more for Gatsby he had vanished, and I was alone again in the unquiet darkness.

CHAPTER II

ABOUT HALF WAY between West Egg and New York the motor road hastily joins the railroad and runs beside it for a quarter of a mile, so as to shrink away from a certain desolate area of land. This is a valley of ashes—a fantastic farm where ashes grow like wheat into ridges and hills and grotesque gardens; where ashes take the forms of houses and chimneys and rising smoke and, finally, with a transcendent effort, of ash-grey men who move dimly and already crumbling through the powdery air. Occasionally a line of grey cars crawls along an invisible track, gives out a ghastly creak, and comes to rest, and immediately the ash-grey men swarm up with leaden spades and stir up an impenetrable cloud, which screens their obscure operations from your sight.

But above the grey land and the spasms of bleak dust which drift endlessly over it, you perceive, after a moment, the eyes of Doctor T. J. Eckleburg. The eyes of Doctor T. J. Eckleburg are blue and gigantic—their retinas are one yard high. They look out of no face, but, instead, from a pair of enormous yellow spectacles which pass over a nonexistent nose. Evidently some wild wag of an oculist set them there to fatten his practice in the borough of Queens, and then sank down himself into eternal blindness, or forgot them and moved away. But his eyes, dimmed a little by many paintless days, under sun and rain, brood on over the solemn dumping ground.

The valley of ashes is bounded on one side by a small foul river, and, when the drawbridge is up to let barges through, the passengers on waiting trains can stare at the dismal scene for as long as half an hour. There is always a halt there of at least a minute, and it was because of this that I first met Tom Buchanan's mistress.

The fact that he had one was insisted upon wherever he was known. His acquaintances resented the fact that he turned up in popular cafés with her and, leaving her at a table, sauntered about, chatting with whomsoever he knew. Though I was curious to see her, I had no desire to meet her —but I did. I went up to New York with Tom on the train one afternoon, and when we stopped by the ash-heaps he jumped to his feet and, taking hold of my elbow, literally forced me from the car.

'We're getting off,' he insisted. 'I want you to meet my girl.'

I think he'd tanked up a good deal at luncheon, and his determination to have my company bordered on violence. The supercilious assumption was that on Sunday afternoon I had nothing better to do.

I followed him over a low whitewashed railroad fence, and we walked back a hundred yards along the road under Doctor Eckleburg's persistent stare. The only building in sight was a small block of yellow brick sitting on the edge of the waste land, a sort of compact Main Street ministering to it, and contiguous to absolutely nothing. One of the three shops it contained was for rent and another was an all-night restaurant, approached by a trail of ashes; the third was a garage—*Repairs*. GEORGE B. WILSON. *Cars bought and sold.* —and I followed Tom inside.

The interior was unprosperous and bare; the only car visible was the dust-covered wreck of a Ford which crouched in a dim corner. It had occurred to me that this shadow of a garage must be a blind, and that sumptuous and romantic apartments were concealed overhead, when the proprietor himself appeared in the door of an office, wiping his hands on a piece of waste. He was a blond, spiritless man, anaemic, and faintly handsome. When he saw us a damp gleam of hope sprang into his light blue eyes.

'Hello, Wilson, old man,' said Tom, slapping him jovially on the shoulder. 'How's business?'

'I can't complain,' answered Wilson unconvincingly. 'When are you going to sell me that car?'

'Next week; I've got my man working on it now.'

'Works pretty slow, don't he?'

'No, he doesn't,' said Tom coldly. 'And if you feel that way about it, maybe I'd better sell it somewhere else after all.'

'I don't mean that,' explained Wilson quickly. 'I just meant——'

His voice faded off and Tom glanced impatiently around the garage. Then I heard footsteps on a stairs, and in a moment the thickish figure of a woman blocked out the light from the office door. She was in the middle thirties, and faintly stout, but she carried her flesh sensuously, as some women can. Her face, above a spotted dress of dark blue crêpe-de-chine, contained no facet or gleam of beauty, but there was an immediately perceptible vitality about her as if the nerves of her body were continually smouldering. She smiled slowly and, walking through her husband as if he were a ghost, shook hands with Tom, looking him flush in the eye. Then she wet her lips, and without turning around spoke to her husband in a soft, coarse, voice:

'Get some chairs, why don't you, so somebody can sit down.'

'Oh, sure,' agreed Wilson hurriedly, and went towards the little office mingling immediately with the cement colour of the walls. A white ashen dust veiled his dark suit and his pale hair as it veiled everything in the vicinity—except his wife, who moved close to Tom.

'I want to see you,' said Tom intently. 'Get on the next train.'

'All right.'

'I'll meet you by the news-stand on the lower level.'

She nodded and moved away from him just as George Wilson emerged with two chairs from his office door.

We waited for her down the road and out of sight. It was

a few days before the Fourth of July, and a grey, scrawny Italian child was setting torpedoes in a row along the railroad track.

'Terrible place, isn't it,' said Tom, exchanging a frown with Doctor Eckleburg.

'Awful.'

'It does her good to get away.'

'Doesn't her husband object?'

'Wilson? He thinks she goes to see her sister in New York. He's so dumb he doesn't know he's alive.'

So Tom Buchanan and his girl and I went up together to New York—or not quite together, for Mrs. Wilson sat discreetly in another car. Tom deferred that much to the sensibilities of those East Eggers who might be on the train.

She had changed her dress to a brown figured muslin, which stretched tight over her rather wide hips as Tom helped her to the platform in New York. At the news-stand she bought a copy of *Town Tattle* and a moving-picture magazine, and in the station drug-store some cold cream and a small flask of perfume. Upstairs, in the solemn echoing drive she let four taxicabs drive away before she selected a new one, lavender-coloured with grey upholstery, and in this we slid out from the mass of the station into the glowing sunshine. But immediately she turned sharply from the window and, leaning forward, tapped on the front glass.

'I want to get one of those dogs,' she said earnestly. 'I want to get one for the apartment. They're nice to have—a dog.'

We backed up to a grey old man who bore an absurd resemblance to John D. Rockefeller. In a basket swung from his neck cowered a dozen very recent puppies of an indeterminate breed.

'What kind are they?' asked Mrs. Wilson eagerly, as he came to the taxi-window.

'All kinds. What kind do you want, lady?'

'I'd like to get one of those police dogs; I don't suppose you got that kind?'

The man peered doubtfully into the basket, plunged in his hand and drew one up, wriggling, by the back of the neck.

'That's no police dog,' said Tom.

'No, it's not exactly a police dog,' said the man with disappointment in his voice. 'It's more of an Airedale.' He passed his hand over the brown washrag of a back. 'Look at that coat. Some coat. That's a dog that'll never bother you with catching cold.'

'I think it's cute,' said Mrs. Wilson enthusiastically. 'How much is it?'

'That dog?' He looked at it admiringly. 'That dog will cost you ten dollars.'

The Airedale—undoubtedly there was an Airedale concerned in it somewhere, though its feet were startlingly white—changed hands and settled down into Mrs. Wilson's lap, where she fondled the weatherproof coat with rapture.

'Is it a boy or a girl?' she asked delicately.

'That dog? That dog's a boy.'

'It's a bitch,' said Tom decisively. 'Here's your money. Go and buy ten more dogs with it.'

We drove over to Fifth Avenue, warm and soft, almost pastoral, on the summer Sunday afternoon. I wouldn't have been surprised to see a great flock of white sheep turn the corner.

'Hold on,' I said, 'I have to leave you here.'

'No you don't,' interposed Tom quickly. 'Myrtle'll be hurt if you don't come up to the apartment. Won't you Myrtle?'

'Come on,' she urged. 'I'll telephone my sister Catherine. She's said to be very beautiful by people who ought to know.'

'Well, I'd like to, but——'

We went on, cutting back again over the Park towards the West Hundreds. At 158th Street the cab stopped at one slice in a long white cake of apartment-houses. Throwing a regal homecoming glance around the neighbourhood, Mrs.

Wilson gathered up her dog and her other purchases, and went haughtily in.

'I'm going to have the McKees come up,' she announced as we rose in the elevator. 'And, of course, I got to call up my sister, too.'

The apartment was on the top floor—a small living-room, a small dining-room, a small bedroom, and a bath. The living-room was crowded to the doors with a set of tapestried furniture entirely too large for it, so that to move about was to stumble continually over scenes of ladies swinging in the gardens of Versailles. The only picture was an over-enlarged photograph, apparently a hen sitting on a blurred rock. Looked at from a distance, however, the hen resolved itself into a bonnet, and the countenance of a stout old lady beamed down into the room. Several old copies of *Town Tattle* lay on the table together with a copy of *Simon Called Peter*, and some of the small scandal magazines of Broadway. Mrs. Wilson was first concerned with the dog. A reluctant elevator-boy went for a box full of straw and some milk to which he added on his own initiative a tin of large, hard dog-biscuits—one of which decomposed apathetically in the saucer of milk all afternoon. Meanwhile Tom brought out a bottle of whiskey from a locked bureau door.

I have been drunk just twice in my life, and the second time was that afternoon; so everything that happened has a dim, hazy cast over it, although until after eight o'clock the apartment was full of cheerful sun. Sitting on Tom's lap Mrs. Wilson called up several people on the telephone; then there were no cigarettes, and I went out to buy some at the drugstore on the corner. When I came back they had both disappeared, so I sat down discreetly in the living-room and read a chapter of *Simon Called Peter*—either it was terrible stuff or the whiskey distorted things, because it didn't make any sense to me.

Just as Tom and Myrtle (after the first drink Mrs. Wilson and I called each other by our first names) reappeared, company commenced to arrive at the apartment-door.

The sister, Catherine, was a slender, worldly girl of about

2*

thirty, with a solid, sticky bob of red hair, and a complexion powdered milky white. Her eyebrows had been plucked and then drawn on again at a more rakish angle but the efforts of nature towards the restoration of the old alignment gave a blurred air to her face. When she moved about there was an incessant clicking as innumerable pottery bracelets jingled up and down upon her arms. She came in with such a proprietary haste, and looked around so possessively at the furniture that I wondered if she lived here. But when I asked her she laughed immoderately, repeated my question aloud, and told me she lived with a girl friend at an hotel.

Mr. McKee was a pale, feminine man from the flat below. He had just shaved, for there was a white spot of lather on his cheekbone, and he was most respectful in his greeting to everyone in the room. He informed me that he was in the 'artistic game,' and I gathered later that he was a photographer and had made the dim enlargement of Mrs. Wilson's mother which hovered like an ectoplasm on the wall. His wife was shrill, languid, handsome, and horrible. She told me with pride that her husband had photographed her a hundred and twenty-seven times since they had been married.

Mrs. Wilson had changed her costume some time before, and was now attired in an elaborate afternoon dress of cream-coloured chiffon, which gave out a continual rustle as she swept about the room. With the influence of the dress her personality had also undergone a change. The intense vitality that had been so remarkable in the garage was converted into impressive hauteur. Her laughter, her gestures, her assertions became more violently affected moment by moment, and as she expanded the room grew smaller around her, until she seemed to be revolving on a noisy, creaking pivot through the smoky air.

'My dear,' she told her sister in a high, mincing shout, 'most of these fellas will cheat you every time. All they think of is money. I had a woman up here last week to look at my feet, and when she gave me the bill you'd of thought she had my appendicitus out.'

'What was the name of the woman?' asked Mrs. McKee.

'Mrs. Eberhardt. She goes around looking at people's feet in their own homes.'

'I like your dress,' remarked Mrs. McKee, 'I think it's adorable.'

Mrs. Wilson rejected the compliment by raising her eyebrow in disdain.

'It's just a crazy old thing,' she said. 'I just slip it on sometimes when I don't care what I look like.'

'But it looks wonderful on you, if you know what I mean,' pursued Mrs. McKee. 'If Chester could only get you in that pose I think he could make something of it.'

We all looked in silence at Mrs. Wilson, who removed a strand of hair from over her eyes and looked back at us with a brilliant smile. Mr. McKee regarded her intently with his head on one side, and then moved his hand back and forth slowly in front of his face.

'I should change the light,' he said after a moment. 'I'd like to bring out the modelling of the features. And I'd try to get hold of all the back hair.'

'I wouldn't think of changing the light,' cried Mrs. McKee. 'I think it's——'

Her husband said '*Sh!*' and we all looked at the subject again, whereupon Tom Buchanan yawned audibly and got to his feet.

'You McKees have something to drink,' he said. 'Get some more ice and mineral water, Myrtle, before everybody goes to sleep.'

'I told that boy about the ice.' Myrtle raised her eyebrows in despair at the shiftlessness of the lower orders. 'These people! You have to keep after them all the time.'

She looked at me and laughed pointlessly. Then she flounced over to the dog, kissed it with ecstasy, and swept into the kitchen, implying that a dozen chefs awaited her orders there.

'I've done some nice things out on Long Island,' asserted Mr. McKee.

Tom looked at him blankly.

'Two of them we have framed downstairs.'

'Two what?' demanded Tom.

'Two studies. One of them I call *Montauk Point—The Gulls*, and the other I call *Montauk Point—The Sea*.'

The sister Catherine sat down beside me on the couch.

'Do you live down on Long Island, too?' she inquired.

'I live at West Egg.'

'Really? I was down there at a party about a month ago. At a man named Gatsby's. Do you know him?'

'I live next door to him.'

'Well, they say he's a nephew or a cousin of Kaiser Wilhelm's. That's where all his money comes from.'

'Really?'

She nodded.

'I'm scared of him. I'd hate to have him get anything on me.'

This absorbing information about my neighbour was interrupted by Mrs. McKee's pointing suddenly at Catherine:

'Chester, I think you could do something with *her*,' she broke out, but Mr. McKee only nodded in a bored way, and turned his attention to Tom.

'I'd like to do more work on Long Island, if I could get the entry. All I ask is that they should give me a start.'

'Ask Myrtle,' said Tom, breaking into a short shout of laughter as Mrs. Wilson entered with a tray. 'She'll give you a letter of introduction, won't you, Myrtle?'

'Do what?' she asked, startled.

'You'll give McKee a letter of introduction to your husband, so he can do some studies of him.' His lips moved silently for a moment as he invented. '*George B. Wilson at the Gasoline Pump*, or something like that.'

Catherine leaned close to me and whispered in my ear:

'Neither of them can stand the person they're married to.'

'Can't they?'

'Can't *stand* them.' She looked at Myrtle and then at Tom. 'What I say is, why go on living with them if they can't stand them? If I was them I'd get a divorce and get married to each other right away.'

'Doesn't she like Wilson either?'

The answer to this was unexpected. It came from Myrtle, who had overheard the question, and it was violent and obscene.

'You see,' cried Catherine triumphantly. She lowered her voice again. 'It's really his wife that's keeping them apart. She's a Catholic, and they don't believe in divorce.'

Daisy was not a Catholic, and I was a little shocked at the elaborateness of the lie.

'When they do get married,' continued Catherine, 'they're going West to live for a while until it blows over.'

'It'd be more discreet to go to Europe.'

'Oh, do you like Europe?' she exclaimed surprisingly. 'I just got back from Monte Carlo.'

'Really.'

'Just last year. I went over there with another girl.'

'Stay long?'

'No, we just went to Monte Carlo and back. We went by way of Marseilles. We had over twelve hundred dollars when we started, but we got gypped out of it all in two days in the private rooms. We had an awful time getting back, I can tell you. God, how I hated that town!'

The late afternoon sky bloomed in the window for a moment like the blue honey of the Mediterranean—then the shrill voice of Mrs. McKee called me back into the room.

'I almost made a mistake, too,' she declared vigorously. 'I almost married a little kike who'd been after me for years. I knew he was below me. Everybody kept saying to me: "Lucille, that man's 'way below you!" But if I hadn't met Chester, he'd of got me sure.'

'Yes, but listen,' said Myrtle Wilson, nodding her head up and down, 'at least you didn't marry him.'

'I know I didn't.'

'Well, I married him,' said Myrtle, ambiguously. 'And that's the difference between your case and mine.'

'Why did you, Myrtle?' demanded Catherine. 'Nobody forced you to.'

Myrtle considered.

'I married him because I thought he was a gentleman,' she said finally. 'I thought he knew something about breeding, but he wasn't fit to lick my shoe.'

'You were crazy about him for a while,' said Catherine.

'Crazy about him!' cried Myrtle incredulously. 'Who said I was crazy about him? I never was any more crazy about him than I was about that man there.'

She pointed suddenly at me, and everyone looked at me accusingly. I tried to show by my expression that I expected no affection.

'The only *crazy* I was was when I married him. I knew right away I made a mistake. He borrowed somebody's best suit to get married in, and never even told me about it, and the man came after it one day when he was out: "Oh, is that your suit?" I said. "This is the first I ever heard about it." But I gave it to him and then I lay down and cried to beat the band all afternoon.'

'She really ought to get away from him,' resumed Catherine to me. 'They've been living over that garage for eleven years. And Tom's the first sweetie she ever had.'

The bottle of whiskey—a second one—was now in constant demand by all present, excepting Catherine, who 'felt just as good on nothing at all.' Tom rang for the janitor and sent him for some celebrated sandwiches, which were a complete supper in themselves. I wanted to get out and walk eastward towards the park through the soft twilight, but each time I tried to go I became entangled in some wild, strident argument which pulled me back, as if with ropes, into my chair. Yet high over the city our line of yellow windows must have contributed their share of human secrecy to the casual watcher in the darkening streets, and I saw him too, looking up and wondering. I was within and without, simultaneously enchanted and repelled by the inexhaustible variety of life.

Myrtle pulled her chair close to mine, and suddenly her warm breath poured over me the story of her first meeting with Tom.

'It was on the two little seats facing each other that are always the last ones left on the train. I was going up to New York to see my sister and spend the night. He had on a dress suit and patent leather shoes, and I couldn't keep my eyes off him, but every time he looked at me I had to pretend to be looking at the advertisement over his head. When we came into the station he was next to me, and his white shirt-front pressed against my arm, and so I told him I'd have to call a policeman, but he knew I lied. I was so excited that when I got into a taxi with him I didn't hardly know I wasn't getting into a subway train. All I kept thinking about, over and over, was "You can't live forever; you can't live forever."'

She turned to Mrs. McKee and the room rang full of her artificial laughter.

'My dear,' she cried, 'I'm going to give you this dress as soon as I'm through with it. I've got to get another one to-morrow. I'm going to make a list of all the things I've got to get. A massage and a wave, and a collar for the dog, and one of those cute little ash-trays where you touch a spring, and a wreath with a black silk bow for mother's grave that'll last all summer. I got to write down a list so I won't forget all the things I got to do.'

It was nine o'clock—almost immediately afterwards I looked at my watch and found it was ten. Mr. McKee was asleep on a chair with his fists clenched in his lap, like a photograph of a man of action. Taking out my handkerchief I wiped from his cheek the spot of dried lather that had worried me all the afternoon.

The little dog was sitting on the table looking with blind eyes through the smoke, and from time to time groaning faintly. People disappeared, reappeared, made plans to go somewhere, and then lost each other, searched for each other, found each other a few feet away. Sometime towards midnight Tom Buchanan and Mrs. Wilson stood face to face discussing in impassioned voices, whether Mrs. Wilson had any right to mention Daisy's name.

'Daisy! Daisy! Daisy!' shouted Mrs. Wilson. 'I'll say it whenever I want to! Daisy! Dai——'

Making a short deft movement, Tom Buchanan broke her nose with his open hand.

Then there were bloody towels upon the bathroom floor, and women's voices scolding, and high over the confusion a long broken wail of pain. Mr. McKee awoke from his doze and started in a daze towards the door. When he had gone halfway he turned around and stared at the scene—his wife and Catherine scolding and consoling as they stumbled here and there among the crowded furniture with articles of aid, and the despairing figure on the couch, bleeding fluently, and trying to spread a copy of *Town Tattle* over the tapestry scenes of Versailles. Then Mr. McKee turned and continued on out the door. Taking my hat from the chandelier, I followed.

'Come to lunch some day,' he suggested, as we groaned down in the elevator.

'Where?'

'Anywhere.'

'Keep your hands off the lever,' snapped the elevator boy.

'I beg your pardon,' said Mr. McKee with dignity, 'I didn't know I was touching it.'

'All right,' I agreed, 'I'll be glad to.'

. . . I was standing beside his bed and he was sitting up between the sheets, clad in his underwear, with a great portfolio in his hands.

'Beauty and the Beast . . . Loneliness . . . Old Grocery Horse . . . Brook'n Bridge. . . .'

Then I was lying half asleep in the cold lower level of the Pennsylvania Station, staring at the morning *Tribune*, and waiting for the four o'clock train.

CHAPTER III

THERE WAS MUSIC from my neighbour's house through the summer nights. In his blue gardens men and girls came and went like moths among the whisperings and the champagne and the stars. At high tide in the afternoon I watched his guests diving from the tower of his raft, or taking the sun on the hot sand of his beach while his two motor-boats slit the waters of the Sound, drawing aquaplanes over cataracts of foam. On week-ends his Rolls-Royce became an omnibus, bearing parties to and from the city between nine in the morning and long past midnight, while his station wagon scampered like a brisk yellow bug to meet all trains. And on Mondays eight servants, including an extra gardener, toiled all day with mops and scrubbing-brushes and hammers and garden-shears, repairing the ravages of the night before.

Every Friday five crates of oranges and lemons arrived from a fruiterer in New York—every Monday these same oranges and lemons left his back door in a pyramid of pulpless halves. There was a machine in the kitchen which could extract the juice of two hundred oranges in half an hour if a little button was pressed two hundred times by a butler's thumb.

At least once a fortnight a corps of caterers came down with several hundred feet of canvas and enough coloured lights to make a Christmas tree of Gatsby's enormous garden. On buffet tables, garnished with glistening hors-d'œuvre, spiced baked hams crowded against salads of harlequin designs and pastry pigs and turkeys bewitched to a dark gold. In the main hall a bar with a real brass rail was set up, and stocked with gins and liquors and with cordials so long forgotten that most of his female guests were too young to know one from another.

By seven o'clock the orchestra has arrived, no thin five-piece affair, but a whole pitful of oboes and trombones and saxophones and viols and cornets and piccolos, and low and high drums. The last swimmers have come in from the beach now and are dressing upstairs; the cars from New York are parked five deep in the drive, and already the halls and salons and verandas are gaudy with primary colours, and hair bobbed in strange new ways, and shawls beyond the dreams of Castile. The bar is in full swing, and floating rounds of cocktails permeate the garden outside, until the air is alive with chatter and laughter, and casual innuendo and introductions forgotten on the spot, and enthusiastic meetings between women who never knew each other's names.

The lights grow brighter as the earth lurches away from the sun, and now the orchestra is playing yellow cocktail music, and the opera of voices pitches a key higher. Laughter is easier minute by minute, spilled with prodigality, tipped out at a cheerful word. The groups change more swiftly, swell with new arrivals, dissolve and form in the same breath; already there are wanderers, confident girls who weave here and there among the stouter and more stable, become for a sharp, joyous moment the centre of a group, and then, excited with triumph, glide on through the sea-change of faces and voices and colour under the constantly changing light.

Suddenly one of these gypsies, in trembling opal, seizes a cocktail out of the air, dumps it down for courage and, moving her hands like Frisco, dances out alone on the canvas platform. A momentary hush; the orchestra leader varies his rhythm obligingly for her, and there is a burst of chatter as the erroneous news goes around that she is Gilda Gray's understudy from the *Follies*. The party has begun.

I believe that on the first night I went to Gatsby's house I was one of the few guests who had actually been invited. People were not invited—they went there. They got into automobiles which bore them out to Long Island, and somehow they ended up at Gatsby's door. Once there they were introduced by somebody who knew Gatsby, and after that they conducted themselves according to the rules of behaviour associated with an amusement park. Sometimes they came and went without having met Gatsby at all, came for the party with a simplicity of heart that was its own ticket of admission.

I had been actually invited. A chauffeur in a uniform of robin's-egg blue crossed my lawn early that Saturday morning with a surprisingly formal note from his employer: the honour would be entirely Gatsby's, it said, if I would attend his 'little party' that night. He had seen me several times, and had intended to call on me long before, but a peculiar combination of circumstances had prevented it—signed Jay Gatsby, in a majestic hand.

Dressed up in white flannels I went over to his lawn a little while after seven, and wandered around rather ill at ease among swirls and eddies of people I didn't know—though here and there was a face I had noticed on the commuting train. I was immediately struck by the number of young Englishmen dotted about; all well dressed, all looking a little hungry, and all talking in low, earnest voices to solid and prosperous Americans. I was sure that they were selling something: bonds or insurance or automobiles. They were at least agonizingly aware of the easy money in the vicinity and convinced that it was theirs for a few words in the right key.

As soon as I arrived I made an attempt to find my host, but the two or three people of whom I asked his whereabouts stared at me in such an amazed way, and denied so vehemently any knowledge of his movements, that I slunk off in the direction of the cocktail table—the only place in the garden where a single man could linger without looking purposeless and alone.

I was on my way to get roaring drunk from sheer embarrassment when Jordan Baker came out of the house and stood at the head of the marble steps, leaning a little backward and looking with contemptuous interest down into the garden.

Welcome or not, I found it necessary to attach myself to someone before I should begin to address cordial remarks to the passers-by.

'Hello!' I roared, advancing towards her. My voice seemed unnaturally loud across the garden.

'I thought you might be here,' she responded absently as I came up. 'I remembered you lived next door to——'

She held my hand impersonally, as a promise that she'd take care of me in a minute, and gave ear to two girls in twin yellow dresses, who stopped at the foot of the steps.

'Hello!' they cried together. 'Sorry you didn't win.'

That was for the golf tournament. She had lost in the finals the week before.

'You don't know who we are,' said one of the girls in yellow, 'but we met you here about a month ago.'

'You've dyed your hair since then,' remarked Jordan, and I started, but the girls had moved casually on and her remark was addressed to the premature moon, produced like the supper, no doubt, out of a caterer's basket. With Jordan's slender golden arm resting in mine, we descended the steps and sauntered about the garden. A tray of cocktails floated at us through the twilight, and we sat down at a table with the two girls in yellow and three men, each one introduced to us as Mr. Mumble.

'Do you come to these parties often?' inquired Jordan of the girl beside her.

'The last one was the one I met you at,' answered the girl, in an alert confident voice. She turned to her companion: 'Wasn't it for you, Lucille?'

It was for Lucille, too.

'I like to come,' Lucille said. 'I never care what I do, so I always have a good time. When I was here last I tore my gown on a chair, and he asked me my name and address—inside of a week I got a package from Croirier's with a new evening gown in it.'

'Did you keep it?' asked Jordan.

'Sure I did. I was going to wear it to-night, but it was too big in the bust and had to be altered. It was gas blue and lavender beads. Two hundred and sixty-five dollars.'

'There's something funny about a fellow that'll do a

thing like that,' said the other girl eagerly. 'He doesn't want any trouble with *any*body.'

'Who doesn't?' I inquired.

'Gatsby. Somebody told me——'

The two girls and Jordan leaned together confidentially.

'Somebody told me they thought he killed a man once.'

A thrill passed over all of us. The three Mr. Mumbles bent forward and listened eagerly.

'I don't think it's so much *that*,' argued Lucille sceptically; 'it's more that he was a German spy during the war.'

One of the men nodded in confirmation.

'I heard that from a man who knew all about him, grew up with him in Germany,' he assured us positively.

'Oh, no,' said the first girl, 'it couldn't be that, because he was in the American army during the war.' As our credulity switched back to her she leaned forward with enthusiasm. 'You look at him sometimes when he thinks nobody's looking at him. I'll bet he killed a man.'

She narrowed her eyes and shivered. Lucille shivered. We all turned and looked around for Gatsby. It was testimony to the romantic speculation he inspired that there were whispers about him from those who had found little that it was necessary to whisper about in this world.

The first supper—there would be another one after midnight—was now being served, and Jordan invited me to join her own party, who were spread around a table on the other side of the garden. There were three married couples and Jordan's escort, a persistent undergraduate given to violent innuendo, and obviously under the impression that sooner or later Jordan was going to yield him up her person to a greater or lesser degree. Instead of rambling, this party had preserved a dignified homogeneity, and assumed to itself the function of representing the staid nobility of the countryside—East Egg condescending to West Egg, and carefully on guard against its spectroscopic gaiety.

'Let's get out,' whispered Jordan, after a somehow wasteful and inappropriate half-hour; 'this is much too polite for me.'

We got up, and she explained that we were going to find the host: I had never met him, she said, and it was making me uneasy. The undergraduate nodded in a cynical, melancholy way.

The bar, where we glanced first, was crowded, but Gatsby was not there. She couldn't find him from the top of the steps, and he wasn't on the veranda. On a chance we tried an important-looking door, and walked into a high Gothic library, panelled with carved English oak, and probably transported complete from some ruin overseas.

A stout, middle-aged man, with enormous owl-eyed spectacles, was sitting somewhat drunk on the edge of a great table, staring with unsteady concentration at the shelves of books. As we entered he wheeled excitedly around and examined Jordan from head to foot.

'What do you think?' he demanded impetuously.

'About what?'

He waved his hand towards the book-shelves.

'About that. As a matter of fact you needn't bother to ascertain. I ascertained. They're real.'

'The books?'

He nodded.

'Absolutely real—have pages and everything. I thought they'd be a nice durable cardboard. Matter of fact, they're absolutely real. Pages and— Here! Lemme show you.'

Taking our scepticism for granted, he rushed to the book-cases and returned with Volume One of the 'Stoddard Lectures.'

'See!' he cried triumphantly. 'It's a bona-fide piece of printed matter. It fooled me. This fella's a regular Belasco. It's a triumph. What thoroughness! What realism! Knew when to stop, too—didn't cut the pages. But what do you want? What do you expect?'

He snatched the book from me and replaced it hastily on its shelf, muttering that if one brick was removed the whole library was liable to collapse.

'Who brought you?' he demanded. 'Or did you just come? I was brought. Most people were brought.'

Jordan looked at him alertly, cheerfully, without answering.

'I was brought by a woman named Roosevelt,' he continued. 'Mrs. Claude Roosevelt. Do you know her? I met her somewhere last night. I've been drunk for about a week now, and I thought it might sober me up to sit in a library.'

'Has it?'

'A little bit, I think. I can't tell yet. I've only been here an hour. Did I tell you about the books? They're real. They're——'

'You told us.'

We shook hands with him gravely and went back outdoors.

There was dancing now on the canvas in the garden; old men pushing young girls backwards in eternal graceless circles, superior couples holding each other tortuously, fashionably, and keeping in the corners—and a great number of single girls dancing individualistically or relieving the orchestra for a moment of the burden of the banjo or the traps. By midnight the hilarity had increased. A celebrated tenor had sung in Italian, and a notorious contralto had sung in jazz, and between the numbers people were doing 'stunts' all over the garden, while happy, vacuous bursts of laughter rose towards the summer sky. A pair of stage twins, who turned out to be the girls in yellow, did a baby act in costume, and champagne was served in glasses bigger than finger-bowls. The moon had risen higher, and floating in the Sound was a triangle of silver scales, trembling a little to the stiff, tinny drip of the banjoes on the lawn.

I was still with Jordan Baker. We were sitting at a table with a man of about my age and a rowdy little girl, who gave way upon the slightest provocation to uncontrollable laughter. I was enjoying myself now. I had taken two finger-bowls of champagne, and the scene had changed before my eyes into something significant, elemental, and profound.

At a lull in the entertainment the man looked at me and smiled.

'Your face is familiar,' he said, politely. 'Weren't you in the First Division during the war?'

'Why, yes. I was in the Twenty-eighth Infantry.'

'I was in the Sixteenth until June nineteen-eighteen. I knew I'd seen you somewhere before.'

We talked for a moment about some wet, grey little villages in France. Evidently he lived in this vicinity, for he told me that he had just bought a hydroplane, and was going to try it out in the morning.

'Want to go with me, old sport? Just near the shore along the Sound.'

'What time?'

'Any time that suits you best.'

It was on the tip of my tongue to ask his name when Jordan looked around and smiled.

'Having a gay time now?' she inquired.

'Much better.' I turned again to my new acquaintance. 'This is an unusual party for me. I haven't even seen the host. I live over there—' I waved my hand at the invisible hedge in the distance, 'and this man Gatsby sent over his chauffeur with an invitation.'

For a moment he looked at me as if he failed to understand.

'I'm Gatsby,' he said suddenly.

'What!' I exclaimed. 'Oh, I beg your pardon.'

'I thought you knew, old sport. I'm afraid I'm not a very good host.'

He smiled understandingly—much more than understandingly. It was one of those rare smiles with a quality of eternal reassurance in it, that you may come across four or five times in life. It faced—or seemed to face—the whole eternal world for an instant, and then concentrated on *you* with an irresistible prejudice in your favour. It understood you just as far as you wanted to be understood, believed in you as you would like to believe in yourself, and assured you that it had precisely the impression of you that, at your best, you hoped to convey. Precisely at that point it vanished—and I was looking at an elegant young roughneck, a year or two over thirty, whose elaborate formality of speech just missed being absurd. Some time before he introduced himself I'd got a strong impression that he was picking his words with care.

Almost at the moment when Mr. Gatsby identified himself, a butler hurried towards him with the information that Chicago was calling him on the wire. He excused himself with a small bow that included each of us in turn.

'If you want anything just ask for it, old sport,' he urged me. 'Excuse me. I will rejoin you later.'

When he was gone I turned immediately to Jordan—constrained to assure her of my surprise. I had expected that Mr. Gatsby would be a florid and corpulent person in his middle years.

'Who is he?' I demanded. 'Do you know?'

'He's just a man named Gatsby.'

'Where is he from, I mean? And what does he do?'

'Now *you're* started on the subject,' she answered with a wan smile. 'Well, he told me once he was an Oxford man.'

A dim background started to take shape behind him, but at her next remark it faded away.

'However, I don't believe it.'

'Why not?'

'I don't know,' she insisted, 'I just don't think he went there.'

Something in her tone reminded me of the other girl's 'I think he killed a man,' and had the effect of stimulating my curiosity. I would have accepted without question the information that Gatsby sprang from the swamps of Louisiana or from the lower East Side of New York. That was comprehensible. But young men didn't—at least in my provincial inexperience I believed they didn't—drift coolly out of nowhere and buy a palace on Long Island Sound.

'Anyhow, he gives large parties,' said Jordan, changing the subject with an urban taste for the concrete. 'And I like large parties. They're so intimate. At small parties there isn't any privacy.'

There was the boom of a brass drum, and the voice of the orchestra leader rang out suddenly above the echolalia of the garden.

'Ladies and gentlemen,' he cried. 'At the request of Mr. Gatsby we are going to play for you Mr. Vladimir Tostoff's latest work, which attracted so much attention at Carnegie Hall last May. If you read the papers, you know there was a big sensation.' He smiled with jovial condescension, and added: 'Some sensation!' Whereupon everybody laughed.

'The piece is known,' he concluded lustily, 'as Vladimir Tostoff's *Jazz History of the World*.'

The nature of Mr. Tostoff's composition eluded me, because just as it began my eyes fell on Gatsby, standing alone on the marble steps and looking from one group to another with approving eyes. His tanned skin was drawn attractively tight on his face and his short hair looked as though it were trimmed every day. I could see nothing sinister about him. I wondered if the fact that he was not drinking helped to set him off from his guests, for it seemed to me that he grew more correct as the fraternal hilarity increased. When the *Jazz History of the World* was over, girls were putting their heads on men's shoulders in a puppyish, convivial way, girls were swooning backward playfully into men's arms, even into groups, knowing that someone would arrest their falls—but no one swooned backward on Gatsby, and no French bob touched Gatsby's shoulder, and no singing quartets were formed with Gatsby's head for one link.

'I beg your pardon.'

Gatsby's butler was suddenly standing beside us.

'Miss Baker?' he inquired. 'I beg your pardon, but Mr. Gatsby would like to speak to you alone.'

'With me?' she exclaimed in surprise.

'Yes, madame.'

She got up slowly, raising her eyebrows at me in astonishment, and followed the butler towards the house. I noticed that she wore her evening-dress, all her dresses, like sports clothes—there was a jauntiness about her movements as if she had first learned to walk upon golf courses on clean, crisp mornings.

I was alone and it was almost two. For some time confused and intriguing sounds had issued from a long, many-windowed room which overhung the terrace. Eluding Jordan's undergraduate, who was now engaged in an obstetrical conversation with two chorus girls, and who implored me to join him, I went inside.

The large room was full of people. One of the girls in yellow was playing the piano, and beside her stood a tall, red-haired young lady from a famous chorus, engaged in song. She had drunk a quantity of champagne, and during the course of her song she had decided, ineptly, that everything was very, very sad—she was not only singing, she was weeping too. Whenever there was a pause in the song she filled it with gasping, broken sobs, and then took up the lyric again in a quavering soprano. The tears coursed down her cheeks—not freely, however, for when they came into contact with her heavily beaded eyelashes they assumed an inky colour, and pursued the rest of their way in slow black rivulets. A humorous suggestion was made that she sing the notes on her face, whereupon she threw up her hands, sank into a chair, and went off into a deep vinous sleep.

'She had a fight with a man who says he's her husband,' explained a girl at my elbow.

I looked around. Most of the remaining women were now having fights with men said to be their husbands. Even Jordan's party, the quartet from East Egg, were rent asunder by dissension. One of the men was talking with curious intensity to a young actress, and his wife, after attempting to laugh at the situation in a dignified and indifferent way, broke down entirely and resorted to flank attacks—at intervals she appeared suddenly at his side like an angry diamond, and hissed: 'You promised!' into his ear.

The reluctance to go home was not confined to wayward men. The hall was at present occupied by two deplorably sober men and their highly indignant wives. The wives were sympathizing with each other in slightly raised voices.

'Whenever he sees I'm having a good time he wants to go home.'

'Never heard anything so selfish in my life.'

'We're always the first ones to leave.'

'So are we.'

'Well, we're almost the last to-night,' said one of the men sheepishly. 'The orchestra left half an hour ago.'

In spite of the wives' agreement that such malevolence was beyond credibility, the dispute ended in a short struggle, and both wives were lifted, kicking, into the night.

As I waited for my hat in the hall the door of the library opened and Jordan Baker and Gatsby came out together. He was saying some last word to her, but the eagerness in his manner tightened abruptly into formality as several people approached him to say good-bye.

Jordan's party were calling impatiently to her from the porch, but she lingered for a moment to shake hands.

'I've just heard the most amazing thing,' she whispered. 'How long were we in there?'

'Why, about an hour.'

'It was . . . simply amazing,' she repeated abstractedly. 'But I swore I wouldn't tell it and here I am tantalizing you.' She yawned gracefully in my face. 'Please come and see me. . . . Phone book. . . . Under the name of Mrs. Sigourney Howard. . . . My aunt. . . .' She was hurrying off as she talked—her brown hand waved a jaunty salute as she melted into her party at the door.

Rather ashamed that on my first appearance I had stayed so late, I joined the last of Gatsby's guests, who were clustered around him. I wanted to explain that I'd hunted for him early in the evening and to apologize for not having known him in the garden.

'Don't mention it,' he enjoined me eagerly. 'Don't give it another thought, old sport.' The familiar expression held no more familiarity than the hand which reassuringly brushed my shoulder. 'And don't forget we're going up in the hydroplane to-morrow morning, at nine o'clock.'

Then the butler, behind his shoulder:

'Philadelphia wants you on the 'phone, sir.'

'All right, in a minute. Tell them I'll be right there. . . .
Good night.'

'Good night.'

'Good night.' He smiled—and suddenly there seemed to
be a pleasant significance in having been among the last to
go, as if he had desired it all the time. 'Good night, old
sport. . . . Good night.'

But as I walked down the steps I saw that the evening
was not quite over. Fifty feet from the door a dozen headlights illuminated a bizarre and tumultuous scene. In the
ditch beside the road, right side up, but violently shorn of
one wheel, rested a new coupé which had left Gatsby's
drive not two minutes before. The sharp jut of a wall
accounted for the detachment of the wheel, which was now
getting considerable attention from half a dozen curious
chauffeurs. However, as they had left their cars blocking
the road, a harsh, discordant din from those in the rear had
been audible for some time, and added to the already violent
confusion of the scene.

A man in a long duster had dismounted from the wreck
and now stood in the middle of the road, looking from the
car to the tyre and from the tyre to the observers in a
pleasant, puzzled way.

'See!' he explained. 'It went in the ditch.'

The fact was infinitely astonishing to him, and I recognized first the unusual quality of wonder, and then the man
—it was the late patron of Gatsby's library.

'How'd it happen?'

He shrugged his shoulders.

'I know nothing whatever about mechanics,' he said
decisively.

'But how did it happen? Did you run into the wall?'

'Don't ask me,' said Owl Eyes, washing his hands of the
whole matter. 'I know very little about driving—next to
nothing. It happened, and that's all I know.'

'Well, if you're a poor driver you oughtn't to try driving
at night.'

'But I wasn't even trying,' he explained indignantly, 'I wasn't even trying.'

An awed hush fell upon the bystanders.

'Do you want to commit suicide?'

'You're lucky it was just a wheel! A bad driver and not even *try*ing!'

'You don't understand,' explained the criminal. 'I wasn't driving. There's another man in the car.'

The shock that followed this declaration found voice in a sustained 'Ah-h-h!' as the door of the coupé swung slowly open. The crowd—it was now a crowd—stepped back involuntarily, and when the door had opened wide there was a ghostly pause. Then, very gradually, part by part, a pale, dangling individual stepped out of the wreck, pawing tentatively at the ground with a large uncertain dancing shoe.

Blinded by the glare of the headlights and confused by the incessant groaning of the horns, the apparition stood swaying for a moment before he perceived the man in the duster.

'Wha's matter?' he inquired calmly. 'Did we run outa gas?'

'Look!'

Half a dozen fingers pointed at the amputated wheel— he stared at it for a moment, and then looked upward as though he suspected that it had dropped from the sky.

'It came off,' someone explained.

He nodded.

'At first I din' notice we'd stopped.'

A pause. Then, taking a long breath and straightening his shoulders, he remarked in a determined voice:

'Wonder'ff tell me where there's a gas'line station?'

At least a dozen men, some of them a little better off than he was, explained to him that wheel and car were no longer joined by any physical bond.

'Back out,' he suggested after a moment. 'Put her in reverse.'

'But the *wheel's* off!'

He hesitated.

'No harm in trying,' he said.

The caterwauling horns had reached a crescendo and I turned away and cut across the lawn towards home. I glanced back once. A wafer of a moon was shining over Gatsby's house, making the night fine as before, and surviving the laughter and the sound of his still glowing garden. A sudden emptiness seemed to flow now from the windows and the great doors, endowing with complete isolation the figure of the host, who stood on the porch, his hand up in a formal gesture of farewell.

Reading over what I have written so far, I see I have given the impression that the events of three nights several weeks apart were all that absorbed me. On the contrary, they were merely casual events in a crowded summer, and, until much later, they absorbed me infinitely less than my personal affairs.

Most of the time I worked. In the early morning the sun threw my shadow westward as I hurried down the white chasms of lower New York to the Probity Trust. I knew the other clerks and young bond-salesmen by their first names, and lunched with them in dark, crowded restaurants on little pig sausages and mashed potatoes and coffee. I even had a short affair with a girl who lived in Jersey City and worked in the accounting department, but her brother began throwing mean looks in my direction, so when she went on her vacation in July I let it blow quietly away.

I took dinner usually at the Yale Club—for some reason it was the gloomiest event of my day—and then I went upstairs to the library and studied investments and securities for a conscientious hour. There were generally a few rioters around, but they never came into the library, so it was a good place to work. After that, if the night was mellow, I strolled down Madison Avenue past the old Murray Hill Hotel, and over 33rd Street to the Pennsylvania Station.

I began to like New York, the racy, adventurous feel of it at night, and the satisfaction that the constant flicker of men and women and machines gives to the restless eye. I liked to walk up Fifth Avenue and pick out romantic women from the crowd and imagine that in a few minutes I was going to enter into their lives, and no one would ever know or disapprove. Sometimes, in my mind, I followed them to their apartments on the corners of hidden streets, and they turned and smiled back at me before they faded through a door into warm darkness. At the enchanted metropolitan twilight I felt a haunting loneliness sometimes, and felt it in others—poor young clerks who loitered in front of windows waiting until it was time for a solitary restaurant dinner—young clerks in the dusk, wasting the most poignant moments of night and life.

Again at eight o'clock, when the dark lanes of the Forties were lined five deep with throbbing taxicabs, bound for the theatre district, I felt a sinking in my heart. Forms leaned together in the taxis as they waited, and voices sang, and there was laughter from unheard jokes, and lighted cigarettes made unintelligible circles inside. Imagining that I, too, was hurrying towards gaiety and sharing their intimate excitement, I wished them well.

For a while I lost sight of Jordan Baker, and then in midsummer I found her again. At first I was flattered to go places with her, because she was a golf champion, and everyone knew her name. Then it was something more. I wasn't actually in love, but I felt a sort of tender curiosity. The bored haughty face that she turned to the world concealed something—most affectations conceal something eventually, even though they don't in the beginning—and one day I found what it was. When we were on a house-party together up in Warwick, she left a borrowed car out in the rain with the top down, and then lied about it—and suddenly I remembered the story about her that had eluded me that night at Daisy's. At her first big golf tournament there was a row that nearly reached the newspapers—a suggestion that she had moved her ball from a bad lie in the semi-final round. The thing approached the proportions of a scandal—then died away. A caddy retracted his statement, and the only other witness admitted that he might have been mistaken. The incident and the name had remained together in my mind.

Jordan Baker instinctively avoided clever, shrewd men, and now I saw that this was because she felt safer on a plane where any divergence from a code would be thought impossible. She was incurably dishonest. She wasn't able to endure being at a disadvantage and, given this unwillingness, I suppose she had begun dealing in subterfuges when she was very young in order to keep that cool, insolent smile turned to the world and yet satisfy the demands of her hard, jaunty body.

It made no difference to me. Dishonesty in a woman is a thing you never blame deeply—I was casually sorry, and then I forgot. It was on that same house-party that we had a curious conversation about driving a car. It started because she passed so close to some workmen that our fender flicked a button on one man's coat.

'You're a rotten driver,' I protested. 'Either you ought to be more careful, or you oughtn't to drive at all.'

'I am careful.'

'No, you're not.'

'Well, other people are,' she said lightly.

'What's that got to do with it?'

'They'll keep out of my way,' she insisted. 'It takes two to make an accident.'

'Suppose you met somebody just as careless as yourself.'

'I hope I never will,' she answered. 'I hate careless people. That's why I like you.'

Her grey, sun-strained eyes stared straight ahead, but she had deliberately shifted our relations, and for a moment I thought I loved her. But I am slow-thinking and full of interior rules that act as brakes on my desires, and I knew that first I had to get myself definitely out of that tangle back home. I'd been writing letters once a week and signing them: 'Love, Nick,' and all I could think of was how, when that certain girl played tennis, a faint moustache of perspiration appeared on her upper lip. Nevertheless there was a

vague understanding that had to be tactfully broken off
before I was free.

Everyone suspects himself of at least one of the cardinal
virtues, and this is mine: I am one of the few honest people
that I have ever known.

CHAPTER IV

ON SUNDAY MORNING while church bells rang in the
villages along-shore, the world and its mistress returned to
Gatsby's house and twinkled hilariously on his lawn.

'He's a bootlegger,' said the young ladies, moving
somewhere between his cocktails and his flowers. 'One
time he killed a man who had found out that he was nephew
to Von Hindenburg and second cousin to the devil. Reach
me a rose, honey, and pour me a last drop into that there
crystal glass.'

Once I wrote down on the empty spaces of a timetable
the names of those who came to Gatsby's house that
summer. It is an old timetable now, disintegrating at its
folds, and headed 'This schedule in effect July 5th, 1922'.
But I can still read the grey names, and they will give you
a better impression than my generalities of those who
accepted Gatsby's hospitality and paid him the subtle
tribute of knowing nothing whatever about him.

From East Egg, then, came the Chester Beckers and the
Leeches, and a man named Bunsen, whom I knew at Yale,
and Doctor Webster Civet, who was drowned last summer
up in Maine. And the Hornbeams and the Willie Voltaires,
and a whole clan named Blackbuck, who always gathered in
a corner and flipped up their noses like goats at whosoever
came near. And the Ismays and the Chrysties (or rather
Hubert Auerbach and Mr. Chrystie's wife), and Edgar
Beaver, whose hair, they say, turned cotton-white one
winter afternoon for no good reason at all.

Clarence Endive was from East Egg, as I remember. He

came only once, in white knickerbockers, and had a fight with a bum named Etty in the garden. From farther out on the Island came the Cheadles and the O. R. P. Schraeders, and the Stonewall Jackson Abrams of Georgia, and the Fishguards and the Ripley Snells. Snell was there three days before he went to the penitentiary, so drunk out on the gravel drive that Mrs. Ulysses Swett's automobile ran over his right hand. The Dancies came, too, and S. B. Whitebait, who was well over sixty, and Maurice A. Flink, and the Hammerheads, and Beluga the tobacco importer, and Beluga's girls.

From West Egg came the Poles and the Mulreadys and Cecil Roebuck and Cecil Schoen and Gulick the State senator and Newton Orchid, who controlled Films Par Excellence, and Eckhaust and Clyde Cohen and Don S. Schwartze (the son) and Arthur McCarty, all connected with the movies in one way or another. And the Catlips and the Bembergs and G. Earl Muldoon, brother to that Muldoon who afterwards strangled his wife. Da Fontano the promoter came there, and Ed Legros and James B. ('Rot-Gut') Ferret and the De Jongs and Ernest Lilly— they came to gamble, and when Ferret wandered into the garden it meant he was cleaned out and Associated Traction would have to fluctuate profitably next day.

A man named Klipspringer was there so often and so long that he became known as 'the boarder'—I doubt if he had any other home. Of theatrical people there were Gus Waize and Horace O'Donavan and Lester Myer and George Duckweed and Francis Bull. Also from New York were the Chromes and the Backhyssons and the Dennickers and Russell Betty and the Corrigans and the Kellehers and the Dewers and the Scullys and S. W. Belcher and the Smirkes and the young Quinns, divorced now, and Henry L. Palmetto, who killed himself by jumping in front of a sub-way train in Times Square.

Benny McClenahan arrived always with four girls. They were never quite the same ones in physical person, but they were so identical one with another that it inevitably seemed that they had been there before. I have forgotten their names—Jacqueline, I think, or else Consuela, or Gloria or Judy or June, and their last names were either the melodious names of flowers and months or the sterner ones of the great American capitalists whose cousins, if pressed, they would confess themselves to be.

In addition to all these I can remember that Faustina O'Brien came there at least once and the Baedeker girls and young Brewer, who had his nose shot off in the war, and Mr. Albrucksburger and Miss Haag, his fiancée, and Ardita Fitz-Peters and Mr. P. Jewett, once head of the American Legion, and Miss Claudia Hip, with a man reputed to be her chauffeur, and a prince of something, whom we called Duke, and whose name, if I ever knew it, I have forgotten.

All these people came to Gatsby's house in the summer.

At nine o'clock, one morning late in July, Gatsby's gorgeous car lurched up the rocky drive to my door and gave out a burst of melody from its three-noted horn. It was the first time he had called on me, though I had gone to two of his parties, mounted in his hydroplane, and, at his urgent invitation, made frequent use of his beach.

'Good morning, old sport. You're having lunch with me to-day and I thought we'd ride up together.'

He was balancing himself on the dashboard of his car with the resourcefulness of movement that is so peculiarly American—that comes, I suppose, with the absence of lifting work in youth and, even more, with the formless grace of our nervous, sporadic games. This quality was continually breaking through his punctilious manner in the shape of restlessness. He was never quite still; there was always a tapping foot somewhere or the impatient opening and closing of a hand.

He saw me looking with admiration at his car.

'It's pretty, isn't it, old sport?' He jumped off to give me a better view. 'Haven't you ever seen it before?'

I'd seen it. Everybody had seen it. It was a rich cream colour, bright with nickel, swollen here and there in its monstrous length with triumphant hat-boxes and supper-boxes and tool-boxes, and terraced with a labyrinth of wind-shields that mirrored a dozen suns. Sitting down behind many layers of glass in a sort of green leather conservatory, we started to town.

I had talked with him perhaps half a dozen times in the past month and found, to my disappointment, that he had little to say. So my first impression, that he was a person of some undefined consequence, had gradually faded and he had become simply the proprietor of an elaborate roadhouse next door.

And then came that disconcerting ride. We hadn't reached West Egg Village before Gatsby began leaving his elegant sentences unfinished and slapping himself indecisively on the knee of his caramel-coloured suit.

'Look here, old sport,' he broke out surprisingly, 'what's your opinion of me, anyhow?'

A little overwhelmed, I began the generalized evasions which that question deserves.

'Well, I'm going to tell you something about my life,' he interrupted. 'I don't want you to get a wrong idea of me from all these stories you hear.'

So he was aware of the bizarre accusations that flavoured conversation in his halls.

'I'll tell you God's truth.' His right hand suddenly ordered divine retribution to stand by. 'I am the son of some wealthy people in the Middle West—all dead now. I was brought up in America but educated at Oxford, because all my ancestors have been educated there for many years. It is a family tradition.'

He looked at me sideways—and I knew why Jordan Baker had believed he was lying. He hurried the phrase 'educated at Oxford,' or swallowed it, or choked on it, as though it had bothered him before. And with this doubt, his whole statement fell to pieces, and I wondered if there wasn't something a little sinister about him, after all.

'What part of the Middle West?' I inquired casually.

'San Francisco.'

'I see.'

'My family all died and I came into a good deal of money.'

His voice was solemn, as if the memory of that sudden extinction of a clan still haunted him. For a moment I suspected that he was pulling my leg, but a glance at him convinced me otherwise.

'After that I lived like a young rajah in all the capitals of Europe—Paris, Venice, Rome—collecting jewels, chiefly rubies, hunting big game, painting a little, things for myself only, and trying to forget something very sad that had happened to me long ago.'

With an effort I managed to restrain my incredulous laughter. The very phrases were worn so threadbare that they evoked no image except that of a turbaned 'character' leaking sawdust at every pore as he pursued a tiger through the Bois de Boulogne.

'Then came the war, old sport. It was a great relief, and I tried very hard to die, but I seemed to bear an enchanted life. I accepted a commission as first lieutenant when it began. In the Argonne Forest I took the remains of my machine-gun battalion so far forward that there was a half mile gap on either side of us where the infantry couldn't advance. We stayed there two days and two nights, a hundred and thirty men with sixteen Lewis guns, and when the infantry came up at last they found the insignia of three German divisions among the piles of dead. I was promoted to be a major, and every Allied government gave me a decoration—even Montenegro, little Montenegro down on the Adriatic Sea!'

Little Montenegro! He lifted up the words and nodded at them—with his smile. The smile comprehended Montenegro's troubled history and sympathized with the brave struggles of the Montenegrin people. It appreciated fully the chain of national circumstances which had elicited this tribute from Montenegro's warm little heart. My incredulity was submerged in fascination now; it was like skimming hastily through a dozen magazines.

He reached in his pocket, and a piece of metal, slung on a ribbon, fell into my palm.

'That's the one from Montenegro.'

To my astonishment, the thing had an authentic look. 'Orderi de Danilo,' ran the circular legend, 'Montenegro, Nicolas Rex.'

'Turn it.'

'Major Jay Gatsby,' I read, 'For Valour Extraordinary.'

'Here's another thing I always carry. A souvenir of Oxford days. It was taken in Trinity Quad—the man on my left is now the Earl of Doncaster.'

It was a photograph of half a dozen young men in blazers loafing in an archway through which were visible a host of spires. There was Gatsby, looking a little, not much, younger—with a cricket bat in his hand.

Then it was all true. I saw the skins of tigers flaming in his palace on the Grand Canal; I saw him opening a chest of rubies to ease, with their crimson-lighted depths, the gnawings of his broken heart.

'I'm going to make a big request of you to-day,' he said, pocketing his souvenirs with satisfaction, 'so I thought you ought to know something about me. I didn't want you to think I was just some nobody. You see, I usually find myself among strangers because I drift here and there trying to forget the sad thing that happened to me.' He hesitated. 'You'll hear about it this afternoon.'

'At lunch?'

'No, this afternoon. I happened to find out that you're taking Miss Baker to tea.'

'Do you mean you're in love with Miss Baker?'

'No, old sport, I'm not. But Miss Baker has kindly consented to speak to you about this matter.'

I hadn't the faintest idea what 'this matter' was, but I was more annoyed than interested. I hadn't asked Jordan to tea in order to discuss Mr. Jay Gatsby. I was sure the request would be something utterly fantastic, and for a moment I was sorry I'd ever set foot upon his overpopulated lawn.

He wouldn't say another word. His correctness grew on

him as we neared the city. We passed Port Roosevelt, where there was a glimpse of red-belted ocean-going ships, and sped along a cobbled slum lined with the dark, undeserted saloons of the faded-gilt nineteen-hundreds. Then the valley of ashes opened out on both sides of us, and I had a glimpse of Mrs. Wilson straining at the garage pump with panting vitality as we went by.

With fenders spread like wings we scattered light through half Astoria—only half, for as we twisted among the pillars of the elevated I heard the familiar 'jug-jug-*spat*!' of a motorcycle, and a frantic policeman rode alongside.

'All right, old sport,' called Gatsby. We slowed down. Taking a white card from his wallet, he waved it before the man's eyes.

'Right you are,' agreed the policeman, tipping his cap 'Know you next time, Mr. Gatsby. Excuse *me!*'

'What was that?' I inquired. 'The picture of Oxford?'

'I was able to do the commissioner a favour once, and he sends me a Christmas card every year.'

Over the great bridge, with the sunlight through the girders making a constant flicker upon the moving cars, with the city rising up across the river in white heaps and sugar lumps all built with a wish out of non-olfactory money. The city seen from the Queensboro Bridge is always the city seen for the first time, in its first wild promise of all the mystery and the beauty in the world.

A dead man passed us in a hearse heaped with blooms, followed by two carriages with drawn blinds, and by more cheerful carriages for friends. The friends looked out at us with the tragic eyes and short upper lips of south-eastern Europe, and I was glad that the sight of Gatsby's splendid car was included in their sombre holiday. As we crossed Blackwell's Island a limousine passed us, driven by a white chauffeur, in which sat three modish negroes, two bucks and a girl. I laughed aloud as the yolks of their eyeballs rolled towards us in haughty rivalry.

'Anything can happen now that we've slid over this bridge,' I thought; 'anything at all. . . .'

Even Gatsby could happen, without any particular wonder.

Roaring noon. In a well-fanned Forty-second Street cellar I met Gatsby for lunch. Blinking away the brightness of the street outside, my eyes picked him out obscurely in the ante-room, talking to another man.

'Mr. Carraway, this is my friend Mr. Wolfsheim.'

A small, flat-nosed Jew raised his large head and regarded me with two fine growths of hair which luxuriated in either nostril. After a moment I discovered his tiny eyes in the half-darkness.

'—So I took one look at him,' said Mr. Wolfsheim, shaking my hand earnestly, 'and what do you think I did?'

'What?' I inquired politely.

But evidently he was not addressing me, for he dropped my hand and covered Gatsby with his expressive nose.

'I handed the money to Katspaugh and I said: "All right, Katspaugh, don't pay him a penny till he shuts his mouth." He shut it then and there.'

Gatsby took an arm of each of us and moved forward into the restaurant, whereupon Mr. Wolfsheim swallowed a new sentence he was starting and lapsed into a somnambulatory abstraction.

'Highballs?' asked the head waiter.

'This is a nice restaurant here,' said Mr. Wolfsheim, looking at the Presbyterian nymphs on the ceiling. 'But I like across the street better!'

'Yes, highballs,' agreed Gatsby, and then to Mr. Wolfsheim: 'It's too hot over there.'

'Hot and small—yes,' said Mr. Wolfsheim, 'but full of memories.'

'What place is that?' I asked.

'The old Metropole.'

'The old Metropole,' brooded Mr. Wolfsheim gloomily. 'Filled with faces dead and gone. Filled with friends gone now forever. I can't forget so long as I live the night they

3*

shot Rosy Rosenthal there. It was six of us at the table, and Rosy had eat and drunk a lot all evening. When it was almost morning the waiter came up to him with a funny look and says somebody wants to speak to him outside. "All right," says Rosy, and begins to get up, and I pulled him down in his chair.

'"Let the bastards come in here if they want you, Rosy, but don't you, so help me, move outside this room."

'It was four o'clock in the morning then, and if we'd of raised the blinds we'd of seen daylight.'

'Did he go?' I asked innocently.

'Sure he went.' Mr. Wolfsheim's nose flashed at me indignantly. 'He turned around in the door and says: "Don't let that waiter take away my coffee!" Then he went out on the sidewalk, and they shot him three times in his full belly and drove away.'

'Four of them were electrocuted,' I said, remembering.

'Five, with Becker.' His nostrils turned to me in an interested way. 'I understand you're looking for a business gonnegtion.'

The juxtaposition of these two remarks was startling. Gatsby answered for me:

'Oh, no,' he exclaimed, 'this isn't the man.'

'No?' Mr. Wolfsheim seemed disappointed.

'This is just a friend. I told you we'd talk about that some other time.'

'I beg your pardon,' said Mr. Wolfsheim, 'I had a wrong man.'

A succulent hash arrived, and Mr. Wolfsheim, forgetting the more sentimental atmosphere of the old Metropole, began to eat with ferocious delicacy. His eyes, meanwhile, roved very slowly all around the room—he completed the arc by turning to inspect the people directly behind. I think that, except for my presence, he would have taken one short glance beneath our own table.

'Look here, old sport,' said Gatsby leaning towards me, 'I'm afraid I made you a little angry this morning in the car.'

There was the smile again, but this time I held out against it.

'I don't like mysteries,' I answered, 'and I don't understand why you won't come out frankly and tell me what you want. Why has it all got to come through Miss Baker?'

'Oh, it's nothing underhand,' he assured me. 'Miss Baker's a great sportswoman, you know, and she'd never do anything that wasn't all right.'

Suddenly he looked at his watch, jumped up, and hurried from the room, leaving me with Mr. Wolfsheim at the table.

'He has to telephone,' said Mr. Wolfsheim, following him with his eyes. 'Fine fellow, isn't he? Handsome to look at and a perfect gentleman.'

'Yes.'

'He's an Oggsford man.'

'Oh!'

'He went to Oggsford College in England. You know Oggsford College?'

'I've heard of it.'

'It's one of the most famous colleges in the world.'

'Have you known Gatsby for a long time?' I inquired.

'Several years,' he answered in a gratified way. 'I made the pleasure of his acquaintance just after the war. But I knew I had discovered a man of fine breeding after I talked with him an hour. I said to myself: "There's the kind of man you'd like to take home and introduce to your mother and sister."' He paused. 'I see you're looking at my cuff buttons.'

I hadn't been looking at them, but I did now. They were composed of oddly familiar pieces of ivory.

'Finest specimens of human molars,' he informed me.

'Well!' I inspected them. 'That's a very interesting idea.'

'Yeah.' He flipped his sleeves up under his coat. 'Yeah, Gatsby's very careful about women. He would never so much as look at a friend's wife.'

When the subject of this instinctive trust returned to the table and sat down Mr. Wolfsheim drank his coffee with a jerk and got to his feet.

'I have enjoyed my lunch,' he said, 'and I'm going to run off from you two young men before I outstay my welcome.'

'Don't hurry, Meyer,' said Gatsby, without enthusiasm. Mr. Wolfsheim raised his hand in a sort of benediction.

'You're very polite, but I belong to another generation,' he announced solemnly. 'You sit here and discuss your sports and your young ladies and your——' He supplied an imaginary noun with another wave of his hand. 'As for me, I am fifty years old, and I won't impose myself on you any longer.'

As he shook hands and turned away his tragic nose was trembling. I wondered if I had said anything to offend him.

'He becomes very sentimental sometimes,' explained Gatsby. 'This is one of his sentimental days. He's quite a character around New York—a denizen of Broadway.'

'Who is he, anyhow, an actor?'

'No.'

'A dentist?'

'Meyer Wolfsheim? No, he's a gambler.' Gatsby hesitated, then added coolly: 'He's the man who fixed the World's Series back in 1919.'

'Fixed the World's Series?' I repeated.

The idea staggered me. I remembered, of course, that the World's Series had been fixed in 1919, but if I had thought of it at all I would have thought of it as a thing that merely *happened*, the end of some inevitable chain. It never occurred to me that one man could start to play with the faith of fifty million people—with the singlemindedness of a burglar blowing a safe.

'How did he happen to do that?' I asked after a minute.

'He just saw the opportunity.'

'Why isn't he in jail?'

'They can't get him, old sport. He's a smart man.'

I insisted on paying the check. As the waiter brought my change I caught sight of Tom Buchanan across the crowded room.

'Come along with me for a minute,' I said; 'I've got to say hello to someone.'

When he saw us Tom jumped up and took half a dozen steps in our direction.

'Where've you been?' he demanded eagerly. 'Daisy's furious because you haven't called up.'

'This is Mr. Gatsby, Mr. Buchanan.'

They shook hands briefly, and a strained, unfamiliar look of embarrassment came over Gatsby's face.

'How've you been, anyhow?' demanded Tom of me. 'How'd you happen to come up this far to eat?'

'I've been having lunch with Mr. Gatsby.'

I turned towards Mr. Gatsby, but he was no longer there.

One October day in nineteen-seventeen——

(said Jordan Baker that afternoon, sitting up very straight on a straight chair in the tea-garden at the Plaza Hotel)

—I was walking along from one place to another, half on the sidewalks and half on the lawns. I was happier on the lawns because I had on shoes from England with rubber nobs on the soles that bit into the soft ground. I had on a new plaid skirt also that blew a little in the wind, and whenever this happened the red, white, and blue banners in front of all the houses stretched out stiff and said *tut-tut-tut-tut*, in a disapproving way.

The largest of the banners and the largest of the lawns belonged to Daisy Fay's house. She was just eighteen, two years older than me, and by far the most popular of all the young girls in Louisville. She dressed in white, and had a little white roadster, and all day long the telephone rang in her house and excited young officers from Camp Taylor demanded the privilege of monopolizing her that night. 'Anyways, for an hour!'

When I came opposite her house that morning her white roadster was beside the curb, and she was sitting in it with a lieutenant I had never seen before. They were so engrossed in each other that she didn't see me until I was five feet away.

'Hello, Jordan,' she called unexpectedly. 'Please come here.'

I was flattered that she wanted to speak to me, because of all the older girls I admired her most. She asked me if I was going to the Red Cross and make bandages. I was. Well, then, would I tell them that she couldn't come that day? The officer looked at Daisy while she was speaking, in a way that every young girl wants to be looked at some time, and because it seemed romantic to me I have remembered the incident ever since. His name was Jay Gatsby, and I didn't lay eyes on him again for over four years—even after I'd met him on Long Island I didn't realize it was the same man.

That was nineteen-seventeen. By the next year I had a few beaux myself, and I began to play in tournaments, so I didn't see Daisy very often. She went with a slightly older crowd—when she went with anyone at all. Wild rumours were circulating about her—how her mother had found her packing her bag one winter night to go to New York and say good-bye to a soldier who was going overseas. She was effactually prevented, but she wasn't on speaking terms with her family for several weeks. After that she didn't play around with the soldiers any more, but only with a few flat-footed, short-sighted young men in town, who couldn't get into the army at all.

By the next autumn she was gay again, gay as ever. She had a début after the Armistice, and in February she was presumably engaged to a man from New Orleans. In June she married Tom Buchanan of Chicago, with more pomp and circumstance than Louisville ever knew before. He came down with a hundred people in four private cars, and hired a whole floor of the Muhlbach Hotel, and the day before the wedding he gave her a string of pearls valued at three hundred and fifty thousand dollars.

I was a bridesmaid. I came into her room half an hour before the bridal dinner, and found her lying on her bed as lovely as the June night in her flowered dress—and as drunk as a monkey. She had a bottle of Sauterne in one hand and a letter in the other.

''Gratulate me,' she muttered. 'Never had a drink before, but oh how I do enjoy it.'

'What's the matter, Daisy?'

I was scared, I can tell you; I'd never seen a girl like that before.

'Here, deares'.' She groped around in a waste-basket she had with her on the bed and pulled out the string of pearls. 'Take 'em downstairs and give 'em back to whoever they belong to. Tell 'em all Daisy's change' her mine. Say: "Daisy's change' her mine!"'

She began to cry—she cried and cried. I rushed out and found her mother's maid, and we locked the door and got her into a cold bath. She wouldn't let go of the letter. She took it into the tub with her and squeezed it up into a wet ball, and only let me leave it in the soap-dish when she saw that it was coming to pieces like snow.

But she didn't say another word. We gave her spirits of ammonia and put ice on her forehead and hooked her back into her dress, and half an hour later, when we walked out of the room, the pearls were around her neck and the incident was over. Next day at five o'clock she married Tom Buchanan without so much as a shiver, and started off on a three months' trip to the South Seas.

I saw them in Santa Barbara when they came back, and I thought I'd never seen a girl so mad about her husband. If he left the room for a minute she'd look around uneasily, and say: 'Where's Tom gone?' and wear the most abstracted expression until she saw him coming in the door. She used to sit on the sand with his head in her lap by the hour, rubbing her fingers over his eyes and looking at him with unfathomable delight. It was touching to see them together —it made you laugh in a hushed, fascinated way. That was in August. A week after I left Santa Barbara Tom ran into a wagon on the Ventura road one night, and ripped a front wheel off his car. The girl who was with him got into the papers, too, because her arm was broken—she was one of the chambermaids in the Santa Barbara Hotel.

The next April Daisy had her little girl, and they went to France for a year. I saw them one spring in Cannes, and later in Deauville, and then they came back to Chicago to settle down. Daisy was popular in Chicago, as you know. They moved with a fast crowd, all of them young and rich and wild, but she came out with an absolutely perfect reputation. Perhaps because she doesn't drink. It's a great advantage not to drink among hard-drinking people. You can hold your tongue, and, moreover, you can time any little irregularity of your own so that everybody else is so blind that they don't see or care. Perhaps Daisy never went in for amour at all—and yet there's something in that voice of hers. . . .

Well, about six weeks ago, she heard the name Gatsby for the first time in years. It was when I asked you—do you remember?—if you knew Gatsby in West Egg. After you had gone home she came into my room and woke me up, and said: 'What Gatsby?' and when I described him—I was half asleep—she said in the strangest voice that it must be the man she used to know. It wasn't until then that I connected this Gatsby with the officer in her white car.

When Jordan Baker had finished telling all this we had left the Plaza for half an hour and were driving in a victoria through Central Park. The sun had gone down behind the tall apartments of the movie stars in the West Fifties, and the clear voices of children, already gathered like crickets on the grass, rose through the hot twilight:

> '*I'm the Sheik of Araby.*
> *Your love belongs to me.*
> *At night when you're asleep*
> *Into your tent I'll creep——*'

'It was a strange coincidence,' I said.

'But it wasn't a coincidence at all.'

'Why not?'

'Gatsby bought that house so that Daisy would be just across the bay.'

Then it had not been merely the stars to which he had aspired on that June night. He came alive to me, delivered suddenly from the womb of his purposeless splendour.

'He wants to know,' continued Jordan, 'if you'll invite Daisy to your house some afternoon and then let him come over.'

The modesty of the demand shook me. He had waited five years and bought a mansion where he dispensed starlight to casual moths—so that he could 'come over' some afternoon to a stranger's garden.

'Did I have to know all this before he could ask such a little thing?'

'He's afraid, he's waited so long. He thought you might be offended. You see, he's regular tough underneath it all.'

Something worried me.

'Why didn't he ask you to arrange a meeting?'

'He wants her to see his house,' she explained. 'And your house is right next door.'

'Oh!'

'I think he half expected her to wander into one of his parties, some night,' went on Jordan, 'but she never did. Then he began asking people casually if they knew her, and I was the first one he found. It was that night he sent for me at his dance, and you should have heard the elaborate way he worked up to it. Of course, I immediately suggested a luncheon in New York—and I thought he'd go mad:

'"I don't want to do anything out of the way!" he kept saying. "I want to see her right next door."

'When I said you were a particular friend of Tom's, he started to abandon the whole idea. He doesn't know very much about Tom, though he says he's read a Chicago paper for years just on the chance of catching a glimpse of Daisy's name.'

It was dark now, and as we dipped under a little bridge I put my arm around Jordan's golden shoulder and drew her towards me and asked her to dinner. Suddenly I wasn't thinking of Daisy and Gatsby any more, but of this clean, hard, limited person, who dealt in universal scepticism, and who leaned back jauntily just within the circle of my arm. A phrase began to beat in my ears with a sort of heady excitement: 'There are only the pursued, the pursuing, the busy and the tired.'

'And Daisy ought to have something in her life,' murmured Jordan to me.

'Does she want to see Gatsby?'

'She's not to know about it. Gatsby doesn't want her to know. You're just supposed to invite her to tea.'

We passed a barrier of dark trees, and then the façade of Fifty-ninth Street, a block of delicate pale light, beamed down into the park. Unlike Gatsby and Tom Buchanan, I had no girl whose disembodied face floated along the dark cornices and blinding signs, and so I drew up the girl beside me, tightening my arms. Her wan, scornful mouth smiled, and so I drew her up again closer, this time to my face.

CHAPTER V

WHEN I CAME HOME to West Egg that night I was afraid for a moment that my house was on fire. Two o'clock and the whole corner of the peninsula was blazing with light, which fell unreal on the shrubbery and made thin elongating glints upon the roadside wires. Turning a corner, I saw that it was Gatsby's house, lit from tower to cellar.

At first I thought it was another party, a wild rout that had resolved itself into 'hide-and-seek' or 'sardines-in-the-box' with all the house thrown open to the game. But there wasn't a sound. Only wind in the trees, which blew the wires and made the lights go off and on again as if the house had winked into the darkness. As my taxi groaned away I saw Gatsby walking towards me across his lawn.

'Your place looks like the World's Fair,' I said.

'Does it?' He turned his eyes towards it absently. 'I have been glancing into some of the rooms. Let's go to Coney Island, old sport. In my car.'

'It's too late.'

'Well, suppose we take a plunge in the swimming-pool? I haven't made use of it all summer.'

'I've got to go to bed.'

'All right.'

He waited, looking at me with suppressed eagerness.

'I talked with Miss Baker,' I said after a moment. 'I'm going to call up Daisy to-morrow and invite her over here to tea.'

'Oh, that's all right,' he said carelessly. 'I don't want to put you to any trouble.'

'What day would suit you?'

'What day would suit *you*?' he corrected me quickly. 'I don't want to put you to any trouble, you see.'

'How about the day after to-morrow?'

He considered for a moment. Then, with reluctance:

'I want to get the grass cut,' he said.

We both looked down at the grass—there was a sharp line where my ragged lawn ended and the darker, well-kept expanse of his began. I suspected that he meant my grass.

'There's another little thing,' he said uncertainly, and hesitated.

'Would you rather put it off for a few days?' I asked.

'Oh, it isn't about that. At least—' He fumbled with a series of beginnings. 'Why, I thought—why, look here, old sport, you don't make much money, do you?'

'Not very much.'

This seemed to reassure him and he continued more confidently.

'I thought you didn't if you'll pardon my—you see, I carry on a little business on the side, a sort of side line, you understand. And I thought that if you don't make very much— You're selling bonds, aren't you, old sport?'

'Trying to.'

'Well, this would interest you. It wouldn't take up much of your time and you might pick up a nice bit of money. It happens to be a rather confidential sort of thing.'

I realize now that under different circumstances that

conversation might have been one of the crises of my life. But, because the offer was obviously and tactlessly for a service to be rendered, I had no choice except to cut him off there.

'I've got my hands full,' I said. 'I'm much obliged but I couldn't take on any more work.'

'You wouldn't have to do any business with Wolfsheim.' Evidently he thought that I was shying away from the 'gonnegtion' mentioned at lunch, but I assured him he was wrong. He waited a moment longer, hoping I'd begin a conversation, but I was too absorbed to be responsive, so he went unwillingly home.

The evening had made me light-headed and happy; I think I walked into a deep sleep as I entered my front door. So I don't know whether or not Gatsby went to Coney Island, or for how many hours he 'glanced into rooms' while his house blazed gaudily on. I called up Daisy from the office next morning, and invited her to come to tea.

'Don't bring Tom,' I warned her.

'What?'

'Don't bring Tom.'

'Who is "Tom"?' she asked innocently.

The day agreed upon was pouring rain. At eleven o'clock a man in a raincoat, dragging a lawn-mower, tapped at my front door and said that Mr. Gatsby had sent him over to cut my grass. This reminded me that I had forgotten to tell my Finn to come back, so I drove into West Egg Village to search for her among soggy whitewashed alleys and to buy some cups and lemons and flowers.

The flowers were unnecessary, for at two o'clock a greenhouse arrived from Gatsby's, with innumerable receptacles to contain it. An hour later the front door opened nervously, and Gatsby, in a white flannel suit, silver shirt, and gold-coloured tie, hurried in. He was pale, and there were dark signs of sleeplessness beneath his eyes.

'Is everything all right?' he asked immediately.

'The grass looks fine, if that's what you mean.'

'What grass?' he inquired blankly. 'Oh, the grass in the

yard.' He looked out the window at it, but, judging from his expression, I don't believe he saw a thing.

'Looks very good,' he remarked vaguely. 'One of the papers said they thought the rain would stop about four. I think it was *The Journal*. Have you got everything you need in the shape of—of tea?'

I took him into the pantry, where he looked a little reproachfully at the Finn. Together we scrutinized the twelve lemon cakes from the delicatessen shop.

'Will they do?' I asked.

'Of course, of course! They're fine!' and he added hollowly, '. . . old sport.'

The rain cooled about half-past three to a damp mist, through which occasional thin drops swam like dew. Gatsby looked with vacant eyes through a copy of Clay's *Economics*, starting at the Finnish tread that shook the kitchen floor, and peering towards the bleared windows from time to time as if a series of invisible but alarming happenings were taking place outside. Finally he got up and informed me, in an uncertain voice, that he was going home.

'Why's that?'

'Nobody's coming to tea. It's too late!' He looked at his watch as if there was some pressing demand on his time elsewhere. 'I can't wait all day.'

'Don't be silly; it's just two minutes to four.'

He sat down miserably, as if I had pushed him, and simultaneously there was the sound of a motor turning into my lane. We both jumped up, and, a little harrowed myself, I went out into the yard.

Under the dripping bare lilac-trees a large open car was coming up the drive. It stopped. Daisy's face, tipped sideways beneath a three-cornered lavender hat, looked at me with a bright ecstatic smile.

'Is this absolutely where you live, my dearest one?'

The exhilarating ripple of her voice was a wild tonic in the rain. I had to follow the sound of it for a moment, up and down, with my ear alone, before any words came through. A damp streak of hair lay like a dash of blue paint across her cheek, and her hand was wet with glistening drops as I took it to help her from the car.

'Are you in love with me,' she said low in my ear, 'or why did I have to come alone?'

'That's the secret of Castle Rackrent. Tell your chauffeur to go far away and spend an hour.'

'Come back in an hour, Ferdie.' Then in a grave murmur : 'His name is Ferdie.'

'Does the gasoline affect his nose?'

'I don't think so,' she said innocently. 'Why?'

We went in. To my overwhelming surprise the living-room was deserted.

'Well, that's funny,' I exclaimed.

'What's funny?'

She turned her head as there was a light dignified knocking at the front door. I went out and opened it. Gatsby, pale as death, with his hands plunged like weights in his coat pockets, was standing in a puddle of water glaring tragically into my eyes.

With his hands still in his coat pockets he stalked by me into the hall, turned sharply as if he were on a wire, and disappeared into the living-room. It wasn't a bit funny. Aware of the loud beating of my own heart I pulled the door to against the increasing rain.

For half a minute there wasn't a sound. Then from the living-room I heard a sort of choking murmur and part of a laugh, followed by Daisy's voice on a clear artificial note :

'I certainly am awfully glad to see you again.'

A pause; it endured horribly. I had nothing to do in the hall, so I went into the room.

Gatsby, his hands still in his pockets, was reclining against the mantelpiece in a strained counterfeit of perfect ease, even of boredom. His head leaned back so far that it rested against the face of a defunct mantelpiece clock, and from this position his distraught eyes stared down at Daisy, who was sitting, frightened but graceful, on the edge of a stiff chair.

'We've met before,' muttered Gatsby. His eyes glanced

momentarily at me, and his lips parted with an abortive attempt at a laugh. Luckily the clock took this moment to tilt dangerously at the pressure of his head, whereupon he turned and caught it with trembling fingers and set it back in place. Then he sat down, rigidly, his elbow on the arm of the sofa and his chin in his hand.

'I'm sorry about the clock,' he said.

My own face had now assumed a deep tropical burn. I couldn't muster up a single commonplace out of the thousand in my head.

'It's an old clock,' I told them idiotically.

I think we all believed for a moment that it had smashed in pieces on the floor.

'We haven't met for many years,' said Daisy, her voice as matter-of-fact as it could ever be.

'Five years next November.'

The automatic quality of Gatsby's answer set us all back at least another minute. I had them both on their feet with the desperate suggestion that they help me make tea in the kitchen when the demoniac Finn brought it in on a tray.

Amid the welcome confusion of cups and cakes a certain physical decency established itself. Gatsby got himself into a shadow and, while Daisy and I talked, looked conscientiously from one to the other of us with tense, unhappy eyes. However, as calmness wasn't an end in itself, I made an excuse at the first possible moment, and got to my feet.

'Where are you going?' demanded Gatsby in immediate alarm.

'I'll be back.'

'I've got to speak to you about something before you go.'

He followed me wildly into the kitchen, closed the door, and whispered: 'Oh, God!' in a miserable way.

'What's the matter?'

'This is a terrible mistake,' he said, shaking his head from side to side, 'a terrible, terrible mistake.'

'You're just embarrassed, that's all,' and luckily I added: 'Daisy's embarrassed too.'

'She's embarrassed?' he repeated incredulously.

'Just as much as you are.'

'Don't talk so loud.'

'You're acting like a little boy,' I broke out impatiently. 'Not only that, but you're rude. Daisy's sitting in there all alone.'

He raised his hand to stop my words, looked at me with unforgettable reproach, and, opening the door cautiously, went back into the other room.

I walked out the back way—just as Gatsby had when he had made his nervous circuit of the house half an hour before—and ran for a huge black knotted tree, whose massed leaves made a fabric against the rain. Once more it was pouring, and my irregular lawn, well-shaved by Gatsby's gardener, abounded in small muddy swamps and prehistoric marshes. There was nothing to look at from under the tree except Gatsby's enormous house, so I stared at it, like Kant at his church steeple, for half an hour. A brewer had built it early in the 'period' craze a decade before, and there was a story that he'd agreed to pay five years' taxes on all the neighbouring cottages if the owners would have their roofs thatched with straw. Perhaps their refusal took the heart out of his plan to Found a Family— he went into an immediate decline. His children sold his house with the black wreath still on the door. Americans, while willing, even eager, to be serfs, have always been obstinate about being peasantry.

After half an hour, the sun shone again, and the grocer's automobile rounded Gatsby's drive with the raw material for his servants' dinner—I felt sure he wouldn't eat a spoonful. A maid began opening the upper windows of his house, appeared momentarily in each, and, leaning from the large central bay, spat meditatively into the garden. It was time I went back. While the rain continued it had seemed like the murmur of their voices, rising and swelling a little now and then with gusts of emotion. But in the new silence I felt that silence had fallen within the house too.

I went in—after making every possible noise in the

kitchen, short of pushing over the stove—but I don't believe they heard a sound. They were sitting at either end of the couch, looking at each other as if some question had been asked, or was in the air, and every vestige of embarrassment was gone. Daisy's face was smeared with tears, and when I came in she jumped up and began wiping at it with her handkerchief before a mirror. But there was a change in Gatsby that was simply confounding. He literally glowed; without a word or a gesture of exultation a new well-being radiated from him and filled the little room.

'Oh, hello old sport,' he said, as if he hadn't seen me for years. I thought for a moment he was going to shake hands.

'It's stopped raining.'

'Has it?' When he realized what I was talking about, that there were twinkle-bells of sunshine in the room, he smiled like a weather man, like an ecstatic patron of recurrent light, and repeated the news to Daisy. 'What do you think of that? It's stopped raining.'

'I'm glad, Jay.' Her throat, full of aching, grieving beauty, told only of her unexpected joy.

'I want you and Daisy to come over to my house,' he said, 'I'd like to show her around.'

'You're sure you want me to come?'

'Absolutely, old sport.'

Daisy went upstairs to wash her face—too late I thought with humiliation of my towels—while Gatsby and I waited on the lawn.

'My house looks well, doesn't it?' he demanded. 'See how the whole front of it catches the light.'

I agreed that it was splendid.

'Yes.' His eyes went over it, every arched door and square tower. 'It took me just three years to earn the money that bought it.'

'I thought you inherited your money.'

'I did, old sport,' he said automatically, 'but I lost most of it in the big panic—the panic of the war.'

I think he hardly knew what he was saying, for when I asked him what business he was in he answered: 'That's my affair,' before he realized that it wasn't an appropriate reply.

'Oh, I've been in several things,' he corrected himself. 'I was in the drug business and then I was in the oil business. But I'm not in either one now.' He looked at me with more attention. 'Do you mean you've been thinking over what I proposed the other night?'

Before I could answer, Daisy came out of the house and two rows of brass buttons on her dress gleamed in the sunlight.

'That huge place *there*?' she cried pointing.

'Do you like it?'

'I love it, but I don't see how you live there all alone.'

'I keep it always full of interesting people, night and day. People who do interesting things. Celebrated people.'

Instead of taking the short cut along the Sound we went down to the road and entered by the big postern. With enchanting murmurs Daisy admired this aspect or that of the feudal silhouette against the sky, admired the gardens, the sparkling odour of jonquils and the frothy odour of hawthorn and plum blossoms and the pale gold odour of kiss-me-at-the-gate. It was strange to reach the marble steps and find no stir of bright dresses in and out of the door, and hear no sound but bird voices in the trees.

And inside, as we wandered through Marie Antoinette music-rooms and Restoration Salons, I felt that there were guests concealed behind every couch and table, under orders to be breathlessly silent until we had passed through. As Gatsby closed the door of 'the Merton College Library' I could have sworn I heard the owl-eyed man break into ghostly laughter.

We went upstairs, through period bedrooms swathed in rose and lavender silk and vivid with new flowers, through dressing-rooms and poolrooms, and bathrooms, with sunken baths—intruding into one chamber where a dishevelled man in pyjamas was doing liver exercises on the floor. It was Mr. Klipspringer, the 'boarder.' I had seen him wandering hungrily about the beach that morning. Finally we came to

Gatsby's own apartment, a bedroom and a bath, and an Adam study, where we sat down and drank a glass of some Chartreuse he took from a cupboard in the wall.

He hadn't once ceased looking at Daisy, and I think he revalued everything in his house according to the measure of response it drew from her well-loved eyes. Sometimes, too, he stared around at his possessions in a dazed way, as though in her actual and astounding presence none of it was any longer real. Once he nearly toppled down a flight of stairs.

His bedroom was the simplest room of all—except where the dresser was garnished with a toilet set of pure dull gold. Daisy took the brush with delight, and smoothed her hair, whereupon Gatsby sat down and shaded his eyes and began to laugh.

'It's the funniest thing, old sport,' he said hilariously. 'I can't—When I try to——'

He had passed visibly through two states and was entering upon a third. After his embarrassment and his unreasoning joy he was consumed with wonder at her presence. He had been full of the idea so long, dreamed it right through to the end, waited with his teeth set, so to speak, at an inconceivable pitch of intensity. Now, in the reaction, he was running down like an overwound clock.

Recovering himself in a minute he opened for us two hulking patent cabinets which held his massed suits and dressing-gowns and ties, and his shirts, piled like bricks in stacks a dozen high.

'I've got a man in England who buys me clothes. He sends over a selection of things at the beginning of each season, spring and fall.'

He took out a pile of shirts and began throwing them, one by one, before us, shirts of sheer linen and thick silk and fine flannel, which lost their folds as they fell and covered the table in many-coloured disarray. While we admired he brought more and the soft rich heap mounted higher—shirts with stripes and scrolls and plaids in coral and apple-green and lavender and faint orange, with monograms of Indian blue. Suddenly, with a strained sound, Daisy bent her head into the shirts and began to cry stormily.

'They're such beautiful shirts,' she sobbed, her voice muffled in the thick folds. 'It makes me sad because I've never seen such—such beautiful shirts before.'

After the house, we were to see the grounds and the swimming-pool, and the hydroplane and the mid-summer flowers—but outside Gatsby's window it began to rain again, so we stood in a row looking at the corrugated surface of the Sound.

'If it wasn't for the mist we could see your home across the bay,' said Gatsby. 'You always have a green light that burns all night at the end of your dock.'

Daisy put her arm through his abruptly, but he seemed absorbed in what he had just said. Possibly it had occurred to him that the colossal significance of that light had now vanished forever. Compared to the great distance that had separated him from Daisy it had seemed very near to her, almost touching her. It had seemed as close as a star to the moon. Now it was again a green light on a dock. His count of enchanted objects had diminished by one.

I began to walk about the room, examining various indefinite objects in the half darkness. A large photograph of an elderly man in yachting costume attracted me, hung on the wall over his desk.

'Who's this?'

'That? That's Mr. Dan Cody, old sport.'

The name sounded faintly familiar.

'He's dead now. He used to be my best friend years ago.'

There was a small picture of Gatsby, also in yachting costume, on the bureau—Gatsby with his head thrown back defiantly—taken apparently when he was about eighteen.

'I adore it,' exclaimed Daisy. 'The pompadour! You never told me you had a pompadour—or a yacht.'

'Look at this,' said Gatsby quickly. 'Here's a lot of clippings—about you.'

They stood side by side examining it. I was going to ask to see the rubies when the phone rang, and Gatsby took up the receiver.

'Yes. . . . Well, I can't talk now. . . . I can't talk now, old sport. . . . I said a *small* town. . . . He must know what a small town is. . . . Well, he's no use to us if Detroit is his idea of a small town. . . .'

He rang off.

'Come here *quick*!' cried Daisy at the window.

The rain was still falling, but the darkness had parted in the west, and there was a pink and golden billow of foamy clouds above the sea.

'Look at that,' she whispered, and then after a moment: 'I'd like to just get one of those pink clouds and put you in it and push you around.'

I tried to go then, but they wouldn't hear of it; perhaps my presence made them feel more satisfactorily alone.

'I know what we'll do,' said Gatsby, 'we'll have Klipspringer play the piano.'

He went out of the room calling 'Ewing!' and returned in a few minutes accompanied by an embarrassed, slightly worn young man, with shell-rimmed glasses and scanty blond hair. He was now decently clothed, in a 'sport shirt', open at the neck, sneakers, and duck trousers of a nebulous hue.

'Did we interrupt your exercises?' inquired Daisy politely.

'I was asleep,' cried Mr. Klipspringer, in a spasm of embarrassment. 'That is, I'd *been* asleep. Then I got up . . .'

'Klipspringer plays the piano,' said Gatsby, cutting him off. 'Don't you, Ewing, old sport?'

'I don't play well. I don't—I hardly play at all, I'm all out of prac——'

'We'll go downstairs,' interrupted Gatsby. He flipped a switch. The grey windows disappeared as the house glowed full of light.

In the music-room Gatsby turned on a solitary lamp beside the piano. He lit Daisy's cigarette from a trembling match, and sat down with her on a couch far across the room, where there was no light save what the gleaming floor bounded in from the hall.

When Klipspringer had played *The Love Nest* he turned around on the bench and searched unhappily for Gatsby in the gloom.

'I'm all out of practice, you see. I told you I couldn't play. I'm all out of prac——'

'Don't talk so much, old sport,' commanded Gatsby. 'Play!'

> *'In the morning,*
> *In the evening,*
> *Ain't we got fun——'*

Outside the wind was loud and there was a faint flow of thunder along the Sound. All the lights were going on in West Egg now; the electric trains, men-carrying, were plunging home through the rain from New York. It was the hour of a profound human change, and excitement was generating on the air.

> *'One thing's sure and nothing's surer*
> *The rich get richer and the poor get—children.*
> *In the meantime,*
> *In between time——'*

As I went over to say good-bye I saw that the expression of bewilderment had come back into Gatsby's face, as though a faint doubt had occurred to him as to the quality of his present happiness. Almost five years! There must have been moments even that afternoon when Daisy tumbled short of his dreams—not through her own fault, but because of the colossal vitality of his illusion. It had gone beyond her, beyond everything. He had thrown himself into it with a creative passion, adding to it all the time, decking it out with every bright feather that drifted his way. No amount of fire or freshness can challenge what a man can store up in his ghostly heart.

As I watched him he adjusted himself a little, visibly.

His hand took hold of hers, and as she said something low in his ear he turned towards her with a rush of emotion. I think that voice held him most, with its fluctuating, feverish warmth, because it couldn't be over-dreamed— that voice was a deathless song.

They had forgotten me, but Daisy glanced up and held out her hand; Gatsby didn't know me now at all. I looked once more at them and they looked back at me, remotely, possessed by intense life. Then I went out of the room and down the marble steps into the rain, leaving them there together.

CHAPTER VI

ABOUT THIS TIME an ambitious young reporter from New York arrived one morning at Gatsby's door and asked him if he had anything to say.

'Anything to say about what?' inquired Gatsby politely.

'Why—any statement to give out.'

It transpired after a confused five minutes that the man had heard Gatsby's name around his office in a connection which he either wouldn't reveal or didn't fully understand. This was his day off and with laudable initiative he had hurried out 'to see.'

It was a random shot, and yet the reporter's instinct was right. Gatsby's notoriety, spread about by the hundreds who had accepted his hospitality and so become authorities upon his past, had increased all summer until he fell just short of being news. Contemporary legends such as the 'underground pipe-line to Canada' attached themselves to him, and there was one persistent story that he didn't live in a house at all, but in a boat that looked like a house and was moved secretly up and down the Long Island shore. Just why these inventions were a source of satisfaction to James Gatz of North Dakota isn't easy to say.

James Gatz—that was really, or at least legally, his name.

He had changed it at the age of seventeen and at the specific moment that witnessed the beginning of his career—when he saw Dan Cody's yacht drop anchor over the most insidious flat on Lake Superior. It was James Gatz who had been loafing along the beach that afternoon in a torn green jersey and a pair of canvas pants, but it was already Jay Gatsby who borrowed a rowboat, pulled out the *Tuolomee*, and informed Cody that a wind might catch him and break him up in half an hour.

I suppose he'd had the name ready for a long time, even then. His parents were shiftless and unsuccessful farm people—his imagination had never really accepted them as his parents at all. The truth was that Jay Gatsby of West Egg, Long Island, sprang from his Platonic conception of himself. He was a son of God—a phrase which, if it means anything, means just that—and he must be about His Father's business, the service of a vast, vulgar, and meretricious beauty. So he invented just the sort of Jay Gatsby that a seventeen-year-old boy would be likely to invent, and to this conception he was faithful to the end.

For over a year he had been beating his way along the south shore of Lake Superior as a clam-digger and a salmon-fisher or in any other capacity that brought him food and bed. His brown, hardening body lived naturally through the half-fierce, half-lazy work of the bracing days. He knew women early, and since they spoiled him he became contemptuous of them, of young virgins because they were ignorant, of the others because they were hysterical about things which in his overwhelming self-absorption he took for granted.

But his heart was in a constant, turbulent riot. The most grotesque and fantastic conceits haunted him in his bed at night. A universe of ineffable gaudiness spun itself out in his brain while the clock ticked on the wash-stand and the moon soaked with wet light his tangled clothes upon the floor. Each night he added to the pattern of his fancies until drowsiness closed down upon some vivid scene with an oblivious embrace. For a while these reveries provided an outlet for his imagination; they were a satisfactory hint of the unreality of reality, a promise that the rock of the world was founded securely on a fairy's wing.

An instinct towards his future glory had led him, some months before, to the small Lutheran College of St. Olaf's in southern Minnesota. He stayed there two weeks, dismayed at its ferocious indifference to the drums of his destiny, to destiny itself, and despising the janitor's work with which he was to pay his way through. Then he drifted back to Lake Superior, and he was still searching for something to do on the day that Dan Cody's yacht dropped anchor in the shallows alongshore.

Cody was fifty years old then, a product of the Nevada silver fields, of the Yukon, of every rush for metal since seventy-five. The transactions in Montana copper that made him many times a millionaire found him physically robust but on the verge of soft-mindedness, and, suspecting this, an infinite number of women tried to separate him from his money. The none too savoury ramifications by which Ella Kaye, the newspaper woman, played Madame de Maintenon to his weakness and sent him to sea in a yacht, were common property of the turgid journalism of 1902. He had been coasting along all too hospitable shores for five years when he turned up as James Gatz's destiny in Little Girl Bay.

To young Gatz, resting on his oars and looking up at the railed deck, that yacht represented all the beauty and glamour in the world. I suppose he smiled at Cody—he had probably discovered that people liked him when he smiled. At any rate Cody asked him a few questions (one of them elicited the brand new name) and found that he was quick and extravagantly ambitious. A few days later he took him to Duluth and bought him a blue coat, six pairs of white duck trousers, and a yachting cap. And when the *Tuolomee* left for the West Indies and the Barbary Coast Gatsby left too.

He was employed in a vague personal capacity—while he remained with Cody he was in turn steward, mate, skipper, secretary, and even jailor, for Dan Cody sober knew what lavish doings Dan Cody drunk might soon be about, and he provided for such contingencies by reposing more and more trust in Gatsby. The arrangement lasted five years, during which the boat went three times around the Continent. It might have lasted indefinitely except for the fact that Ella Kaye came on board one night in Boston and a week later Dan Cody inhospitably died.

I remember the portrait of him up in Gatsby's bedroom, a grey, florid man with a hard, empty face—the pioneer debauchee, who during one phase of American life brought back to the Eastern seaboard the savage violence of the frontier brothel and saloon. It was indirectly due to Cody that Gatsby drank so little. Sometimes in the course of gay parties women used to rub champagne into his hair; for himself he formed the habit of letting liquor alone.

And it was from Cody that he inherited money—a legacy of twenty-five thousand dollars. He didn't get it. He never understood the legal device that was used against him, but what remained of the millions went intact to Ella Kaye. He was left with his singularly appropriate education; the vague contour of Jay Gatsby had filled out to the substantiality of a man.

He told me all this very much later, but I've put it down here with the idea of exploding those first wild rumours about his antecedents, which weren't even faintly true. Moreover he told it to me at a time of confusion, when I had reached the point of believing everything and nothing about him. So I take advantage of this short halt, while Gatsby, so to speak, caught his breath, to clear this set of misconceptions away.

It was a halt, too, in my association with his affairs. For several weeks I didn't see him or hear his voice on the phone —mostly I was in New York, trotting around with Jordan and trying to ingratiate myself with her senile aunt—but finally I went over to his house one Sunday afternoon. I hadn't been there two minutes when somebody brought Tom Buchanan in for a drink. I was startled, naturally, but the really surprising thing was that it hadn't happened before.

They were a party of three on horseback—Tom and a man named Sloane and a pretty woman in a brown riding-habit, who had been there previously.

'I'm delighted to see you,' said Gatsby, standing on his porch. 'I'm delighted that you dropped in.'

As though they cared!

'Sit right down. Have a cigarette or a cigar.' He walked around the room quickly, ringing bells. 'I'll have something to drink for you in just a minute.'

He was profoundly affected by the fact that Tom was there. But he would be uneasy anyhow until he had given them something, realizing in a vague way that that was all they came for. Mr. Sloane wanted nothing. A lemonade? No, thanks. A little champagne? Nothing at all, thanks. . . . I'm sorry——

'Did you have a nice ride?'

'Very good roads around here.'

'I suppose the automobiles——'

'Yeah.'

Moved by an irresistible impulse, Gatsby turned to Tom, who had accepted the introduction as a stranger.

'I believe we've met somewhere before, Mr. Buchanan.'

'Oh, yes,' said Tom, gruffly polite, but obviously not remembering. 'So we did. I remember very well.'

'About two weeks ago.'

'That's right. You were with Nick here.'

'I know your wife,' continued Gatsby, almost aggressively.

'That so?'

Tom turned to me.

'You live near here, Nick?'

'Next door.'

'That so?'

Mr. Sloane didn't enter into the conversation, but lounged back haughtily in his chair; the woman said nothing either—until unexpectedly, after two highballs, she became cordial.

'We'll all come over to your next party, Mr. Gatsby,' she suggested. 'What do you say?'

'Certainly; I'd be delighted to have you.'

'Be ver' nice,' said Mr. Sloane, without gratitude. 'Well —think ought to be starting home.'

'Please don't hurry,' Gatsby urged them. He had control of himself now, and he wanted to see more of Tom. 'Why don't you—why don't you stay for supper? I wouldn't be surprised if some other people dropped in from New York.'

'You come to supper with *me*,' said the lady enthusiastically. 'Both of you.'

This included me. Mr. Sloane got to his feet.

'Come along,' he said—but to her only.

'I mean it,' she insisted. 'I'd love to have you. Lots of room.'

Gatsby looked at me questioningly. He wanted to go, and he didn't see that Mr. Sloane had determined he shouldn't.

'I'm afraid I won't be able to,' I said.

'Well, you come,' she urged, concentrating on Gatsby.

Mr. Sloane murmured something close to her ear.

'We won't be late if we start now,' she insisted aloud.

'I haven't got a horse,' said Gatsby. 'I used to ride in the army, but I've never bought a horse. I'll have to follow you in my car. Excuse me for just a minute.'

The rest of us walked out on the porch, where Sloane and the lady began an impassioned conversation aside.

'My God, I believe the man's coming,' said Tom. 'Doesn't he know she doesn't want him?'

'She says she does want him.'

'She has a big dinner party and he won't know a soul there.' He frowned. 'I wonder where in the devil he met Daisy. By God, I may be old-fashioned in my ideas, but women run around too much these days to suit me. They meet all kinds of crazy fish.'

Suddenly Mr. Sloane and the lady walked down the steps and mounted their horses.

'Come on,' said Mr. Sloane to Tom, 'we're late. We've

got to go.' And then to me: 'Tell him we couldn't wait, will you?'

Tom and I shook hands, the rest of us exchanged a cool nod, and they trotted quickly down the drive, disappearing under the August foliage just as Gatsby, with hat and light overcoat in hand, came out the front door.

Tom was evidently perturbed at Daisy's running around alone, for on the following Saturday night he came with her to Gatsby's party. Perhaps his presence gave the evening its peculiar quality of oppressiveness—it stands out in my memory from Gatsby's other parties that summer. There were the same people, or at least the same sort of people, the same profusion of champagne, the same many-coloured, many-keyed commotion, but I felt an unpleasantness in the air, a pervading harshness that hadn't been there before. Or perhaps I had merely grown used to it, grown to accept West Egg as a world complete in itself, with its own standards and its own great figures, second to nothing because it had no consciousness of being so, and now I was looking at it again, through Daisy's eyes. It is invariably saddening to look through new eyes at things upon which you have expended your own powers of adjustment.

They arrived at twilight, and, as we strolled out among the sparkling hundreds, Daisy's voice was playing murmurous tricks in her throat.

'These things excite me *so*,' she whispered. 'If you want to kiss me any time during the evening, Nick, just let me know and I'll be glad to arrange it for you. Just mention my name. Or present a green card. I'm giving out green——'

'Look around,' suggested Gatsby.

'I'm looking around. I'm having a marvellous——'

'You must see the faces of many people you've heard about.'

Tom's arrogant eyes roamed the crowd.

'We don't go around very much,' he said; 'in fact, I was just thinking I don't know a soul here.'

'Perhaps you know that lady,' Gatsby indicated a gorgeous, scarcely human orchid of a woman who sat in

state under a white-plum tree. Tom and Daisy stared, with
that particularly unreal feeling that accompanies the
recognition of a hitherto ghostly celebrity of the movies.

'She's lovely,' said Daisy.

'The man bending over her is her director.'

He took them ceremoniously from group to group:

'Mrs. Buchanan . . . and Mr. Buchanan—' After an
instant's hesitation he added: 'the polo player.'

'Oh, no,' objected Tom quickly, 'not me.'

But evidently the sound of it pleased Gatsby, for Tom
remained 'the polo player' for the rest of the evening.

'I've never met so many celebrities,' Daisy exclaimed.
'I liked that man—what was his name?—with the sort of
blue nose.'

Gatsby identified him, adding that he was a small
producer.

'Well, I liked him anyhow.'

'I'd a little rather not be the polo player,' said Tom
pleasantly, 'I'd rather look at all these famous people in—
in oblivion.'

Daisy and Gatsby danced. I remember being surprised
by his graceful, conservative fox-trot—I had never seen
him dance before. Then they sauntered over to my house
and sat on the steps for half an hour, while at her request,
I remained watchfully in the garden. 'In case there's a fire,
or a flood,' she explained, 'or any act of God.'

Tom appeared from his oblivion as we were sitting down
to supper together. 'Do you mind if I eat with some people
over here?' he said. 'A fellow's getting off some funny
stuff.'

'Go ahead,' answered Daisy genially, 'and if you want to
take down any addresses here's my little gold pencil.' . . .
She looked around after a moment and told me the girl was
'common but pretty,' and I knew that except for the half-
hour she'd been alone with Gatsby she wasn't having a good
time.

We were at a particularly tipsy table. That was my fault
—Gatsby had been called to the phone, and I'd enjoyed

these same people only two weeks before. But what had amused me then turned septic on the air now.

'How do you feel, Miss Baedeker?'

The girl addressed was trying, unsuccessfully, to slump against my shoulder. At this inquiry she sat up and opened her eyes.

'Wha'?'

A massive and lethargic woman, who had been urging Daisy to play golf with her at the local club to-morrow, spoke in Miss Baedeker's defence:

'Oh, she's all right now. When she's had five or six cock-tails she always starts screaming like that. I tell her she ought to leave it alone.'

'I do leave it alone,' affirmed the accused hollowly.

'We heard you yelling, so I said to Doc Civet here: "There's somebody that needs your help, Doc."'

'She's much obliged, I'm sure,' said another friend, without gratitude, 'but you got her dress all wet when you stuck her head in the pool.'

'Anything I hate is to get my head stuck in a pool,' mumbled Miss Baedeker. 'They almost drowned me once over in New Jersey.'

'Then you ought to leave it alone,' countered Doctor Civet.

'Speak for yourself!' cried Miss Baedeker violently. 'Your hand shakes. I wouldn't let you operate on me!'

It was like that. Almost the last thing I remember was standing with Daisy and watching the moving-picture director and his Star. They were still under the white-plum tree and their faces were touching except for a pale, thin ray of moonlight between. It occurred to me that he had been very slowly bending towards her all evening to attain this proximity, and even while I watched I saw him stoop one ultimate degree and kiss at her cheek.

'I like her,' said Daisy, 'I think she's lovely.'

But the rest offended her—and inarguably, because it wasn't a gesture but an emotion. She was appalled by West Egg, this unprecedented 'place' that Broadway had begotten upon a Long Island fishing village—appalled by its raw vigour that chafed under the old euphemisms and by the too obtrusive fate that herded its inhabitants along a short-cut from nothing to nothing. She saw something awful in the very simplicity she failed to understand.

I sat on the front steps with them while they waited for their car. It was dark here; only the bright door sent ten square feet of light volleying out into the soft black morning. Sometimes a shadow moved against a dressing-room blind above, gave way to another shadow, an indefinite procession of shadows, that rouged and powdered in an invisible glass.

'Who is this Gatsby anyhow?' demanded Tom suddenly. 'Some big bootlegger?'

'Where'd you hear that?' I inquired.

'I didn't hear it. I imagined it. A lot of these newly rich people are just big bootleggers, you know.'

'Not Gatsby,' I said shortly.

He was silent for a moment. The pebbles of the drive crunched under his feet.

'Well, he certainly must have strained himself to get this menagerie together.'

A breeze stirred the grey haze of Daisy's fur collar.

'At least they are more interesting than the people we know,' she said with an effort.

'You didn't look so interested.'

'Well, I was.'

Tom laughed and turned to me.

'Did you notice Daisy's face when that girl asked her to put her under a cold shower?'

Daisy began to sing with the music in a husky, rhythmic whisper, bringing out a meaning in each word that it had never had before and would never have again. When the melody rose, her voice broke up sweetly, following it, in a way contralto voices have, and each change tipped out a little of her warm human magic upon the air.

'Lots of people come who haven't been invited,' she said suddenly. 'That girl hadn't been invited. They simply force their way in and he's too polite to object.'

'I'd like to know who he is and what he does,' insisted Tom. 'And I think I'll make a point of finding out.'

'I can tell you right now,' she answered. 'He owned some drug-stores, a lot of drug-stores. He built them up himself.'

The dilatory limousine came rolling up the drive.

'Good night, Nick,' said Daisy.

Her glance left me and sought the lighted top of the steps, where *Three O'Clock in the Morning*, a neat, sad little waltz of that year, was drifting out the open door. After all, in the very casualness of Gatsby's party there were romantic possibilities totally absent from her world. What was it up there in the song that seemed to be calling her back inside? What would happen now in the dim, incalculable hours? Perhaps some unbelievable guest would arrive, a person infinitely rare and to be marvelled at, some authentically radiant young girl who with one fresh glance at Gatsby, one moment of magical encounter, would blot out those five years of unwavering devotion.

I stayed late that night, Gatsby asked me to wait until he was free, and I lingered in the garden until the inevitable swimming party had run up, chilled and exalted, from the black beach, until the lights were extinguished in the guest-rooms overhead. When he came down the steps at last the tanned skin was drawn unusually tight on his face, and his eyes were bright and tired.

'She didn't like it,' he said immediately.

'Of course she did.'

'She didn't like it,' he insisted. 'She didn't have a good time.'

He was silent, and I guessed at his unutterable depression.

'I feel far away from her,' he said. 'It's hard to make her understand.'

'You mean about the dance?'

'The dance?' He dismissed all the dances he had given with a snap of his fingers. 'Old sport, the dance is unimportant.'

He wanted nothing less of Daisy than that she should go

4*

to Tom and say: 'I never loved you.' After she had obliterated four years with that sentence they could decide upon the more practical measures to be taken. One of them was that, after she was free, they were to go back to Louisville and be married from her house—just as if it were five years ago.

'And she doesn't understand,' he said. 'She used to be able to understand. We'd sit for hours——'

He broke off and began to walk up and down a desolate path of fruit rinds and discarded favours and crushed flowers.

'I wouldn't ask too much of her,' I ventured. 'You can't repeat the past.'

'Can't repeat the past?' he cried incredulously. 'Why of course you can!'

He looked around him wildly, as if the past were lurking here in the shadow of his house, just out of reach of his hand.

'I'm going to fix everything just the way it was before,' he said, nodding determinedly. 'She'll see.'

He talked a lot about the past, and I gathered that he wanted to recover something, some idea of himself perhaps, that had gone into loving Daisy. His life had been confused and disordered since then, but if he could once return to a certain starting place and go over it all slowly, he could find out what that thing was. . . .

. . . One autumn night, five years before, they had been walking down the street when the leaves were falling, and they came to a place where there were no trees and the sidewalk was white with moonlight. They stopped here and turned towards each other. Now it was a cool night with that mysterious excitement in it which comes at the two changes of the year. The quiet lights in the houses were humming out into the darkness and there was a stir and bustle among the stars. Out of the corner of his eye Gatsby saw that the blocks of the sidewalks really formed a ladder and mounted to a secret place above the trees—he could climb to it, if he climbed alone, and once there he could suck on the pap of life, gulp down the incomparable milk of wonder.

His heart beat faster and faster as Daisy's white face came up to his own. He knew that when he kissed this girl, and forever wed his unutterable visions to her perishable breath, his mind would never romp again like the mind of God. So he waited, listening for a moment longer to the tuning-fork that had been struck upon a star. Then he kissed her. At his lips' touch she blossomed for him like a flower and the incarnation was complete.

Through all he said, even through his appalling sentimentality, I was reminded of something—an elusive rhythm, a fragment of lost words, that I had heard somewhere a long time ago. For a moment a phrase tried to take shape in my mouth and my lips parted like a dumb man's, as though there was more struggling upon them than a wisp of startled air. But they made no sound, and what I had almost remembered was uncommunicable forever.

CHAPTER VII

IT WAS when curiosity about Gatsby was at its highest that the lights in his house failed to go on one Saturday night—and, as obscurely as it had begun, his career as Trimalchio was over. Only gradually did I become aware that the automobiles which turned expectantly into his drive stayed for just a minute and then drove sulkily away. Wondering if he were sick I went over to find out—an unfamiliar butler with a villainous face squinted at me suspiciously from the door.

'Is Mr. Gatsby sick?'

'Nope.' After a pause he added 'sir' in a dilatory, grudging way.

'I hadn't seen him around, and I was rather worried. Tell him Mr. Carraway came over.'

'Who?' he demanded rudely.

'Carraway.'

'Carraway. All right, I'll tell him.'

Abruptly he slammed the door.

My Finn informed me that Gatsby had dismissed every servant in his house a week ago and replaced them with half a dozen others, who never went into West Egg Village to be bribed by the tradesmen, but ordered moderate supplies over the telephone. The grocery boy reported that the kitchen looked like a pigsty, and the general opinion in the village was that the new people weren't servants at all.

Next day Gatsby called me on the phone.

'Going away?' I inquired.

'No, old sport.'

'I hear you fired all your servants.'

'I wanted somebody who wouldn't gossip. Daisy comes over quite often—in the afternoons.'

So the whole caravansary had fallen in like a card house at the disapproval in her eyes.

'They're some people Wolfsheim wanted to do something for. They're all brothers and sisters. They used to run a small hotel.'

'I see.'

He was calling up at Daisy's request—would I come to lunch at her house to-morrow? Miss Baker would be there. Half an hour later Daisy herself telephoned and seemed relieved to find that I was coming. Something was up. And yet I couldn't believe that they would choose this occasion for a scene—especially for the rather harrowing scene that Gatsby had outlined in the garden.

The next day was broiling, almost the last, certainly the warmest, of the summer. As my train emerged from the tunnel into sunlight, only the hot whistles of the National Biscuit Company broke the simmering hush at noon. The straw seats of the car hovered on the edge of combustion; the woman next to me perspired delicately for a while into her white shirtwaist, and then, as her newspaper dampened under her fingers, lapsed despairingly into deep heat with a desolate cry. Her pocket-book slapped to the floor.

'Oh, my!' she gasped.

I picked it up with a weary bend and handed it back to her, holding it at arm's length and by the extreme tip of the corners to indicate that I had no designs upon it—but everyone near by, including the woman, suspected me just the same.

'Hot!' said the conductor to familiar faces. 'Some weather! . . . Hot! . . . Hot! . . . Hot! . . . Is it hot enough for you? Is it not? Is it . . .?'

My commutation ticket came back to me with a dark stain from his hand. That anyone should care in this heat whose flushed lips he kissed, whose head made damp the pyjama pocket over his heart!

. . . Through the hall of the Buchanan's house blew a faint wind, carrying the sound of the telephone bell out to Gatsby and me as we waited at the door.

'The master's body!' roared the butler into the mouthpiece. 'I'm sorry, madame, but we can't furnish it—it's far too hot to touch this noon!'

What he really said was: 'Yes . . . Yes . . . I'll see.'

He set down the receiver and came towards us, glistening slightly, to take our stiff straw hats.

'Madame expects you in the salon!' he cried, needlessly indicating the direction. In this heat every extra gesture was an affront to the common store of life.

The room, shadowed well with awnings, was dark and cool. Daisy and Jordan lay upon an enormous couch, like silver idols weighing down their own white dresses against the singing breeze of the fans.

'We can't move,' they said together.

Jordan's fingers, powdered white over their tan, rested for a moment in mine.

'And Mr. Thomas Buchanan, the athlete?' I inquired.

Simultaneously I heard his voice, gruff, muffled, husky, at the hall telephone.

Gatsby stood in the centre of the crimson carpet and gazed around with fascinated eyes. Daisy watched him and laughed, her sweet, exciting laugh; a tiny gust of powder rose from her bosom into the air.

'The rumour is,' whispered Jordan, 'that that's Tom's girl on the telephone.'

We were silent. The voice in the hall rose high with annoyance: 'Very well, then, I won't sell you the car at all . . . I'm under no obligations to you at all . . . and as for your bothering me about it at lunch time, I won't stand that at all!'

'Holding down the receiver,' said Daisy cynically.

'No, he's not,' I assured her. 'It's a bona-fide deal. I happen to know about it.'

Tom flung open the door, blocked out its space for a moment with his thick body, and hurried into the room.

'Mr. Gatsby!' He put out his broad, flat hand with well-concealed dislike. 'I'm glad to see you, sir. . . . Nick. . . .'

'Make us a cold drink,' cried Daisy.

As he left the room again she got up and went over to Gatsby, and pulled his face down, kissing him on the mouth.

'You know I love you,' she murmured.

'You forget there's a lady present,' said Jordan.

Daisy looked around doubtfully.

'You kiss Nick too.'

'What a low, vulgar girl!'

'I don't care!' cried Daisy, and began to clog on the brick fireplace. Then she remembered the heat and sat down guiltily on the couch just as a freshly laundered nurse leading a little girl came into the room.

'Bles-sed pre-cious,' she crooned, holding out her arms. 'Come to your own mother that loves you.'

The child, relinquished by the nurse, rushed across the room and rooted shyly into her mother's dress.

'The bles-sed pre-cious! Did mother get powder on your old yellowy hair? Stand up now, and say—How-de-do.'

Gatsby and I in turn leaned down and took the small reluctant hand. Afterwards he kept looking at the child with surprise. I don't think he had ever really believed in its existence before.

'I got dressed before luncheon,' said the child, turning eagerly to Daisy.

'That's because your mother wanted to show you off.'
Her face bent into the single wrinkle of the small white
neck. 'You dream, you. You absolute little dream.'

'Yes,' admitted the child calmly. 'Aunt Jordan's got on
a white dress, too.'

'How do you like mother's friends?' Daisy turned her
around so that she faced Gatsby. 'Do you think they're
pretty?'

'Where's Daddy?'

'She doesn't look like her father,' explained Daisy. 'She
looks like me. She's got my hair and shape of the face.'

Daisy sat back upon the couch. The nurse took a step
forward and held out her hand.

'Come, Pammy.'

'Good-bye, sweetheart!'

With a reluctant backward glance the well-disciplined
child held to her nurse's hand and was pulled out of the
door, just as Tom came back, preceding four gin rickeys
that clicked full of ice.

Gatsby took up his drink.

'They certainly look cool,' he said, with visible
tension.

We drank in long, greedy swallows.

'I read somewhere that the sun's getting hotter every
year,' said Tom genially. 'It seems that pretty soon the
earth's going to fall into the sun—or wait a minute—it's
just the opposite—the sun's getting colder every year.'

'Come outside,' he suggested to Gatsby, 'I'd like you to
have a look at the place.'

I went with them out to the veranda. On the green Sound,
stagnant in the heat, one small sail crawled slowly towards
the fresher sea. Gatsby's eyes followed it momentarily; he
raised his hand and pointed across the bay.

'I'm right across from you.'

'So you are.'

Our eyes lifted over the rose-beds and the hot lawn and
the weedy refuse of the dog-days along-shore. Slowly the
white wings of the boat moved against the blue cool limit

of the sky. Ahead lay the scalloped ocean and the abounding blessed isles.

'There's sport for you,' said Tom, nodding. 'I'd like to be out there with him for about an hour.'

We had luncheon in the dining-room, darkened too against the heat, and drank down nervous gaiety with the cold ale.

'What'll we do with ourselves this afternoon?' cried Daisy, 'and the day after that, and the next thirty years?'

'Don't be morbid,' Jordan said. 'Life starts all over again when it gets crisp in the fall.'

'But it's so hot,' insisted Daisy, on the verge of tears, 'and everything's so confused. Let's all go to town!'

Her voice struggled on through the heat, beating against it, moulding its senselessness into forms.

'I've heard of making a garage out of a stable,' Tom was saying to Gatsby, 'but I'm the first man who ever made a stable out of a garage.'

'Who wants to go to town?' demanded Daisy insistently. Gatsby's eyes floated towards her. 'Ah,' she cried, 'you look so cool.'

Their eyes met, and they stared together at each other, alone in space. With an effort she glanced down at the table.

'You always look so cool,' she repeated.

She had told him that she loved him, and Tom Buchanan saw. He was astounded. His mouth opened a little, and he looked at Gatsby, and then back at Daisy as if he had just recognized her as someone he knew a long time ago.

'You resemble the advertisement of the man,' she went on innocently. 'You know the advertisement of the man——'

'All right,' broke in Tom quickly, 'I'm perfectly willing to go to town. Come on—we're all going to town.'

He got up, his eyes still flashing between Gatsby and his wife. No one moved.

'Come on!' His temper cracked a little. 'What's the matter, anyhow? If we're going to town, let's start.'

His hand, trembling with his effort at self-control, bore

to his lips the last of his glass of ale. Daisy's voice got us to our feet and out on to the blazing gravel drive.

'Are we just going to go?' she objected. 'Like this? Aren't we going to let anyone smoke a cigarette first?'

'Everybody smoked all through lunch.'

'Oh, let's have fun,' she begged him. 'It's too hot to fuss.'

He didn't answer.

'Have it your own way,' she said. 'Come on, Jordan.'

They went upstairs to get ready while we three men stood there shuffling the hot pebbles with our feet. A silver curve of the moon hovered already in the western sky. Gatsby started to speak, changed his mind, but not before Tom wheeled and faced him expectantly.

'Have you got your stables here?' asked Gatsby with an effort.

'About a quarter of a mile down the road.'

'Oh.'

A pause.

'I don't see the idea of going to town,' broke out Tom savagely. 'Women get these notions in their heads——'

'Shall we take anything to drink?' called Daisy from an upper window.

'I'll get some whiskey,' answered Tom. He went inside.

Gatsby turned to me rigidly:

'I can't say anything in his house, old sport.'

'She's got an indiscreet voice,' I remarked. 'It's full of——' I hesitated.

'Her voice is full of money,' he said suddenly.

That was it. I'd never understood before. It was full of money—that was the inexhaustible charm that rose and fell in it, the jingle of it, the cymbal's song of it. . . . High in a white palace the king's daughter, the golden girl. . . .

Tom came out of the house wrapping a quart bottle in a towel, followed by Daisy and Jordan wearing small tight hats of metallic cloth and carrying light capes over their arms.

'Shall we all go in my car?' suggested Gatsby. He felt the hot, green leather of the seat. 'I ought to have left it in the shade.'

'Is it standard shift?' demanded Tom.

'Yes.'

'Well, you take my coupé and let me drive your car to town.'

The suggestion was distasteful to Gatsby.

'I don't think there's much gas,' he objected.

'Plenty of gas,' said Tom boisterously. He looked at the gauge. 'And if it runs out I can stop at a drug-store. You can buy anything at a drug-store nowadays.'

A pause followed this apparently pointless remark. Daisy looked at Tom frowning, and an indefinable expression, at once definitely unfamiliar and vaguely recognizable, as if I had only heard it described in words, passed over Gatsby's face.

'Come on, Daisy,' said Tom, pressing her with his hand towards Gatsby's car. 'I'll take you in this circus wagon.'

He opened the door, but she moved out from the circle of his arm.

'You take Nick and Jordan. We'll follow you in the coupé.'

She walked close to Gatsby, touching his coat with her hand. Jordan and Tom and I got into the front seat of Gatsby's car, Tom pushed the unfamiliar gears tentatively, and we shot off into the oppressive heat, leaving them out of sight behind.

'Did you see that?' demanded Tom.

'See what?'

He looked at me keenly, realizing that Jordan and I must have known all along.

'You think I'm pretty dumb, don't you?' he suggested. 'Perhaps I am, but I have a—almost a second sight, some-times, that tells me what to do. Maybe you don't believe that, but science——'

He paused. The immediate contingency overtook him, pulled him back from the edge of the theoretical abyss.

'I've made a small investigation of this fellow,' he continued. 'I could have gone deeper if I'd known——'

'Do you mean you've been to a medium?' inquired Jordan humorously.

'What?' Confused, he stared at us as we laughed. 'A medium?'

'About Gatsby.'

'About Gatsby! No, I haven't. I said I'd been making a small investigation of his past.'

'And you found he was an Oxford man,' said Jordan helpfully.

'An Oxford man!' He was incredulous. 'Like hell he is! He wears a pink suit.'

'Nevertheless he's an Oxford man.'

'Oxford, New Mexico,' snorted Tom contemptuously, 'or something like that.'

'Listen, Tom. If you're such a snob, why did you invite him to lunch?' demanded Jordan crossly.

'Daisy invited him; she knew him before we were married—God knows where!'

We were all irritable now with the fading ale, and aware of it we drove for a while in silence. Then as Doctor T. J. Eckleburg's faded eyes came into sight down the road, I remembered Gatsby's caution about gasoline.

'We've got enough to get us to town,' said Tom.

'But there's a garage right here,' objected Jordan. 'I don't want to get stalled in this baking heat.'

Tom threw on both brakes impatiently, and we slid to an abrupt dusty stop under Wilson's sign. After a moment the proprietor emerged from the interior of his establishment and gazed hollow-eyed at the car.

'Let's have some gas!' cried Tom roughly. 'What do you think we stopped for—to admire the view?'

'I'm sick,' said Wilson without moving. 'Been sick all day.'

'What's the matter?'

'I'm all run down.'

'Well, shall I help myself?' Tom demanded. 'You sounded well enough on the phone.'

With an effort Wilson left the shade and support of the

doorway and, breathing hard, unscrewed the cap of the tank. In the sunlight his face was green.

'I didn't mean to interrupt your lunch,' he said. 'But I need money pretty bad, and I was wondering what you were going to do with your old car.'

'How do you like this one?' inquired Tom. 'I bought it last week.'

'It's a nice yellow one,' said Wilson, as he strained at the handle.

'Like to buy it?'

'Big chance,' Wilson smiled faintly. 'No, but I could make some money on the other.'

'What do you want money for, all of a sudden?'

'I've been here too long. I want to get away. My wife and I want to go West.'

'Your wife does?' exclaimed Tom, startled.

'She's been talking about it for ten years.' He rested for a moment against the pump, shading his eyes. 'And now she's going whether she wants to or not. I'm going to get her away.'

The coupé flashed by us with a flurry of dust and the flash of a waving hand.

'What do I owe you?' demanded Tom harshly.

'I just got wised up to something funny the last two days,' remarked Wilson. 'That's why I want to get away. That's why I been bothering you about the car.'

'What do I owe you?'

'Dollar twenty.'

The relentless beating heat was beginning to confuse me and I had a bad moment there before I realized that so far his suspicions hadn't alighted on Tom. He had discovered that Myrtle had some sort of life apart from him in another world, and the shock had made him physically sick. I stared at him and then at Tom, who had made a parallel discovery less than an hour before—and it occurred to me that there was no difference between men, in intelligence or race, so profound as the difference between the sick and the well. Wilson was so sick that he looked guilty, unforgivably guilty—as if he had just got some poor girl with child.

'I'll let you have that car,' said Tom. 'I'll send it over to-morrow afternoon.'

That locality was always vaguely disquieting, even in the broad glare of afternoon, and now I turned my head as though I had been warned of something behind. Over the ashheaps the giant eyes of Doctor T. J. Eckleburg kept their vigil, but I perceived, after a moment, that the other eyes were regarding us less than twenty feet away.

In one of the windows over the garage the curtains had been moved aside a little, and Myrtle Wilson was peering down at the car. So engrossed was she that she had no consciousness of being observed, and one emotion after another crept into her face like objects into a slowly developing picture. Her expression was curiously familiar—it was an expression I had often seen on women's faces, but on Myrtle Wilson's face it seemed purposeless and inexplicable until I realized that her eyes, wide with jealous terror, were fixed not on Tom, but on Jordan Baker, whom she took to be his wife.

There is no confusion like the confusion of a simple mind, and as we drove away Tom was feeling the hot whips of panic. His wife and his mistress, until an hour ago secure and inviolate, were slipping precipitately from his control. Instinct made him step on the accelerator with the double purpose of overtaking Daisy and leaving Wilson behind, and we sped along towards Astoria at fifty miles an hour, until, among the spidery girders of the elevated, we came in sight of the easy-going blue coupé.

'Those big movies around Fiftieth Street are cool,' suggested Jordan. 'I love New York on summer afternoons when everyone's away. There's something very sensuous about it—overripe, as if all sorts of funny fruits were going to fall into your hands.'

The word 'sensuous' had the effect of further disquieting Tom, but before he could invent a protest the coupé came to a stop, and Daisy signalled us to draw up alongside.

'Where are we going?' she cried.

'How about the movies?'

'It's so hot,' she complained. 'You go. We'll ride around and meet you after.' With an effort her wit rose faintly, 'We'll meet you on some corner. I'll be the man smoking two cigarettes.'

'We can't argue about it here,' Tom said impatiently, as a truck gave out a cursing whistle behind us. 'You follow me to the south side of Central Park, in front of the Plaza.'

Several times he turned his head and looked back for their car, and if the traffic delayed them he slowed up until they came into sight. I think he was afraid they would dart down a side street and out of his life forever.

But they didn't. And we all took the less explicable step of engaging the parlour of a suite in the Plaza Hotel.

The prolonged and tumultuous argument that ended by herding us into that room eludes me, though I have a sharp physical memory that, in the course of it, my underwear kept climbing like a damp snake around my legs and intermittent beads of sweat raced cool across my back. The notion originated with Daisy's suggestion that we hire five bathrooms and take cold baths, and then assumed more tangible form as 'a place to have a mint julep.' Each of us said over and over that it was a 'crazy idea'—we all talked at once to a baffled clerk and thought, or pretended to think, that we were being very funny. . . .

The room was large and stifling, and, though it was already four o'clock, opening the windows admitted only a gust of hot shrubbery from the Park. Daisy went to the mirror and stood with her back to us, fixing her hair.

'It's a swell suite,' whispered Jordan respectfully, and everyone laughed.

'Open another window,' commanded Daisy, without turning around.

'There aren't any more.'

'Well, we'd better telephone for an axe——'

'The thing to do is to forget about the heat,' said Tom impatiently. 'You make it ten times worse by crabbing about it.'

He unrolled the bottle of whiskey from the towel and put it on the table.

'Why not let her alone, old sport?' remarked Gatsby. 'You're the one that wanted to come to town.'

There was a moment of silence. The telephone book slipped from its nail and splashed to the floor, whereupon Jordan whispered, 'Excuse me'—but this time no one laughed.

'I'll pick it up,' I offered.

'I've got it.' Gatsby examined the parted string, muttered 'Hum!' in an interested way, and tossed the book on a chair.

'That's a great expression of yours, isn't it?' said Tom sharply.

'What is?'

'All this "old sport" business. Where'd you pick that up?'

'Now see here, Tom,' said Daisy, turning around from the mirror, 'if you're going to make personal remarks I won't stay here a minute. Call up and order some ice for the mint julep.'

As Tom took up the receiver the compressed heat exploded into sound and we were listening to the portentous chords of Mendelssohn's Wedding March from the ballroom below.

'Imagine marrying anybody in this heat!' cried Jordan dismally.

'Still—I was married in the middle of June,' Daisy remembered, 'Louisville in June! Somebody fainted. Who was it fainted, Tom?'

'Biloxi,' he answered shortly.

'A man named Biloxi. "Blocks" Biloxi, and he made boxes—that's a fact—and he was from Biloxi, Tennessee.'

'They carried him into my house,' appended Jordan, 'because we lived just two doors from the church. And he stayed three weeks, until Daddy told him he had to get out. The day after he left Daddy died.' After a moment she added. 'There wasn't any connection.'

'I used to know a Bill Biloxi from Memphis,' I remarked.

'That was his cousin. I knew his whole family history before he left. He gave me an aluminium putter that I use to-day.'

The music had died down as the ceremony began and now a long cheer floated in at the window, followed by intermittent cries of 'Yea—ea—ea!' and finally by a burst of jazz as the dancing began.

'We're getting old,' said Daisy. 'If we were young we'd rise and dance.'

'Remember Biloxi,' Jordan warned her. 'Where'd you know him, Tom?'

'Biloxi?' He concentrated with an effort. 'I didn't know him. He was a friend of Daisy's.'

'He was not,' she denied. 'I'd never seen him before. He came down in the private car.'

'Well, he said he knew you. He said he was raised in Louisville. Asa Bird brought him around at the last minute and asked if we had room for him.'

Jordan smiled.

'He was probably bumming his way home. He told me he was president of your class at Yale.'

Tom and I looked at each other blankly.

'Biloxi?'

'First place, we didn't have any president——'

Gatsby's foot beat a short, restless tattoo and Tom eyed him suddenly.

'By the way, Mr. Gatsby, I understand you're an Oxford man.'

'Not exactly.'

'Oh, yes, I understand you went to Oxford.'

'Yes—I went there.'

A pause. Then Tom's voice incredulous and insulting:

'You must have gone there about the time Biloxi went to New Haven.'

Another pause. A waiter knocked and came in with crushed mint and ice, but the silence was unbroken by his 'thank you' and the soft closing of the door. This tremendous detail was to be cleared up at last.

'I told you I went there,' said Gatsby.

'I heard you, but I'd like to know when.'

'It was in nineteen-nineteen. I only stayed five months. That's why I can't really call myself an Oxford man.'

Tom glanced around to see if we mirrored his unbelief. But we were all looking at Gatsby.

'It was an opportunity they gave to some of the officers after the Armistice,' he continued. 'We could go to any of the universities in England or France.'

I wanted to get up and slap him on the back. I had one of those renewals of complete faith in him that I'd experienced before.

Daisy rose, smiling faintly, and went to the table.

'Open the whiskey, Tom,' she ordered, 'and I'll make you a mint julep. Then you won't seem so stupid to yourself. . . . Look at the mint!'

'Wait a minute,' snapped Tom, 'I want to ask Mr. Gatsby one more question.'

'Go on,' Gatsby said politely.

'What kind of a row are you trying to cause in my house anyhow?'

They were out in the open at last and Gatsby was content.

'He isn't causing a row,' Daisy looked desperately from one to the other. 'You're causing a row. Please have a little self-control.'

'Self-control!' repeated Tom incredulously. 'I suppose the latest thing is to sit back and let Mr. Nobody from Nowhere make love to your wife. Well, if that's the idea you can count me out. . . . Nowadays people begin by sneering at family life and family institutions, and next they'll throw everything overboard and have intermarriage between black and white.'

Flushed with his impassioned gibberish, he saw himself standing alone on the last barrier of civilization.

'We're all white here,' murmured Jordan.

'I know I'm not very popular. I don't give big parties.

I suppose you've got to make your house into a pigsty in order to have any friends—in the modern world.'

Angry as I was, as we all were, I was tempted to laugh whenever he opened his mouth. The transition from libertine to prig was so complete.

'I've got something to tell *you*, old sport—' began Gatsby. But Daisy guessed at his intention.

'Please, don't!' she interrupted helplessly. 'Please let's all go home. Why don't we all go home?'

'That's a good idea.' I got up. 'Come on, Tom. Nobody wants a drink.'

'I want to know what Mr. Gatsby has to tell me.'

'Your wife doesn't love you,' said Gatsby. 'She's never loved you. She loves me.'

'You must be crazy!' exclaimed Tom automatically.

Gatsby sprang to his feet, vivid with excitement.

'She never loved you, do you hear?' he cried. 'She only married you because I was poor and she was tired of waiting for me. It was a terrible mistake, but in her heart she never loved anyone except me!'

At this point Jordan and I tried to go, but Tom and Gatsby insisted with competitive firmness that we remain —as though neither of them had anything to conceal and it would be a privilege to partake vicariously of their emotions.

'Sit down, Daisy,' Tom's voice groped unsuccessfully for the paternal note. 'What's been going on? I want to hear all about it.'

'I told you what's been going on,' said Gatsby. 'Going on for five years—and you didn't know.'

Tom turned to Daisy sharply.

'You've been seeing this fellow for five years?'

'Not seeing,' said Gatsby. 'No, we couldn't meet. But both of us loved each other all that time, old sport, and you didn't know. I used to laugh sometimes'—but there was no laughter in his eyes—'to think that you didn't know.'

'Oh—that's all.' Tom tapped his thick fingers together like a clergyman and leaned back in his chair.

'You're crazy!' he exploded. 'I can't speak about what happened five years ago because I didn't know Daisy then—and I'll be damned if I see how you got within a mile of her unless you brought the groceries to the back door. But all the rest of that's a God damned lie. Daisy loved me when she married me and she loves me now.'

'No,' said Gatsby, shaking his head.

'She does, though. The trouble is that sometimes she gets foolish ideas in her head and doesn't know what she's doing.' He nodded sagely. 'And what's more I love Daisy too. Once in a while I go off on a spree and make a fool of myself, but I always come back, and in my heart I love her all the time.'

'You're revolting,' said Daisy. She turned to me, and her voice, dropping an octave lower, filled the room with thrilling scorn: 'Do you know why we left Chicago? I'm surprised that they didn't treat you to the story of that little spree.'

Gatsby walked over and stood beside her.

'Daisy, that's all over now,' he said earnestly. 'It doesn't matter any more. Just tell him the truth—that you never loved him—and it's all wiped out forever.'

She looked at him blindly. 'Why—how could I love him—possibly?'

'You never loved him.'

She hesitated. Her eyes fell on Jordan and me with a sort of appeal, as though she realized at last what she was doing—and as though she had never, all along, intended doing anything at all. But it was done now. It was too late.

'I never loved him,' she said, with perceptible reluctance.

'Not at Kapiolani?' demanded Tom suddenly.

'No.'

From the ballroom beneath, muffled and suffocating chords were drifting up on hot waves of air.

'Not that day I carried you down from the Punch Bowl to keep your shoes dry?' There was a husky tenderness in his tone. . . . 'Daisy?'

'Please don't.' Her voice was cold, but the rancour was

gone from it. She looked at Gatsby. 'There, Jay,' she said
—but her hand as she tried to light a cigarette was trembling.
Suddenly she threw the cigarette and the burning match on
the carpet.

'Oh, you want too much!' she cried to Gatsby. 'I love
you now—isn't that enough? I can't help what's past.' She
began to sob helplessly. 'I did love him once—but I loved
you too.'

Gatsby's eyes opened and closed.

'You loved me *too*?' he repeated.

'Even that's a lie,' said Tom savagely. 'She didn't know
you were alive. Why—there're things between Daisy and
me that you'll never know, things that neither of us can
ever forget.'

The words seemed to bite physically into Gatsby.

'I want to speak to Daisy alone,' he insisted. 'She's all
excited now——'

'Even alone I can't say I never loved Tom,' she admitted
in a pitiful voice. 'It wouldn't be true.'

'Of course it wouldn't,' agreed Tom.

She turned to her husband.

'As if it mattered to you,' she said.

'Of course it matters. I'm going to take better care of you
from now on.'

'You don't understand,' said Gatsby, with a touch of
panic. 'You're not going to take care of her any more.'

'I'm not?' Tom opened his eyes wide and laughed. He
could afford to control himself now. 'Why's that?'

'Daisy's leaving you.'

'Nonsense.'

'I am, though,' she said with a visible effort.

'She's not leaving me!' Tom's words suddenly leaned
down over Gatsby. 'Certainly not for a common swindler
who'd have to steal the ring he put on her finger.'

'I won't stand this!' cried Daisy. 'Oh, please let's get
out.'

'Who are you, anyhow?' broke out Tom. 'You're one of
that bunch that hangs around with Meyer Wolfsheim—

that much I happen to know. I've made a little investigation into your affairs—and I'll carry it further to-morrow.'

'You can suit yourself about that, old sport,' said Gatsby steadily.

'I found out what your "drug-stores" were.' He turned to us and spoke rapidly. 'He and this Wolfsheim bought up a lot of side-street drug-stores here and in Chicago and sold grain alcohol over the counter. That's one of his little stunts. I picked him for a bootlegger the first time I saw him, and I wasn't far wrong.'

'What about it?' said Gatsby politely. 'I guess your friend Walter Chase wasn't too proud to come in on it.'

'And you left him in the lurch, didn't you? You let him go to jail for a month over in New Jersey. God! You ought to hear Walter on the subject of *you*.'

'He came to us dead broke. He was very glad to pick up some money, old sport.'

'Don't you call me "old sport"!' cried Tom. Gatsby said nothing. 'Walter could have you up on the betting laws too, but Wolfsheim scared him into shutting his mouth.'

That unfamiliar yet recognizable look was back again in Gatsby's face.

'That drug-store business was just small change,' continued Tom slowly, 'but you've got something on now that Walter's afraid to tell me about.'

I glanced at Daisy, who was staring terrified between Gatsby and her husband, and at Jordan, who had begun to balance an invisible but absorbing object on the tip of her chin. Then I turned back to Gatsby—and was startled at his expression. He looked—and this is said in all contempt for the babbled slander of his garden—as if he had 'killed a man.' For a moment the set of his face could be described in just that fantastic way.

It passed, and he began to talk excitedly to Daisy, denying everything, defending his name against accusations that had not been made. But with every word she was drawing further and further into herself, so he gave that up, and only the dead dream fought on as the afternoon slipped away, trying to touch what was no longer tangible, struggling unhappily, undespairingly, towards that lost voice across the room.

The voice begged again to go.

'*Please*, Tom! I can't stand this any more.'

Her frightened eyes told that whatever intentions, whatever courage she had had, were definitely gone.

'You two start on home, Daisy,' said Tom. 'In Mr. Gatsby's car.'

She looked at Tom, alarmed now, but he insisted with magnanimous scorn.

'Go on. He won't annoy you. I think he realizes that his presumptuous little flirtation is over.'

They were gone, without a word, snapped out, made accidental, isolated, like ghosts, even from our pity.

After a moment Tom got up and began wrapping the unopened bottle of whiskey in the towel.

'Want any of this stuff? Jordan? . . . Nick?'

I didn't answer.

'Nick?' He asked again.

'What?'

'Want any?'

'No . . . I just remembered that to-day's my birthday.'

I was thirty. Before me stretched the portentous, menacing road of a new decade.

It was seven o'clock when we got into the coupé with him and started for Long Island. Tom talked incessantly, exulting and laughing, but his voice was as remote from Jordan and me as the foreign clamour on the sidewalk or the tumult of the elevated overhead. Human sympathy has its limits, and we were content to let all their tragic arguments fade with the city lights behind. Thirty—the promise of a decade of loneliness, a thinning list of single men to know, a thinning brief-case of enthusiasm, thinning hair. But there was Jordan beside me, who, unlike Daisy, was too wise ever to carry well-forgotten dreams from age to age. As we passed over the dark bridge her wan face fell lazily against my coat's shoulder and the formidable stroke of thirty died away with the reassuring pressure of her hand.

So we drove on towards death through the cooling twilight.

The young Greek, Michaelis, who ran the coffee joint beside the ashheaps was the principal witness at the inquest. He had slept through the heat until after five, when he strolled over to the garage, and found George Wilson sick in his office—really sick, pale as his own pale hair and shaking all over. Michaelis advised him to go to bed, but Wilson refused, saying that he'd miss a lot of business if he did. While his neighbour was trying to persuade him a violent racket broke out overhead.

'I've got my wife locked in up there,' explained Wilson calmly. 'She's going to stay there till the day after tomorrow, and then we're going to move away.'

Michaelis was astonished; they had been neighbours for four years, and Wilson had never seemed faintly capable of such a statement. Generally he was one of these worn-out men: when he wasn't working, he sat on a chair in the doorway and stared at the people and the cars that passed along the road. When anyone spoke to him he invariably laughed in an agreeable, colourless way. He was his wife's man and not his own.

So naturally Michaelis tried to find out what had happened, but Wilson wouldn't say a word—instead he began to throw curious suspicious glances at his visitor and ask him what he'd been doing at certain times on certain days. Just as the latter was getting uneasy, some workmen came past the door bound for his restaurant, and Michaelis took the opportunity to get away, intending to come back later. But he didn't. He supposed he forgot to, that's all. When he came outside again, a little after seven, he was reminded of the conversation because he heard Mrs. Wilson's voice, loud and scolding, downstairs in the garage.

'Beat me!' he heard her cry. 'Throw me down and beat me, you dirty little coward!'

A moment later she rushed out into the dusk, waving her hands and shouting—before he could move from his door the business was over.

The 'death car' as the newspapers called it, didn't stop; it came out of the gathering darkness, wavered tragically for a moment, and then disappeared around the next bend. Mavromichaelis wasn't even sure of its colour—he told the first policeman that it was light green. The other car, the one going towards New York, came to rest a hundred yards beyond, and its driver hurried back to where Myrtle Wilson, her life violently extinguished, knelt in the road and mingled her thick dark blood with the dust.

Michaelis and this man reached her first, but when they had torn open her shirtwaist, still damp with perspiration, they saw that her left breast was swinging loose like a flap, and there was no need to listen for the heart beneath. The mouth was wide open and ripped a little at the corners, as though she had choked a little in giving up the tremendous vitality she had stored so long.

We saw the three or four automobiles and the crowd when we were still some distance away.

'Wreck!' said Tom. 'That's good. Wilson'll have a little business at last.'

He slowed down, but still without any intention of stopping, until, as we came nearer, the hushed, intent faces of the people at the garage door made him automatically put on his brakes.

'We'll take a look,' he said doubtfully, 'just a look.'

I became aware now of a hollow, wailing sound which issued incessantly from the garage, a sound which as we got out of the coupé and walked towards the door resolved itself into the words 'Oh, my God!' uttered over and over in a gasping moan.

'There's some bad trouble here,' said Tom excitedly.

He reached up on tiptoes and peered over a circle of heads into the garage, which was lit only by a yellow light in a swinging metal basket overhead. Then he made a harsh sound in his throat, and with a violent thrusting movement of his powerful arms pushed his way through.

The circle closed up again with a running murmur of

expostulation; it was a minute before I could see anything at all. Then new arrivals deranged the line, and Jordan and I were pushed suddenly inside.

Myrtle Wilson's body, wrapped in a blanket, and then in another blanket, as though she suffered from a chill in the hot night, lay on a work-table by the wall, and Tom, with his back to us, was bending over it, motionless. Next to him stood a motorcycle policeman taking down names with much sweat and correction in a little book. At first I couldn't find the source of the high, groaning words that echoed clamourously through the bare garage—then I saw Wilson standing on the raised threshold of his office, swaying back and forth and holding to the doorposts with both hands. Some man was talking to him in a low voice and attempting, from time to time, to lay a hand on his shoulder, but Wilson neither heard nor saw. His eyes would drop slowly from the swinging light to the laden table by the wall, and then jerk back to the light again, and he gave out incessantly his high, horrible call:

'Oh, my Ga-od! Oh, my Ga-od! Oh, Ga-od! Oh, my Ga-od!'

Presently Tom lifted his head with a jerk and, after staring around the garage with glazed eyes, addressed a mumbled incoherent remark to the policeman.

'M-a-y—' the policeman was saying, '—o———'

'No, r—' corrected the man, 'M-a-v-r-o———'

'Listen to me!' muttered Tom fiercely.

'r' said the policeman, 'o———'

'g———'

'g—' He looked up as Tom's broad hand fell sharply on his shoulder. 'What you want, fella?'

'What happened?—that's what I want to know.'

'Auto hit her. Ins'antly killed.'

'Instantly killed,' repeated Tom, staring.

'She ran out ina road. Son-of-a-bitch didn't even stopus car.'

'There was two cars,' said Michaelis, 'one comin', one goin', see?'

5+s.f.

'Going where?' asked the policeman keenly.

'One goin' each way. Well she'—his hand rose towards the blankets but stopped half way and fell to his side—'she ran out there an' the one comin' from N'York knock right into her, goin' thirty or forty miles an hour.'

'What's the name of this place here?' demanded the officer.

'Hasn't got any name.'

A pale well-dressed negro stepped near.

'It was a yellow car,' he said, 'big yellow car. New.'

'See the accident?' asked the policeman.

'No, but the car passed me down the road, going faster'n forty. Going fifty, sixty.'

'Come here and let's have your name. Look out now. I want to get his name.'

Some words of this conversation must have reached Wilson, swaying in the office door, for suddenly a new theme found voice among his gasping cries:

'You don't have to tell me what kind of car it was! I know what kind of car it was!'

Watching Tom, I saw the wad of muscle back of his shoulder tighten under his coat. He walked quickly over to Wilson and, standing in front of him, seized him firmly by the upper arms.

'You've got to pull yourself together,' he said with soothing gruffness.

Wilson's eyes fell upon Tom; he started up on his tiptoes and then would have collapsed to his knees had not Tom held him upright.

'Listen,' said Tom, shaking him a little. 'I just got here a minute ago, from New York. I was bringing you that coupé we've been talking about. That yellow car I was driving this afternoon wasn't mine—do you hear? I haven't seen it all afternoon.'

Only the negro and I were near enough to hear what he said, but the policeman caught something in the tone and looked over with truculent eyes.

'What's all that?' he demanded.

'I'm a friend of his.' Tom turned his head but kept his hands firm on Wilson's body. 'He says he knows the car that did it. . . . It was a yellow car.'

Some dim impulse moved the policeman to look suspiciously at Tom.

'And what colour's your car?'

'It's a blue car, a coupé.'

'We've come straight from New York,' I said.

Someone who had been driving a little behind us confirmed this, and the policeman turned away.

'Now, if you'll let me have that name again correct——'

Picking up Wilson like a doll, Tom carried him into the office, set him down in a chair, and came back.

'If somebody'll come here and sit with him,' he snapped authoritatively. He watched while the two men standing closest glanced at each other and went unwillingly into the room. Then Tom shut the door on them and came down the single step, his eyes avoiding the table. As he passed close to me he whispered: 'Let's get out.'

Self-consciously, with his authoritative arms breaking the way, we pushed through the still gathering crowd, passing a hurried doctor, case in hand, who had been sent for in wild hope half an hour ago.

Tom drove slowly until we were beyond the bend—then his foot came down hard, and the coupé raced along through the night. In a little while I heard a low husky sob, and saw that the tears were overflowing down his face.

'The God damned coward!' he whimpered. 'He didn't even stop his car.'

The Buchanans' house floated suddenly towards us through the dark rustling trees. Tom stopped beside the porch and looked up at the second floor, where two windows bloomed with light among the vines.

'Daisy's home,' he said. As we got out of the car he glanced at me and frowned slightly.

'I ought to have dropped you in West Egg, Nick. There's nothing we can do to-night.'

A change had come over him, and he spoke gravely, and with decision. As we walked across the moonlight gravel to the porch he disposed of the situation in a few brisk phrases.

'I'll telephone for a taxi to take you home, and while you're waiting you and Jordan better go in the kitchen and have them get you some supper—if you want any.' He opened the door. 'Come in.'

'No, thanks. But I'd be glad if you'd order me the taxi. I'll wait outside.'

Jordan put her hand on my arm.

'Won't you come in, Nick?'

'No, thanks.'

I was feeling a little sick and I wanted to be alone. But Jordan lingered for a moment more.

'It's only half-past nine,' she said.

I'd be damned if I'd go in; I'd had enough of all of them for one day, and suddenly that included Jordan too. She must have seen something of this in my expression, for she turned abruptly away and ran up the porch steps into the house. I sat down for a few minutes with my head in my hands, until I heard the phone taken up inside and the butler's voice calling a taxi. Then I walked slowly down the drive away from the house, intending to wait by the gate.

I hadn't gone twenty yards when I heard my name and Gatsby stepped from between two bushes into the path. I must have felt pretty weird by that time, because I could think of nothing except the luminosity of his pink suit under the moon.

'What are you doing?' I inquired.

'Just standing here, old sport.'

Somehow, that seemed a despicable occupation. For all I knew he was going to rob the house in a moment; I wouldn't have been surprised to see sinister faces, the faces of 'Wolfsheim's people', behind him in the dark shrubbery.

'Did you see any trouble on the road?' he asked after a minute.

'Yes.'

He hesitated.

'Was she killed?'

'Yes.'

'I thought so; I told Daisy I thought so. It's better that the shock should all come at once. She stood it pretty well.'

He spoke as if Daisy's reaction was the only thing that mattered.

'I got to West Egg by a side road,' he went on, 'and left the car in my garage. I don't think anybody saw us, but of course I can't be sure.'

I disliked him so much by this time that I didn't find it necessary to tell him he was wrong.

'Who was the woman?' he inquired.

'Her name was Wilson. Her husband owns the garage. How the devil did it happen?'

'Well, I tried to swing the wheel——' He broke off, and suddenly I guessed at the truth.

'Was Daisy driving?'

'Yes,' he said after a moment, 'but of course I'll say I was. You see, when we left New York she was very nervous and she thought it would steady her to drive—and this woman rushed out at us just as we were passing a car coming the other way. It all happened in a minute, but it seemed to me that she wanted to speak to us, thought we were somebody she knew. Well, first Daisy turned away from the woman towards the other car, and then she lost her nerve and turned back. The second my hand reached the wheel I felt the shock—it must have killed her instantly.'

'It ripped her open——'

'Don't tell me, old sport.' He winced. 'Anyhow—Daisy stepped on it. I tried to make her stop, but she couldn't, so I pulled on the emergency brake. Then she fell over into my lap and I drove on.'

'She'll be all right to-morrow,' he said presently. 'I'm just going to wait here and see if he tries to bother her about that unpleasantness this afternoon. She's locked herself into her room, and if he tries any brutality she's going to turn the light out and on again.'

'He won't touch her,' I said. 'He's not thinking about her.'

'I don't trust him, old sport.'

'How long are you going to wait?'

'All night, if necessary. Anyhow, till they all go to bed.'

A new point of view occurred to me. Suppose Tom found out that Daisy had been driving. He might think he saw a connection in it—he might think anything. I looked at the house; there were two or three bright windows downstairs and the pink glow from Daisy's room on the second floor.

'You wait here,' I said. 'I'll see if there's any sign of a commotion.'

I walked back along the border of the lawn, traversed the gravel softly, and tiptoed up the veranda steps. The drawing-room curtains were open, and I saw that the room was empty. Crossing the porch where we had dined that June night three months before, I came to a small rectangle of light which I guessed was the pantry window. The blind was drawn, but I found a rift at the sill.

Daisy and Tom were sitting opposite each other at the kitchen table, with a plate of cold fried chicken between them, and two bottles of ale. He was talking intently across the table at her, and in his earnestness his hand had fallen upon and covered her own. Once in a while she looked up at him and nodded in agreement.

They weren't happy, and neither of them had touched the chicken or the ale—and yet they weren't unhappy either. There was an unmistakable air of natural intimacy about the picture, and anybody would have said that they were conspiring together.

As I tiptoed from the porch I heard my taxi feeling its way along the dark drive towards the house. Gatsby was waiting where I had left him in the drive.

'Is it all quiet up there?' he asked anxiously.

'Yes, it's all quiet.' I hesitated. 'You'd better come home and get some sleep.'

He shook his head.

'I want to wait here till Daisy goes to bed. Good night, old sport.'

He put his hands in his coat pockets and turned back eagerly to his scrutiny of the house, as though my presence marred the sacredness of the vigil. So I walked away and left him standing there in the moonlight—watching over nothing.

CHAPTER VIII

I COULDN'T SLEEP all night; a fog-horn was groaning incessantly on the Sound, and I tossed half-sick between grotesque reality and savage, frightening dreams. Towards dawn I heard a taxi go up Gatsby's drive, and immediately I jumped out of bed and began to dress—I felt that I had something to tell him, something to warn him about, and morning would be too late.

Crossing his lawn, I saw that his front door was still open and he was leaning against a table in the hall, heavy with dejection or sleep.

'Nothing happened,' he said wanly. 'I waited, and about four o'clock she came to the window and stood there for a minute and then turned out the light.'

His house had never seemed so enormous to me as it did that night when we hunted through the great rooms for cigarettes. We pushed aside curtains that were like pavilions, and felt over innumerable feet of dark wall for electric light switches—once I tumbled with a sort of splash upon the keys of a ghostly piano. There was an inexplicable amount of dust everywhere, and the rooms were musty, as though they hadn't been aired for many days. I found the humidor on an unfamiliar table, with two stale, dry cigarettes inside. Throwing open the French windows of the drawing-room, we sat smoking out into the darkness.

'You ought to go away,' I said. 'It's pretty certain they'll trace your car.'

'Go away *now*, old sport?'

'Go to Atlantic City for a week, or up to Montreal.'

He wouldn't consider it. He couldn't possibly leave Daisy until he knew what she was going to do. He was clutching at some last hope and I couldn't bear to shake him free.

It was this night that he told me the strange story of his youth with Dan Cody—told it to me because 'Jay Gatsby' had broken up like glass against Tom's hard malice, and the long secret extravaganza was played out. I think that he would have acknowledged anything now, without reserve, but he wanted to talk about Daisy.

She was the first 'nice girl' he had ever known. In various unrevealed capacities he had come in contact with such people, but always with indiscernible barbed wire between. He found her excitingly desirable. He went to her house, at first with other officers from Camp Taylor, then alone. It amazed him—he had never been in such a beautiful house before. But what gave it an air of breathless intensity was that Daisy lived there—it was as casual a thing to her as his tent out at camp was to him. There was a ripe mystery about it, a hint of bedrooms upstairs more beautiful and cool than other bedrooms, of gay and radiant activities taking place through its corridors, and of romances that were not musty and laid away already in lavender, but fresh and breathing and redolent of this year's shining motor-cars and of dances whose flowers were scarcely withered. It excited him, too, that many men had already loved Daisy— it increased her value in his eyes. He felt their presence all about the house, pervading the air with the shades and echoes of still vibrant emotions.

But he knew that he was in Daisy's house by a colossal accident. However glorious might be his future as Jay Gatsby, he was at present a penniless young man without a past, and at any moment the invisible cloak of his uniform might slip from his shoulders. So he made the most of his time. He took what he could get, ravenously and un-scrupulously—eventually he took Daisy one still October night, took her because he had no real right to touch her hand.

He might have despised himself, for he had certainly taken her under false pretences. I don't mean that he had traded on his phantom millions, but he had deliberately given Daisy a sense of security; he let her believe that he was a person from much the same strata as herself—that he was fully able to take care of her. As a matter of fact, he had no such facilities—he had no comfortable family standing behind him, and he was liable at the whim of an impersonal government to be blown anywhere about the world.

But he didn't despise himself and it didn't turn out as he had imagined. He had intended, probably, to take what he could and go—but now he found that he had committed himself to the following of a grail. He knew that Daisy was extraordinary, but he didn't realize just how extraordinary a 'nice' girl could be. She vanished into her rich house, into her rich, full life, leaving Gatsby—nothing. He felt married to her, that was all.

When they met again, two days later, it was Gatsby who was breathless, who was, somehow, betrayed. Her porch was bright with the bought luxury of star-shine; the wicker of the settee squeaked fashionably as she turned towards him and he kissed her curious and lovely mouth. She had caught a cold, and it made her voice huskier and more charming than ever, and Gatsby was overwhelmingly aware of the youth and mystery that wealth imprisons and pre-serves, of the freshness of many clothes, and of Daisy, gleaming like silver, safe and proud above the hot struggles of the poor.

'I can't describe to you how surprised I was to find out I loved her, old sport. I even hoped for a while that she'd throw me over, but she didn't, because she was in love with me too. She thought I knew a lot because I knew different things from her. . . . Well, there I was, 'way off my ambitions, getting deeper in love every minute, and all of a sudden I didn't care. What was the use of doing great things if I could have a better time telling her what I was going to do?'

On the last afternoon before he went abroad, he sat with Daisy in his arms for a long, silent time. It was a cold fall day, with fire in the room and her cheeks flushed. Now and then she moved and he changed his arm a little, and once he kissed her dark shining hair. The afternoon had made them tranquil for a while, as if to give them a deep memory for the long parting the next day promised. They had never been closer in their month of love, nor communicated more profoundly one with another, than when she brushed silent lips against his coat's shoulder or when he touched the end of her fingers, gently, as though she were asleep.

He did extraordinarily well in the war. He was a captain before he went to the front, and following the Argonne battles he got his majority and the command of the divisional machine-guns. After the Armistice he tried frantically to get home, but some complication or misunderstanding sent him to Oxford instead. He was worried now—there was a quality of nervous despair in Daisy's letters. She didn't see why he couldn't come. She was feeling the pressure of the world outside, and she wanted to see him and feel his presence beside her and be reassured that she was doing the right thing after all.

For Daisy was young and her artificial world was redolent of orchids and pleasant, cheerful snobbery and orchestras which set the rhythm of the year, summing up the sadness and suggestiveness of life in new tunes. All night the saxophones wailed the hopeless comment of the *Beale Street Blues* while a hundred pairs of golden and silver slippers shuffled the shining dust. At the grey tea hour there were always rooms that throbbed incessantly with this low, sweet fever, while fresh faces drifted here and there like rose petals blown by the sad horns around the floor.

Through this twilight universe Daisy began to move again with the season; suddenly she was again keeping half a dozen dates a day with half a dozen men, and drowsing asleep at dawn with the beads and chiffon of an evening dress tangled among dying orchids on the floor beside her bed. And all the time something within her was crying for a decision. She wanted her life shaped now, immediately —and the decision must be made by some force—of love, of money, of unquestionable practicality—that was close at hand.

That force took shape in the middle of spring with the arrival of Tom Buchanan. There was a wholesome bulkiness about his person and his position, and Daisy was flattered. Doubtless there was a certain struggle and a certain relief. The letter reached Gatsby while he was still at Oxford.

It was dawn now on Long Island and we went about opening the rest of the windows downstairs, filling the house with grey-turning, gold-turning light. The shadow of a tree fell abruptly across the dew and ghostly birds began to sing among the blue leaves. There was a slow, pleasant movement in the air, scarcely a wind, promising a cool, lovely day.

'I don't think she ever loved him,' Gatsby turned around from a window and looked at me challengingly. 'You must remember, old sport, she was very excited this afternoon. He told her those things in a way that frightened her—that made it look as if I was some kind of cheap sharper. And the result was she hardly knew what she was saying.'

He sat down gloomily.

'Of course she might have loved him just for a minute, when they were first married—and loved me more even then, do you see?'

Suddenly he came out with a curious remark.

'In any case,' he said, 'it was just personal.'

What could you make of that, except to suspect some intensity in his conception of the affair that couldn't be measured?

He came back from France when Tom and Daisy were still on their wedding trip, and made a miserable but irresistible journey to Louisville on the last of his army pay.

He stayed there a week, walking the streets where their footsteps had clicked together through the November night and revisiting the out-of-the-way places to which they had driven in her white car. Just as Daisy's house had always seemed to him more mysterious and gay than other houses, so his idea of the city itself, even though she was gone from it, was pervaded with a melancholy beauty.

He left, feeling that if he had searched harder, he might have found her—that he was leaving her behind. The day-coach—he was penniless now—was hot. He went out to the open vestibule and sat down on a folding-chair, and the station slid away and the backs of unfamiliar buildings moved by. Then out into the spring fields, where a yellow trolley raced them for a minute with people in it who might once have seen the pale magic of her face along the casual street.

The track curved and now it was going away from the sun, which, as it sank lower, seemed to spread itself in benediction over the vanishing city where she had drawn her breath. He stretched out his hand desperately as if to snatch only a wisp of air, to save a fragment of the spot that she had made lovely for him. But it was all going by too fast now for his blurred eyes and he knew that he had lost that part of it, the freshest and the best, forever.

It was nine o'clock when we finished breakfast and went out on the porch. The night had made a sharp difference in the weather and there was an autumn flavour in the air. The gardener, the last one of Gatsby's former servants, came to the foot of the steps.

'I'm going to drain the pool to-day, Mr. Gatsby. Leaves'll start falling pretty soon, and then there's always trouble with the pipes.'

'Don't do it to-day,' Gatsby answered. He turned to me apologetically. 'You know, old sport, I've never used that pool all summer.'

I looked at my watch and stood up.

'Twelve minutes to my train.'

I didn't want to go to the city. I wasn't worth a decent

stroke of work, but it was more than that—I didn't want to leave Gatsby. I missed that train, and then another, before I could get myself away.

'I'll call you up,' I said finally.

'Do, old sport.'

'I'll call you about noon.'

We walked slowly down the steps.

'I suppose Daisy'll call too.' He looked at me anxiously, as if he hoped I'd corroborate this.

'I suppose so.'

'Well, good-bye.'

We shook hands and I started away. Just before I reached the hedge I remembered something and turned around.

'They're a rotten crowd,' I shouted across the lawn. 'You're worth the whole damn bunch put together.'

I've always been glad I said that. It was the only compliment I ever gave him, because I disapproved of him from beginning to end. First he nodded politely, and then his face broke into that radiant and understanding smile, as if we'd been in ecstatic cahoots on that fact all the time. His gorgeous pink rag of a suit made a bright spot of colour against the white steps, and I thought of the night when I first came to his ancestral home, three months before. The lawn and drive had been crowded with the faces of those who guessed at his corruption—and he had stood on those steps, concealing his incorruptible dream, as he waved them good-bye.

I thanked him for his hospitality. We were always thanking him for that—I and the others.

'Good-bye,' I called. 'I enjoyed breakfast, Gatsby.'

Up in the city, I tried for a while to list the quotations on an interminable amount of stock, then I fell asleep in my swivel-chair. Just before noon the phone woke me, and I started up with sweat breaking out on my forehead. It was Jordan Baker; she often called me up at this hour because the uncertainty of her own movements between hotels and clubs and private houses made her hard to find in any other way. Usually her voice came over the wire as something fresh and cool, as if a divot from a green golf-links had come sailing in at the office window, but this morning it seemed harsh and dry.

'I've left Daisy's house,' she said. 'I'm at Hempstead, and I'm going down to Southampton this afternoon.'

Probably it had been tactful to leave Daisy's house, but the act annoyed me, and her next remark made me rigid.

'You weren't so nice to me last night.'

'How could it have mattered then?'

Silence for a moment. Then:

'However—I want to see you.'

'I want to see you, too.'

'Suppose I don't go to Southampton, and come into town this afternoon?'

'No—I don't think this afternoon.'

'Very well.'

'It's impossible this afternoon. Various——'

We talked like that for a while, and then abruptly we weren't talking any longer. I don't know which of us hung up with a sharp click, but I know I didn't care. I couldn't have talked to her across a tea-table that day if I never talked to her again in this world.

I called Gatsby's house a few minutes later, but the line was busy. I tried four times; finally an exasperated central told me the wire was being kept open for long distance from Detroit. Taking out my time-table, I drew a small circle around the three-fifty train. Then I leaned back in my chair and tried to think. It was just noon.

When I passed the ashheaps on the train that morning I had crossed deliberately to the other side of the car. I supposed there'd be a curious crowd around there all day with little boys searching for dark spots in the dust, and some garrulous man telling over and over what had happened, until it became less and less real even to him and he could tell it no longer, and Myrtle Wilson's tragic achievement was forgotten. Now I want to go back a little and tell what happened at the garage after we left there the night before.

They had difficulty in locating the sister, Catherine. She must have broken her rule against drinking that night, for when she arrived she was stupid with liquor and unable to understand that the ambulance had already gone to Flushing. When they convinced her of this, she immediately fainted, as if that was the intolerable part of the affair. Someone, kind or curious, took her in his car and drove her in the wake of her sister's body.

Until long after midnight a changing crowd lapped up against the front of the garage, while George Wilson rocked himself back and forth on the couch inside. For a while the door of the office was open, and everyone who came into the garage glanced irresistibly through it. Finally someone said it was a shame, and closed the door. Michaelis and several other men were with him; first, four or five men, later two or three men. Still later Michaelis had to ask the last stranger to wait there fifteen minutes longer, while he went back to his own place and made a pot of coffee. After that, he stayed there alone with Wilson until dawn.

About three o'clock the quality of Wilson's incoherent muttering changed—he grew quieter and began to talk about the yellow car. He announced that he had a way of finding out whom the yellow car belonged to, and then he blurted out that a couple of months ago his wife had come from the city with her face bruised and her nose swollen.

But when he heard himself say this, he flinched and began to cry 'Oh, my God!' again in his groaning voice. Michaelis made a clumsy attempt to distract him.

'How long have you been married, George? Come on there, try and sit still a minute and answer my question. How long have you been married?'

'Twelve years.'

'Ever had any children? Come on, George, sit still—I asked you a question. Did you ever have any children?'

The hard brown beetles kept thudding against the dull light, and whenever Michaelis heard a car go tearing along the road outside it sounded to him like the car that hadn't stopped a few hours before. He didn't like to go into the garage, because the work bench was stained where the body had been lying, so he moved uncomfortably around the office—he knew every object in it before morning—and from time to time sat down beside Wilson trying to keep him more quiet.

'Have you got a church you go to sometimes, George? Maybe even if you haven't been there for a long time? Maybe I could call up the church and get a priest to come over and he could talk to you, see?'

'Don't belong to any.'

'You ought to have a church, George, for times like this. You must have gone to church once. Didn't you get married in a church? Listen, George, listen to me. Didn't you get married in a church?'

'That was a long time ago.'

The effort of answering broke the rhythm of his rocking —for a moment he was silent. Then the same half-knowing, half-bewildered look came back into his faded eyes.

'Look in the drawer there,' he said, pointing at the desk.

'Which drawer?'

'That drawer—that one.'

Michaelis opened the drawer nearest his hand. There was nothing in it but a small, expensive dog-leash, made of leather and braided silver. It was apparently new.

'This?' he inquired, holding it up.

Wilson stared and nodded.

'I found it yesterday afternoon. She tried to tell me about it, but I knew it was something funny.'

'You mean your wife bought it?'

'She had it wrapped in tissue paper on her bureau.'

Michaelis didn't see anything odd in that, and he gave Wilson a dozen reasons why his wife might have bought the dog-leash. But conceivably Wilson had heard some of these same explanations before, from Myrtle, because he began saying 'Oh, my God!' again in a whisper—his comforter left several explanations in the air.

'Then he killed her,' said Wilson. His mouth dropped open suddenly.

'Who did?'

'I have a way of finding out.'

'You're morbid, George,' said his friend. 'This has been a strain to you and you don't know what you're saying. You'd better try and sit quiet till morning.'

'He murdered her.'

'It was an accident, George.'

Wilson shook his head. His eyes narrowed and his mouth widened slightly with the ghost of a superior 'Hm!'

'I know,' he said definitely, 'I'm one of these trusting fellas and I don't think any harm to *no*body, but when I get to know a thing I know it. It was the man in that car. She ran out to speak to him and he wouldn't stop.'

Michaelis had seen this too, but it hadn't occurred to him that there was any special significance in it. He believed that Mrs. Wilson had been running away from her husband, rather than trying to stop any particular car.

'How could she of been like that?'

'She's a deep one,' said Wilson, as if that answered the question. 'Ah-h-h——'

He began to rock again, and Michaelis stood twisting the leash in his hand.

'Maybe you got some friend that I could telephone for, George?'

This was a forlorn hope—he was almost sure that Wilson had no friend: there was not enough of him for his wife. He was glad a little later when he noticed a change in the room, a blue quickening by the window, and realized that dawn wasn't far off. About five o'clock it was blue enough outside to snap off the light.

Wilson's glazed eyes turned out to the ashheaps, where small grey clouds took on fantastic shapes and scurried here and there in the faint dawn wind.

'I spoke to her,' he muttered, after a long silence. 'I told her she might fool me but she couldn't fool God. I took her to the window'—with an effort he got up and walked to

the rear window and leaned with his face pressed against it
—'and I said "God knows what you've been doing, everything you've been doing. You may fool me, but you can't
fool God!"'

Standing behind him, Michaelis saw with a shock that he
was looking at the eyes of Doctor T. J. Eckleburg, which
had just emerged, pale and enormous, from the dissolving
night.

'God sees everything,' repeated Wilson.

'That's an advertisement,' Michaelis assured him.
Something made him turn away from the window and look
back into the room. But Wilson stood there a long time, his
face close to the window pane, nodding into the twilight.

By six o'clock Michaelis was worn out, and grateful for
the sound of a car stopping outside. It was one of the
watchers of the night before who had promised to come
back, so he cooked breakfast for three, which he and the
other man ate together. Wilson was quieter now, and
Michaelis went home to sleep; when he awoke four hours
later and hurried back to the garage, Wilson was gone.

His movements—he was on foot all the time—were
afterwards traced to Port Roosevelt and than to Gad's Hill,
where he bought a sandwich that he didn't eat, and a cup
of coffee. He must have been tired and walking slowly, for
he didn't reach Gad's Hill until noon. Thus far there was
no difficulty in accounting for his time—there were boys
who had seen a man 'acting sort of crazy,' and motorists at
whom he stared oddly from the side of the road. Then for
three hours he disappeared from view. The police, on the
strength of what he said to Michaelis, that he 'had a way of
finding out,' supposed that he spent that time going from
garage to garage thereabouts, inquiring for a yellow car.
On the other hand, no garage man who had seen him ever
came forward, and perhaps he had an easier, surer way of
finding out what he wanted to know. By half-past two he
was in West Egg, where he asked someone the way to
Gatsby's house. So by that time he knew Gatsby's
name.

At two o'clock Gatsby put on his bathing-suit and left word with the butler that if anyone phoned word was to be brought to him at the pool. He stopped at the garage for a pneumatic mattress that had amused his guests during the summer, and the chauffeur helped him pump it up. Then he gave instructions that the open car wasn't to be taken out under any circumstances—and this was strange, because the front right fender needed repair.

Gatsby shouldered the mattress and started for the pool. Once he stopped and shifted it a little, and the chauffeur asked him if he needed help, but he shook his head and in a moment disappeared among the yellowing trees.

No telephone message arrived, but the butler went without his sleep and waited for it until four o'clock—until long after there was anyone to give it to if it came. I have an idea that Gatsby himself didn't believe it would come, and perhaps he no longer cared. If that was true he must have felt that he had lost the old warm world, paid a high price for living too long with a single dream. He must have looked up at an unfamiliar sky through frightening leaves and shivered as he found what a grotesque thing a rose is and how raw the sunlight was upon the scarcely created grass. A new world, material without being real, where poor ghosts, breathing dreams like air, drifted fortuitously about . . . like that ashen, fantastic figure gliding towards him through the amorphous trees.

The chauffeur—he was one of Wolfsheim's protégés—heard the shots—afterwards he could only say that he hadn't thought anything much about them. I drove from the station directly to Gatsby's house and my rushing anxiously up the front steps was the first thing that alarmed any one. But they knew then, I firmly believe. With scarcely a word said, four of us, the chauffeur, butler, gardener, and I, hurried down to the pool.

There was a faint, barely perceptible movement of the water as the fresh flow from one end urged its way towards the drain at the other. With little ripples that were hardly the shadows of waves, the laden mattress moved irregularly down the pool. A small gust of wind that scarcely corrugated the surface was enough to disturb its accidental course with its accidental burden. The touch of a cluster of leaves revolved it slowly, tracing, like the leg of transit, a thin red circle in the water.

It was after we started with Gatsby towards the house that the gardener saw Wilson's body a little way off in the grass, and the holocaust was complete.

CHAPTER IX

AFTER TWO YEARS I remember the rest of that day, and that night and the next day, only as an endless drill of police and photographers and newspaper men in and out of Gatsby's front door. A rope stretched across the main gate and a policeman by it kept out the curious, but little boys soon discovered that they could enter through my yard, and there were always a few of them clustered open-mouthed about the pool. Someone with a positive manner, perhaps a detective, used the expression 'madman' as he bent over Wilson's body that afternoon, and the adventitious authority of his voice set the key for the newspaper reports next morning.

Most of those reports were a nightmare—grotesque, circumstantial, eager, and untrue. When Michaelis's testimony at the inquest brought to light Wilson's suspicions of his wife I thought the whole tale would shortly be served up in racy pasquinade—but Catherine, who might have said anything, didn't say a word. She showed a surprising amount of character about it too—looked at the coroner with determined eyes under that corrected brow of hers, and swore that her sister had never seen Gatsby, that her sister was completely happy with her husband, that her sister had been into no mischief whatever. She convinced herself of it, and cried into her handkerchief, as if the very suggestion was more than she could endure. So Wilson was reduced to a man 'deranged by grief' in order that the case might remain in its simplest form. And it rested there.

But all this part of it seemed remote and unessential. I found myself on Gatsby's side, and alone. From the moment I telephoned news of the catastrophe to West Egg village, every surmise about him, and every practical question, was referred to me. At first I was surprised and confused; then, as he lay in his house and didn't move or breathe or speak, hour upon hour, it grew upon me that I was responsible, because no one else was interested—interested, I mean, with that intense personal interest to which everyone has some vague right at the end.

I called up Daisy half an hour after we found him, called her instinctively and without hesitation. But she and Tom had gone away early that afternoon, and taken baggage with them.

'Left no address?'

'No.'

'Say when they'd be back?'

'No.'

'Any idea where they are? How I could reach them?'

'I don't know. Can't say.'

I wanted to get somebody for him. I wanted to go into the room where he lay and reassure him: 'I'll get somebody for you, Gatsby. Don't worry. Just trust me and I'll get somebody for you——'

Meyer Wolfsheim's name wasn't in the phone book. The butler gave me his office address on Broadway, and I called Information, but by the time I had the number it was long after five, and no one answered the phone.

'Will you ring again?'

'I've rung them three times.'

'It's very important.'

'Sorry. I'm afraid no one's there.'

I went back to the drawing-room and thought for an instant that they were chance visitors, all these official people who suddenly filled it. But, though they drew back the sheet and looked at Gatsby with shocked eyes, his protest continued in my brain:

'Look here, old sport, you've got to get somebody for
me. You've got to try hard. I can't go through this
alone.'

Someone started to ask me questions, but I broke away
and going upstairs looked hastily through the unlocked parts
of his desk—he'd never told me definitely that his parents
were dead. But there was nothing—only the picture of
Dan Cody, a token of forgotten violence, staring down from
the wall.

Next morning I sent the butler to New York with a letter
to Wolfsheim, which asked for information and urged him
to come out on the next train. That request seemed super-
fluous when I wrote it. I was sure he'd start when he saw
the newspapers, just as I was sure there'd be a wire from
Daisy before noon—but neither a wire nor Mr. Wolfsheim
arrived; no one arrived except more police and photographers and newspaper men. When the butler brought
back Wolfsheim's answer I began to have a feeling of
defiance, of scornful solidarity between Gatsby and me
against them all.

DEAR MR. CARRAWAY. This has been one of the most
terrible shocks of my life to me I hardly can believe it
that it is true at all. Such a mad act as that man did
should make us all think. I cannot come down now as
I am tied up in some very important business and cannot get mixed up in this thing now. If there is anything
I can do a little later let me know in a letter by Edgar.
I hardly know where I am when I hear about a
thing like this and am completely knocked down and
out.

                    Yours truly
                    MEYER WOLFSHEIM

and then hasty addenda beneath:

Let me know about the funeral etc. do not know his
family at all.

When the phone rang that afternoon and Long Distance said Chicago was calling I thought this would be Daisy at last. But the connection came through as a man's voice, very thin and far away.

'This is Slagle speaking . . .'

'Yes?' The name was unfamiliar.

'Hell of a note, isn't it? Get my wire?'

'There haven't been any wires.'

'Young Parke's in trouble,' he said rapidly. 'They picked him up when he handed the bonds over the counter. They got a circular from New York giving 'em the numbers just five minutes before. What d'you know about that, hey? You never can tell in these hick towns——'

'Hello!' I interrupted breathlessly. 'Look here—this isn't Mr. Gatsby. Mr. Gatsby's dead.'

There was a long silence on the other end of the wire, followed by an exclamation . . . then a quick squawk as the connection was broken.

I think it was on the third day that a telegram signed Henry C. Gatz arrived from a town in Minnesota. It said only that the sender was leaving immediately and to postpone the funeral until he came.

It was Gatsby's father, a solemn old man, very helpless and dismayed, bundled up in a long cheap ulster against the warm September day. His eyes leaked continuously with excitement, and when I took the bag and umbrella from his hands he began to pull so incessantly at his sparse grey beard that I had difficulty in getting off his coat. He was on the point of collapse, so I took him into the music room and made him sit down while I sent for something to eat. But he wouldn't eat, and the glass of milk spilled from his trembling hand.

'I saw it in the Chicago newspaper,' he said. 'It was all in the Chicago newspaper. I started right away.'

'I didn't know how to reach you.'

His eyes, seeing nothing, moved ceaselessly about the room.

'It was a madman,' he said. 'He must have been mad.'

'Wouldn't you like come coffee?' I urged him.

'I don't want anything. I'm all right now, Mr.——'

'Carraway.'

'Well, I'm all right now. Where have they got Jimmy?'

I took him into the drawing-room, where his son lay, and left him there. Some little boys had come up on the steps and were looking into the hall; when I told them who had arrived, they went reluctantly away.

After a little while Mr. Gatz opened the door and came out, his mouth ajar, his face flushed slightly, his eyes leaking isolated and unpunctual tears. He had reached an age where death no longer has the quality of ghastly surprise, and when he looked around him now for the first time and saw the height and splendour of the hall and the great rooms opening out from it into other rooms, his grief began to be mixed with an awed pride. I helped him to a bedroom upstairs; while he took off his coat and vest I told him that all arrangements had been deferred until he came.

'I didn't know what you'd want, Mr. Gatsby——'

'Gatz is my name.'

'—Mr. Gatz. I thought you might want to take the body West.'

He shook his head.

'Jimmy always liked it better down East. He rose up to his position in the East. Were you a friend of my boy's, Mr.——?'

'We were close friends.'

'He had a big future before him, you know. He was only a young man, but he had a lot of brain power here.'

He touched his head impressively, and I nodded.

'If he'd of lived, he'd of been a great man. A man like James J. Hill. He'd of helped build up the country.'

'That's true,' I said, uncomfortably.

He fumbled at the embroidered coverlet, trying to take it from the bed, and lay down stiffly—was instantly asleep.

That night an obviously frightened person called up, and

demanded to know who I was before he would give his name.

'This is Mr. Carraway,' I said.

'Oh!' He sounded relieved. 'This is Klipspringer.'

I was relieved too, for that seemed to promise another friend at Gatsby's grave. I didn't want it to be in the papers and draw a sightseeing crowd, so I'd been calling up a few people myself. They were hard to find.

'The funeral's to-morrow,' I said. 'Three o'clock, here at the house. I wish you'd tell anybody who'd be interested.'

'Oh, I will,' he broke out hastily. 'Of course I'm not likely to see anybody, but if I do.'

His tone made me suspicious.

'Of course you'll be there yourself.'

'Well, I'll certainly try. What I called up about is——'

'Wait a minute,' I interrupted. 'How about saying you'll come?'

'Well, the fact is—the truth of the matter is that I'm staying with some people up here in Greenwich, and they rather expect me to be with them to-morrow. In fact, there's a sort of picnic or something. Of course I'll do my very best to get away.'

I ejaculated an unrestrained 'Huh!' and he must have heard me, for he went on nervously:

'What I called up about was a pair of shoes I left there. I wonder if it'd be too much trouble to have the butler send them on. You see, they're tennis shoes, and I'm sort of helpless without them. My address is care of B. F.——'

I didn't hear the rest of the name, because I hung up the receiver.

After that I felt a certain shame for Gatsby—one gentleman to whom I telephoned implied that he had got what he deserved. However, that was my fault, for he was one of those who used to sneer most bitterly at Gatsby on the courage of Gatsby's liquor, and I should have known better than to call him.

The morning of the funeral I went up to New York to see Meyer Wolfsheim; I couldn't seem to reach him any other way. The door that I pushed open, on the advice of an elevator boy, was marked 'The Swastika Holding Company,' and at first there didn't seem to be anyone inside. But when I'd shouted 'hello' several times in vain, an argument broke out behind a partition, and presently a lovely Jewess appeared at an interior door and scrutinized me with black hostile eyes.

'Nobody's in,' she said. 'Mr. Wolfsheim's gone to Chicago.'

The first part of this was obviously untrue, for someone had begun to whistle 'The Rosary,' tunelessly, inside.

'Please say that Mr. Carraway wants to see him.'

'I can't get him back from Chicago, can I?'

At this moment a voice, unmistakably Wolfsheim's, called 'Stella!' from the other side of the door.

'Leave your name on the desk,' she said quickly. 'I'll give it to him when he gets back.'

'But I know he's there.'

She took a step towards me and began to slide her hands indignantly up and down her hips.

'You young men think you can force your way in here any time,' she scolded. 'We're getting sickantired of it. When I say he's in Chicago, he's in Chicago.'

I mentioned Gatsby.

'Oh-h!' She looked at me over again. 'Will you just— What was your name?'

She vanished. In a moment Meyer Wolfsheim stood solemnly in the doorway, holding out both hands. He drew me into his office, remarking in a reverent voice that it was a sad time for all of us, and offered me a cigar.

'My memory goes back to when first I met him,' he said. 'A young major just out of the army and covered over with medals he got in the war. He was so hard up he had to keep on wearing his uniform because he couldn't buy some regular clothes. First time I saw him was when he come into Winebrenner's poolroom at Forty-third Street and asked for a job. He hadn't eat anything for a couple of days.

"Come on have some lunch with me," I said. He ate more than four dollars' worth of food in half an hour.'

'Did you start him in business?' I inquired.

'Start him! I made him.'

'Oh.'

'I raised him up out of nothing, right out of the gutter. I saw right away he was a fine-appearing, gentlemanly young man, and when he told me he was an Oggsford I knew I could use him good. I got him to join up in the American Legion and he used to stand high there. Right off he did some work for a client of mine up to Albany. We were so thick like that in everything'—he held up two bulbous fingers—'always together.'

I wondered if this partnership had included the World's Series transaction in 1919.

'Now he's dead,' I said after a moment. 'You were his closest friend, so I know you'll want to come to his funeral this afternoon.'

'I'd like to come.'

'Well, come then.'

The hair in his nostrils quivered slightly, and as he shook his head his eyes filled with tears.

'I can't do it—I can't get mixed up in it,' he said.

'There's nothing to get mixed up in. It's all over now.'

'When a man gets killed I never like to get mixed up in it in any way. I keep out. When I was a young man it was different—if a friend of mine died, no matter how, I stuck with them to the end. You may think that's sentimental, but I mean it—to the bitter end.'

I saw that for some reason of his own he was determined not to come, so I stood up.

'Are you a college man?' he inquired suddenly.

For a moment I thought he was going to suggest a 'gonnegtion,' but he only nodded and shook my hand.

'Let us learn to show our friendship for a man when he is alive and not after he is dead,' he suggested. 'After that, my own rule is to let everything alone.'

When I left his office the sky had turned dark and I got back to West Egg in a drizzle. After changing my clothes I went next door and found Mr. Gatz walking up and down excitedly in the hall. His pride in his son and in his son's possessions was continually increasing and now he had something to show me.

'Jimmy sent me this picture.' He took out his wallet with trembling fingers. 'Look there.'

It was a photograph of the house, cracked in the corners and dirty with many hands. He pointed out every detail to me eagerly. 'Look there!' and then sought admiration from my eyes. He had shown it so often that I think it was more real to him now than the house itself.

'Jimmy sent it to me. I think it's a very pretty picture. It shows up well.'

'Very well. Had you seen him lately?'

'He came out to see me two years ago and bought me the house I live in now. Of course we was broke up when he run off from home, but I see now there was a reason for it. He knew he had a big future in front of him. And ever since he made a success he was very generous with me.'

He seemed reluctant to put away the picture, held it for another minute, lingeringly, before my eyes. Then he returned the wallet and pulled from his pocket a ragged old copy book called *Hopalong Cassidy*.

'Look here, this is a book he had when he was a boy. It just shows you.'

He opened it at the back cover and turned it around for me to see. On the last fly-leaf was printed the word SCHEDULE, and the date September 12, 1906. And underneath:

Rise from bed	6.00	A.M.
Dumbbell exercise and wall-scaling .	6.15–6.30	,,
Study electricity, etc.	7.15–8.15	,,
Work	8.30–4.30	P.M.
Baseball and sports	4.30–5.00	,,
Practice elocution, pose and how to attain it	5.00–6.00	,,
Study needed inventions . . .	7.00–9.00	,,

GENERAL RESOLVES

No wasting time at Shafters or [a name, indecipherable]
No more smokeing or chewing.
Bath every other day
Read one improving book or magazine per week
Save $5.00 [crossed out] $3.00 per week
Be better to parents

'I come across this book by accident,' said the old man.
'It just shows you, don't it?

'Jimmy was bound to get ahead. He always had some
resolves like this or something. Do you notice what he's got
about improving his mind? He was always great for that.
He told me I et like a hog once, and I beat him for it.'

He was reluctant to close the book, reading each item
aloud and then looking eagerly at me. I think he rather
expected me to copy down the list for my own use.

A little before three the Lutheran minister arrived from
Flushing, and I began to look involuntarily out the windows
for other cars. So did Gatsby's father. And as the time passed
and the servants came in and stood waiting in the hall, his
eyes began to blink anxiously, and he spoke of the rain in a
worried, uncertain way. The minister glanced several times
at his watch, so I took him aside and asked him to wait for
half an hour. But it wasn't any use. Nobody came.

About five o'clock our procession of three cars reached
the cemetery and stopped in a thick drizzle beside the gate
—first a motor hearse, horribly black and wet, then Mr.
Gatz and the minister and I in the limousine, and a little
later four or five servants and the postman from West Egg,
in Gatsby's station wagon, all wet to the skin. As we started
through the gate into the cemetery I heard a car stop and
then the sound of someone splashing after us over the soggy
ground. I looked around. It was the man with owl-eyed
glasses whom I had found marvelling over Gatsby's books
in the library one night three months before.

I'd never seen him since then. I don't know how he knew about the funeral, or even his name. The rain poured down his thick glasses, and he took them off and wiped them to see the protecting canvas unrolled from Gatsby's grave.

I tried to think about Gatsby then for a moment, but he was already too far away, and I could only remember, without resentment, that Daisy hadn't sent a message or a flower. Dimly I heard someone murmur 'Blessed are the dead that the rain falls on,' and then the owl-eyed man said 'Amen to that,' in a brave voice.

We straggled down quickly through the rain to the cars. Owl-eyes spoke to me by the gate.

'I couldn't get to the house,' he remarked.

'Neither could anybody else.'

'Go on!' He started. 'Why, my God! they used to go there by the hundreds.'

He took off his glasses and wiped them again, outside and in.

'The poor son-of-a-bitch,' he said.

One of my most vivid memories is of coming back West from prep school and later from college at Christmas time. Those who went farther than Chicago would gather in the old dim Union Station at six o'clock of a December evening, with a few Chicago friends, already caught up into their own holiday gaieties, to bid them a hasty good-bye. I remember the fur coats of the girls returning from Miss This-or-That's and the chatter of frozen breath and the hands waving overhead as we caught sight of old acquaintances, and the matchings of invitations: 'Are you going to the Ordways'? the Herseys'? the Schultzes'?' and the long green tickets clasped tight in our gloved hands. And last the murky yellow cars of the Chicago, Milwaukee & St. Paul railroad looking cheerful as Christmas itself on the tracks beside the gate.

When we pulled out into the winter night and the real snow, our snow, began to stretch out beside us and twinkle against the windows, and the dim lights of small Wisconsin stations moved by, a sharp wild brace came suddenly into the air. We drew in deep breaths of it as we walked back from dinner through the cold vestibules, unutterably aware of our identity with this country for one strange hour, before we melted indistinguishably into it again.

That's my Middle West—not the wheat or the prairies or the lost Swede towns, but the thrilling returning trains of my youth, and the street lamps and sleigh bells in the frosty dark and the shadows of holly wreaths thrown by lighted windows on the snow. I am part of that, a little solemn with the feel of those long winters, a little complacent from growing up in the Carraway house in a city where dwellings are still called through decades by a family's name. I see now that this has been a story of the West, after all—Tom and Gatsby, Daisy and Jordan and I, were all Westerners, and perhaps we possessed some deficiency in common which made us subtly unadaptable to Eastern life.

Even when the East excited me most, even when I was most keenly aware of its superiority to the bored, sprawling, swollen towns beyond the Ohio, with their interminable inquisitions which spared only the children and the very old —even then it had always for me a quality of distortion. West Egg, especially, still figures in my more fantastic dreams. I see it as a night scene by El Greco: a hundred houses, at once conventional and grotesque, crouching under a sullen, overhanging sky and a lustreless moon. In the foreground four solemn men in dress suits are walking along the sidewalk with a stretcher on which lies a drunken woman in a white evening dress. Her hand, which dangles over the side, sparkles cold with jewels. Gravely the men turn in at a house—the wrong house. But no one knows the woman's name, and no one cares.

After Gatsby's death the East was haunted for me like that, distorted beyond my eyes' power of correction. So when the blue smoke of brittle leaves was in the air and the wind blew the wet laundry stiff on the line I decided to come back home.

There was one thing to be done before I left, an awkward,

unpleasant thing that perhaps had better have been let alone. But I wanted to leave things in order and not just trust that obliging and indifferent sea to sweep my refuse away. I saw Jordan Baker and talked over and around what had happened to us together, and what had happened afterward to me, and she lay perfectly still, listening, in a big chair.

She was dressed to play golf, and I remember thinking she looked like a good illustration, her chin raised a little jauntily, her hair the colour of an autumn leaf, her face the same brown tint as the fingerless glove on her knee. When I had finished she told me without comment that she was engaged to another man. I doubted that, though there were several she could have married at a nod of her head, but I pretended to be surprised. For just a minute I wondered if I wasn't making a mistake, then I thought it all over again quickly and got up to say good-bye.

'Nevertheless you did throw me over,' said Jordan suddenly. 'You threw me over on the telephone. I don't give a damn about you now, but it was a new experience for me, and I felt a little dizzy for a while.'

We shook hands.

'Oh, and do you remember'—she added—'a conversation we had once about driving a car?'

'Why—not exactly.'

'You said a bad driver was only safe until she met another bad driver? Well, I met another bad driver, didn't I? I mean it was careless of me to make such a wrong guess. I thought you were rather an honest, straightforward person. I thought it was your secret pride.'

'I'm thirty,' I said. 'I'm five years too old to lie to myself and call it honour.'

She didn't answer. Angry, and half in love with her, and tremendously sorry, I turned away.

One afternoon late in October I saw Tom Buchanan. He was walking ahead of me along Fifth Avenue in his alert, aggressive way, his hands out a little from his body as if to fight off interference, his head moving sharply here and there, adapting itself to his restless eyes. Just as I slowed up to avoid overtaking him he stopped and began frowning into the windows of a jewellery store. Suddenly he saw me and walked back, holding out his hand.

'What's the matter, Nick? Do you object to shaking hands with me?'

'Yes. You know what I think of you.'

'You're crazy, Nick,' he said quickly. 'Crazy as hell. I don't know what's the matter with you.'

'Tom,' I inquired, 'what did you say to Wilson that afternoon?'

He stared at me without a word, and I knew I had guessed right about those missing hours. I started to turn away, but he took a step after me and grabbed my arm.

'I told him the truth,' he said. 'He came to the door while we were getting ready to leave, and when I sent down word that we weren't in he tried to force his way upstairs. He was crazy enough to kill me if I hadn't told him who owned the car. His hand was on a revolver in his pocket every minute he was in the house—' He broke off defiantly. 'What if I did tell him? That fellow had it coming to him. He threw dust into your eyes just like he did in Daisy's, but he was a tough one. He ran over Myrtle like you'd run over a dog and never even stopped his car.'

There was nothing I could say, except the one unutterable fact that it wasn't true.

'And if you think I didn't have my share of suffering—look here, when I went to give up that flat and saw that damn box of dog biscuits sitting there on the sideboard, I sat down and cried like a baby. By God it was awful——'

I couldn't forgive him or like him, but I saw that what he had done was, to him, entirely justified. It was all very careless and confused. They were careless people, Tom and Daisy—they smashed up things and creatures and then retreated back into their money or their vast carelessness, or whatever it was that kept them together, and let other people clean up the mess they had made. . . .

I shook hands with him; it seemed silly not to for I felt

6+s.f.

suddenly as though I were talking to a child. Then he went into the jewellery store to buy a pearl necklace—or perhaps only a pair of cuff buttons—rid of my provincial squeamishness forever.

Gatsby's house was still empty when I left—the grass on his lawn had grown as long as mine. One of the taxi drivers in the village never took a fare past the entrance gate without stopping for a minute and pointing inside; perhaps it was he who drove Daisy and Gatsby over to East Egg the night of the accident, and perhaps he had made a story about it all his own. I didn't want to hear it and I avoided him when I got off the train.

I spent my Saturday nights in New York, because those gleaming, dazzling parties of his were with me so vividly that I could still hear the music and the laughter, faint and incessant, from his garden, and the cars going up and down his drive. One night I did hear a material car there, and saw its lights stop at his front steps. But I didn't investigate. Probably it was some final guest who had been away at the ends of the earth and didn't know that the party was over.

On the last night, with my trunk packed and my car sold to the grocer, I went over and looked at that huge incoherent failure of a house once more. On the white steps an obscene word, scrawled by some boy with a piece of brick, stood out clearly in the moonlight, and I erased it, drawing my shoe raspingly along the stone. Then I wandered down to the beach and sprawled out on the sand.

Most of the big shore places were closed now and there were hardly any lights except the shadowy, moving glow of a ferryboat across the Sound. And as the moon rose higher the inessential houses began to melt away until gradually I became aware of the old island here that flowered once for Dutch sailors' eyes—a fresh, green breast of the new world. Its vanished trees, the trees that had made way for Gatsby's house, had once pandered in whispers to the last and greatest of all human dreams; for a transitory enchanted moment man must have held his breath in the presence of this continent, compelled into an æsthetic contemplation he neither understood nor desired, face to face for the last time in history with something commensurate to his capacity for wonder.

And as I sat there brooding on the old, unknown world, I thought of Gatsby's wonder when he first picked out the green light at the end of Daisy's dock. He had come a long way to this blue lawn, and his dream must have seemed so close that he could hardly fail to grasp it. He did not know that it was already behind him, somewhere back in that vast obscurity beyond the city, where the dark fields of the republic rolled on under the night.

Gatsby believed in the green light, the orgiastic future that year by year recedes before us. It eluded us then, but that's no matter—to-morrow we will run faster, stretch out our arms farther. . . . And one fine morning——

So we beat on, boats against the current, borne back ceaselessly into the past.

THE
LAST TYCOON

[1941]

THE
LAST TYCOON

CHAPTER I

THOUGH I HAVEN'T ever been on the screen I was
brought up in pictures. Rudolph Valentino came to my fifth
birthday party—or so I was told. I put this down only to
indicate that even before the age of reason I was in a position to watch the wheels go round.

I was going to write my memoirs once, *The Producer's
Daughter*, but at eighteen you never quite get around to anything like that. It's just as well—it would have been as flat
as an old column of Lolly Parsons'. My father was in the
picture business as another man might be in cotton or steel,
and I took it tranquilly. At the worst I accepted Hollywood
with the resignation of a ghost assigned to a haunted house.
I knew what you were supposed to think about it but I was
obstinately unhorrified.

This is easy to say, but harder to make people understand.
When I was at Bennington some of the English teachers who
pretended an indifference to Hollywood or its products,
really *hated* it. Hated it way down deep as a threat to their
existence. Even before that, when I was in a convent, a
sweet little nun asked me to get her a script of a screen play
so she could 'teach her class about movie writing' as she
had taught them about the essay and the short story. I got
the script for her, and I suppose she puzzled over it and
puzzled over it, but it was never mentioned in class, and
she gave it back to me with an air of offended surprise
and not a single comment. That's what I half expect to
happen to this story.

You can take Hollywood for granted like I did, or you

can dismiss it with the contempt we reserve for what we
don't understand. It can be understood too, but only dimly
and in flashes. Not half a dozen men have ever been able to
keep the whole equation of pictures in their heads. And
perhaps the closest a woman can come to the set-up is to
try and understand one of those men.

   The world from an aeroplane I knew. Father always had
us travel back and forth that way from school and college.
After my sister died when I was a junior, I travelled to and
fro alone, and the journey always made me think of her,
made me somewhat solemn and subdued. Sometimes there
were picture people I knew on board the plane, and
occasionally there was an attractive college boy—but not
often during the depression. I seldom really fell asleep
during the trip, what with thoughts of Eleanor and the
sense of that sharp rip between coast and coast—at
least not till we had left those lonely little airports in
Tennessee.

   This trip was so rough that the passengers divided early
into those who turned in right away and those who didn't
want to turn in at all. There were two of these latter right
across from me, and I was pretty sure from their fragmentary
conversation that they were from Hollywood—one of them
because he looked like it: a middle-aged Jew, who alter-
nately talked with nervous excitement or else crouched as if
ready to spring, in a harrowing silence; the other a pale,
plain, stocky man of thirty, whom I was sure I had seen
before. He had been to the house or something. But it
might have been when I was a little girl, and so I wasn't
offended that he didn't recognize me.

   The stewardess—she was tall, handsome and flashing
dark, a type that they seemed to run to—asked me if she
could make up my berth.

   '—and, dear, do you want an aspirin?' She perched on
the side of the seat and rocked precariously to and fro with
the June hurricane. '—or nembutal?'

   'No.'

   'I've been so busy with everyone else that I've had no

time to ask you.' She sat down beside me and buckled us both in. 'Do you want some gum?'

This reminded me to get rid of the piece that had been boring me for hours. I wrapped it in a piece of magazine and put it into the automatic ash-holder.

'I can always tell people are nice,' the stewardess said approvingly, 'if they wrap their gum in paper before they put it in there.'

We sat for a while in the half-light of the swaying car. It was vaguely like a swanky restaurant at that twilight time between meals. We were all lingering—and not quite on purpose. Even the stewardess, I think, had to keep reminding herself why she was there.

She and I talked about a young actress I knew, whom she had flown West with two years before. It was in the very lowest time of the depression, and the young actress kept staring out the window in such an intent way that the stewardess was afraid she was contemplating a leap. It appeared though that she was not afraid of poverty, but only of revolution.

'I know what mother and *I* are going to do,' she confided to the stewardess. 'We're coming out to the Yellowstone and we're just going to live simply till it all blows over. Then we'll come back. They don't kill artists—you know?'

The proposition pleased me. It conjured up a pretty picture of the actress and her mother being fed by kind Tory bears who brought them honey, and by gentle fawns who fetched extra milk from the does and then lingered near to make pillows for their heads at night. In turn I told the stewardess about the lawyer and the director who told their plans to Father one night in those brave days. If the bonus army conquered Washington, the lawyer had a boat hidden in the Sacramento River, and he was going to row upstream for a few months and then come back 'because they always needed lawyers after a revolution to straighten out the legal side.'

The director had tended more towards defeatism. He had an old suit, shirt and shoes in waiting—he never did say

6*

whether they were his own or whether he got them from the prop department—and he was going to Disappear into the Crowd. I remember Father saying: 'But they'll look at your hands! They'll know you haven't done manual work for years. And they'll ask for your union card'. And I remember how the director's face fell, and how gloomy he was while he ate his dessert, and how funny and puny they sounded to me.

'Is your father an actor, Miss Brady?' asked the stewardess. 'I've certainly heard the name.'

At the name Brady, both the men across the aisle looked up. Sidewise—that Hollywood look, that always seems thrown over one shoulder. Then the young, pale, stocky man unbuttoned his safety strap and stood in the aisle beside us.

'Are you Cecilia *Bra*dy?' he demanded accusingly, as if I'd been holding out on him. 'I *thought* I recognized you. I'm Wylie White.'

He could have omitted this—for at the same moment a new voice said, 'Watch your step, Wylie!', and another man brushed by him in the aisle and went forward in the direction of the cockpit. Wylie White started, and a little too late called after him defiantly:

'I only take orders from the pilot.'

I recognized the kind of pleasantry that goes on between the powers in Hollywood and their satellites.

The stewardess reproved him:

'Not so loud, please—some of the passengers are asleep.'

I saw now that the other man across the aisle, the middle-aged Jew, was on his feet also, staring, with shameless economic lechery, after the man who had just gone by. Or rather at the back of the man, who gestured sideways with his hand in a sort of farewell, as he went out of my sight.

'I asked the stewardess: 'Is he the as*sis*tant pilot?'

She was unbuckling our belt, about to abandon me to Wylie White.

'No. That's Mr. Smith. He has the private compartment, the "bridal suite"—only he has it alone. The assistant pilot is always in uniform.' She stood up: 'I want to find out if we're going to be grounded in Nashville.'

Wylie White was aghast.

'Why?'

'It's a storm coming up the Mississippi Valley.'

'Does that mean we'll have to stay here all *night*?'

'If this keeps up!'

A sudden dip indicated that it would. It tipped Wylie White into the seat opposite me, shunted the stewardess precipitately down in the direction of the cockpit, and plunked the Jewish man into a sitting position. After the studied, unruffled exclamations of distaste that befitted the air-minded, we settled down. There was an introduction.

'Miss Brady—Mr. Schwartz,' said Wylie White. 'He's a great friend of your father's, too.'

Mr. Schwartz nodded so vehemently that I could almost hear him saying: 'It's true. As God is my judge, it's true!'

He might have said this right out loud at one time in his life—but he was obviously a man to whom something had happened. Meeting him was like encountering a friend who has been in a fist fight or collision, and got flattened. You stare at your friend and say: 'What happened to you?' And he answers something unintelligible through broken teeth and swollen lips. He can't even tell you about it.

Mr. Schwartz was physically unmarked; the exaggerated Persian nose and oblique eye-shadow were as congenital as the tip-tilted Irish redness around my father's nostrils.

'Nashville!' cried Wylie White. 'That means we go to an hotel. We don't get to the coast till to-morrow night—if then. My God! I was born in Nashville.'

'I should think you'd like to see it again.'

'Never—I've kept away for fifteen years. I hope I'll *nev*er see it again.'

But he would—for the plane was unmistakably going down, down, down, like Alice in the rabbit hole. Cupping my hand against the window I saw the blur of the city far away on the left. The green sign 'Fasten your belts—No smoking' had been on since we first rode into the storm.

'Did you hear what he said?' said Schwartz from one of his fiery silences across the aisle.

'Hear what?' asked Wylie.

'Hear what he's calling himself,' said Schwartz. 'Mr. *Smith*!'

'Why not?' asked Wylie.

'Oh, nothing,' said Schwartz quickly. 'I just thought it was funny, Smith.' I never heard a laugh with less mirth in it : 'Smith!'

I suppose there has been nothing like the airports since the days of the stage-stops—nothing quite as lonely, as sombre-silent. The old red-brick depots were built right into the towns they marked—people didn't get off at those isolated stations unless they lived there. But airports lead you way back in history like oases, like the stops on the great trade routes. The sight of air travellers strolling in ones and twos into midnight airports will draw a small crowd any night up to two. The young people look at the planes, the older ones look at the passengers with a watchful incredulity. In the big trans-continental planes we were the coastal rich, who casually alighted from our cloud in mid-America. High adventure might be among us, disguised as a movie star. But mostly it wasn't. And I always wished fervently that we looked more interesting than we did—just as I often have at premières, when the fans look at you with scornful reproach because you're not a star.

On the ground Wylie and I were suddenly friends because he held out his arm to steady me when I got out of the plane. From then on, he made a dead set for me—and I didn't mind. From the moment we walked into the airport it had become plain that if we were stranded here we were stranded here together. (It wasn't like the time I lost my boy—the time my boy played the piano with that girl Reina in a little New England farmhouse near Bennington, and I realized at last I wasn't wanted. Guy Lombardo was on the air playing *Top Hat* and *Cheek to Cheek*, and she taught him the melodies. The keys falling like leaves and her hands splayed over his as she showed him a black chord. I was a freshman then.)

When we went into the airport Mr. Schwartz was along
with us, too, but he seemed in a sort of dream. All the time
we were trying to get accurate information at the desk, he
kept staring at the door that led out to the landing field, as
if he were afraid the plane would leave without him. Then
I excused myself for a few minutes and something happened
that I didn't see, but when I came back he and White were
standing close together, White talking and Schwartz looking
twice as much as if a great truck had just backed up over
him. He didn't stare at the door to the landing field any
more. I heard the end of Wylie White's remark . . .

'—I told you to shut up. It serves you right.'

'I only said——'

He broke off as I came up and asked if there was any
news. It was then half-past two in the morning.

'A little,' said Wylie White. 'They don't think we'll be
able to start for three hours anyhow, so some of the softies
are going to an hotel. But I'd like to take you out to the
Hermitage, Home of Andrew Jackson.'

'How could we see it in the dark?' demanded Schwartz.

'Hell, it'll be sunrise in two hours.'

'You two go,' said Schwartz.

'All right—you take the bus to the hotel. It's still waiting
—*he's* in there.' Wylie's voice had a taunt in it. 'Maybe it'd
be a good thing.'

'No, I'll go along with you,' said Schwartz hastily.

We took a taxi in the sudden country dark outside, and
he seemed to cheer up. He patted my knee-cap encourag-
ingly.

'I should go along,' he said, 'I should be chaperone.
Once upon a time when I was in the big money, I had a
daughter—a beautiful daughter.'

He spoke as if she had been sold to creditors as a tangible
asset.

'You'll have another,' Wylie assured him. 'You'll get it
all back. Another turn of the wheel and you'll be where
Cecilia's papa is, won't he, Cecilia?'

'Where is this Hermitage?' asked Schwartz presently.

'Far away at the end of nowhere? Will we miss the plane?'

'Skip it,' said Wylie. 'We ought to've brought the stewardess along for you. Didn't you admire the stewardess? *I* thought she was pretty cute.'

We drove for a long time over a bright level countryside, just a road and a tree and a shack and a tree, and then suddenly along a winding twist of woodland. I could feel even in the darkness that the trees of the woodland were green —that it was all different from the dusty olive-tint of California. Somewhere we passed a negro driving three cows ahead of him, and they mooed as he scatted them to the side of the road. They were real cows, with warm, fresh, silky flanks, and the negro grew gradually real out of the darkness with his big brown eyes staring at us close to the car, as Wylie gave him a quarter. He said '*Thank* you —thank you,' and stood there, and the cows mooed again into the night as we drove off.

I thought of the first sheep I ever remember seeing— hundreds of them, and how our car drove suddenly into them on the back lot of the old Laemmle studio. They were unhappy about being in pictures, but the men in the car with us kept saying:

'Swell?'

'Is that what you wanted, Dick?'

'Isn't that swell?' And the man named Dick kept standing up in the car as if he were Cortez or Balboa, looking over that grey fleecy undulation. If I ever knew what picture they were in, I have long forgotten.

We had driven an hour. We crossed a brook over an old rattley iron bridge laid with planks. Now there were roosters crowing and blue-green shadows stirring every time we passed a farmhouse.

'I told you it'd be morning soon,' said Wylie. 'I was born near here—the son of impoverished southern paupers. The family mansion is now used as an outhouse. We had four servants—my father, my mother and my two sisters. I refused to join the guild, and so I went to Memphis to start my career, which has now reached a dead end.' He put his arm around me: 'Cecilia, will you marry me, so I can share the Brady fortune?'

He was disarming enough, so I let my head lie on his shoulder.

'What do you do, Cecilia. Go to school?'

'I go to Bennington. I'm a junior.'

'Oh, I beg your pardon. I should have known, but I never had the advantage of college training. But a *junior*— why I read in *Esquire* that juniors have nothing to learn, Cecilia.'

'Why do people think that college girls——'

'Don't apologize—knowledge is power.'

'You'd know from the way you talk that we were on our way to Hollywood,' I said. 'It's always years and years behind the times.'

He pretended to be shocked.

'You mean girls in the East have no private lives?'

'That's the point. They *have* got private lives. You're bothering me, let go.'

'I can't. It might wake Schwartz, and I think this is the first sleep he's had for weeks. Listen, Cecilia: I once had an affair with the wife of a producer. A very short affair. When it was over she said to me in no uncertain terms, she said: "Don't you ever tell about this or I'll have you thrown out of Hollywood. My husband's a much more important man than you!"'

I liked him again now, and presently the taxi turned down a long lane fragrant with honeysuckle and narcissus, and stopped beside the great grey hulk of the Andrew Jackson house. The driver turned around to tell us something about it, but Wylie shushed him, pointing at Schwartz, and we tiptoed out of the car.

'You can't get into the Mansion now,' the taxi man told us politely.

Wylie and I went and sat against the wide pillars of the steps.

'What about Mr. Schwartz,' I asked. 'Who is he?'

'To hell with Schwartz. He was the head of some combine once—First National? Paramount? United Artists? Now he's down and out. But he'll be back. You can't flunk out of pictures unless you're a dope or a drunk.'

'You don't like Hollywood,' I suggested.

'Yes I do. Sure I do. Say! This isn't anything to talk about on the steps of Andrew Jackson's house—at dawn.'

'I *like* Hollywood,' I persisted.

'It's all right. It's a mining town in lotus land. Who said that? I did. It's a good place for toughies, but I went there from Savannah, Georgia. I went to a garden party the first day. My host shook hands and left me. It was all there— that swimming pool, green moss at two dollars an inch, beautiful felines having drinks and fun——

'—And nobody spoke to me. Not a soul. I spoke to half a dozen people but they didn't answer. That continued for an hour, two hours—then I got up from where I was sitting and ran out at a dog trot like a crazy man. I didn't feel I had any rightful identity until I got back to the hotel and the clerk handed me a letter addressed to me in my name.'

Naturally I hadn't ever had such an experience, but looking back on parties I'd been to, I realized that such things could happen. We don't go for strangers in Hollywood unless they wear a sign saying that their axe has been thoroughly ground elsewhere, and that in any case it's not going to fall on our necks—in other words, unless they're a celebrity. And they'd better look out even then.

'You should have risen above it,' I said smugly. 'It's not a slam at *you* when people are rude—it's a slam at the people they've met before.'

'Such a pretty girl—to say such wise things.'

There was an eager to-do in the eastern sky, and Wylie could see me plain—thin with good features and lots of style, and the kicking fetus of a mind. I wonder what I looked like in that dawn, five years ago. A little rumpled and pale, I suppose, but at that age, when one has the young illusion that most adventures are good, I needed only a bath and a change to go on for hours.

Wylie stared at me with really flattering appreciation—and then suddenly we were not alone. Mr. Schwartz wandered apologetically into the pretty scene.

'I fell upon a large metal handle,' he said, touching the corner of his eye.

Wylie jumped up.

'Just in time, Mr. Schwartz,' he said. 'The tour is just starting. Home of Old Hickory—America's tenth president. The victor of New Orleans, opponent of the National Bank, and inventor of the Spoils System.'

Schwartz looked towards me as towards a jury.

'There's a writer for you,' he said. 'Knows everything and at the same time he knows nothing.'

'What's that?' said Wylie, indignant.

It was my first inkling that he was a writer. And while I like writers—because if you ask a writer anything, you usually get an answer—still it belittled him in my eyes. Writers aren't people exactly. Or, if they're any good, they're a whole *lot* of people trying so hard to be one person. It's like actors, who try so pathetically not to look in mirrors. who lean *back*ward trying—only to see their faces in the reflecting chandeliers.

'Ain't writers like that, Cecilia?' demanded Schwartz. 'I have no words for them. I only know it's true.'

Wylie looked at him with slowly gathering indignation. 'I've heard that before,' he said. 'Look, Manny, I'm a more practical man than you any day! I've sat in an office and listened to some mystic stalk up and down for hours spouting tripe that'd land him on a nut-farm anywhere outside of California—and then at the end tell me how *practical* he was, and *I* was a dreamer—and would I kindly go away and make sense out of what he'd said.'

Mr. Schwartz's face fell into its more disintegrated alignments. One eye looked upwards through the tall elms. He raised his hand and bit without interest at the cuticle on his second finger. There was a bird flying about the chimney of the house, and his glance followed it. It perched on the chimney pot like a raven, and Mr. Schwartz's eyes remained fixed upon it as he said: 'We can't get in, and it's time for you two to go back to the plane.'

It was still not quite dawn. The Hermitage looked like a nice big white box, but a little lonely and vacated still after a hundred years. We walked back to the car. Only after we had gotten in, and Mr. Schwartz had surprisingly shut the taxi door on us, did we realize he didn't intend to come along.

'I'm not going to the Coast—I decided that when I woke up. So I'll stay here, and afterwards the driver could come back for me.'

'Going back East?' said Wylie with surprise. 'Just because——'

'I have decided,' said Schwartz, faintly smiling. 'Once I used to be a regular man of decision—you'd be surprised.' He felt in his pocket, as the taxi driver warmed up the engine. 'Will you give this note to Mr. Smith?'

'Shall I come in two hours?' the driver asked Schwartz.

'Yes . . . sure. I shall be glad to entertain myself looking around.'

I kept thinking of him all the way back to the airport—trying to fit him into that early hour and into that landscape. He had come a long way from some Ghetto to present himself at that raw shrine. Manny Schwartz and Andrew Jackson—it was hard to say them in the same sentence. It was doubtful if he knew who Andrew Jackson was as he wandered around, but perhaps he figured that if people had preserved his house Andrew Jackson must have been someone who was large and merciful, able to understand. At both ends of life man needed nourishment: a breast—a shrine. Something to lay himself beside when no one wanted him further, and shoot a bullet into his head.

Of course we did not know this for twenty hours. When we got to the airport we told the purser that Mr. Schwartz was not continuing, and then forgot about him. The storm had wandered away into Eastern Tennessee and broken against the mountains, and we were taking off in less than an hour. Sleepy-eyed travellers appeared from the hotel, and I dozed a few minutes on one of those Iron Maidens they use for couches. Slowly the idea of a perilous journey was recreated out of the debris of our failure : a new stewardess, tall, handsome, flashing dark, exactly like the other except she wore seersucker instead of French red-and-blue, went briskly past us with a suitcase. Wylie sat beside me as we waited.

'Did you give the note to Mr. Smith?' I asked, half asleep.

'Yeah.'

'Who is Mr. Smith? I suspect he spoiled Mr. Schwartz's trip.'

'It was Schwartz's fault.'

'I'm prejudiced against steam-rollers,' I said. 'My father tries to be a steam-roller around the house, and I tell him to save it for the studio.'

I wondered if I was being fair; words are the palest counters at that time in the morning. 'Still, he steam-rollered me into Bennington and I've always been grateful for that.'

'There would be quite a crash,' Wylie said, 'if steam-roller Brady met steam-roller Smith.'

'Is Mr. Smith a competitor of Father's?'

'Not exactly. I should say no. But if he was a competitor I know where my money would be.'

'On Father?'

'I'm afraid not.'

It was too early in the morning for family patriotism. The pilot was at the desk with the purser and he shook his head as they regarded a prospective passenger who had put two nickels in the electric phonograph and lay alcoholically on a bench fighting off sleep. The first song he had chosen, *Lost*, thundered through the room, followed, after a slight interval, by his other choice, *Gone*, which was equally dogmatic and final. The pilot shook his head emphatically and walked over to the passenger.

'Afraid we're not going to be able to carry you this time, old man.'

'Wha'?'

The drunk sat up, awful-looking, yet discernibly attractive, and I was sorry for him in spite of his passionately ill-chosen music.

'Go back to the hotel and get some sleep. There'll be another plane to-night.'

'Only going up in ee *air*.'

'Not this time, old man.'

In his disappointment the drunk fell off the bench—and above the phonograph, a loudspeaker summoned us respectable people outside. In the corridor of the plane I ran into Monroe Stahr and fell all over him, or wanted to. There was a man any girl would go for, with or without encouragement. I was emphatically with*out* it, but he liked me and sat down opposite till the plane took off.

'Let's all ask for our money back,' he suggested. His dark eyes took me in, and I wondered what they would look like if he fell in love. They were kind, aloof and, though they often reasoned with you gently, somewhat superior. It was no fault of theirs if they saw so much. He darted in and out of the role of 'one of the boys' with dexterity—but on the whole I should say he wasn't one of them. But he knew how to shut up, how to draw into the background, how to listen. From where he stood (and though he was not a tall man, it always seemed high up) he watched the multitudinous practicalities of his world like a proud young shepherd to whom night and day had never mattered. He was born sleepless, without a talent for rest or the desire for it.

We sat in unembarrassed silence—I had known him since he became Father's partner a dozen years ago, when I was seven and Stahr was twenty-two. Wylie was across the aisle and I didn't know whether or not to introduce them, but Stahr kept turning his ring so abstractedly that he made me feel young and invisible, and I didn't dare. I never dared look quite away from him or quite *at* him, unless I had something important to say—and I knew he affected many other people in the same manner.

'I'll *give* you this ring, Cecilia.'

'I beg your pardon. I didn't realize that I was——'

'I've got half a dozen like it.'

He handed it to me, a gold nugget with the letter S in bold relief. I had been thinking how oddly its bulk contrasted with his fingers, which were delicate and slender like the rest of his body, and like his slender face with the arched eyebrows and the dark curly hair. He looked spiritual at times, but he was a fighter—somebody out of his past knew him when he was one of a gang of kids in the Bronx, and gave me a description of how he walked always at the head of his gang, this rather frail boy, occasionally throwing a command backward out of the corner of his mouth.

Stahr folded my hand over the ring, stood up and addressed Wylie.

'Come up to the bridal suite,' he said. 'See you later, Cecilia.'

Before they went out of hearing, I heard Wylie's question: 'Did you open Schwartz's note?' And Stahr:

'Not yet.'

I must be slow, for only then did I realize that Stahr was Mr. Smith.

Afterwards Wylie told me what was in the note. Written by the headlights of the taxi, it was almost illegible.

DEAR MONROE, You are the best of them all I have always admired your mentality so when you turn against me I know it's no use! I must be no good and am not going to continue the journey let me warn you once again look out! I know.

Your friend
MANNY.

Stahr read it twice, and raised his hand to the morning stubble on his chin.

'He's a nervous wreck,' he said. 'There's nothing to be done—absolutely nothing. I'm sorry I was short with him —but I don't like a man to approach me telling me it's for *my* sake.'

'Maybe it was,' said Wylie.

'It's poor technique.'

'I'd fall for it,' said Wylie. 'I'm vain as a woman. If anybody pretends to be interested in me, I'll ask for more. I like advice.'

Stahr shook his head distastefully. Wylie kept on ribbing him—he was one of those to whom this privilege was permitted.

'You fall for some kinds of flattery,' he said. 'This "little Napoleon stuff."'

'It makes me sick,' said Stahr, 'but it's not as bad as some man trying to help you.'

'If you don't like advice, why do you pay *me*?'

'That's a question of merchandise,' said Stahr. 'I'm a merchant. I want to buy what's in your mind.'

'You're no merchant,' said Wylie. 'I knew a lot of them when I was a publicity man, and I agree with Charles Francis Adams.'

'What did he say?'

'He knew them all—Gould, Vanderbilt, Carnegie, Astor —and he said there wasn't one he'd care to meet again in the hereafter. Well—they haven't improved since then, and that's why I say you're no merchant.'

'Adams was probably a sourbelly,' said Stahr. 'He wanted to be head man himself, but he didn't have the judgment or else the character.'

'He had brains,' said Wylie rather tartly.

'It takes more than brains. You writers and artists poop out and get all mixed up, and somebody has to come in and straighten you out.' He shrugged his shoulders. 'You seem to take things so personally, hating people and worshipping them—always thinking people are so important—especially yourselves. You just ask to be kicked around. I like people and I like them to like me, but I wear my heart where God put it—on the inside.'

He broke off.

'What did I say to Schwartz in the airport? Do you remember—exactly?

'You said, "Whatever you're after, the answer is No!"'

Stahr was silent.

'He was sunk,' said Wylie, 'but I laughed him out of it. We took Billy Brady's daughter for a ride.'

Stahr rang for the stewardess.

'That pilot,' he said, 'would he mind if I sat up in front with him a while?'

'That's against the rules, Mr. Smith.'

'Ask him to step in here a minute when he's free.'

Stahr sat up front all afternoon. While we slid off the endless desert and over the table-lands, dyed with many colours like the white sands we dyed with colours when I was a child. Then in the late afternoon, the peaks themselves —the Mountains of the Frozen Saw—slid under our propellers and we were close to home.

When I wasn't dozing I was thinking that I wanted to marry Stahr, that I wanted to make him love me. Oh, the conceit! What on earth did I have to offer? But I didn't think like that then. I had the pride of young women, which draws its strength from such sublime thoughts as 'I'm as good as *she* is.' For my purposes I was just as beautiful as the great beauties who must have inevitably thrown themselves at his head. My little spurt of intellectual interest was of course making me fit to be a brilliant ornament of any salon.

I know now it was absurd. Though Stahr's education was founded on nothing more than a night-school course in stenography, he had a long time ago run ahead through trackless wastes of perception into fields where very few men were able to follow him. But in my reckless conceit I matched my grey eyes against his brown ones for guile, my young golf-and-tennis heart-beats against his, which must be slowing a little after years of over-work. And I planned and I contrived and I plotted—any women can tell you—but it never came to anything, as you will see. I still like to think that if he'd been a poor boy and nearer my age I could have managed it, but of course the real truth was that I had nothing to offer that he didn't have; some of my more romantic ideas actually stemmed from pictures—*42nd Street*, for example, had a great influence on me. It's more than possible that some of the pictures which Stahr himself conceived had shaped me into what I was.

So it was rather hopeless. Emotionally, at least, people can't live by taking in each other's washing.

But at that time it was different: Father might help, the stewardess might help. She might go up in the cockpit and say to Stahr: 'If I ever saw love, it's in that girl's eyes.'

The pilot might help: 'Man, are you blind? Why don't you go back there?'

Wylie White might help—instead of standing in the aisle looking at me doubtfully, wondering whether I was awake or asleep.

'Sit down,' I said. 'What's new?—where are we?'

'Up in the air.'

'Oh, so that's it. Sit down.' I tried to show a cheerful interest: 'What are you writing?'

'Heaven help me, I am writing about a Boy Scout—*The* Boy Scout.'

'Is it Stahr's idea?'

'I don't know—he told me to look into it. He may have ten writers working ahead of me or behind me, a system which he so thoughtfully invented. So you're in love with him?'

'I should say not,' I said indignantly. 'I've known him all my life.'

'Desperate, eh? Well, I'll arrange it if you'll use all your influence to advance me. I want a unit of my own.'

I closed my eyes and drifted off. When I woke up, the stewardess was putting a blanket over me.

'Almost there,' she said.

Out the window I could see by the sunset that we were in a greener land.

'I just heard something funny,' she volunteered, 'up in the cockpit—that Mr. Smith—or Mr. Stahr—I never remember seeing his name—'

'It's never on any pictures,' I said.

'Oh. Well, he's been asking the pilots a lot about flying—I mean he's interested? You *know*?'

'I know.'

'I mean one of them told me he bet he could teach Mr. Stahr solo flying in ten minutes. He has such a fine mentality, that's what he said.'

I was getting impatient.

'Well, what was so funny?'

'Well, finally one of the pilots asked Mr. Smith if he liked his business, and Mr. Smith said, "Sure. Sure I like it. It's nice being the only sound nut in a hatful of cracked ones."'

The stewardess doubled up with laughter—and I could have spit at her.

'I mean calling all those people a hatful of nuts. I mean *cracked* nuts.' Her laughter stopped with unexpected suddenness, and her face was grave as she stood up. 'Well, I've got to finish my chart.'

'Good-bye.'

Obviously Stahr had put the pilots right up on the throne with him and let them rule with him for a while. Years later I travelled with one of those same pilots and he told me one thing Stahr had said.

He was looking down at the mountains.

'Suppose you were a railroad man,' he said. 'You have to send a train through there somewhere. Well, you get your surveyors' reports, and you find there's three or four or half a dozen gaps, and not one is better than the other. You've got to decide—on what basis? You can't test the best way—except by doing it. So you just do it.'

The pilot thought he had missed something.

'How do you mean?'

'You choose some one way for no reason at all—because that mountain's pink or the blueprint is a better blue. You see?'

The pilot considered that this was very valuable advice. But he doubted if he'd ever be in a position to apply it.

'What I wanted to know,' he told me ruefully, 'is how he ever got to be Mr. Stahr.'

I'm afraid Stahr could never have answered that one; for the embryo is not equipped with a memory. But I could answer a little. He had flown up very high to see, on strong wings, when he was young. And while he was up there he had looked on all the kingdoms, with the kind of eyes that can stare straight into the sun. Beating his wings tenaciously—finally frantically—and keeping on beating them, he had stayed up there longer than most of us, and then, remembering all he had seen from his great height of how things were, he had settled gradually to earth.

The motors were off, and all our five senses began to readjust themselves for landing. I could see a line of lights for the Long Beach Naval Station ahead and to the left, and on the right a twinkling blur for Santa Monica. The California moon was out, huge and orange over the Pacific. However I happened to feel about these things—and they were home, after all—I know that Stahr must have felt much more. These were the things I had first opened my eyes on, like the sheep on the back lot of the old Laemmle studio; but this was where Stahr had come to earth after that extraordinary illuminating flight where he saw which way we were going, and how we looked doing it, and how much of it mattered. You could say that this was where an accidental wind blew him, but I don't think so. I would rather think that in a 'long shot' he saw a new way of measuring our jerky hopes and graceful rogueries and awkward sorrows, and that he came here from choice to be with us to the end. Like the plane coming down into the Glendale airport, into the warm darkness.

CHAPTER II

IT WAS NINE O'CLOCK of a July night and there were still some extras in the drug-store across from the studio— I could see them bent over the pin-games inside—as I parked my car. 'Old' Johnny Swanson stood on the corner in his semi-cowboy clothes, staring gloomily past the moon. Once he had been as big in pictures as Tom Mix or Bill Hart—now it was too sad to speak to him, and I hurried across the street and through the front gate.

There is never a time when a studio is absolutely quiet. There is always a night shift of technicians in the laboratories and dubbing rooms and people on the maintenance staff dropping in at the commissary. But the sounds are all different—the padded hush of tyres, the quiet tick of a motor running idle, the naked cry of a soprano singing into a nightbound microphone. Around a corner I came upon a man in rubber boots washing down a car in a wonderful white light—a fountain among the dead industrial shadows. I slowed up as I saw Mr. Marcus being hoisted into his car in front of the administration building, because he took so long to say anything, even good night—and while I waited I realized that the soprano was singing, *Come, come, I love you only* over and over; I remember this because she kept singing the same line during the earthquake. That didn't come for five minutes yet.

Father's offices were in the old building with the long balconies and iron rails with their suggestion of a perpetual tightrope. Father was on the second floor, with Stahr on one side and Mr. Marcus on the other—this evening there were lights all along the row. My stomach dipped a little at the proximity to Stahr, but that was in pretty good control now—I'd seen him only once in the month I'd been home.

There were a lot of strange things about Father's office, but I'll make it brief. In the outer part were three poker-faced secretaries who had sat there like witches ever since I could remember—Birdy Peters, Maude something, and Rosemary Schmiel; I don't know whether this was her name, but she was the dean of the trio, so to speak, and under her desk was the kick-lock that admitted you to Father's throne room. All three of the secretaries were passionate capitalists, and Birdy had invented the rule that if typists were seen eating together more than once in a single week, they were hauled up on the carpet. At that time the studios feared mob rule.

I went on in. Nowadays all chief executives have huge drawing rooms, but my father's was the first. It was also the first to have one-way glass in the big French windows, and I've heard a story about a trap in the floor that would drop unpleasant visitors to an oubliette below, but believe it to be an invention. There was a big painting of Will Rogers, hung conspicuously and intended, I think, to suggest Father's essential kinship with Hollywood's St. Francis; there was a signed photograph of Minna Davis, Stahr's dead wife, and photos of other studio celebrities and big chalk drawings of mother and me. To-night the one-way French windows were open and a big moon, rosy-gold with a haze around, was wedged helpless in one of them. Father and Jacques La Borwitz and Rosemary Schmiel were down at the end around a big circular desk.

What did Father look like? I couldn't describe him except for once in New York when I met him where I didn't expect to; I was aware of a bulky, middle-aged man who looked a little ashamed of himself, and I wished he'd move on—and then I saw he was Father. Afterwards I was shocked at my impression. Father can be very magnetic—he had a tough jaw and an Irish smile.

But as for Jacques La Borwitz, I shall spare you. Let me just say he was an assistant producer, which is something like a commissar, and let it go at that. Where Stahr picked up such mental cadavers or had them forced upon him—or especially how he got any use out of them—has always amazed me, as it amazed everyone fresh from the East who slapped up against them. Jacques La Borwitz had his points, no doubt, but so have the sub-microscopic protozoa, so has a dog prowling for a bitch and a bone. Jacques La—oh my!

From their expressions I was sure they had been talking about Stahr. Stahr had ordered something or forbidden something, or defied Father or junked one of La Borwitz' pictures or something catastrophic, and they were sitting there in protest at night in a community of rebellion and helplessness. Rosemary Schmiel sat pad in hand, as if ready to write down their dejection.

'I'm to drive you home dead or alive,' I told Father. 'All those birthday presents rotting away in their packages!'

'A birthday!' cried Jacques in a flurry of apology. 'How old? I didn't know.'

'Forty-three,' said Father distinctly.

He was older than that—four years—and Jacques knew it; I saw him note it down in his account book to use some time. Out here these account books are carried open in the hand. One can see the entries being made without recourse to lip-reading, and Rosemary Schmiel was compelled in emulation to make a mark on her pad. As she rubbed it out, the earth quaked under us.

We didn't get the full shock like at Long Beach, where the upper storeys of shops were spewed into the streets and small hotels drifted out to sea—but for a full minute our bowels were one with the bowels of the earth—like some nightmare attempt to attach our navel cords again and jerk us back to the womb of creation.

Mother's picture fell off the wall, revealing a small safe —Rosemary and I grabbed frantically for each other and did a strange screaming waltz across the room. Jacques fainted or at least disappeared, and Father clung to his desk and shouted, 'Are you all right?' Outside the window the singer came to the climax of *I love you only*, held it a moment and then, I swear, started it all over. Or maybe they were playing it back to her from the recording machine.

The room stood still, shimmying a little. We made our way to the door, suddenly including Jacques, who had reappeared, and tottered out dizzily through the anteroom on to the iron balcony. Almost all the lights were out, and from here and there we could hear cries and calls. Momentarily we stood waiting for a second shock—then, as with a common impulse, we went into Stahr's entry and through to his office.

The office was big, but not as big as Father's. Stahr sat on the side of his couch rubbing his eyes. When the quake came he had been asleep, and he wasn't sure yet whether he had dreamed it. When we convinced him he thought it was all rather funny—until the telephones began to ring. I watched him as unobtrusively as possible. He was grey with fatigue while he listened to the phone and dictagraph; but as the reports came in, his eyes began to pick up shine.

'A couple of water mains have burst,' he said to Father, '—they're heading into the back lot.'

'Gray's shooting in the French Village,' said Father.

'It's flooded around the Station, too, and in the Jungle and the City Corner. What the hell—nobody seems to be hurt.' In passing, he shook my hands gravely: 'Where've you been, Cecilia?'

'You going out there, Monroe?' Father asked.

'When all the news is in: One of the power lines is off, too —I've sent for Robinson.'

He made me sit down with him on the couch and tell about the quake again.

'You look tired,' I said, cute and motherly.

'Yes,' he agreed, 'I've got no place to go in the evenings, so I just work.'

'I'll arrange some evenings for you.'

'I used to play poker with a gang,' he said thoughtfully, 'before I was married. But they all drank themselves to death.'

Miss Doolan, his secretary, came in with fresh bad news.

'Robby'll take care of everything when he comes,' Stahr assured Father. He turned to me. 'Now there's a man—that Robinson. He was a trouble-shooter—fixed the telephone wires in Minnesota blizzards—nothing stumps him. He'll be here in a minute—you'll like Robby.'

He said it as if it had been his life-long intention to bring us together, and he had arranged the whole earthquake with just that in mind.

'Yes, you'll like Robby,' he repeated. 'When do you go back to college?'

'I've just come home.'

'You get the whole summer?'

'I'm sorry,' I said. 'I'll go back as soon as I can.'

I was in a mist. It hadn't failed to cross my mind that he might have some intention about me, but if it was so, it was in an exasperatingly early stage—I was merely 'a good property.' And the idea didn't seem so attractive at that moment—like marrying a doctor. He seldom left the studio before eleven.

'How long,' he asked my father, 'before she graduates from college. That's what I was trying to say.'

And I think I was about to sing out eagerly that I needn't go back at all, that I was quite educated already—when the totally admirable Robinson came in. He was a bowlegged young redhead, all ready to go.

'This is Robby, Cecilia,' said Stahr. 'Come on, Robby.'

So I met Robby. I can't say it seemed like fate—but it was. For it was Robby who later told me how Stahr found his love that night.

Under the moon the back lot was thirty acres of fairyland—not because the locations really looked like African jungles and French châteaux and schooners at anchor and Broadway at night, but because they looked like the torn picture books of childhood, like fragments of stories dancing in an open fire. I never lived in a house with an attic, but a back lot must be something like that, and at night of course in an enchanted distorted way, it all comes true.

When Stahr and Robby arrived, clusters of lights had already picked out the danger spots in the flood.

'We'll pump it out into the swamp on Thirty-Sixth Street,' said Robby after a moment. 'It's city property—but isn't this an act of God? Say—look there!'

On top of a huge head of the Goddess Siva, two women were floating down the current of an impromptu river. The idol had come unloosed from a set of Burma, and it meandered earnestly on its way, stopping sometimes to waddle and bump in the shallows with the other debris of the tide. The two refugees had found sanctuary along a scroll of curls on its bald forehead and seemed at first glance to be sightseers on an interesting bus-ride through the scene of the flood.

'Will you look at that, Monroe!' said Robby. 'Look at those dames!'

Dragging their legs through sudden bogs, they made their way to the bank of the stream. Now they could see the women, looking a little scared but brightening at the prospect of rescue.

'We ought to let 'em drift out to the waste pipe,' said Robby gallantly, 'but DeMille needs that head next week.'

He wouldn't have hurt a fly, though, and presently he was hip deep in the water, fishing for them with a pole and succeeding only in spinning it in a dizzy circle. Help arrived, and the impression quickly got around that one of them was very pretty, and then that they were people of importance. But they were just strays, and Robby waited disgustedly to give them hell while the thing was brought finally into control and beached.

'Put that head back!' he called up to them. 'You think it's a souvenir?'

One of the women came sliding smoothly down the cheek of the idol, and Robby caught her and set her on solid ground; the other one hesitated and then followed. Robby turned to Stahr for judgment.

'What'll we do with them, chief?'

Stahr did not answer. Smiling faintly at him from not four feet away was the face of his dead wife, identical even to the expression. Across the four feet of moonlight, the eyes he knew looked back at him, a curl blew a little on a familiar forehead; the smile lingered, changed a little according to pattern; the lips parted—the same. An awful fear went over him, and he wanted to cry aloud. Back from the still sour room, the muffled glide of the limousine hearse, the falling concealing flowers, from out there in the dark—here now warm and glowing. The river passed him in a rush, the great spotlights swooped and blinked—and then he heard another voice speak that was not Minna's voice.

'We're sorry,' said the voice. 'We followed a truck in through a gate.'

A little crowd had gathered—electricians, grips, truckers, and Robby began to nip at them like a sheep dog.

'. . . get the big pumps on the tanks on Stage 4 . . . put a cable around this head . . . raft it up on a couple of two by fours . . . get the water out of the jungle first, for Christ's sake . . . that big 'A' pipe, lay it down . . . all that stuff is plastic. . . .'

Stahr stood watching the two women as they threaded their way after a policeman towards an exit gate. Then he took a tentative step to see if the weakness had gone out of his knees. A loud tractor came bumping through the slush, and men began streaming by him—every second one glancing at him, smiling, speaking: 'Hello, Monroe . . . Hello, Mr. Stahr . . . wet night, Mr. Stahr . . . Monroe . . . Monroe . . . Stahr . . . Stahr . . . Stahr.'

He spoke and waved back as the people streamed by in the darkness, looking, I suppose, a little like the Emperor and the Old Guard. There is no world so but it has its heroes, and Stahr was the hero. Most of these men had been here a long time—through the beginnings and the great upset, when sound came, and the three years of depression, he had seen that no harm came to them. The old loyalties were trembling now, there were clay feet everywhere; but still he was their man, the last of the princes. And their greeting was a sort of low cheer as they went by.

CHAPTER III

BETWEEN THE NIGHT I got back and the quake, I'd made many observations.

About Father, for example. I loved Father—in a sort of irregular graph with many low swoops—but I began to see that his strong will didn't fill him out as a passable man. Most of what he accomplished boiled down to shrewd. He had acquired with luck and shrewdness a quarter interest in a booming circus—together with young Stahr. That was his life's effort—all the rest was an instinct to hang on. Of course, he talked that double talk to Wall Street about how mysterious it was to make a picture, but Father didn't know the ABC's of dubbing or even cutting. Nor had he learned much about the feel of America as a bar boy in Ballyhegan, nor did he have any more than a drummer's sense of a story. On the other hand, he didn't have concealed paresis like——; he came to the studio before noon, and, with a suspiciousness developed like a muscle, it was hard to put anything over on him.

Stahr had been his luck—and Stahr was something else again. He was a marker in industry like Edison and Lumière and Griffith and Chaplin. He led pictures way up past the range and power of the theatre, reaching a sort of golden age, before the censorship.

Proof of his leadership was the spying that went on around him—not just for inside information or patented process secrets—but spying on his scent for a trend in taste, his guess as to how things were going to be. Too much of his vitality was taken by the mere parrying of these attempts. It made his work secret in part, often devious, slow—and hard to describe as the plans of a general, where the psychological factors become too tenuous and we end by merely adding up the successes and failures. But I have determined to give you a glimpse of him functioning, which is my excuse for what follows. It is drawn partly from a paper I wrote in college on *A Producer's Day* and partly from my imagination. More often I have blocked in the ordinary events myself, while the stranger ones are true.

In the early morning after the flood, a man walked up to the outside balcony of the Administration Building. He lingered there some time, according to an eyewitness, then mounted to the iron railing and dove head first to the pavement below. Breakage—one arm.

Miss Doolan, Stahr's secretary, told him about it when he buzzed for her at nine. He had slept in his office without hearing the small commotion.

'Pete Zavras!' Stahr exclaimed, '—the camera man?'

'They took him to a doctor's office. It won't be in the paper.'

'Hell of a thing,' he said. 'I knew he'd gone to pot—but I don't know why. He was all right when we used him two years ago—why should he come here? How did he get in?'

'He bluffed it with his old studio pass,' said Catherine Doolan. She was a dry hawk, the wife of an assistant director. 'Perhaps the quake had something to do with it.'

'He was the best camera man in town,' Stahr said. When he had heard of the hundreds dead at Long Beach, he was still haunted by the abortive suicide at dawn. He told Catherine Doolan to trace the matter down.

The first dictagraph messages blew in through the warm morning. While he shaved and had coffee, he talked and listened. Robby had left a message: 'If Mr. Stahr wants me tell him to hell with it I'm in bed.' An actor was sick or thought so; the Governor of California was bringing a party out; a supervisor had beaten up his wife for the prints and must be 'reduced to a writer'—these three affairs were Father's job—unless the actor was under personal contract to Stahr. There was early snow on a location in Canada with the company already there—Stahr raced over the possibilities of salvage, reviewing the story of the picture. Nothing. Stahr called Catherine Doolan.

'I want to speak to the cop who put two women off the back lot last night. I think his name's Malone.'

'Yes, Mr. Stahr. I've got Joe Wyman—about the trousers.'

'Hello, Joe,' said Stahr. 'Listen—two people at the sneak preview complained that Morgan's fly was open for half the picture . . . of course they're exaggerating, but even if it's only ten feet . . . no, we can't find the people, but I want that picture run over and over until you find that footage.

Get a lot of people in the projection room—somebody'll spot it.'

> *Tout passe.—L'art robuste*
> *Seul a l'éternité.*

'And there's the Prince from Denmark,' said Catherine Doolan. 'He's very handsome.' She was impelled to add pointlessly, '—for a tall man.'

'Thanks,' Stahr said. 'Thank you, Catherine, I appreciate it that I am now the handsomest small man on the lot. Send the Prince out on the sets and tell him we'll lunch at one.'

'And Mr. George Boxley—looking very angry in a British way.'

'I'll see him for ten minutes.'

As she went out, he asked: 'Did Robby phone in?'

'No.'

'Call sound, and if he's been heard from, call him and ask him this. Ask him this—did he hear that woman's name last night? Either of those women. Or anything so they could be traced.'

'Anything else?'

'No, but tell him it's important while he still remembers. What were they? I mean what kind of people—ask him that, too. I mean were they——'

She waited, scratching his words on her pad without looking.

'—oh, were they—questionable? Were they theatrical? Never mind—skip that. Just ask if he knows how they can be traced.'

The policeman, Malone, had known nothing. Two dames, and he had hustled 'em, you betcha. One of them was sore. Which one? One of them. They had a car, a Chevvy—he thought of taking the licence. Was it—the good looker who was sore? It was one of them.

Not which one—he had noticed nothing. Even on the lot here Minna was forgotten. In three years. So much for that, then.

Stahr smiled at Mr. George Boxley. It was a kindly fatherly smile Stahr had developed inversely when he was a young man pushed into high places. Originally it had been a smile of respect towards his elders, then as his own decisions grew rapidly to displace theirs, a smile so that they should not feel it—finally emerging as what it was : a smile of kindness—sometimes a little hurried and tired, but always there—towards anyone who had not angered him within the hour. Or anyone he did not intend to insult, aggressive and outright.

Mr. Boxley did not smile back. He came in with the air of being violently dragged, though no one apparently had a hand on him. He stood in front of a chair, and again it was as if two invisible attendants seized his arms and set him down forcibly into it. He sat there morosely. Even when he lit a cigarette on Stahr's invitation, one felt that the match was held to it by exterior forces he disdained to control.

Stahr looked at him courteously.

'Something not going well, Mr. Boxley?'

The novelist looked back at him in thunderous silence.

'I read your letter,' said Stahr. The tone of the pleasant young headmaster was gone. He spoke as to an equal, with a faint two-edged deference.

'I can't get what I write on paper,' broke out Boxley. 'You've all been very decent, but it's a sort of conspiracy. Those two hacks you've teamed me with listen to what I say, but they spoil it—they seem to have a vocabulary of about a hundred words.'

'Why don't you write it yourself?' asked Stahr.

'I have. I sent you some.'

'But it was just talk, back and forth,' said Stahr mildly. 'Interesting talk but nothing more.'

Now it was all the two ghostly attendants could do to hold Boxley in the deep chair. He struggled to get up; he uttered a single quiet bark which had some relation to laughter but none to amusement, and said :

'I don't think you people read things. The men are duelling when the conversation takes place. At the end one of them falls into a well and has to be hauled up in a bucket.'

He barked again and subsided.

'Would you write that in a book of your own, Mr. Boxley?'

'What? Naturally not.'

'You'd consider it too cheap.'

'Movie standards are different,' said Boxley, hedging.

'Do you ever go to them?'

'No—almost never.'

'Isn't it because people are always duelling and falling down wells?'

'Yes—and wearing strained facial expressions and talking incredible and unnatural dialogue.'

'Slip the dialogue for a minute,' said Stahr. 'Granted your dialogue is more graceful than what these hacks can write—that's why we brought you out here. But let's imagine something that isn't either bad dialogue or jumping down a well. Has your office got a stove in it that lights with a match?'

'I think it has,' said Boxley stiffly, '—but I never use it.'

'Suppose you're in your office. You've been fighting duels or writing all day and you're too tired to fight or write any more. You're sitting there staring—dull, like we all get sometimes. A pretty stenographer that you've seen before comes into the room and you watch her—idly. She doesn't see you, though you're very close to her. She takes off her gloves, opens her purse and dumps it out on a table——'

Stahr stood up, tossing his key-ring on his desk.

'She has two dimes and a nickel—and a cardboard match box. She leaves the nickel on the desk, puts the two dimes back into her purse and takes her black gloves to the stove, opens it and puts them inside. There is one match in the match box and she starts to light it kneeling by the stove. You notice that there's a stiff wind blowing in the window—but just then your telephone rings. The girl picks it up, says hello—listens—and says deliberately into the phone, "I've never owned a pair of black gloves in my life."

She hangs up, kneels by the stove again, and just as she lights the match, you glance around very suddenly and see that there's another man in the office, watching every move the girl makes——'

Stahr paused. He picked up his keys and put them in his pocket.

'Go on,' said Boxley, smiling. 'What happens?'

'I don't know,' said Stahr. 'I was just making pictures.'

Boxley felt he was being put in the wrong.

'It's just melodrama,' he said.

'Not necessarily,' said Stahr. 'In any case, nobody has moved violently or talked cheap dialogue or had any facial expression at all. There was only one bad line, and a writer like you could improve it. But you were interested.'

'What was the nickel for?' asked Boxley evasively.

'I don't know,' said Stahr. Suddenly he laughed. 'Oh, yes—the nickel was for the movies.'

The two invisible attendants seemed to release Boxley. He relaxed, leaned back in his chair and laughed.

'What in hell do you pay me for?' he demanded. 'I don't understand the damn stuff.'

'You will,' said Stahr grinning, 'or you wouldn't have asked about the nickel.'

A dark saucer-eyed man was waiting in the outer office as they came out.

'Mr. Boxley, this is Mr. Mike Van Dyke,' Stahr said. 'What is it, Mike?'

'Nothing,' Mike said. 'I just came up to see if you were real.'

'Why don't you go to work?' Stahr said. 'I haven't had a laugh in the rushes for days.'

'I'm afraid of a nervous breakdown.'

'You ought to keep in form,' Stahr said. 'Let's see you peddle your stuff.' He turned to Boxley: 'Mike's a gag man —he was out here when I was in the cradle. Mike, show Mr. Boxley a double wing, clutch, kick and scram.'

'Here?' asked Mike.

'Here.'

'There isn't much room. I wanted to ask you about——'

'There's lots of room.'

'Well,' he looked around tentatively. 'You shoot the gun.'

Miss Doolan's assistant, Katy, took a paper bag, blew it open.

'It was a routine,' Mike said to Boxley, '——back in the Keystone days.' He turned to Stahr: 'Does he know what a routine is?'

'It means an act,' Stahr explained. 'Georgie Jessel talks about "Lincoln's Gettysburg routine."'

Katy poised the neck of the blown-up bag in her mouth. Mike stood with his back to her.

'Ready?' Katy asked. She brought her hands down on the side. Immediately Mike grabbed his bottom with both hands, jumped in the air, slid his feet out on the floor one after the other, remaining in place and flapping his arms twice like a bird——

'Double wing,' said Stahr.

——and then ran out the screen door which the office boy held open for him and disappeared past the window of the balcony.

'Mr. Stahr,' said Miss Doolan, 'Mr. Hanson is on the phone from New York.'

Ten minutes later he clicked his dictagraph, and Miss Doolan came in. There was a male star waiting to see him in the outer office, Miss Doolan said.

'Tell him I went out by the balcony,' Stahr advised her.

'All right. He's been in four times this week. He seems very anxious.'

'Did he give you any hint of what he wanted? Isn't it something he can see Mr. Brady about?'

'He didn't say. You have a conference coming up. Miss Meloney and Mr. White are outside. Mr. Broaca is next door in Mr. Reinmund's office.'

'Send Mr. Roderiguez in,' said Stahr. 'Tell him I can see him only for a minute.'

When the handsome actor came in, Stahr remained standing.

'What is it that can't wait?' he asked pleasantly.

The actor waited carefully till Miss Doolan had gone out.

'Monroe, I'm through,' he said. 'I had to see you.'

'Through!' said Stahr. 'Have you seen *Variety*? Your picture's held over at Roxy's and did thirty-seven thousand in Chicago last week.'

'That's the worst of it. That's the tragedy. I get everything I want, and now it means nothing.'

'Well, go on, explain.'

'There's nothing between Esther and me any more. There never can be again.'

'A row.'

'Oh, no—worse—I can't bear to mention it. My head's in a daze. I wander around like a madman. I go through my part as if I was asleep.'

'I haven't noticed it,' said Stahr. 'You were great in your rushes yesterday.'

'Was I? That just shows you nobody ever guesses.'

'Are you trying to tell me that you and Esther are separating?'

'I suppose it'll come to that. Yes—inevitably—it will.'

'What was it?' demanded Stahr impatiently. 'Did she come in without knocking?'

'Oh, there's nobody else. It's just—me. I'm through.'

Stahr got it suddenly.

'How do you know?'

'It's been true for six weeks.'

'It's your imagination,' said Stahr. 'Have you been to a doctor?'

The actor nodded.

'I've tried everything. I even—one day in desperation I went down to—to Claris. But it was hopeless. I'm washed up.'

Stahr had an impish temptation to tell him to go to Brady about it. Brady handled all matters of public relations. Or

7*

was this private relations. He turned away for a moment, got his face in control, turned back.

'I've been to Pat Brady,' said the star, as if guessing the thought. 'He gave me a lot of phoney advice and I tried it all, but nothing doing. Esther and I sit opposite each other at dinner, and I'm ashamed to look at her. She's been a good sport about it, but I'm ashamed. I'm ashamed all day long. I think *Rainy Day* grossed twenty-five thousand in Des Moines and broke all records in St. Louis and did twenty-seven thousand in Kansas City. My fan mail's way up, and there I am afraid to go home at night, afraid to go to bed.'

Stahr began to be faintly oppressed. When the actor first came in, Stahr had intended to invite him to a cocktail party, but now it scarcely seemed appropriate. What would he want with a cocktail party with this hanging over him? In his mind's eye he saw him wandering haunted from guest to guest with a cocktail in his hand and his grosses up twenty-seven thousand.

'So I came to you, Monroe. I never saw a situation where you didn't know a way out. I said to myself: even if he advises me to kill myself, I'll ask Monroe.'

The buzzer sounded on Stahr's desk—he switched on the dictagraph and heard Miss Doolan's voice.

'Five minutes, Mr. Stahr.'

'I'm sorry,' said Stahr. 'I'll need a few minutes more.'

'Five hundred girls marched to my house from the high school,' the actor said gloomily, 'and I stood behind the curtains and watched them. I couldn't go out.'

'You sit down,' said Stahr. 'We'll take plenty of time and talk this over.'

In the outer office, two members of the conference group had already waited ten minutes—Wylie White and Jane Meloney. The latter was a dried-up little blonde of fifty about whom one could hear the fifty assorted opinions of Hollywood—'a sentimental dope,' 'the best writer on construction in Hollywood,' 'a veteran,' 'that old hack,' 'the smartest woman on the lot,' 'the cleverest plagiarist in the biz.'; and, of course, in addition she was variously described as a nymphomaniac, a virgin, a pushover, a Lesbian and a faithful wife. Without being an old maid, she was, like most self-made women, rather old maidish. She had ulcers of the stomach, and her salary was over a hundred thousand a year. A complicated treatise could be written on whether she was 'worth it' or more than that or nothing at all. Her value lay in such ordinary assets as the bare fact that she was a woman and adaptable, quick and trustworthy, 'knew the game' and was without egotism. She had been a great friend of Minna's, and over a period of years Stahr had managed to stifle what amounted to a sharp physical revulsion.

She and Wylie waited in silence—occasionally addressing a remark to Miss Doolan. Every few minutes Reinmund, the supervisor, called up from his office, where he and Broaca, the director, were waiting. After ten minutes Stahr's button went on, and Miss Doolan called Reinmund and Broaca; simultaneously Stahr and the actor came out of Stahr's office with Stahr holding the man's arm. He was so wound up now that when Wylie White asked him how he was he opened his mouth and began to tell him then and there.

'Oh, I've had an awful time,' he said, but Stahr interrupted sharply.

'No, you haven't. Now you go along and do the role the way I said.'

'Thank you, Monroe.'

Jane Meloney looked after him without speaking.

'Somebody been catching flies on him?' she asked—a phrase for stealing scenes.

'I'm sorry I kept you waiting,' Stahr said. 'Come on in.'

It was noon already and the conferees were entitled to exactly an hour of Stahr's time. No less, for such a conference could only be interrupted by a director who was held up in his shooting; seldom much more, because every eight days the company must release a production as complex and costly as Reinhardt's *Miracle*.

Occasionally, less often than five years ago, Stahr would work all through the night on a single picture. But after such a spree he felt badly for days. If he could go from problem to problem, there was a certain rebirth of vitality with each change. And like those sleepers who can wake whenever they wish, he had set his psychological clock to run one hour.

The cast assembled included, besides the writers, Reinmund, one of the most favoured of the supervisors, and John Broaca, the picture's director.

Broaca, on the surface, was all engineer—large and without nerves, quietly resolute, popular. He was an ignoramus, and Stahr often caught him making the same scenes over and over—one scene about a rich young girl occurred in all his pictures with the same action, the same business. A bunch of large dogs entered the room and jumped around the girl. Later the girl went to a stable and slapped a horse on the rump. The explanation was probably not Freudian; more likely that at a drab moment in youth he had looked through a fence and seen a beautiful girl with dogs and horses. As a trademark for glamour it was stamped on his brain forever.

Reinmund was a handsome young opportunist, with a fairly good education. Originally a man of some character, he was being daily forced by his anomalous position into devious ways of acting and thinking. He was a bad man now, as men go. At thirty he had none of the virtues which either gentile Americans or Jews are taught to think admirable. But he got his pictures out in time, and by manifesting an almost homosexual fixation on Stahr, seemed to have dulled Stahr's usual acuteness. Stahr liked him—considered him a good all-round man.

Wylie White, of course, in any country would have been recognizable as an intellectual of the second order. He was civilized and voluble, both simple and acute, half dazed and half saturnine. His jealousy of Stahr showed only in unguarded flashes, and was mingled with admiration and even affection.

'The production date for this picture is two weeks from Saturday,' said Stahr. 'I think basically it's all right—much improved.'

Reinmund and the two writers exchanged a glance of congratulation.

'Except for one thing,' said Stahr, thoughtfully. 'I don't see why it should be produced at all, and I've decided to put it away.'

There was a moment of shocked silence—and then murmurs of protest, stricken queries.

'It's not your fault,' Stahr said. 'I thought there was something there that wasn't there—that was all.' He hesitated, looking regretfully at Reinmund : 'It's too bad—it was a good play. We paid fifty thousand for it.'

'What's the matter with it, Monroe?' asked Broaca bluntly.

'Well, it hardly seems worth while to go into it,' said Stahr.

Reinmund and Wylie White were both thinking of the professional effect on them. Reinmund had two pictures to his account this year—but Wylie White needed a credit to start his comeback to the scene. Jane Meloney was watching Stahr closely from little skull-like eyes.

'Couldn't you give us some clue,' Reinmund asked. 'This is a good deal of a blow, Monroe.'

'I just wouldn't put Margaret Sullavan in it,' said Stahr. 'Or Colman either. I wouldn't advise them to play it——'

'Specifically, Monroe,' begged Wylie White. 'What didn't you like? The scenes? the dialogue? the humour? construction?'

Stahr picked up the script from his desk, let it fall as if it were, physically, too heavy to handle.

'I don't like the people,' he said. 'I wouldn't like to meet them—if I knew they were going to be somewhere, I'd go somewhere else.'

Reinmund smiled, but there was worry in his eyes.

'Well, that's a damning criticism,' he said. 'I thought the people were rather interesting.'

'So did I,' said Broaca. 'I thought Em was very sympathetic.'

'Did you?' asked Stahr sharply. 'I could just barely believe she was alive. And when I came to the end, I said to myself, "So what?"'

'There must be something to do,' Reinmund said. 'Naturally we feel bad about this. This is the structure we agreed on——'

'But it's not the story,' said Stahr. 'I've told you many times that the first thing I decide is the *kind* of story I want. We change in every other regard, but once that is set we've got to work towards it with every line and movement. This is not the kind of a story I want. The story we bought had shine and glow—it was a happy story. This is all full of doubt and hesitation. The hero and heroine stop loving each other over trifles—then they start up again over trifles. After the first sequence, you don't care if she never sees him again or he her.'

'That's my fault,' said Wylie suddenly. 'You see, Monroe, I don't think stenographers have the same dumb admiration for their bosses they had in 1929. They've been laid off—they've seen their bosses jittery. The world has moved on, that's all.'

Stahr looked at him impatiently, gave a short nod.

'That's not under discussion,' he said. 'The premise of this story is that the girl did have dumb admiration for her boss, if you want to call it that. And there wasn't any evidence that he'd ever been jittery. When you make her doubt him in any way, you have a different kind of story. Or rather you haven't anything at all. These people are extraverts—get that straight—and I want them to extravert all over the lot. When I want to do a Eugene O'Neill play, I'll buy one.'

Jane Meloney, who had never taken her eyes off Stahr, knew it was going to be all right now. If he had really been going to abandon the picture, he wouldn't have gone at it like this. She had been in this game longer than any of them except Broaca, with whom she had had a three-day affair twenty years ago.

Stahr turned to Reinmund.

'You ought to have understood from the casting, Reiny, what kind of a picture I wanted. I started marking the lines that Corliss and McKelway couldn't say and got tired of it. Remember this in the future—if I order a limousine, I want that kind of car. And the fastest midget racer you ever saw wouldn't do. Now—' He looked around. '—shall we go any farther? Now that I've told you I don't even like the kind of picture this is? Shall we go on? We've got two weeks. At the end of that time I'm going to put Corliss and McKelway into this or something else—is it worth while?'

'Well, naturally,' said Reinmund, 'I think it is. I feel bad about this. I should have warned Wylie. I thought he had some good ideas.'

'Monroe's right,' said Broaca bluntly. 'I felt this was wrong all the time, but I couldn't put my finger on it.'

Wylie and Rose looked at him contemptuously and exchanged a glance.

'Do you writers think you can get hot on it again?' asked Stahr, not unkindly. 'Or shall I try somebody fresh?'

'I'd like another shot,' said Wylie.

'How about you, Jane?'

She nodded briefly.

'What do you think of the girl?' asked Stahr.

'Well—naturally I'm prejudiced in her favour.'

'You better forget it,' said Stahr warningly. 'Ten million Americans would put thumbs down on that girl if she walked on the screen. We've got an hour and twenty-five minutes on the screen—you show a woman being unfaithful to a man for one-third of that time and you've given the impression that she's one-third whore.'

'Is that a big proportion?' asked Jane slyly, and they laughed.

'It is for me,' said Stahr thoughtfully, 'even if it wasn't for the Hays office. If you want to paint a scarlet letter on her back, it's all right, but that's another story. Not this story. This is a future wife and mother. However—*however*——'

He pointed his pencil at Wylie White.

'—this has as much passion as that Oscar on my desk.'

'What the hell!' said Wylie. 'She's full of it. Why she goes to——'

'She's loose enough,' said Stahr, '—but that's all. There's one scene in the play better than all this you cooked up, and you've left it out. When she's trying to make the time pass by changing her watch.'

'It didn't seem to fit,' Wylie apologized.

'Now,' said Stahr, 'I've got about fifty ideas. I'm going to call Miss Doolan.' He pressed a button. '—And if there's anything you don't understand, speak up——'

Miss Doolan slid in almost imperceptibly. Pacing the floor swiftly, Stahr began. In the first place he wanted to tell them what kind of a girl she was—what kind of a girl he approved of here. She was a perfect girl with a few small faults as in the play, but a perfect girl not because the public wanted her that way but because it was the kind of girl that he, Stahr, liked to see in this sort of picture. Was that clear? It was no character role. She stood for health, vitality, ambition and love. What gave the play its importance was entirely a situation in which she found herself. She became possessed of a secret that affected a great many lives. There was a right thing and a wrong thing to do—at first it was not plain which was which, but when it was, she went right away and did it. That was the kind of story this was—thin, clean and shining. No doubts.

'She has never heard the word labour troubles,' he said with a sigh. 'She might be living in 1929. Is it plain what kind of girl I want?'

'It's very plain, Monroe.'

'Now about the things she does,' said Stahr. 'At all times, at all moments when she is on the screen in our sight, she wants to sleep with Ken Willard. Is that plain, Wylie?'

'Passionately plain.'

'Whatever she does, it is in place of sleeping with Ken

Willard. If she walks down the street she is walking to sleep with Ken Willard, if she eats her food it is to give her strength to sleep with Ken Willard. *But* at no time do you give the impression that she would even consider sleeping with Ken Willard unless they were properly sanctified. I'm ashamed of having to tell you these kindergarten facts, but they have somehow leaked out of the story.'

He opened the script and began to go through it page by page. Miss Doolan's notes would be typed in quintuplicate and given to them, but Jane Meloney made notes of her own. Broaca put his hand up to his half-closed eyes—he could remember 'when a director was something out here,' when writers were gag-men or eager and ashamed young reporters full of whiskey—a director was all there was then. No supervisor—no Stahr.

He started wide-awake as he heard his name.

'It would be nice, John, it you could put the boy on a pointed roof and let him walk around and keep the camera on him. You might get a nice feeling—not danger, not suspense, not pointing for anything—a kid on the roof in the morning.'

Broaca brought himself back in the room.

'All right,' he said, '—just an element of danger.'

'Not exactly,' said Stahr. 'He doesn't start to fall off the roof. Break into the next scene with it.'

'Through the window,' suggested Jane Meloney. 'He could climb in his sister's window.'

'That's a good transition,' said Stahr. 'Right into the diary scene.'

Broaca was wide-awake now.

'I'll shoot up at him,' he said. 'Let him go away from the camera. Just a fixed shot from quite a distance—let him go away from the camera. Don't follow him. Pick him up in a close shot and let him go away again. No attention on him except against the whole roof and the sky.' He liked the shot —it was a director's shot that didn't come up on every page any more. He might use a crane—it would be cheaper in the end than building the roof on the ground with a process sky.

That was one thing about Stahr—the literal sky was the limit. He had worked with Jews too long to believe legends that they were small with money.

'In the third sequence have him hit the priest,' Stahr said.

'What!' Wylie cried, '—and have the Catholics on our neck.'

'I've talked to Joe Breen. Priests have been hit. It doesn't reflect on them.'

His quiet voice ran on—stopped abruptly as Miss Doolan glanced at the clock.

'Is that too much to do before Monday?' he asked Wylie.

Wylie looked at Jane and she looked back, not even bothering to nod. He saw their week-end melting away, but he was a different man from when he entered the room. When you were paid fifteen hundred a week, emergency work was one thing you did not skimp, nor when your picture was threatened. As a 'free lance' writer Wylie had failed from lack of caring, but here was Stahr to care, for all of them. The effect would not wear off when he left the office—not anywhere within the walls of the lot. He felt a great purposefulness. The mixture of common sense, wise sensibility, theatrical ingenuity, and a certain half-naive conception of the common weal which Stahr had just stated aloud, inspired him to do his part, to get his block of stone in place, even if the effort were foredoomed, the result as dull as a pyramid.

Out of the window Jane Meloney watched the trickle streaming towards the commissary. She would have her lunch in her office and knit a few rows while it came. The man was coming at one-fifteen with the French perfume smuggled over the Mexican border. That was no sin—it was like prohibition.

Broaca watched as Reinmund fawned upon Stahr. He sensed that Reinmund was on his way up. He received seven hundred and fifty a week for his partial authority over directors, writers and stars who got much more. He wore a pair of cheap English shoes he had bought near the Beverly

Wilshire, and Broaca hoped they hurt his feet, but soon now he would order his shoes from Peel's and put away his little green Alpine hat with a feather. Broaca was years ahead of him. He had a fine record in the war, but he had never felt quite the same with himself since he had let Ike Franklin strike him in the face with his open hand.

There was smoke in the room, and behind it, behind his great desk, Stahr was withdrawing further and further, in all courtesy, still giving Reinmund an ear and Miss Doolan an ear. The conference was over.

[*Stahr was to have received the Danish Prince Agge, who 'wanted to learn about pictures from the beginning' and who in the author's cast of characters is described as an 'early Fascist.'*]

'Mr. Marcus calling from New York,' said Miss Doolan.

'What do you mean?' demanded Stahr. 'Why, I saw him here last night.'

'Well, he's on the phone—it's a New York call and Miss Jacobs' voice. It's his office.'

Stahr laughed.

'I'm seeing him at lunch,' he said. 'There's no aeroplane fast enough to take him there.'

Miss Doolan returned to the phone. Stahr lingered to hear the outcome.

'It's all right,' said Miss Doolan presently. 'It was a mistake. Mr. Marcus called East this morning to tell them about the quake and the flood on the back lot, and it seems he asked them to ask you about it. It was a new secretary who didn't understand Mr. Marcus. I think she got mixed up.'

'I think she did,' said Stahr grimly.

Prince Agge did not understand either of them, but, looking for the fabulous, he felt it was something triumphantly American. Mr. Marcus, whose quarters could be seen across the way, had called his New York office to ask Stahr about the flood. The Prince imagined some intricate relationship without realizing that the transaction had taken place entirely within the once brilliant steel-trap mind of Mr. Marcus, which was intermittently slipping.

'I think she was a very new secretary,' repeated Stahr. 'Any other messages?'

'Mr. Robinson called in,' Miss Doolan said, as he started for the commissary. 'One of the women told him her name, but he's forgotten it—he thinks it was Smith or Brown or Jones.'

'That's a great help.'

'And he remembers she says she just moved to Los Angeles.'

'I remember she had a silver belt,' Stahr said, 'with stars cut out of it.'

'I'm still trying to find out more about Pete Zavras. I talked to his wife.'

'What did she say?'

'Oh, they've had an awful time—given up their house—she's been sick——'

'Is the eye-trouble hopeless?'

'She didn't seem to know anything about the state of his eyes. She didn't even know he was going blind.'

'That's funny.'

He thought about it on the way to luncheon, but it was as confusing as the actor's trouble this morning. Troubles about people's health didn't seem within his range—he gave no thought to his own. In the lane beside the commissary he stepped back as an open electric truck crammed with girls in the bright costumes of the Regency came rolling in from the back lot. The dresses were fluttering in the wind, the young painted faces looked at him curiously, and he smiled as it went by.

Eleven men and their guest, Prince Agge, sat at lunch in the private dining-room of the studio commissary. They were the money men—they were the rulers; and unless there was a guest, they ate in broken silence, sometimes asking questions about each other's wives and children, sometimes discharging a single absorption from the forefront of their consciousness. Eight out of the ten were Jews —five of the ten were foreign-born, including a Greek and an Englishman; and they had all known each other for a long time: there was a rating in the group, from old Marcus down to old Leanbaum, who had bought the most fortunate block of stock in the business and never was allowed to spend over a million a year producing.

Old Marcus still managed to function with disquieting resilience. Some never-atrophying instinct warned him of danger, of gangings up against him—he was never so dangerous himself as when others considered him surrounded. His grey face had attained such immobility that even those who were accustomed to watch the reflex of the inner corner of his eye could no longer see it. Nature had grown a little white whisker there to conceal it; his armour was complete.

As he was the oldest, Stahr was the youngest of the group—not by many years at this date, though he had first sat with most of these men when he was a boy wonder of twenty-two. Then, more than now, he had been a money man among money men. Then he had been able to figure costs in his head with a speed and accuracy that dazzled them—for they were not wizards or even experts in that regard, despite the popular conception of Jews in finance. Most of them owed their success to different and incompatible qualities. But in a group a tradition carries along the less adept, and they were content to look at Stahr for the sublimated auditing, and experience a sort of glow as if they had done it themselves, like rooters at a football game.

Stahr, as will presently be seen, had grown away from that particular gift, though it was always there.

Prince Agge sat between Stahr and Mort Fleishacker, the company lawyer, and across from Joe Popolos the theatre owner. He was hostile to Jews in a vague general way that he tried to cure himself of. As a turbulent man, serving his time in the Foreign Legion, he thought that Jews were too fond of their own skins. But he was willing to concede that they might be different in America under different circumstances, and certainly he found Stahr was much of a man in every way. For the rest—he thought most business men were dull dogs—for final reference he reverted always to the blood of Bernadotte in his veins.

My father—I will call him Mr. Brady, as Prince Agge did when he told me of this luncheon—was worried about a picture, and when Leanbaum went out early, he came up and took his chair opposite.

'How about the South America picture idea, Monroe?' he asked.

Prince Agge noticed a blink of attention towards them as distinct as if a dozen pairs of eyelashes had made the sound of batting wings. Then silence again.

'We're going ahead with it,' said Stahr.

'With that same budget?' Brady asked.

Stahr nodded.

'It's out of proportion,' said Brady. 'There won't be any miracle in these bad times—no *Hell's Angels* or *Ben Hur*, when you throw it away and get it back.'

Probably the attack was planned, for Popolos, the Greek, took up the matter in a sort of double talk.

'It's not adoptable, Monroe, in as we wish adopt to this times in as it changes. It what could be done as we run the gamut of prosperity is scarcely conceptuable now.'

'What do you think, Mr. Marcus?' asked Stahr.

All eyes followed his down the table, but, as if forewarned, Mr. Marcus had already signalled his private waiter behind him that he wished to rise, and was even now in a basket-like position in the waiter's arms. He looked at them with such helplessness that it was hard to realize that in the evenings he sometimes went dancing with his young Canadian girl.

'Monroe is our production genius,' he said. 'I count upon Monroe and lean heavily upon him. I have not seen the flood myself.'

There was a moment of silence as he moved from the room.

'There's not a two million dollar gross in the country now,' said Brady.

'Is not,' agreed Popolos. 'Even as if so you could grab them by the head and push them by and in, is not.'

'Probably not,' agreed Stahr. He paused as if to make sure that all were listening. 'I think we can count on a million and a quarter from the road-show. Perhaps a million and a half altogether. And a quarter of a million abroad.'

Again there was silence—this time puzzled, a little confused. Over his shoulder Stahr asked the waiter to be connected with his office on the phone.

'But your budget?' said Fleishacker. 'Your budget is seventeen hundred and fifty thousand, I understand. And your expectations only add up to that without profits.'

'Those aren't my expectations,' said Stahr. 'We're not sure of more than a million and a half.'

The room had grown so motionless that Pringe Agge could hear a grey chunk of ash fall from a cigar in mid-air. Fleishacker started to speak, his face fixed with amazement, but a phone had been handed over Stahr's shoulder.

'Your office, Mr. Stahr.'

'Oh, yes—oh, hello, Miss Doolan. I've figured it out about Zavras. It's one of these lousy rumours—I'll bet my shirt on it. . . . Oh, you did. Good . . . good. Now here's what to do: send him to my oculist this afternoon—Dr. John Kennedy—and have him get a report and have it photostated—you understand?'

He hung up—turned with a touch of passion to the table at large.

'Did any of you ever hear a story that Pete Zavras was going blind?'

There were a couple of nods. But most of those present were poised breathlessly on whether Stahr had slipped on his figures a minute before.

'It's pure bunk. He says he's never even been to an oculist—never knew why the studios turned against him,' said Stahr. 'Somebody didn't like him or somebody talked too much, and he's been out of work for a year.'

There was a conventional murmur of sympathy. Stahr signed the check and made as though to get up.

'Excuse me, Monroe,' said Fleishacker persistently, while Brady and Popolos watched. 'I'm fairly new here, and perhaps I fail to comprehend implicitly and explicitly.' He was talking fast, but the veins on his forehead bulged with pride at the big words from N.Y.U. 'Do I understand you to say you expect to gross a quarter million short of your budget?'

'It's a quality picture,' said Stahr with assumed innocence.

It had dawned on them all now, but they still felt there was a trick in it. Stahr really thought it would make money. No one in his senses——

'For two years we've played safe,' said Stahr. 'It's time we made a picture that'll lose some money. Write it off as good will—this'll bring in new customers.'

Some of them still thought he meant it was a flyer and a favourable one, but he left them in no doubt.

'It'll lose money,' he said as he stood up, his jaw just slightly out and his eyes smiling and shining. 'It would be a bigger miracle than *Hell's Angels* if it broke even. But we have a certain duty to the public, as Pat Brady has said at Academy dinners. It's a good thing for the production schedule to slip in a picture that'll lose money.'

He nodded at Prince Agge. As the latter made his bows quickly, he tried to take in with a last glance the general effect of what Stahr said, but he could tell nothing. The eyes, not so much downcast as fixed upon an indefinite distance just above the table, were all blinking quickly now, but there was not a whisper in the room.

Coming out of the private dining-room, they passed through a corner of the commissary proper. Prince Agge drank it in—eagerly. It was gay with gypsies and with citizens and soldiers, with the sideburns and braided coats of the First Empire. From a little distance they were men who lived and walked a hundred years ago, and Agge wondered how he and the men of his time would look as extras in some future costume picture.

Then he saw Abraham Lincoln, and his whole feeling suddenly changed. He had been brought up in the dawn of Scandinavian socialism when Nicolay's biography was much read. He had been told Lincoln was a great man whom he should admire, and he hated him instead, because he was forced upon him. But now seeing him sitting here, his legs crossed, his kindly face fixed on a forty-cent dinner, including dessert, his shawl wrapped around him as if to protect himself from the erratic air-cooling—now Prince Agge, who was in America at last, stared as a tourist at the mummy of Lenin in the Kremlin. This, then, was Lincoln. Stahr had walked on far ahead of him, turned waiting for him—but still Agge stared.

This, then, he thought, was what they all meant to be.

Lincoln suddenly raised a triangle of pie and jammed it in his mouth, and, a little frightened, Prince Agge hurried to join Stahr.

'I hope you're getting what you want,' said Stahr, feeling he had neglected him. 'We'll have some rushes in half an hour and then you can go on to as many sets as you want.'

'I should rather stay with you,' said Prince Agge.

'I'll see what there is for me,' said Stahr. 'Then we'll go on together.'

There was the Japanese consul on the release of a spy story which might offend the national sensibilities of Japan. There were phone calls and telegrams. There was some further information from Robby.

'Now he remembers the name of the woman. He's sure it was Smith,' said Miss Doolan. 'He asked her if she wanted to come on the lot and get some dry shoes, and she said no —so she can't sue.'

'That's pretty bad for a total recall—"Smith." That's a great help.' He thought a moment: 'Ask the phone company for a list of Smiths that have taken new phones here in the last month. Call them all.'

'All right.'

CHAPTER IV

'How are you, Monroe,' said Red Ridingwood. 'I'm glad you came down.'

Stahr walked past him, heading across the great stage towards the set of a brilliant room that would be used to-morrow. Director Ridingwood followed, realizing after a moment that, however fast he walked Stahr managed to be a step or two ahead. He recognized the indication of dis-pleasure—he had used it himself. He had had his own studio once and he had used everything. There was no stop Stahr could pull that would surprise him. His task was the delivery of situations, and Stahr by effective business could not out-play him on his own grounds. Goldwyn had once interfered with him, and Ridingwood had led Goldwyn into trying to act out a part in front of fifty people—with the result that he had anticipated : his own authority had been restored.

Stahr reached the brilliant set and stopped.

'It's no good,' said Ridingwood. 'No imagination. I don't care how you light it——'

'Why did you call me about it?' Stahr asked, standing close to him. 'Why didn't you take it up with Art?'

'I didn't ask you to come down, Monroe.'

'You wanted to be your own supervisor.'

'I'm sorry, Monroe,' said Ridingwood patiently, 'but I didn't ask you to come down.'

Stahr turned suddenly and walked back towards the camera set-up. The eyes and open mouths of a group of visitors moved momentarily off the heroine of the picture, took in Stahr, and then moved vacantly back to the heroine again. They were Knights of Columbus. They had seen the host carried in procession, but this was the dream made flesh.

Stahr stopped beside her chair. She wore a low gown which displayed the bright eczema of her chest and back. Before each take, the blemished surface was plastered over with an emollient, which was removed immediately after the take. Her hair was of the colour and viscosity of drying blood, but there was starlight that actually photographed in her eyes.

Before Stahr could speak, he heard a helpful voice behind him:

'She's radiunt. Absolutely radiunt.'

It was an assistant director, and the intention was delicate compliment. The actress was being complimented so that she did not have to strain her poor skin to bend and hear. Stahr was being complimented for having her under contract. Ridingwood was being remotely complimented.

'Everything all right?' Stahr asked her pleasantly.

'Oh, it's fine,' she agreed, '——except for the ——ing publicity men.'

He winked at her gently.

'We'll keep them away,' he said.

Her name had become currently synonymous with the expression 'bitch.' Presumably she had modelled herself after one of those queens in the Tarzan comics who rule mysteriously over a nation of blacks. She regarded the rest of the world as black. She was a necessary evil, borrowed for a single picture.

Ridingwood walked with Stahr towards the door of the stage.

'Everything's all right,' the director said. 'She's as good as she can be.'

They were out of hearing range, and Stahr stopped suddenly and looked at Red with blazing eyes.

'You've been photographing crap,' he said. 'Do you know what she reminds me of in the rushes—"Miss Foodstuffs."'

'I'm trying to get the best performance——'

'Come along with me,' said Stahr abruptly.

'With you? Shall I tell them to rest?'

'Leave it as it is,' said Stahr, pushing the padded outer door.

His car and chauffeur waited outside. Minutes were precious most days.

'Get in,' said Stahr.

Red knew now it was serious. He even knew all at once what was the matter. The girl had got the whip hand on him the first day with her cold lashing tongue. He was a peace-loving man and he had let her walk through her part cold rather than cause trouble.

Stahr spoke into his thoughts.

'You can't handle her,' he said. 'I told you what I wanted. I wanted her *mean*—and she comes out bored, I'm afraid we'll have to call it off, Red.'

'The picture?'

'No. I'm putting Harley on it.'

'All right, Monroe.'

'I'm sorry, Red. We'll try something else another time.'

The car drew up in front of Stahr's office.

'Shall I finish this take?' said Red.

'It's being done now,' said Stahr grimly. 'Harley's in there.'

'What the hell——'

'He went in when we came out. I had him read the script last night.'

'Now listen, Monroe——'

'It's my busy day, Red,' said Stahr, tersely. 'You lost interest about three days ago.'

It was a sorry mess, Ridingwood thought. It meant he would have slight, very slight loss of position—it probably meant that he could not have a third wife just now as he had planned. There wasn't even the satisfaction of raising a row about it—if you disagreed with Stahr, you did not advertise it. Stahr was his world's great customer, who was always—almost always—right.

'How about my coat?' he asked suddenly. 'I left it over a chair on the set.'

'I know you did,' said Stahr. 'Here it is.'

He was trying so hard to be charitable about Ridingwood's lapse that he had forgotten that he had it in his hand.

'Mr. Stahr's Projection Room' was a miniature picture

theatre with four rows of overstuffed chairs. In front of the front row ran long tables with dim lamps, buzzers and telephones. Against the wall was an upright piano, left there since the early days of sound. The room had been redecorated and reupholstered only a year before, but already it was ragged again with work and hours.

Here Stahr sat at two-thirty and again at six-thirty watching the lengths of film taken during the day. There was often a savage tensity about the occasion—he was dealing with *faits accomplis*—the net result of months of buying, planning, writing and rewriting, casting, constructing, lighting, rehearsing and shooting—the fruit of brilliant hunches or of counsels of despair, of lethargy, conspiracy and sweat. At this point the tortuous manœuvre was staged and in suspension—these were reports from the battle-line.

Besides Stahr, there were present the representatives of all technical departments, together with the supervisors and unit managers of the pictures concerned. The directors did not appear at these showings—officially because their work was considered done, actually because few punches were pulled here as money ran out in silver spools. There had evolved a delicate staying away.

The staff was already assembled. Stahr came in and took his place quickly, and the murmur of conversation died away. As he sat back and drew his thin knee up beside him in the chair, the lights in the room went out. There was the flare of a match in the back row—then silence.

On the screen a troop of French Canadians pushed their canoes up a rapids. The scene had been photographed in a studio tank, and at the end of each take, after the director's voice could be heard saying 'Cut,' the actors on the screen relaxed and wiped their brows and sometimes laughed hilariously—and the water in the tank stopped flowing and the illusion ceased. Except to name his choice from each set of takes and to remark that it was 'a good process,' Stahr made no comment.

The next scene, still in the rapids, called for dialogue between the Canadian girl (Claudette Colbert) and the *courrier du bois* (Ronald Colman), with her looking down at him from a canoe. After a few strips had run through, Stahr spoke up suddenly.

'Has the tank been dismantled?'

'Yes, sir.'

'Monroe—they needed it for——'

Stahr cut in peremptorily.

'Have it set up again right away. Let's have that second take again.'

The lights went on momentarily. One of the unit managers left his chair and came and stood in front of Stahr.

'A beautifully acted scene thrown away,' raged Stahr quietly. 'It wasn't centred. The camera was set up so it caught the beautiful top of Claudette's head all the time she was talking. That's just what we want, isn't it? That's just what people go to see—the top of a beautiful girl's head. Tell Tim he could have saved wear and tear by using her stand-in.'

The lights went out again. The unit manager squatted by Stahr's chair to be out of the way. The take was run again.

'Do you see now?' asked Stahr. 'And there's a hair in the picture—there on the right, see it? Find out if it's in the projector or the film.'

At the very end of the take, Claudette Colbert slowly lifted her head, revealing her great liquid eyes.

'That's what we should have had all the way,' said Stahr. 'She gave a fine performance too. See if you can fit it in to-morrow or late this afternoon.'

Pete Zavras would not have made a slip like that. There were not six camera men in the industry you could entirely trust.

The lights went on; the supervisor and unit manager for that picture went out.

'Monroe, this stuff was shot yesterday—it came through late last night.'

The room darkened. On the screen appeared the head of Siva, immense and imperturbable, oblivious to the fact that in a few hours it was to be washed away in a flood. Around it milled a crowd of the faithful.

'When you take that scene again,' said Stahr suddenly, 'put a couple of little kids up on top. You better check about whether it's reverent or not, but I think it's all right. Kids'll do anything.'

'Yes, Monroe.'

A silver belt with stars cut out of it . . . Smith, Jones or Brown. . . . Personal—will the woman with the silver belt who——?

With another picture the scene shifted to New York, a gangster story, and suddenly Stahr became restive.

'That's scene's trash,' he called suddenly in the darkness. 'It's badly written, it's miscast, it accomplishes nothing. Those types aren't tough. They look like a lot of dressed-up lollipops—what the hell is the matter, Lee?'

'The scene was written on the set this morning,' said Lee Kapper. 'Burton wanted to get all the stuff on Stage 6.'

'Well—it's trash. And so is this one. There's no use printing stuff like that. She doesn't believe what she's saying —neither does Cary. "I love you" in a close up—they'll cluck you out of the house! And the girl's overdressed.'

In the darkness a signal was given, the projector stopped, the lights went on. The room waited in utter silence. Stahr's face was expressionless.

'Who wrote the scene?' he asked after a minute.

'Wylie White.'

'Is he sober?'

'Sure he is.'

Stahr considered.

'Put about four writers on that scene to-night,' he said. 'See who we've got. Is Sidney Howard here yet?'

'He got in this morning.'

'Talk to him about it. Explain to him what I want there. The girl is in deadly terror—she's stalling. It's as simple as that. People don't have three emotions at once. And Kapper——'

The art director leaned forward out of the second row.

'Yeah.'

'There's something the matter with that set.'

There were little glances exchanged all over the room.

'What is it, Monroe?'

'You tell *me*,' said Stahr. 'It's crowded. It doesn't carry your eye out. It looks cheap.'

'It wasn't.'

'I know it wasn't. There's not much the matter, but there's something. Go over and take a look to-night. It may be too much furniture—or the wrong kind. Perhaps a window would help. Couldn't you force the perspective in that hall a little more?'

'I'll see what I can do.' Kapper edged his way out of the row, looking at his watch.

'I'll have to get at it right away,' he said. 'I'll work to-night and we'll put it up in the morning.'

'All right. Lee, you can shoot around those scenes, can't you?'

'I think so, Monroe.'

'I take the blame for this. Have you got the fight stuff?'

'Coming up now.'

Stahr nodded. Kapper hurried out, and the room went dark again. On the screen four men staged a terrific socking match in a cellar. Stahr laughed.

'Look at Tracy,' he said. 'Look at him go down after that guy. I bet he's been in a few.'

The men fought over and over. Always the same fight. Always at the end they faced each other smiling, sometimes touching the opponent in a friendly gesture on the shoulder. The only one in danger was the stunt man, a pug who could have murdered the other three. He was in danger only if they swung wild and didn't follow the blows he had taught them. Even so, the youngest actor was afraid for his face and the director had covered his flinches with ingenious angles and interpositions.

And then two men met endlessly in a door, recognized each other and went on. They met, they started, they went on.

Then a little girl read underneath a tree with a boy reading on a limb of the tree above. The little girl was bored and wanted to talk to the boy. He would pay no attention. The core of the apple he was eating fell on the little girl's head.

A voice spoke up out of the darkness:

'It's pretty long, isn't it, Monroe?'

'Not a bit,' said Stahr. 'It's nice. It has nice feeling.'

'I just thought it was long.'

'Sometimes ten feet can be too long—sometimes a scene two hundred feet long can be too short. I want to speak to the cutter before he touches this scene—this is something that'll be remembered in the picture.'

The oracle had spoken. There was nothing to question or argue. Stahr must be right always, not most of the time, but always—or the structure would melt down like gradual butter.

Another hour passed. Dreams hung in fragments at the far end of the room, suffered analysis, passed—to be dreamed in crowds, or else discarded. The end was signalled by two tests, a character man and a girl. After the rushes, which had a tense rhythm of their own, the tests were smooth and finished; the observers settled in their chairs; Stahr's foot slipped to the floor. Opinions were welcome. One of the technical men let it be known that he would willingly cohabit with the girl; the rest were indifferent.

'Somebody sent up a test of that girl two years ago. She must be getting around—but she isn't getting any better. But the man's good. Can't we use him as the old Russian Prince in *Steppes*?'

'He *is* an old Russian Prince,' said the casting director, 'but he's ashamed of it. He's a Red. And that's one part he says he wouldn't play.'

'It's the only part he could play,' said Stahr.

The lights went on. Stahr rolled his gum into its wrapper and put it in an ash-tray. He turned questioningly to his secretary.

'The processes on Stage 2,' she said.

8+s.f.

He looked in briefly at the processes, moving pictures taken against a background of other moving pictures by an ingenious device. There was a meeting in Marcus' office on the subject of *Manon* with a happy ending, and Stahr had his say on that as he had had before—it had been making money without a happy ending for a century and a half. He was obdurate—at this time in the afternoon he was at his most fluent and the opposition faded into another subject: they would lend a dozen stars to the benefit for those the quake had made homeless at Long Beach. In a sudden burst of giving, five of them all at once made up a purse of twenty-five thousand dollars. They gave well, but not as poor men give. It was not charity.

At his office there was word from the oculist to whom he had sent Pete Zavras that the camera man's eyes were 19-20: approximately perfect. He had written a letter that Zavras was having photostated. Stahr walked around his office cockily while Miss Doolan admired him. Prince Agge had dropped in to thank him for his afternoon on the sets, and while they talked, a cryptic word came from a supervisor that some writers named Tarleton had 'found out' and were about to quit.

'These are good writers,' Stahr explained to Prince Agge, 'and we don't have good writers out here.'

'Why, you can hire anyone!' exclaimed his visitor in surprise.

'Oh, we hire them, but when they get out here, they're not good writers—so we have to work with the material we have.'

'Such as what?'

'Anybody that'll accept the system and stay decently sober—we have all sorts of people—disappointed poets, one-hit playwrights—college girls—we put them on an idea in pairs, and if it slows down, we put two more writers working behind them. I've had as many as three pairs working independently on the same idea.'

'Do they like that?'

'Not if they know about it. They're not geniuses—none

of them could make as much any other way. But these
Tarletons are a husband and wife team from the East—
pretty good playwrights. They've just found out they're not
alone on the story and it shocks them—shocks their sense of
unity—that's the word they'll use.'

'But what does make the—the unity?'

Stahr hesitated—his face was grim except that his eyes
twinkled.

'I'm the unity,' he said. 'Come and see us again.'

He saw the Tarletons. He told them he liked their work,
looking at Mrs. Tarleton as if he could read her hand-
writing through the typescript. He told them kindly that
he was taking them from the picture and putting them on
another, where there was less pressure, more time. As he
had half expected, they begged to stay on the first picture,
seeing a quicker credit, even though it was shared with
others. The system was a shame, he admitted—gross, com-
mercial, to be deplored. He had originated it—a fact that he
did not mention.

When they had gone, Miss Doolan came in triumphant.

'Mr. Stahr, the lady with the belt is on the phone.'

Stahr walked into his office alone and sat down behind
his desk and picked up the phone with a great sinking of his
stomach. He did not know what he wanted. He had not
thought about the matter as he had thought about the matter
of Pete Zavras. At first he had only wanted to know if they
were 'professional' people, if the woman was an actress who
had got herself up to look like Minna, as he had once had a
young actress made up like Claudette Colbert and photographed her from the same angles.

'Hello,' he said.

'Hello.'

As he searched the short, rather surprised word for a
vibration of last night, the feeling of terror began to steal
over him, and he choked it off with an effort of will.

'Well—you were hard to find,' he said. '*Smith*—and you
moved here recently. That was all we had. And a silver
belt.'

'Oh, yes,' the voice said, still uneasy, unpoised, 'I had on a silver belt last night.'

Now, where from here?

'Who *are* you?' the voice said, with a touch of flurried bourgeois dignity.

'My name is Monroe Stahr,' he said.

A pause. It was a name that never appeared on the screen, and she seemed to have trouble placing it.

'Oh, yes—yes. You were the husband of Minna Davis.'

'Yes.'

Was it a trick? As the whole vision of last night came back to him—the very skin with that peculiar radiance as if phosphorus had touched it—he thought whether it might not be a trick to reach him from somewhere. Not Minna and yet Minna. The curtains blew suddenly into the room, the papers whispered on his desk, and his heart cringed faintly at the intense reality of the day outside his window. If he could go out now this way, what would happen if he saw her again—the starry veiled expression, the mouth strongly formed for poor brave human laughter.

'I'd like to see you. Would you like to come to the studio?'

Again the hesitancy—then a blank refusal.

'Oh, I don't think I ought to. I'm awfully sorry.'

This last was purely formal, a brush-off, a final axe. Ordinary skin-deep vanity came to Stahr's aid, adding persuasion to his urgency.

'I'd like to see you,' he said. 'There's a reason.'

'Well—I'm afraid that——'

'Could I come and see you?'

A pause again, not from hesitation, he felt, but to assemble her answer.

'There's something you don't know,' she said finally.

'Oh, you're probably married,' he was impatient. 'It has nothing to do with that. I asked you to come here openly, bring your husband if you have one.'

'It's—it's quite impossible.'

'Why?'

'I feel silly even talking to you, but your secretary

insisted—I thought I'd dropped something in the flood last night and you'd found it.'

'I want very much to see you for five minutes.'

'To put me in the movies?'

'That wasn't my idea.'

There was such a long pause that he thought he had offended her.

'Where could I meet you?' she asked unexpectedly.

'Here? At your house?'

'No—somewhere outside.'

Suddenly Stahr could think of no place. His own house —a restaurant. Where did people meet?—a house of assignation, a cocktail bar?

'I'll meet you somewhere at nine o'clock,' she said.

'That's impossible, I'm afraid.'

'Then never mind.'

'All right, then, nine o'clock, but can we make it near here? There's a drug-store on Wilshire——'

It was a quarter to six. There were two men outside who had come every day at this time only to be postponed. This was an hour of fatigue—the men's business was not so important that it must be seen to, nor so insignificant that it could be ignored. So he postponed it again and sat motionless at his desk for a moment, thinking about Russia. Not so much about Russia as about the picture about Russia which would consume a hopeless half hour presently. He knew there were many stories about Russia, not to mention The Story, and he had employed a squad of writers and research men for over a year, but all the stories involved had the wrong feel. He felt it could be told in terms of the American thirteen states, but it kept coming out different, in new terms that opened unpleasant possibilities and problems. He considered he was very fair to Russia—he had no desire to make anything but a sympathetic picture, but it kept turning into a headache.

'Mr. Stahr—Mr. Drummon's outside, and Mr. Kirstoff and Mrs. Cornhill, about the Russian picture.'

'All right—send them in.'

Afterwards from six-thirty to seven-thirty he watched the afternoon rushes. Except for his engagement with the girl, he would ordinarily have spent the early evening in the projection room or the dubbing room, but it had been a late night with the earthquake, and he decided to go to dinner. Coming in through his front office, he found Pete Zavras waiting, his arm in a sling.

'You are the Aeschylus and the Euripides of the moving picture,' said Zavras simply. 'Also the Aristophanes and the Menander.'

He bowed.

'Who are they?' asked Stahr smiling.

'They are my countrymen.'

'I didn't know you made pictures in Greece.'

'You're joking with me, Monroe,' said Zavras. 'I want to say you are as dandy a fellow as they come. You have saved me one hundred per cent.'

'You feel all right now?'

'My arm is nothing. It feels like someone kisses me there. It was worth doing what I did, if this is the outcome.'

'How did you happen to do it here?' Stahr asked curiously.

'Before the Delphic oracle,' said Zavras. 'The Oedipus who solved the riddle. I wish I had my hands on the son-of-a-bitch who started the story.'

'You make me sorry I didn't get an education,' said Stahr.

'It isn't worth a damn,' said Pete. 'I took my baccalaureate in Salonika and look how I ended up.'

'Not quite,' said Stahr.

'If you want anybody's throat cut anytime day or night,' said Zavras, 'my number is in the book.'

Stahr closed his eyes and opened them again. Zavras' silhouette had blurred a little against the sun. He hung on to the table behind him and said in an ordinary voice.

'Good luck, Pete.'

The room was almost black, but he made his feet move, following a pattern, into his office and waited till the door clicked shut before he felt for the pills. The water decanter

clattered against the table; the glass clacked. He sat down
in a big chair, waiting for the benzedrine to take effect before
he went to dinner.

As Stahr walked back from the commissary, a hand waved
at him from an open roadster. From the heads showing over
the back he recognized a young actor and his girl, and
watched them disappear through the gate, already part of
the summer twilight. Little by little he was losing the feel
of such things, until it seemed that Minna had taken their
poignancy with her; his apprehension of splendour was
fading so that presently the luxury of eternal mourning
would depart. A childish association of Minna with the
material heavens made him, when he reached his office,
order out his roadster for the first time this year. The big
limousine seemed heavy with remembered conferences or
exhausted sleep.

Leaving the studio, he was still tense, but the open car
pulled the summer evening up close, and he looked at it.
There was a moon down at the end of the boulevard, and
it was a good illusion that it was a different moon every
evening, every year. Other lights shone in Hollywood since
Minna's death: in the open markets lemons and grapefruit
and green apples slanted a misty glare into the street. Ahead
of him the stop-signal of a car winked violet and at another
crossing he watched it wink again. Everywhere floodlights
raked the sky. On an empty corner two mysterious men
moved a gleaming drum in pointless arcs over the
heavens.

In the drug-store a woman stood by the candy counter.
She was tall, almost as tall as Stahr, and embarrassed.
Obviously it was a situation for her, and if Stahr had not
looked as he did—most considerate and polite—she would
not have gone through with it. They said hello, and walked
out without another word, scarcely a glance—yet before
they reached the curb Stahr knew: this was just exactly a
pretty American woman and nothing more—no beauty like
Minna.

'Where are we going?' she asked. 'I thought there'd be a chauffeur. Never mind—I'm a good boxer.'

'Boxer?'

'That didn't sound very polite.' She forced a smile. 'But you people are supposed to be such *horrors*.'

The conception of himself as sinister amused Stahr— then suddenly it failed to amuse him.

'Why did you want to see me?' she asked as she got in.

He stood motionless, wanting to tell her to get out immediately. But she had relaxed in the car, and he knew the unfortunate situation was of his own making—he shut his teeth and walked around to get in. The street lamp fell full upon her face, and it was difficult to believe that this was the girl of last night. He saw no resemblance to Minna at all.

'I'll run you home,' he said. 'Where do you live?'

'Run me home?' She was startled. 'There's no hurry— I'm sorry if I offended you.'

'No. It was nice of you to come. I've been stupid. Last night I had an idea that you were an exact double for some-one I knew. It was dark and the light was in my eyes.'

She was offended—he had reproached her for not looking like someone else.

'It was just that!' she said. 'That's funny.'

They rode in silence for a minute.

'You were married to Minna Davis, weren't you?' she said with a flash of intuition. 'Excuse me for referring to it.'

He was driving as fast as he could without making it conspicuous.

'I'm quite a different type from Minna Davis,' she said, '—if that's who you meant. You might have referred to the girl who was with me. She looks more like Minna Davis than I do.'

That was of no interest now. The thing was to get this over quick and forget it.

'Could it have been her?' she asked. 'She lives next door.'

'Not possibly,' he said. 'I remember the silver belt you wore.'

'That was me all right.'

They were northwest of Sunset, climbing one of the canyons through the hills. Lighted bungalows rose along the winding road, and the electric current that animated them sweated into the evening air as radio sound.

'You see that last highest light—Kathleen lives there. I live just over the top of the hill.'

A moment later she said, 'Stop here.'

'I thought you said over the top.'

'I want to stop at Kathleen's.'

'I'm afraid I'm——'

'I want to get out here myself,' she said impatiently.

Stahr slid out after her. She started towards a new little house almost roofed over by a single willow tree, and automatically he followed her to the steps. She rang a bell and turned to say good night.

'I'm sorry you were disappointed,' she said.

He was sorry for her now—sorry for them both.

'It was my fault. Good night.'

A wedge of light came out the opening door, and as a girl's voice inquired, 'Who is it?' Stahr looked up.

There she was—face and form and smile against the light from inside. It was Minna's face—the skin with its peculiar radiance as if phosphorus had touched it, the mouth with its warm line that never counted costs—and over all the haunting jollity that had fascinated a generation.

With a leap his heart went out of him as it had the night before, only this time it stayed out there with a vast beneficence.

'Oh, Edna, you can't come in,' the girl said. 'I've been cleaning and the house is full of ammonia smell.'

Edna began to laugh, bold and loud. 'I believe it was you he wanted to see, Kathleen,' she said.

Stahr's eyes and Kathleen's met and tangled. For an instant they made love as no one ever dares to do after. Their glance was slower than an embrace, more urgent than a call.

'He telephoned me,' said Edna. 'It seems he thought ——'

8*

Stahr interrupted, stepping forward into the light.

'I was afraid we were rude at the studio, yesterday evening.'

But there were no words for what he really said. She listened closely without shame. Life flared high in them both —Edna seemed at a distance and in darkness.

'You weren't rude,' said Kathleen. A cool wind blew the brown curls around her forehead. 'We had no business there.'

'I hope you'll both,' Stahr said, 'come and make a tour of the studio.'

'Who are you? Somebody important?'

'He was Minna Davis's husband, he's a producer,' said Edna, as if it were a rare joke, '—and this isn't at all what he just told me. I think he has a crush on you.'

'Shut up, Edna,' said Kathleen sharply.

As if suddenly realizing her offensiveness, Edna said, 'Phone me, will you?' and stalked away towards the road. But she carried their secret with her—she had seen a spark pass between them in the darkness.

'I remember you,' Kathleen said to Stahr. 'You got us out of the flood.'

Now what? The other woman was more missed in her absence. They were alone and on too slim a basis for what had passed already. They existed nowhere. His world seemed far away—she had no world at all except the idol's head, the half open door.

'You're Irish,' he said, trying to build one for her.

She nodded.

'I've lived in London a long time—I didn't think you could tell.'

The wild green eyes of a bus sped up the road in the darkness. They were silent until it went by.

'Your friend Edna didn't like me,' he said. 'I think it was the word Producer.'

'She's just come out here, too. She's a silly creature who means no harm. *I* shouldn't be afraid of you.'

She searched his face. She thought, like everyone, that

he seemed tired—then she forgot it at the impression he gave of a brazier out of doors on a cool night.

'I suppose the girls are all after you to put them on the screen.'

'They've given up,' he said.

This was an understatement—they were all there, he knew, just over his threshold, but they had been there so long that their clamouring voices were no more than the sound of the traffic in the street. But his position remained more than royal: a king could make only one queen; Stahr, at least so they supposed, could make many.

'I'm thinking that it would turn you into a cynic,' she said. 'You didn't want to put me in the pictures?'

'No.'

'That's good. I'm no actress. Once in London a man came up to me in the Carlton and asked me to make a test, but I thought a while and finally I didn't go.'

They had been standing nearly motionless, as if in a moment he would leave and she would go in. Stahr laughed suddenly.

'I feel as if I had my foot in the door—like a collector.'

She laughed, too.

'I'm sorry I can't ask you in. Shall I get my reefer and sit outside?'

'No.' He scarcely knew why he felt it was time to go. He might see her again—he might not. It was just as well this way.

'You'll come to the studio?' he said. 'I can't promise to go around with you, but if you come, you must be sure to send word to my office.'

A frown, the shadow of a hair in breadth, appeared between her eyes.

'I'm not sure,' she said. 'But I'm very much obliged.'

He knew that, for some reason, she would not come—in an instant she had slipped away from him. They both sensed that the moment was played out. He must go, even though he went nowhere, and it left him with nothing.

Practically, vulgarly, he did not have her telephone number —or even her name; but it seemed impossible to ask for them now.

She walked with him to the car, her glowing beauty and her unexplored novelty pressing up against him; but there was a foot of moonlight between them when they came out of the shadow.

'Is this all?' he said spontaneously.

He saw regret in her face—but there was a flick of the lip, also, a bending of the smile towards some indirection, a momentary dropping and lifting of a curtain over a forbidden passage.

'I do hope we'll meet again,' she said almost formally.

'I'd be sorry if we didn't.'

They were distant for a moment. But as he turned his car in the next drive, and came back with her still waiting, and waved and drove on, he felt exalted and happy. He was glad that there was beauty in the world that would not be weighed in the scales of the casting department.

But at home he felt a curious loneliness as his butler made him tea in the samovar. It was the old hurt come back, heavy and delightful. When he took up the first of two scripts that were his evening stint, that presently he would visualize line by line on the screen, he waited a moment, thinking of Minna. He explained to her that it was really nothing, that no one could ever be like she was, that he was sorry.

That was substantially a day of Stahr's. I don't know about the illness, when it started, etc., because he was secretive, but I know he fainted a couple of times that month because Father told me. Prince Agge is my authority for the luncheon in the commissary where he told them he was going to make a picture that would lose money—which was something, considering the men he had to deal with and that he held a big block of stock and had a profit-sharing contract.

And Wylie White told me a lot, which I believed because

he felt Stahr intensely with a mixture of jealousy and admiration. As for me, I was head over heels in love with him then, and you can take what I say for what it's worth.

CHAPTER V

FRESH AS the morning, I went up to see him a week later. Or so I thought; when Wylie called for me, I had gotten into riding clothes to give the impression I'd been out in the dew since early morning.

'I'm going to throw myself under the wheel of Stahr's car, this morning,' I said.

'How about this car?' he suggested. 'It's one of the best cars Mort Fleishacker ever sold second-hand.'

'Not on your flowing veil,' I answered like a book. 'You have a wife in the East.'

'She's the past,' he said. 'You've got one great card, Celia—your valuation of yourself. Do you think anybody would look at you if you weren't Pat Brady's daughter?'

We don't take abuse like our mothers would have. Nothing —no remark from a contemporary means much. They tell you to be smart, they're marrying you for your money, or you tell them. Everything's simpler. Or is it? as we used to say.

But as I turned on the radio and the car raced up Laurel Canyon to *The Thundering Beat of My Heart*, I didn't believe he was right. I had good features except my face was too round, and a skin they seemed to love to touch, and good legs, and I didn't have to wear a brassiere. I haven't a sweet nature, but who was Wylie to reproach me for that?

'Don't you think I'm smart to go in the morning?' I asked.

'Yeah. To the busiest man in California. He'll appreciate it. Why didn't you wake him up at four?'

'That's just it. At night he's tired. He's been looking at

people all day, and some of them not bad. I come in in the morning and start a train of thought.'

'I don't like it. It's brazen.'

'What have you got to offer? And don't be rough.'

'I love you,' he said, without much conviction. 'I love you more than I love your money, and that's plenty. Maybe your father would make me a supervisor.'

'I could marry the last man tapped for Bones this year and live in Southampton.'

I turned the dial and got either *Gone* or *Lost*—there were good songs that year. The music was getting better again. When I was young during the depression, it wasn't so hot, and the best numbers were from the twenties, like Benny Goodman playing *Blue Heaven* or Paul Whiteman with *When Day Is Done*. There were only the bands to listen to. But now I liked almost everything except Father singing *Little Girl, You've Had a Busy Day* to try to create a sentimental father-and-daughter feeling.

Lost and *Gone* were the wrong mood, so I turned again and got *Lovely to Look At*, which was my kind of poetry. I looked back as we crossed the crest of the foothills—with the air so clear you could see the leaves on Sunset Mountain two miles away. It's startling to you sometimes—just air, unobstructed, uncomplicated air.

'*Lovely to look at—de-lightful to know-w,*' I sang.

'Are you going to sing for Stahr?' Wylie said. 'If you do, get in a line about my being a good supervisor.'

'Oh, this'll be only Stahr and me,' I said. 'He's going to look at me and think, "I've never really seen her before."'

'We don't use that line this year,' he said.

'—Then he'll say "Little Cecilia," like he did the night of the earthquake. He'll say he never noticed I have become a woman.'

'You won't have to do a thing.'

'I'll stand there and bloom. After he kisses me as you would a child——'

'That's all in my script,' complained Wylie, 'and I've got to show it to him to-morrow.'

'—he'll sit down and put his face in his hands and say he never thought of me like that.'

'You mean you get in a little fast work during the kiss?'

'I bloom, I told you. How often do I have to tell you I bloom.'

'It's beginning to sound pretty randy to me,' said Wylie. 'How about laying off—I've got to work this morning.'

'Then he says it seems as if he was always meant to be this way.'

'Right in the industry. Producer's blood.' He pretended to shiver. 'I'd hate to have a transfusion of that.'

'Then he says——'

'I know all his lines,' said Wylie. 'What I want to know is what you say.'

'Somebody comes in,' I went on.

'And you jump up quickly off the casting couch, smoothing your skirts.'

'Do you want me to walk out and get home?'

We were in Beverly Hills, getting very beautiful now with the tall Hawaiian pines. Hollywood is a perfectly zoned city, so you know exactly what kind of people economically live in each section, from executives and directors, through technicians in their bungalows, right down to extras. This was the executive section and a very fancy lot of pastry. It wasn't as romantic as the dingiest village of Virginia or New Hampshire, but it looked nice this morning.

'*They asked me how I knew*,' sang the radio, '*—my true love was true.*'

My heart was fire, and smoke was in my eyes and everything, but I figured my chance at about fifty-fifty. I would walk right up on him as if I was either going to walk through him or kiss him on the mouth—and stop a bare foot away and say 'Hello' with disarming understatement.

And I did—though of course it wasn't like I expected: Stahr's beautiful dark eyes looking back into mine, knowing, I am dead sure, everything I was thinking—and not a bit embarrassed. I stood there an hour, I think, without moving, and all he did was twitch the side of his mouth and put his hands in his pockets.

'Will you go with me to the ball to-night?' I asked.

'What ball?'

'The screen-writers' ball down at the Ambassador.'

'Oh, yes.' He considered. 'I can't go with you. I might just come in late. We've got a sneak preview in Glendale.'

How different it all was from what you'd planned. When he sat down, I went over and put my head among his telephones, like a sort of desk appendage, and looked at him; and his dark eyes looked back so kind and nothing. Men don't often know those times when a girl could be had for nothing. All I succeeded in putting into his head was:

'Why don't you get married, Celia?'

Maybe he'd bring up Robby again, try to make a match there.

'What could I do to interest an interesting man?' I asked him.

'Tell him you're in love with him.'

'Should I chase him?'

'Yes,' he said, smiling.

'I don't know. If it isn't there, it isn't there.'

'I'd marry you,' he said unexpectedly. 'I'm lonesome as hell. But I'm too old and tired to undertake anything.'

I went around the desk and stood beside him.

'Undertake me.'

He looked up in surprise, understanding for the first time that I was in deadly earnest.

'Oh, no,' he said. He looked almost miserable for a minute. 'Pictures are my girl. I haven't got much time——' He corrected himself quickly, 'I mean any time.'

'You couldn't love me.'

'It's not that,' he said and—right out of my dream but with a difference: 'I never thought of you that way, Celia. I've known you so long. Somebody told me you were going to marry Wylie White.'

'And you had—no reaction.'

'Yes, I did. I was going to speak to you about it. Wait till he's been sober for two years.'

'I'm not even considering it, Monroe.'

We were way off the track, and just as in my day-dream, somebody came in—only I was quite sure Stahr had pressed a concealed button.

I'll always think of that moment, when I felt Miss Doolan behind me with her pad, as the end of childhood, the end of the time when you cut out pictures. What I was looking at wasn't Stahr but a picture of him I cut out over and over: the eyes that flashed a sophisticated understanding at you and then darted up too soon into his wide brow with its ten thousand plots and plans; the face that was ageing from within, so that there were no casual furrows of worry and vexation but a drawn asceticism as if from a silent self-set struggle—or a long illness. It was handsomer to me than all the rosy tan from Coronado to Del Monte. He was my picture, as sure as if he had been pasted on the inside of my old locker in school. That's what I told Wylie White, and when a girl tells the man she likes second best about the other one—then she's in love.

I noticed the girl long before Stahr arrived at the dance. Not a pretty girl, for there are none of those in Los Angeles —one girl can be pretty, but a dozen are only a chorus. Nor yet a professional beauty—they do all the breathing for everyone, and finally even the men have to go outside for air. Just a girl, with the skin of one of Raphael's corner angels and a style that made you look back twice to see if it were something she had on.

I noticed her and forgot her. She was sitting back behind the pillars at a table whose ornament was a faded semi-star, who, in hopes of being noticed and getting a bit, rose and danced regularly with some scarecrow males. It reminded me shamefully of my first party, where mother made me dance over and over with the same boy to keep in the spotlight. The semi-star spoke to several people at our table, but we were busy being Café Society and she got nowhere at all.

From our angle it appeared that they all wanted something.

'You're expected to fling it around,' said Wylie, '—like in the old days. When they find out you're hanging on to it, they get discouraged. That's what all this brave gloom is about—the only way to keep their self-respect is to be Hemingway characters. But underneath they hate you in a mournful way, and you know it.'

He was right—I knew that since 1933 the rich could only be happy alone together.

I saw Stahr come into the half-light at the top of the wide steps and stand there with his hands in his pockets, looking around. It was late and the lights seemed to have burned a little lower, though they were the same. The floor show was finished, except for a man who still wore a placard which said that at midnight in the Hollywood Bowl Sonja Henie was going to skate on hot soup. You could see the sign as he danced becoming less funny on his back. A few years before there would have been drunks around. The faded actress seemed to be looking for them hopefully over her partner's shoulder. I followed her with my eyes when she went back to her table——

——and there, to my surprise, was Stahr talking to the other girl. They were smiling at each other as if this was the beginning of the world.

Stahr had expected nothing like this when he stood at the head of the steps a few minutes earlier. The 'sneak preview' had disappointed him, and afterwards he had had a scene with Jacques La Borwitz right in front of the theatre, for which he was now sorry. He had started towards the Brady party when he saw Kathleen sitting in the middle of a long white table alone.

Immediately things changed. As he walked towards her, the people shrank back against the walls till they were only murals; the white table lengthened and became an altar where the priestess sat alone. Vitality welled up in him, and he could have stood a long time across the table from her, looking and smiling

The incumbents of the table were crawling back—Stahr and Kathleen danced.

When she came close, his several visions of her blurred; she was momentarily unreal. Usually a girl's skull made her real, but not this time—Stahr continued to be dazzled as they danced out along the floor—to the last edge, where they stepped through a mirror into another dance with new dancers whose faces were familiar but nothing more. In this new region he talked, fast and urgently.

'What's your name?'

'Kathleen Moore.'

'Kathleen Moore,' he repeated.

'I have no telephone, if that's what you're thinking.'

'When will you come to the studio?'

'It's not possible. Truly.'

'Why isn't it? Are you married?'

'No.'

'You're not married?'

'No, nor never have been. But then I may be.'

'Someone there at the table.'

'No.' She laughed. 'What curiosity!'

But she was deep in it with him, no matter what the words were. Her eyes invited him to a romantic communion of unbelievable intensity. As if she realized this, she said, frightened:

'I must go back now. I promised this dance.'

'I don't want to lose you. Couldn't we have lunch or dinner?'

'It's impossible.' But her expression helplessly amended the words to, 'It's just possible. The door is still open by a chink, if you could squeeze past. But quickly—so little time.'

'I must go back,' she repeated aloud. Then she dropped her arms, stopped dancing, and looked at him, a laughing wanton.

'When I'm with you, I don't breathe quite right,' she said.

She turned, picked up her long dress, and stepped back

through the mirror. Stahr followed until she stopped near her table.

'Thank you for the dance,' she said, 'and now really, good night.'

Then she nearly ran.

Stahr went to the table where he was expected and sat down with the Café Society group—from Wall Street, Grand Street, Loudon County, Virginia, and Odessa, Russia. They were all talking with enthusiasm about a horse that had run very fast, and Mr. Marcus was the most enthusiastic of all. Stahr guessed that the Jews had taken over the worship of horses as a symbol—for years it had been the Cossacks mounted and the Jews on foot. Now the Jews had horses, and it gave them a sense of extraordinary well-being and power. Stahr sat pretending to listen and even nodding when something was referred to him, but all the time watching the table behind the pillars. If everything had not happened as it had, even to his connecting the silver belt with the wrong girl, he might have thought it was some elaborate frame-up. But the elusiveness was beyond suspicion. For there in a moment he saw that she was escaping again—the pantomime at the table indicated good-bye. She was leaving, she was gone.

'There,' said Wylie White with malice, 'goes Cinderella. Simply bring the slipper to the Regal Shoe Company, 812 South Broadway.'

Stahr overtook her in the long upper lobby, where middle-aged women sat behind a roped-off space, watching the ballroom entrance.

'Am I responsible for this?' he asked.

'I was going anyhow.' But she added almost resentfully, 'They talked as if I'd been dancing with the Prince of Wales. They all stared at me. One of the men wanted to draw my picture, and another one wanted to see me to-morrow.'

'That's just what I want,' said Stahr gently, 'but I want to see you much more than he does.'

'You insist so,' she said wearily. 'One reason I left

England was that men always wanted their own way. I thought it was different here. Isn't it enough that I don't want to see you?'

'Ordinarily,' agreed Stahr. 'Please believe me, I'm way out of my depth already. I feel like a fool. But I must see you again and talk to you.'

She hesitated.

'There's no reason for feeling like a fool,' she said. 'You're too good a man to feel like a fool. But you should see this for what it is.'

'What is it?'

'You've fallen for me—completely. You've got me in your dreams.'

'I'd forgotten you,' he declared, '—till the moment I walked in that door.'

'Forgotten me with your head perhaps. But I knew the first time I saw you that you were the kind that likes me——'

She stopped herself. Near them a man and woman from the party were saying good-bye: 'Tell her hello—tell her I love her dearly,' said the woman, '—you both—all of you —the children.' Stahr could not talk like that, the way everyone talked now. He could think of nothing further to say as they walked towards the elevator except:

'I suppose you're perfectly right.'

'Oh, you admit it?'

'No, I don't,' he retracted. 'It's just the whole way you're made. What you say—how you walk—the way you look right this minute—' He saw she had melted a little, and his hopes rose. 'To-morrow is Sunday, and usually I work on Sunday, but if there's anything you're curious about in Hollywood, any person you want to meet or see, please let me arrange it.'

They were standing by the elevator. It opened, but she let it go.

'You're very modest,' she said. 'You always talk about showing me the studio and taking me around. Don't you ever stay alone?'

'To-morrow I'll feel very much alone.'

'Oh, the poor man—I could weep for him. He could have all the stars jumping around him and he chooses me.'

He smiled—he had laid himself open to that one.

The elevator came again. She signalled for it to wait.

'I'm a weak woman,' she said. 'If I meet you to-morrow, will you leave me in peace? No, you won't. You'll make it worse. It wouldn't do any good but harm, so I'll say no and thank you.'

She got into the elevator. Stahr got in too, and they smiled as they dropped two floors to the hall, cross-sectioned with small shops. Down at the end, held back by police, was the crowd, their heads and shoulders leaning forward to look down the alley. Kathleen shivered.

'They looked so strange when I came in,' she said, '—as if they were furious at me for not being someone famous.'

'I know another way out,' said Stahr.

They went through a drug-store, down an alley, and came out into the clear cool California night beside the car park. He felt detached from the dance now, and she did, too.

'A lot of picture people used to live down here,' he said. 'John Barrymore and Pola Negri in those bungalows. And Connie Talmadge lived in that tall thin apartment house over the way.'

'Doesn't anybody live here now?'

'The studios moved out into the country,' he said, '—what used to be the country. I had some good times around here, though.'

He did not mention that ten years ago Minna and her mother had lived in another apartment over the way.

'How old are you?' she asked suddenly.

'I've lost track—almost thirty-five, I think.'

'They said at the table you were the boy wonder.'

'I'll be that when I'm sixty,' he said grimly. 'You will meet me to-morrow, won't you?'

'I'll meet you,' she said. 'Where?'

Suddenly there was no place to meet. She would not go

to a party at anyone's house, nor to the country, nor swimming, though she hesitated, nor to a well-known restaurant.
She seemed hard to please, but he knew there was some
reason. He would find out in time. It occurred to him
that she might be the sister or daughter of someone
well-known who was pledged to keep in the background.
He suggested that he come for her and they could
decide.

'That wouldn't do,' she said. 'What about right here?
—the same spot.'

He nodded—pointing up at the arch under which they
stood.

He put her into her car, which would have brought
eighty dollars from any kindly dealer, and watched it rasp
away. Down by the entrance a cheer went up as a favourite
emerged, and Stahr wondered whether to show himself and
say good night.

This is Cecilia taking up the narrative in person. Stahr
came back finally—it was about half past three—and asked
me to dance.

'How are you?' he asked me, just as if he hadn't seen me
that morning. 'I got involved in a long conversation with a
man.'

It was secret, too—he cared that much about it.

'I took him for a drive,' he went on innocently. 'I didn't
realize how much this part of Hollywood had changed.'

'Has it changed?'

'Oh, yes,' he said, '—changed completely. Unrecogniz-
able. I couldn't tell you exactly, but it's all changed—everything. It's like a new city.' After a moment he amplified:
'I had no idea how much it had changed.'

'Who was the man?' I ventured.

'An old friend,' he said vaguely, '—someone I knew a
long time ago.'

I had made Wylie try to find out quietly who she was.
He had gone over and the ex-star had asked him excitedly
to sit down. No: she didn't know who the girl was—a friend

of a friend of someone—even the man who had brought her didn't know.

So Stahr and I danced to the beautiful music of Glen Miller playing *I'm on a See-Saw*. It was good dancing now, with plenty of room. But it was lonely—lonelier than before the girl had gone. For me, as well as for Stahr, she took the evening with her, took along the stabbing pain I had felt —left the great ballroom empty and without emotion. Now it was nothing, and I was dancing with an absent-minded man who told me how much Los Angeles had changed.

They met, next afternoon, as strangers in an unfamiliar country. Last night was gone, the girl he had danced with was gone. A misty rose-and-blue hat with a trifling veil came along the terrace to him, and paused, searching his face. Stahr was strange, too, in a brown suit and a black tie that blocked him out more tangibly than a formal dinner coat, or when he was simply a face and voice in the darkness the night they had first met.

He was the first to be sure it was the same person as before: the upper half of the face that was Minna's, luminous, with creamy temples and opalescent brown—the cool-coloured curly hair. He could have put his arm around her and pulled her close with an almost family familiarity —already he knew the down on her neck, the very set of her backbone, the corners of her eyes, and how she breathed— the very texture of the clothes that she would wear.

'Did you wait here all night,' she said, in a voice that was like a whisper.

'I didn't move—didn't stir.'

Still a problem remained, the same one—there was no special place to go.

'I'd like tea,' she suggested, '—if it's some place you're not known.'

'That sounds as if one of us had a bad reputation.'

'Doesn't it?' she laughed.

'We'll go to the shore,' Stahr suggested. 'There's a place there where I got out once and was chased by a trained seal.'

'Do you think the seal could make tea?'

'Well—he's trained. And I don't think he'll talk—I don't think his training got that far. What in *hell* are you trying to hide?'

After a moment she said lightly: 'Perhaps the future,' in a way that might mean anything or nothing at all.

As they drove away, she pointed at her jalopy in the parking lot.

'Do you think it's safe?'

'I doubt it. I noticed some black-bearded foreigners snooping around.'

Kathleen looked at him alarmed.

'Really?' She saw he was smiling. 'I believe everything you say,' she said. 'You've got such a gentle way about you that I don't see why they're all so afraid of you.' She examined him with approval—fretting a little about his pallor, which was accentuated by the bright afternoon. 'Do you work very hard? Do you really always work on Sundays?'

He responded to her interest—impersonal yet not perfunctory.

'Not always. Once we had—we had a house with a pool and all—and people came on Sunday. I played tennis and swam. I don't swim any more.'

'Why not? It's good for you. I thought all Americans swam.'

'My legs got very thin—a few years ago, and it embarrassed me. There were other things I used to do—lots of things: I used to play handball when I was a kid, and sometimes out here—I had a court that was washed away in a storm.'

'You have a good build,' she said in formal compliment, meaning only that he was made with thin grace.

He rejected this with a shake of his head.

'I enjoy working most,' he said. 'My work is very congenial.'

'Did you always want to be in movies?'

'No. When I was young I wanted to be a chief clerk—the one who knew where everything was.'

She smiled.

'That's odd. And now you're much more than that.'

'No, I'm still a chief clerk,' Stahr said. 'That's my gift, if I have one. Only when I got to be it, I found out that no one knew where anything was. And I found out that you had to know why it was where it was, and whether it should be left there. They began throwing it all at me, and it was a very complex office. Pretty soon I had all the keys. And they wouldn't have remembered what locks they fitted if I'd given them back.'

They stopped for a red light, and a newsboy bleated at him: 'Mickey Mouse Murdered! Randolph Hearst declares war on China!'

'We'll have to buy this paper,' she said.

As they drove on, she straightened her hat and preened herself. Seeing him looking at her, she smiled.

She was alert and calm—qualities that were currently at a premium. There was lassitude in plenty—California was filling up with weary desperadoes. And there were tense young men and women who lived back East in spirit while they carried on a losing battle against the climate. But it was everyone's secret that sustained effort was difficult here —a secret that Stahr scarcely admitted to himself. But he knew that people from other places spurted a pure rill of new energy for a while.

They were very friendly now. She had not made a move or a gesture that was out of keeping with her beauty, that pressed it out of its contour one way or another. It was all proper to itself. He judged her as he would a shot in a picture. She was not trash, she was not confused but clear —in his special meaning of the word, which implied balance, delicacy and proportion, she was 'nice.'

They reached Santa Monica, where there were the stately houses of a dozen picture stars, penned in the middle of a crawling Coney Island. They turned down hill into the wide blue sky and sea and went on along the sea till the beach slid out again from under the bathers in a widening and narrowing yellow strand.

'I'm building a house out here,' Stahr said, '—much further on. I don't know why I'm building it.'

'Perhaps it's for me,' she said.

'Maybe it is.'

'I think it's splendid for you to build a big house for me without even knowing what I looked like.'

'It isn't too big. And it hasn't any roof. I didn't know what kind of roof you wanted.'

'We don't want a roof. They told me it never rained here. It——'

She stopped so suddenly that he knew she was reminded of something.

'Just something that's past,' she said.

'What was it?' he demanded, '—another house without a roof?'

'Yes. Another house without a roof.'

'Were you happy there?'

'I lived with a man,' she said, 'a long, long time—too long. It was one of those awful mistakes people make. I lived with him a long time after I wanted to get out, but he couldn't let me go. He'd try, but he couldn't. So finally I ran away.'

He was listening, weighing but not judging. Nothing changed under the rose and blue hat. She was twenty-five or so. It would have been a waste if she had not loved and been loved.

'We were too close,' she said. 'We should probably have had children—to stand between us. But you can't have children when there's no roof to the house.'

All right, he knew something of her. It would not be like last night when something kept saying, as in a story conference: 'We know nothing about the girl. We don't have to know much—but we have to know something.' A vague background spread behind her, something more tangible than the head of Siva in the moonlight.

They came to the restaurant, forbidding with many Sunday automobiles. When they got out, the trained seal growled reminiscently at Stahr. The man who owned it said that the seal would never ride in the back seat of his car but always climbed over the back and up in front. It was plain that the man was in bondage to the seal, though he had not yet acknowledged it to himself.

'I'd like to see the house you're building,' said Kathleen. 'I don't want tea—tea is the past.'

Kathleen drank a coke instead and they drove on ten miles into a sun so bright that he took out two pairs of cheaters from a compartment. Five miles further on they turned down a small promontory and came to the fuselage of Stahr's house.

A headwind blowing out of the sun threw spray up the rocks and over the car. Concrete mixer, raw yellow wood and builders' rubble waited, an open wound in the seascape for Sunday to be over. They walked around front, where great boulders rose to what would be the terrace.

She looked at the feeble hills behind and winced faintly at the barren glitter, and Stahr saw—

'No use looking for what's not here,' he said cheerfully. 'Think of it as if you were standing on one of those globes with a map on it—I always wanted one when I was a boy.'

'I understand,' she said after a minute. 'When you do that, you can feel the earth turn, can't you?'

He nodded.

'Yes. Otherwise it's all just *mañana*—waiting for the morning or the moon.'

They went in under the scaffolding. One room, which was to be the chief salon, was completed even to the built-in book shelves and the curtain rods and the trap in the floor for the motion picture projection machine. And to her surprise, this opened out to a porch with cushioned chairs in place and a ping-pong table. There was another ping-pong table on the newly laid sod beyond.

'Last week I gave a premature luncheon,' he admitted, 'I had some props brought out—some grass and things. I wanted to see how the place felt.'

She laughed suddenly.

'Isn't that real grass?'

'Oh yes—it's grass.'

Beyond the strip of anticipatory lawn was the excavation for a swimming pool, patronized now by a crowd of seagulls, which saw them and took flight.

'Are you going to live here all alone?' she asked him, '—not even dancing girls?'

'Probably. I used to make plans, but not any more. I thought this would be a nice place to read scripts. The studio is really home.'

'That's what I've heard about American business men.'

He caught a tilt of criticism in her voice.

'You do what you're born to do,' he said gently. 'About once a month somebody tries to reform me, tells me what a barren old age I'll have when I can't work any more. But it's not so simple.'

The wind was rising. It was time to go, and he had his car keys out of his pocket, absent-mindedly jingling them in his hand. There was the silvery 'hey!' of a telephone, coming from somewhere across the sunshine.

It was not from the house, and they hurried here and there around the garden, like children playing warmer and colder—closing in finally on a tool shack by the tennis court. The phone, irked with delay, barked at them suspiciously from the wall. Stahr hesitated.

'Shall I let the damn thing ring?'

'I couldn't. Unless I was sure who it was.'

'Either it's for somebody else or they've made a wild guess.'

He picked up the receiver.

'Hello . . . Long distance from where? Yes, this is Mr. Stahr.'

His manner changed perceptibly. She saw what few people had seen for a decade: Stahr impressed. It was not discordant, because he often pretended to be impressed, but it made him momentarily a little younger.

'It's the President,' he said to her, almost stiffly.

'Of your company?'

'No, of the United States.'

He was trying to be casual for her benefit, but his voice was eager.

'All right, I'll wait,' he said into the phone, and then to Kathleen: 'I've talked to him before.'

She watched. He smiled at her and winked, as an evidence that while he must give this his best attention, he had not forgotten her.

'Hello,' he said presently. He listened. Then he said, 'Hello' again. He frowned.

'Can you talk a little louder,' he said politely, and then: 'Who? . . . What's that?'

She saw a disgusted look come into his face.

'I don't want to talk to him,' he said. 'No!'

He turned to Kathleen:

'Believe it or not, it's an orang-outang.'

He waited while something was explained to him at length; then he repeated:

'I don't want to talk to it, Lew. I haven't got anything to say that would interest an orang-outang.'

He beckoned to Kathleen, and when she came close to the phone, he held the receiver so that she heard odd breathing and a gruff growl. Then a voice:

'This is no phoney, Monroe. It can talk and it's a dead ringer for McKinley. Mr. Horace Wickersham is with me here with a picture of McKinley in his hand——'

Stahr listened patiently.

'We've got a chimp,' he said, after a minute. 'He bit a chunk out of John Gilbert last year. . . . All right, put him on again.'

He spoke formally as if to a child.

'Hello, orang-outang.'

His face changed, and he turned to Kathleen.

'He said "Hello."'

'Ask him his name,' suggested Kathleen.

'Hello, orang-outang—God, what a thing to be!—Do you know your name? . . . He doesn't seem to know his name. . . . Listen, Lew. We're not making anything like

King Kong, and there is no monkey in *The Hairy Ape*. . . .
Of course I'm sure. I'm sorry, Lew, good-bye.'

He was annoyed with Lew because he had thought it
was the President and had changed his manner, acting as if
it were. He felt a little ridiculous, but Kathleen felt sorry
and liked him better because it had been an orang-outang.

They started back along the shore with the sun behind
them. The house seemed kindlier when they left it, as if
warmed by their visit—the hard glitter of the place was more
endurable if they were not bound there like people on the
shiny surface of a moon. Looking back from a curve of the
shore, they saw the sky growing pink behind the indecisive
structure, and the point of land seemed a friendly island,
not without promise of fine hours on a further day.

Past Malibu with its gaudy shacks and fishing barges
they came into the range of human kind again, the cars
stacked and piled along the road, the beaches like ant hills
without a pattern, save for the dark drowned heads that
sprinkled the sea.

Goods from the city were increasing in sight—blankets,
matting, umbrellas, cookstoves, reticules full of clothing—
the prisoners had laid out their shackles beside them on
this sand. It was Stahr's sea if he wanted it, or knew what
to do with it—only by sufferance did these others wet
their feet and fingers in the wild cool reservoirs of man's
world.

Stahr turned off the road by the sea and up a canyon and
along a hill road, and the people dropped away. The hill
became the outskirts of the city. Stopping for gasoline, he
stood beside the car.

'We could have dinner,' he said almost anxiously.

'You have work you could do.'

'No—I haven't planned anything. Couldn't we have
dinner?'

He knew that she had nothing to do either—no planned
evening or special place to go.

She compromised.

'Do you want to get something in that drug-store across the street?'

He looked at it tentatively.

'Is that really what you want?'

'I like to eat in American drug-stores. It seems so queer and strange.'

They sat on high stools and had tomato broth and hot sandwiches. It was more intimate than anything they had done, and they both felt a dangerous sort of loneliness, and felt it in each other. They shared in varied scents of the drug-store, bitter and sweet and sour, and the mystery of the waitress, with only the outer part of her hair dyed and black beneath, and, when it was over, the still life of their empty plates—a sliver of potato, a sliced pickle and an olive stone.

It was dusk in the street, it seemed nothing to smile at him now when they got into the car.

'Thank you so much. It's been a nice afternoon.'

It was not far from her house. They felt the beginning of the hill, and the louder sound of the car in second was the beginning of the end. Lights were on in the climbing bungalows—he turned on the headlights of the car. Stahr felt heavy in the pit of his stomach.

'We'll go out again.'

'No,' she said quickly, as if she had been expecting this. 'I'll write you a letter. I'm sorry I've been so mysterious— it was really a compliment because I like you so much. You should try not to work so hard. You ought to marry again.'

'Oh, that isn't what you should say,' he broke out protestingly. 'This has been you and me to-day. It may have meant nothing to you—it meant a lot to me. I'd like time to tell you about it.'

But if he were to take time it must be in her house, for they were there and she was shaking her head as the car drew up to the door.

'I must go now. I do have an engagement. I didn't tell you.'

'That's not true. But it's all right.'

He walked to the door with her and stood in his own foot-steps of that other night, while she felt in her bag for the key.

'Have you got it?'

'I've got it,' she said.

That was the moment to go in, but she wanted to see him once more and she leaned her head to the left, then to the right, trying to catch his face against the last twilight. She leaned too far and too long, and it was natural when his hand touched the back of her upper arm and shoulder and pressed her forward into the darkness of his throat. She shut her eyes, feeling the bevel of the key in her tight-clutched hand. She said 'Oh' in an expiring sigh, and then 'Oh' again, as he pulled her in close and his chin pushed her cheek around gently. They were both smiling just faintly, and she was frowning, too, as the inch between them melted into darkness.

When they were apart, she shook her head still, but more in wonder than in denial. It came like this then, it was your own fault, now far back, when was the moment? It came like this, and every instant the burden of tearing herself away from them together, from it, was heavier and more unimaginable. He was exultant; she resented and could not blame him, but she would not be part of his exultation, for it was a defeat. So far it was a defeat. And then she thought that if she stopped it being a defeat, broke off and went inside, it was still not a victory. Then it was just nothing.

'This was not my idea,' she said, 'not at all my idea.'

'Can I come in?'

'Oh, no—no.'

'Then let's jump in the car and drive somewhere.'

With relief, she caught at the exact phrasing—to get away from here immediately, that was accomplishment or sounded like it—as if she were fleeing from the spot of a crime. Then they were in the car, going down hill with the breeze cool in their faces, and she came slowly to herself. Now it was all clear in black and white.

'We'll go back to your house on the beach,' she said.

9—S.F.

'Back there?'

'Yes—we'll go back to your house. Don't let's talk. I just want to ride.'

When they got to the coast again the sky was grey, and at Santa Monica a sudden gust of rain bounced over them. Stahr halted beside the road, put on a raincoat, and lifted the canvas top. 'We've got a roof,' he said.

The windshield wiper ticked domestically as a grandfather's clock. Sullen cars were leaving the wet beaches and starting back into the city. Further on they ran into fog—the road lost its boundaries on either side, and the lights of cars coming towards them were stationary until just before they flared past.

They had left a part of themselves behind, and they felt light and free in the car. Fog fizzed in at a chink, and Kathleen took off the rose-and-blue hat in a calm, slow way that made him watch tensely, and put it under a strip of canvas in the back seat. She shook out her hair and, when she saw that Stahr was looking at her, she smiled.

The trained seal's restaurant was only a sheen of light off towards the ocean. Stahr cranked down a window and looked for landmarks, but after a few more miles the fog fell away, and just ahead of them the road turned off that led to his house. Out here a moon showed behind the clouds. There was still a shifting light over the sea.

The house had dissolved a little back into its elements. They found the dripping beams of a doorway and groped over mysterious waist-high obstacles to the single finished room, odorous of sawdust and wet wood. When he took her in his arms, they could just see each other's eyes in the half darkness. Presently his raincoat dropped to the floor.

'Wait,' she said.

She needed a minute. She did not see how any good could come from this, and though this did not prevent her from being happy and desirous, she needed a minute to think how it was, to go back an hour and know how it had happened. She waited in his arms, moving her head a little from side to side as she had before, only more slowly, and never taking her eyes from his. Then she discovered that he was trembling.

He discovered it at the same time, and his arms relaxed. Immediately she spoke to him coarsely and provocatively, and pulled his face down to hers. Then, with her knees she struggled out of something, still standing up and holding him with one arm, and kicked it off beside the coat. He was not trembling now and he held her again, as they knelt down together and slid to the raincoat on the floor.

Afterwards they lay without speaking, and then he was full of such tender love for her that he held her tight till a stitch tore in her dress. The small sound brought them to reality.

'I'll help you up,' he said, taking her hands.

'Not just yet. I was thinking of something.'

She lay in the darkness, thinking irrationally that it would be such a bright indefatigable baby, but presently she let him help her up. . . . When she came back into the room, it was lit from a single electric fixture.

'A one-bulb lighting system,' he said. 'Shall I turn it off?'

'No. It's very nice. I want to see you.'

They sat in the wooden frame of the window seat, with the soles of their shoes touching.

'You seem far away,' she said.

'So do you.'

'Are you surprised?'

'At what?' . .

'That we're two people again. Don't you always think— hope that you'll be one person, and then find you're still two?'

'I feel very close to you.'

'So do I to you,' she said.

'Thank you.'

'Thank *you*.'

They laughed.

'Is this what you wanted?' she asked. 'I mean last night.'

'Not consciously.'

'I wonder when it was settled,' she brooded. 'There's a moment when you needn't, and then there's another moment when you know nothing in the world could keep it from happening.'

This had an experienced ring, and to his surprise he liked her even more. In his mood, which was passionately to repeat yet not recapitulate the past, it was right that it should be that way.

'I *am* rather a trollop,' she said, following his thoughts. 'I suppose that's why I didn't get on to Edna.'

'Who is Edna?'

'The girl you thought was me. The one you phoned to —who lived across the road. She's moved to Santa Barbara.'

'You mean she was a tart?'

'So it seems. She went to what you call call-houses.'

'That's funny.'

'If she had been English, I'd have known right away. But she seemed like everyone else. She only told me just before she went away.'

He saw her shiver and got up, putting the raincoat around her shoulders. He opened a closet and a pile of pillows and beach mattresses fell out on the floor. There was a box of candles, and he lit them around the room, attaching the electric heater where the bulb had been.

'Why was Edna afraid of me?' he asked suddenly.

'Because you were a producer. She had some awful experience or a friend of hers did. Also, I think she was extremely stupid.'

'How did you happen to know her?'

'She came over. Maybe she thought I was a fallen sister. She seemed quite pleasant. She said "Call me Edna" all the time—"Please call me Edna," so finally I called her Edna and we were friends.'

She got off the window seat so he could lay pillows along it and behind her.

'What can I do?' she said. 'I'm a parasite.'

'No, you're not.' He put his arms around her. 'Be still. Get warm.'

They sat for a while quiet.

'I know why you liked me at first,' she said. 'Edna told me.'

'What did she tell you?'

'That I looked like—Minna Davis. Several people have told me that.'

He leaned away from her and nodded.

'It's here,' she said, putting her hands on her cheek-bones and distorting her cheeks slightly. 'Here and here.'

'Yes,' said Stahr. 'It was very strange. You look more like she actually *looked* than how she was on the screen.'

She got up, changing the subject with her gesture as if she were afraid of it.

'I'm warm now,' she said. She went to the closet and peered in, came back wearing a little apron with a crystalline pattern like a snowfall. She stared around critically.

'Of course we've just moved in,' she said, '—and there's a sort of echo.'

She opened the door of the veranda and pulled in two wicker chairs, drying them off. He watched her move, intently, yet half afraid that her body would fail somewhere and break the spell. He had watched women in screen tests and seen their beauty vanish second by second, as if a lovely statue had begun to walk with the meagre joints of a paper doll. But Kathleen was ruggedly set on the balls of her feet —the fragility was, as it should be, an illusion.

'It's stopped raining,' she said. 'It rained the day I came. Such an awful rain—so loud—like horses weeing.'

He laughed.

'You'll like it. Especially if you've got to stay here. Are you going to stay here? Can't you tell me now? What's the mystery?'

She shook her head.

'Not now—it's not worth telling.'

'Come here then.'

She came over and stood near him, and he pressed his cheek against the cool fabric of the apron.

'You're a tired man,' she said, putting her hand in his hair.

'Not that way.'

'I didn't mean that way,' she said hastily. 'I meant you'll work yourself sick.'

'Don't be a mother,' he said.

'All right. What shall I be?'

Be a trollop, he thought. He wanted the pattern of his life broken. If he was going to die soon, like the two doctors said, he wanted to stop being Stahr for a while and hunt for love like men who had no gifts to give, like young nameless men who looked along the streets in the dark.

'You've taken off my apron,' she said gently.

'Yes.'

'Would anyone be passing along the beach? Shall we put out the candles?'

'No, don't put out the candles.'

Afterwards she lay half on a white cushion and smiled up at him.

'I feel like Venus on the half shell,' she said.

'What made you think of that?'

'Look at me—isn't it Botticelli?'

'I don't know,' he said smiling. 'It is if you say so.'

She yawned.

'I've had such a good time. And I'm very fond of you.'

'You know a lot, don't you?'

'What do you mean?'

'Oh, from little things you've said. Or perhaps the way you say them.'

She deliberated.

'Not much,' she said. 'I never went to a university, if that's what you mean. But the man I told you about knew everything and he had a passion for educating me. He made out schedules and made me take courses at the Sorbonne and go to museums. I picked up a little.'

'What was he?'

'He was a painter of sorts and a hell-cat. And a lot besides. He wanted me to read Spengler—everything was for that. All the history and philosophy and harmony was all so I could read Spengler, and then I left him before we got to

Spengler. At the end I think that was the chief reason he didn't want me to go.'

'Who was Spengler?'

'I tell you we didn't get to him,' she laughed, 'and now I'm forgetting everything very patiently, because it isn't likely I'll ever meet anyone like him again.'

'Oh, but you shouldn't forget,' said Stahr, shocked. He had an intense respect for learning, a racial memory of the old *schules*. 'You shouldn't forget.'

'It was just in place of babies.'

'You could teach your babies,' he said.

'Could I?'

'Sure you could. You could give it to them while they were young. When I want to know anything, I've got to ask some drunken writer. Don't throw it away.'

'All right,' she said, getting up. 'I'll tell it to my children. But it's so endless—the more you know, the more there is just beyond, and it keeps on coming. This man could have been anything if he hadn't been a coward and a fool.'

'But you were in love with him.'

'Oh, yes—with all my heart.' She looked through the window, shading her eyes. 'It's light out there. Let's go down to the beach.'

He jumped up, exclaiming:

'Why, I think it's the grunion!'

'What?'

'It's to-night. It's in all the papers.' He hurried out the door, and she heard him open the door of the car. Presently he returned with a newspaper.

'It's at ten-sixteen. That's five minutes.'

'An eclipse or something?'

'Very punctual fish,' he said. 'Leave your shoes and stockings and come with me.'

It was a fine blue night. The tide was at the turn, and the little silver fish rocked off shore waiting for 10.16. A few seconds after the time they came swarming in with the tide, and Stahr and Kathleen stepped over them barefoot as they flicked slip-slop on the sand. A negro man came along the

shore towards them, collecting the grunion quickly, like
twigs, into two pails. They came in twos and threes and
platoons and companies, relentless and exalted and scornful, round the great bare feet of the intruders, as they had
come before Sir Francis Drake had nailed his plaque to the
boulder on the shore.

'I wish for another pail,' the negro man said, resting a
moment.

'You've come a long way out,' said Stahr.

'I used to go to Malibu, but they don't like it, those
moving picture people.'

A wave came in and forced them back, receded swiftly,
leaving the sand alive again.

'Is it worth the trip?' Stahr asked.

'I don't figure it that way. I really come out to read some
Emerson. Have you ever read him?'

'I have,' said Kathleen. 'Some.'

'I've got him inside my shirt. I got some Rosicrucian
literature with me, too, but I'm fed up with them.'

The wind had changed a little—the waves were stronger
further down, and they walked along the foaming edge of
the water.

'What's your work,' the negro asked Stahr.

'I work for the pictures.'

'Oh.' After a moment he added, 'I never go to movies.'

'Why not?' asked Stahr sharply.

'There's no profit. I never let my children go.'

Stahr watched him, and Kathleen watched Stahr pro-
tectively.

'Some of them are good,' she said, against a wave of
spray; but he did not hear her. She felt she could contradict
him and said it again, and this time he looked at her
indifferently.

'Are the Rosicrucian brotherhood against pictures?'
asked Stahr.

'Seems as if they don't know what they *are* for. One week
they for one thing and next week for another.'

Only the little fish were certain. Half an hour had gone,

and still they came. The negro's two pails were full, and finally he went off over the beach towards the road, unaware that he had rocked an industry.

Stahr and Kathleen walked back to the house, and she thought how to drive his momentary blues away.

'Poor old Sambo,' she said.

'What?'

'Don't you call them poor old Sambo?'

'We don't call them anything especially.' After a moment, he said, 'They have pictures of their own.'

In the house she drew on her shoes and stockings before the heater.

'I like California better,' she said deliberately. 'I think I was a bit sex-starved.'

'That wasn't quite all, was it?'

'You know it wasn't.'

'It's nice to be near you.'

She gave a little sigh as she stood up, so small that he did not notice it.

'I don't want to lose you now,' he said. 'I don't know what you think of me or whether you think of me at all. As you've probably guessed, my heart's in the grave—' He hesitated, wondering if this was quite true. '—but you're the most attractive woman I've met since I don't know when. I can't stop looking at you. I don't know now exactly the colour of your eyes, but they make me sorry for everyone in the world——'

'Stop it, stop it!' she cried laughing. 'You'll have me looking in the mirror for weeks. My eyes aren't any colour—they're just eyes to see with, and I'm just as ordinary as I can be. I have nice teeth for an English girl——'

'You have beautiful teeth.'

'—but I couldn't hold a candle to these girls I see here ——'

'*You* stop it,' he said. 'What I said is true, and I'm a cautious man.'

She stood motionless a moment—thinking. She looked

9*

at him, then she looked back into herself, then at him again
—then she gave up her thought.

'We must go,' she said.

Now they were different people as they started back. Four
times they had driven along the shore road to-day, each time
a different pair. Curiosity, sadness and desire were behind
them now; this was a true returning—to themselves and all
their past and future and the encroaching presence of to-
morrow. He asked her to sit close in the car, and she did,
but they did not seem close, because for that you have to
seem to be growing closer. Nothing stands still. It was
on his tongue to ask her to come to the house he rented
and sleep there to-night—but he felt that it would
make him sound lonely. As the car climbed the hill to
her house, Kathleen looked for something behind the seat
cushion.

'What have you lost?'

'It might have fallen out,' she said, feeling through her
purse in the darkness.

'What was it?'

'An envelope.'

'Was it important?'

'No.'

But when they got to her house and Stahr turned on the
dashboard light, she helped take the cushions out and look
again.

'It doesn't matter,' she said, as they walked to the door.
'What's your address where you really live?'

'Just Bel-air. There's no number.'

'Where is Bel-air?'

'It's a sort of development, near Santa Monica. But you'd
better call me at the studio.'

'All right . . . good night, Mr. Stahr.'

'*Mister* Stahr,' he repeated, astonished.

She corrected herself gently.

'Well, then, good night, Stahr. Is that better?'

He felt as though he had been pushed away a little.

'As you like,' he said. He refused to let the aloofness communicate itself. He kept looking at her and moved his head from side to side in her own gesture, saying without words: 'You know what's happened to me.' She sighed. Then she came into his arms and for a moment was his again completely. Before anything could change, Stahr whispered good night and turned away and went to his car.

Winding down the hill, he listened inside himself as if something by an unknown composer, powerful and strange and strong, was about to be played for the first time. The theme would be stated presently, but because the composer was always new, he would not recognize it as the theme right away. It would come in some such guise as the auto horns from the technicolor boulevards below, or be barely audible, a tattoo on the muffled drum of the moon. He strained to hear it, knowing only that music was beginning, new music that he liked and did not understand. It was hard to react to what one could entirely compass—this was new and confusing, nothing one could shut off in the middle and supply the rest from an old score.

Also, and persistently, and bound up with the other, there was the negro on the sand. He was waiting at home for Stahr, with his pails of silver fish, and he would be waiting at the studio in the morning. He had said that he did not allow his children to listen to Stahr's story. He was prejudiced and wrong, and he must be shown somehow, some way. A picture, many pictures, a decade of pictures, must be made to show him he was wrong. Since he had spoken, Stahr had thrown four pictures out of his plans—one that was going into production this week. They were borderline pictures in point of interest, but at least he submitted the borderline pictures to the negro and found them trash. And he put back on his list a difficult picture that he had tossed to the wolves, to Brady and Marcus and the rest, to get his way on something else. He rescued it for the negro man.

When he drove up to his door, the porch lights went on.

and his Philippino came down the steps to put away the car. In the library, Stahr found a list of phone calls:

La Borwitz
Marcus
Harlow
Reinmund
Fairbanks
Brady
Colman
Skouras
Fleishacker, *etc.*

The Philippino came into the room with a letter.
'This fell out of the car,' he said.
'Thanks,' said Stahr. 'I was looking for it.'
'Will you be running a picture to-night, Mr. Stahr?'
'No, thanks—you can go to bed.'
The letter, to his surprise, was addressed to Monroe Stahr, Esq. He started to open it—then it occurred to him that she had wanted to recapture it, and possibly to withdraw it. If she had had a phone, he would have called her for permission before opening it. He held it for a moment. It had been written before they met—it was odd to think that whatever it said was now invalidated; it possessed the interest of a souvenir by representing a mood that was gone.

Still he did not like to read it without asking her. He put it down beside a pile of scripts and sat down with the top script in his lap. He was proud of resisting his first impulse to open the letter. It seemed to prove that he was not 'losing his head.' He had never lost his head about Minna, even in the beginning—it had been the most appropriate and regal match imaginable. She had loved him always and just before she died, all unwilling and surprised, his tenderness had burst and surged forward and he had been in love with her. In love with Minna and death together—with the world in which she looked so alone that he wanted to go with her there.

But 'falling for dames' had never been an obsession—his

brother had gone to pieces over a dame, or rather over dame after dame after dame. But Stahr, in his younger days, had them once and never more than once—like one drink. He had quite another sort of adventure reserved for his mind— something better than a series of emotional sprees. Like many brilliant men, he had grown up dead cold. Beginning at about twelve, probably, with the total rejection common to those of extraordinary mental powers, the 'See here : this is all wrong—a mess—all a lie—and a sham—,' he swept it all away, everything, as men of his type do; and then instead of being a son-of-a-bitch as most of them are, he looked around at the barrenness that was left and said to himself, '*This* will never do.' And so he had learned tolerance, kindness, forbearance, and even affection like lessons.

The Philippino boy brought in a carafe of water and bowls of nuts and fruit, and said good night. Stahr opened the first script and began to read.

He read for three hours—stopping from time to time, editing without a pencil. Sometimes he looked up, warm from some vague happy thought that was not in the script, and it took him a minute each time to remember what it was. Then he knew it was Kathleen, and he looked at the letter— it was nice to have a letter.

It was three o'clock when a vein began to bump in the back of his hand, signalling that it was time to quit. Kathleen was really far away now with the waning night—the different aspects of her telescoped into the memory of a single thrilling stranger, bound to him only by a few slender hours. It seemed perfectly all right to open the letter.

DEAR MR. STAHR,

In half an hour I will be keeping my date with you. When we say good-bye I will hand you this letter. It is to tell you that I am to be married soon and that I won't be able to see you after to-day.

I should have told you last night but it didn't seem

to concern you. And it would seem silly to spend this
beautiful afternoon telling you about it and watching
your interest fade. Let it fade all at once—now. I will
have told you enough to convince you that I am
Nobody's Prize Potato. (I have just learned that expression—from my hostess of last night, who called and
stayed an hour. She seems to believe that everyone is
Nobody's Prize Potato—except you. I think I am
supposed to tell you she thinks this, so give her a job
if you can.)

I am very flattered that anyone who sees so many
lovely women—I can't finish this sentence but you
know what I mean. And I will be late if I don't go to
meet you right now.

> With All Good Wishes
> KATHLEEN MOORE.

Stahr's first feeling was like fear; his second thought was
that the letter was invalidated—she had even tried to
retrieve it. But then he remembered 'Mister Stahr' just at
the end, and that she had asked him his address—she had
probably already written another letter which would also
say good-bye. Illogically he was shocked by the letter's
indifference to what had happened later. He read it again,
realizing that it foresaw nothing. Yet in front of the house
she had decided to let it stand, belittling everything that had
happened, curving her mind away from the fact that there
had been no other man in her consciousness that afternoon.
But he could not even believe this now, and the whole
adventure began to peel away even as he recapitulated it
searchingly to himself. The car, the hill, the hat, the music,
the letter itself, blew off like the scraps of tar paper from the
rubble of his house. And Kathleen departed, packing up
her remembered gestures, her softly moving head, her sturdy
eager body, her bare feet in the wet swirling sand. The skies
paled and faded—the wind and rain turned dreary, washing
the silver fish back to sea. It was only one more day, and
nothing was left except the pile of scripts upon the table.

He went upstairs. Minna died again on the first landing, and he forgot her lingeringly and miserably again, step by step to the top. The empty floor stretched around him—the doors with no one sleeping behind. In his room, Stahr took off his tie, untied his shoes and sat on the side of his bed. It was all closed out, except for something that he could not remember; then he remembered: her car was still down in the parking lot of the hotel. He set his clock to give him six hours' sleep.

This is Cecilia taking up the story. I think it would be most interesting to follow my own movements at this point, as this is a time in my life that I am ashamed of. What people are ashamed of usually makes a good story.

When I sent Wylie over to Martha Dodd's table, he had no success in finding out who the girl was, but it had suddenly become my chief interest in life. Also, I guesssed—correctly—that it would be Martha Dodd's. To have had at your table a girl who is admired by royalty, who may be tagged for a coronet in our little feudal system—and not even know her name!

I had only a speaking acquaintance with Martha, and it would be too obvious to approach her directly, but I went out to the studio Monday and dropped in on Jane Meloney.

Jane Meloney was quite a friend of mine. I thought of her rather as a child thinks of a family dependent. I knew she was a writer, but I grew up thinking that writer and secretary were the same, except that a writer usually smelled of cocktails and came more often to meals. They were spoken of the same way when they were not around—except for a species called playwrights, who came from the East. These were treated with respect if they did not stay long—if they did, they sank with the others into the white collar class.

Jane's office was in the 'old writers' building.' There was one on every lot, a row of iron maidens left over from silent days and still resounding with the dull moans of cloistered hacks and bums. There was the story of the new producer

who had gone down the line one day and then reported
excitedly to the head office.

'Who are those men?'

'They're supposed to be writers.'

'I thought so. Well, I watched them for ten minutes and
there were two of them that didn't write a line.'

Jane was at her typewriter, about to break off for lunch.
I told her frankly that I had a rival.

'It's a dark horse,' I said. 'I can't even find out her name.'

'Oh,' said Jane. 'Well, maybe I know something about
that. I heard something from somebody.'

The somebody, of course, was her nephew, Ned Sollinger,
Stahr's office boy. He had been her pride and hope. She had
sent him through New York University, where he played
on the football team. Then in his first year at medical
school, after a girl turned him down, he dissected out the
least publicized section of a lady corpse and sent it to the
girl. Don't ask me why? In disgrace with fortune and men's
eyes, he had begun life at the bottom again, and was still there.

'What do you know?' I asked.

'It was the night of the earthquake. She fell into the lake
on the back lot, and he dove in and saved her life. Someone
else told me it was his balcony she jumped off of and broke
her arm.'

'Who was she?'

'Well, that's funny, too——'

Her phone rang, and I waited restlessly during a long
conversation she had with Joe Reinmund. He seemed to be
trying to find out over the phone how good she was or
whether she had ever written any pictures at all. And she
was reputed to have been on the set the day Griffith invented
the close-up! While he talked she groaned silently, writhed,
made faces into the receiver, held it all in her lap so that the
voice reached her faintly—and kept up a side chatter to me.

'What is *he* doing—killing time between appointments?
. . . He's asked me every one of these questions ten times . . .
that's all on a memorandum I sent him. . . . '

And into the phone:

'If this goes up to Monroe, it won't be my doing. I want to go right through to the end.'

She shut her eyes in agony again.

'Now he's casting it . . . he's casting the minor characters . . . he's going to have Buddy Ebson. . . . My God, he just hasn't anything to do . . . now he's on Walter Davenport—he means Donald Crisp . . . he's got a big casting directory open in his lap and I can hear him turn the pages . . . he's a big important man this morning, a second Stahr, and for Christ sake I've got two scenes to do before lunch.'

Reinmund quit finally or was interrupted at his end. A waiter came in from the commissary with Jane's luncheon and a Coca-Cola for me—I wasn't lunching that summer. Jane wrote down one sentence on her typewriter before she ate. It interested me the way she wrote. One day I was there when she and a young man had just lifted a story out of *The Saturday Evening Post*—changing the characters and all. Then they began to write it, making each line answer the line before it, and of course it sounded just like people do in life when they're straining to be anything—funny or gentle or brave. I always wanted to see that one on the screen, but I missed it somehow.

I found her as lovable as a cheap old toy. She made three thousand a week, and her husbands all drank and beat her nearly to death. But to-day I had an axe to grind.

'You don't know her name?' I persisted.

'Oh—' said Jane, 'that. Well, he kept calling her up afterwards, and he told Katy Doolan it was the wrong name, after all.'

'I think he found her,' I said. 'Do you know Martha Dodd?'

'Hasn't that little girl had a tough break, though!' she exclaimed with ready theatrical sympathy.

'Could you possibly invite her to lunch to-morrow?'

'Oh, I think she gets enough to eat all right. There's a Mexican——'

I explained that my motives were not charitable. Jane agreed to co-operate. She called Martha Dodd.

We had lunch next day at the Bev Brown Derby, a languid restaurant, patronized for its food by clients who always look as if they'd like to lie down. There is some animation at lunch, where the women put on a show for the first five minutes after they eat, but we were a tepid three-some. I should have come right out with my curiosity. Martha Dodd was an agricultural girl, who had never quite understood what had happened to her and had nothing to show for it except a washed-out look about the eyes. She still believed that the life she had tasted was reality and this was only a long waiting.

'I had a beautiful place in 1928,' she told us, '—thirty acres, with a miniature golf course and a pool and a gorgeous view. All spring I was up to my ass in daisies.'

I ended by asking her to come over and meet Father. This was pure penance for having had 'a mixed motive' and being ashamed of it. One doesn't mix motives in Holly-wood—it is confusing. Everybody understands, and the climate wears you down. A mixed motive is conspicuous waste.

Jane left us at the studio gate, disgusted by my cowardice. Martha had worked up inside to a pitch about her career— not a very high pitch, because of seven years of neglect, but a sort of nervous acquiescence, and I was going to speak strongly to Father. They never did anything for people like Martha, who had made them so much money at one time. They let them slip away into misery eked out with extra work—it would have been kinder to ship them out of town. And Father was being so proud of me this summer. I had to keep him from telling everybody just how I had been brought up so as to produce such a perfect jewel. And Bennington—oh, what an exclusive—dear God, my heart. I assured him there was the usual proportion of natural-born skivvies and biddies tastefully concealed by throw-overs from sex Fifth Avenue; but Father had worked himself up to practically an alumnus. 'You've had everything,' he used to say happily. Everything included roughly the two years in Florence, where I managed against heavy odds to be the only virgin in school, and the courtesy début in Boston, Massachusetts. I was a veritable flower of the fine old cost-and-gross aristocracy.

So I knew he would do something for Martha Dodd, and as we went into his office, I had great dreams of doing something for Johnny Swanson, the cowboy, too, and Evelyn Brent, and all sorts of discarded flowers. Father was a charming and sympathetic man—except for that time I had seen him unexpectedly in New York—and there was something touching about his being my father. After all, he was *my* father—he would do anything in the world for me.

Only Rosemary Schmiel was in the outer office, and she was on Birdy Peter's phone. She waved for me to sit down, but I was full of my plans and, telling Martha to take it easy, I pressed the clicker under Rosemary's desk and went towards the opened door.

'Your father's in conference,' Rosemary called. 'Not in conference, but I ought to——'

By this time I was through the door and a little vestibule and another door, and caught Father in his shirtsleeves, very sweaty and trying to open a window. It was a hot day, but I hadn't realized it was that hot, and thought he was ill.

'No, I'm all right,' he said. 'What is it?'

I told him. I told him the whole theory of people like Martha Dodd, walking up and down his office. How could he use them and guarantee them regular employment? He seemed to take me up excitedly and kept nodding and agreeing, and I felt closer to him than I had for a long time. I came close and kissed him on his cheek. He was trembling and his shirt was soaked through.

'You're not well,' I said, 'or you're in some sort of stew.'

'No, I'm not at all.'

'What is it?'

'Oh, it's Monroe,' he said. 'That goddam little Vine Street Jesus! He's in my hair night and day!'

'What's happened?' I asked, very much cooler.

'Oh, he sits like a little goddam priest or rabbi and says

what he'll do and he won't do. I can't tell you now—I'm
half crazy. Why don't you go along?'

'I won't have you like this.'

'Go along, I tell you!' I sniffed, but he never drank.

'Go and brush your hair,' I said. 'I want you to see
Martha Dodd.'

'In here! I'd never get rid of her.'

'Out there then. Go wash up first. Put on another shirt.'

With an exaggerated gesture of despair, he went into the
little bathroom adjoining. It was hot in the office as if it
had been closed for hours, and maybe that was making him
sick, so I opened two more windows.

'You go along,' Father called from behind the closed door
of the bathroom. 'I'll be there presently.'

'Be awfully nice to her,' I said. 'No charity.'

As if it were Martha speaking for herself, a long low
moan came from somewhere in the room. I was startled—
then transfixed, as it came again, not from the bathroom
where Father was, not from outside, but from a closet in the
wall across from me. How I was brave enough I don't know,
but I ran across to it and opened it, and Father's secretary,
Birdy Peters, tumbled out stark naked—just like a corpse in
the movies. With her came a gust of stifling, stuffy air. She
flopped sideways on the floor, with the one hand still
clutching some clothes, and lay on the floor bathed in sweat
—just as Father came in from the bathroom. I could feel
him standing behind me, and without turning I knew
exactly how he looked, for I had surprised him before.

'Cover her up,' I said, covering her up myself with a
rug from the couch. 'Cover her *up*!'

I left the office. Rosemary Schmiel saw my face as I came
out and responded with a terrified expression. I never saw
her again or Birdy Peters either. As Martha and I went out,
Martha asked: 'What's the matter, dear?'—and when I
didn't say anything: 'You did your best. Probably it was
the wrong time. I'll tell you what I'll do. I'll take you to see
a very nice English girl. Did you see the girl that Stahr
danced with at our table the other night?'

So at the price of a little immersion in the family drains I had what I wanted.

I don't remember much about our call. She wasn't at home was one reason. The screen door of her house was unlocked, and Martha went in calling 'Kathleen' with bright familiarity. The room we saw was bare and formal as an hotel; there were flowers about, but they did not look like sent flowers. Also, Martha found a note on the table, which said: 'Leave the dress. Have gone looking for a job. Will drop by to-morrow.'

Martha read it twice but it didn't seem to be for Stahr, and we waited five minutes. People's houses are very still when they are gone. Not that I expect them to be jumping around, but I leave the observation for what it's worth. Very still. Prim almost, with just a fly holding down the place and paying no attention to you, and the corner of a curtain blowing.

'I wonder what kind of a job,' said Martha. 'Last Sunday she went somewhere with Stahr.'

But I was no longer interested. It seemed awful to be here —producer's blood, I thought in horror. And in quick panic I pulled her out into the placid sunshine. It was no use—I felt just black and awful. I had always been proud of my body—I had a way of thinking of it as geometric which made everything it did seem all right. And there was probably not any kind of place, including churches and office and shrines, where people had not embraced—but no one had ever stuffed me naked into a hole in the wall in the middle of a business day.

'If you were in a drug-store,' said Stahr, '—having a prescription filled——'

'You mean a chemist's?' Boxley asked.

'If you were in a chemist's,' conceded Stahr, 'and you were getting a prescription for some member of your family who was very sick——'

'—Very ill?' queried Boxley.

10 + S.F.

'Very ill. *Then* whatever caught your attention through the window, whatever distracted you and held you would probably be material for pictures.'

'A murder outside the window, you mean.'

'There you go,' said Stahr, smiling. 'It might be a spider working on the pane.'

'Of course—I see.'

'I'm afraid you don't, Mr. Boxley. You see it for *your* medium, but not for ours. You keep the spiders for yourself and you try to pin the murders on us.'

'I might as well leave,' said Boxley. 'I'm no good to you. I've been here three weeks and I've accomplished nothing. I make suggestions, but no one writes them down.'

'I want you to stay. Something in you doesn't like pictures, doesn't like telling a story this way——'

'It's such a damned bother,' exploded Boxley. 'You can't let yourself go——'

He checked himself. He knew that Stahr, the helmsman, was finding time for him in the middle of a constant stiff blow—that they were talking in the always creaking rigging of a ship sailing in great awkward tacks along an open sea. Or else—it seemed at times—they were in a huge quarry—where even the newly-cut marble bore the tracery of old pediments, half-obliterated inscriptions of the past.

'I keep wishing you could start over,' Boxley said. 'It's this mass production.'

'That's the condition,' said Stahr. 'There's always some lousy condition. We're making a life of Rubens—suppose I asked you to do portraits of rich dopes like Bill Brady and me and Garry Cooper and Marcus when you wanted to paint Jesus Christ! Wouldn't you feel you had a condition? Our condition is that we have to take people's own favourite folklore and dress it up and give it back to them. Anything beyond that is sugar. So won't you give us some sugar, Mr. Boxley?'

Boxley knew he could sit with Wylie White to-night at the Troc raging at Stahr, but he had been reading Lord Charnwood and he recognized that Stahr like Lincoln was a leader carrying on a long war on many fronts; almost single-handed he had moved pictures sharply forward through a decade, to a point where the content of the 'A productions' was wider and richer than that of the stage. Stahr was an artist only, as Mr. Lincoln was a general, perforce and as a layman.

'Come down to La Borwitz' office with me,' said Stahr. 'They sure need some sugar there.'

In La Borwitz' office, two writers, a shorthand secretary and a hushed supervisor, sat in a tense smoky stalemate, where Stahr had left them three hours before. He looked at the faces one after another and found nothing. La Borwitz spoke with awed reverence for his defeat.

'We've just got too many characters, Monroe.'

Stahr snorted affably.

'That's the principal idea of the picture.'

He took some change out of his pocket, looked up at the suspended light and tossed up half a dollar, which clanked into the bowl. He looked at the coins in his hands and selected a quarter.

La Borwitz watched miserably; he knew this was a favourite idea of Stahr's and he saw the sands running out. At the moment everyone's back was towards him. Suddenly he brought up his hands from their placid position under the desk and threw them high in the air, so high that they seemed to leave his wrist—and then he caught them neatly as they were descending. After that he felt better. He was in control.

One of the writers had taken out some coins, also, and presently rules were defined. 'You have to toss your coin through the chains without hitting them. Whatever falls into the light is the kitty.'

They played for half an hour—all except Boxley, who sat aside and dug into the script, and the secretary, who kept tally. She calculated the cost of the four men's time, arriving at a figure of sixteen hundred dollars. At the end, La Borwitz was winner by $5.50, and a janitor brought in a step-ladder to take the money out of the light.

Boxley spoke up suddenly.

'You have the stuffings of a turkey here,' he said.

'What!'

'It's not pictures.'

They looked at him in astonishment. Stahr concealed a smile.

'So we've got a real picture man here!' exclaimed La Borwitz.

'A lot of beautiful speeches,' said Boxley boldly, 'but no situations. After all, you know, it's not going to be a novel. And it's too long. I can't exactly describe how I feel, but it's not quite right. And it leaves me cold.'

He was giving them back what had been handed him for three weeks. Stahr turned away, watching the others out of the corner of his eye.

'We don't need *less* characters,' said Boxley. 'We need *more*. As I see it, that's the idea.'

'That's the idea,' said the writers.

'Yes—that's the idea,' said La Borwitz.

Boxley was inspired by the attention he had created.

'Let each character see himself in the other's place,' he said. 'The policeman is about to arrest the thief when he sees that the thief actually has *his* face. I mean, show it that way. You could almost call the thing *Put Yourself in My Place*.'

Suddenly they were at work again—taking up this new theme in turn like hepcats in a swing band and going to town with it. They might throw it out again to-morrow, but life had come back for a moment. Pitching the coins had done it as much as Boxley. Stahr had re-created the proper atmosphere—never consenting to be a driver of the driven, but feeling like and acting like and even sometimes looking like a small boy getting up a show.

He left them, touching Boxley on the shoulder in passing —a deliberate accolade—he didn't want them to gang up on him and break his spirit in an hour.

Doctor Baer was waiting in his inner office. With him was a coloured man with a portable cardiograph like a huge

suitcase. Stahr called it the lie detector. Stahr stripped to
the waist, and the weekly examination began.

'How've you been feeling?'

'Oh—the usual,' said Stahr.

'Been hard at it? Getting any sleep?'

'No—about five hours. If I go to bed early, I just lie
there.'

'Take the sleeping pills.'

'The yellow one gives me a hangover.'

'Take two red ones, then.'

'That's a nightmare.'

'Take one of each—the yellow first.'

'All right—I'll try. How've *you* been?'

'Say—I take care of myself, Monroe, I save myself.'

'The hell you do—you're up all night sometimes.'

'Then I sleep all next day.'

After ten minutes, Baer said:

'Seems O.K. The blood pressure's up five points.'

'Good,' said Stahr. 'That's good, isn't it?'

'That's good. I'll develop the cardiographs to-night.
When are you coming away with me?'

'Oh, some time,' said Stahr lightly. 'In about six weeks
thing'll ease up.'

Baer looked at him with a genuine liking that had grown
over three years.

'You got better in thirty-three when you laid up,' he
said. 'Even for three weeks.'

'I will again.'

No he wouldn't, Baer thought. With Minna's help he
had enforced a few short rests years ago and lately he had
hinted around, trying to find who Stahr considered his
closest friends. Who could take him away and keep him
away? It would almost surely be useless. He was due to die
very soon now. Within six months one could say definitely.
What was the use of developing the cardiograms? You
couldn't persuade a man like Stahr to stop and lie down and
look at the sky for six months. He would much rather die.
He said differently, but what it added up to was the definite

urge towards total exhaustion that he had run into before.
Fatigue was a drug as well as a poison, and Stahr apparently
derived some rare almost physical pleasure from working
lightheaded with weariness. It was a perversion of the life
force he had seen before, but he had almost stopped trying
to interfere with it. He had cured a man or so—a hollow
triumph of killing and preserving the shell.

'You hold your own,' he said.

They exchanged a glance. Did Stahr know? Probably.
But he did not know when—he did not know how soon
now.

'If I hold my own, I can't ask more,' said Stahr.

The coloured man had finished packing the apparatus.

'Next week same time?'

'O.K., Bill,' said Stahr. 'Good-bye.'

As the door closed, Stahr switched open the dictagraph.
Miss Doolan's voice came through immediately.

'Do you know a Miss Kathleen Moore?'

'What do you mean?' he asked startled.

'A Miss Kathleen Moore is on the line. She said you
asked her to call.'

'Well, my God!' he exclaimed. He was swept with
indignant rapture. It had been five days—this would never
do at all.

'She's on now?'

'Yes.'

'Well, all right then.'

In a moment he heard the voice up close to him.

'Are you married?' he asked, low and surly.

'No, not yet.'

His memory blocked out her face and form—as he sat
down, she seemed to lean down to his desk, keeping level
with his eyes.

'What's on your mind?' he asked in the same surly voice.
It was hard to talk that way.

'You did find the letter?' she asked.

'Yes. It turned up that night.'

'That's what I want to speak to you about.'

He found an attitude at length—he was outraged.

'What is there to talk about?' he demanded.

'I tried to write you another letter, but it wouldn't write.'

'I know that, too.'

There was a pause.

'Oh, cheer up!' she said surprisingly. 'This doesn't sound like you. It *is* Stahr, isn't it? That very nice Mr. Stahr?'

'I feel a little outraged,' he said almost pompously. 'I don't see the use of this. I had at least a pleasant memory of you.'

'I don't believe it's you,' she said. 'Next thing you'll wish me luck.' Suddenly she laughed: 'Is this what you planned to say? I know how *awful* it gets when you plan to say anything——'

'I never expected to hear from you again,' he said with dignity; but it was no use, she laughed again—a woman's laugh that is like a child's, just one syllable, a crow and a cry of delight.

'Do you know how you make me feel?' she demanded. 'Like a day in London during a caterpillar plague when a hot furry thing dropped in my mouth.'

'I'm sorry.'

'Oh, please wake up,' she begged. 'I want to see you. I can't explain things on the phone. It was no fun for me either, you understand.'

'I'm very busy. There's a sneak preview in Glendale to-night.'

'Is that an invitation?'

'George Boxley, the English writer, is going with me.' He surprised himself. 'Do you want to come along?'

'How could we talk?'

She considered. 'Why don't you call for me afterwards,' she suggested. 'We could ride around.'

Miss Doolan on the huge dictagraph was trying to cut in on the line with a shooting director—the only interruption ever permitted. He flipped the button and called 'Wait' impatiently into the machine.

'About eleven?' Kathleen was saying confidentially.

The idea of 'riding around' seemed so unwise that if he could have thought of the words to refuse her he would have spoken them, but he did not want to be the caterpillar. Suddenly he had no attitude left except the sense that the day, at least, was complete. He had an evening—a beginning, a middle and an end.

He rapped on the screen door, heard her call from inside, and stood waiting where the level fell away. From below came the whir of a lawn mower—a man was cutting his grass at midnight. The moon was so bright that Stahr could see him plainly, a hundred feet off and down, as he stopped and rested on the handle before pushing it back across his garden. There was a midsummer restlessness abroad—early August with imprudent loves and impulsive crimes. With little more to expect from summer, one tried anxiously to live in the present—or, if there was no present, to invent one.

She came at last. She was all different and delighted. She wore a suit with a skirt that she kept hitching up as they walked down to the car with a brave, gay, stimulating, reckless air of 'Tighten up your belt, baby. Let's get going.' Stahr had brought his limousine with the chauffeur, and the intimacy of the four walls whisking them along a new curve in the dark took away any strangeness at once. In its way, the little trip they made was one of the best times he had ever had in his life. It was certainly one of the times when, if he knew he was going to die, it was not to-night.

She told him her story. She sat beside him cool and gleaming for a while, spinning on excitedly, carrying him to far places with her, meeting and knowing the people she had known. The story was vague at first. 'This Man' was the one she had loved and lived with. 'This American' was the one who had rescued her when she was sinking into a quicksand.

'Who is he—the American?'

Oh, names—what did they matter? No one important

like Stahr, not rich. He had lived in London and now they would live out here. She was going to be a good wife, a real person. He was getting a divorce—not just on account of her—but that was the delay.

'But the first man?' asked Stahr. 'How did you get into that?'

Oh, that was a blessing at first. From sixteen to twenty-one the thing was to eat. The day her stepmother presented her at Court they had one shilling to eat with so as not to feel faint. Sixpence apiece, but the stepmother watched while she ate. After a few months the stepmother died, and she would have sold out for that shilling but she was too weak to go into the streets. London can be harsh—oh, quite.

Was there nobody?

There were friends in Ireland who sent butter. There was a soup kitchen. There was a visit to an uncle, who made advances to her when she had a full stomach, and she held out and got fifty pounds out of him for not telling his wife.

'Couldn't you work?' Stahr asked.

'I worked. I sold cars. Once I sold a car.'

'But couldn't you get a regular job?'

'It's hard—it's different. There was a feeling that people like me forced other people out of jobs. A women struck me when I tried to get a job as chambermaid in an hotel.'

'But you were presented at Court?'

'That was my stepmother who did that—on an off chance. I was nobody. My father was shot by the Black-and-Tans in twenty-two when I was a child. He wrote a book called *Last Blessing*. Did you ever read it?'

'I don't read.'

'I wish you'd buy it for the movies. It's a good little book. I still get a royalty from it—ten shillings a year.'

Then she met 'The Man' and they travelled the world around. She had been to all the places that Stahr made movies of, and lived in cities whose name he had never heard. Then The Man went to seed, drinking and sleeping with the housemaids and trying to force her off on his friends. They all tried to make her stick with him. They said she had saved him and should cleave to him longer now, indefinitely, to the end. It was her duty. They brought enormous pressure to bear. But she had met The American, and so finally she ran away.

'You should have run away before.'

'Well, you see, it was difficult.' She hesitated, and plunged. 'You see, I ran away from a king.'

His moralities somehow collapsed—she had managed to top him. A confusion of thoughts raced through his head— one of them a faint old credo that all royalty was diseased.

'It wasn't the King of England,' she said. 'My king was out of a job as he used to say. There are lots of kings in London.' She laughed—then added almost defiantly, 'He was very attractive until he began drinking and raising hell.'

'What was he king of?'

She told him—and Stahr visualized the face out of old newsreels.

'He was a very learned man,' she said. 'He could have taught all sorts of subjects. But he wasn't much like a king. Not nearly as much as you. None of them were.'

This time Stahr laughed.

'You know what I mean. They all felt old-fashioned. Most of them tried so hard to keep up with things. They were always advised to keep up with things. One was a syndicalist, for instance. And one used to carry around a couple of clippings about a tennis tournament when he was in the semi-finals. I saw those clippings a dozen times.'

They rode through Griffith Park and out past the dark studios of Burbank, past the airports, and along the way to Pasadena past the neon signs of roadside cabarets. Up in his head he wanted her, but it was late and just the ride was an overwhelming joy. They held hands and once she came close into his arms saying, 'Oh, you're *so* nice. I *do* like to be with you.' But her mind was divided—this was not his night as the Sunday afternoon had been his. She was absorbed in herself, stung into excitement by telling of her own adventures; he could not help wondering if he was getting the story she had saved up for The American.

'How long have you known The American?' he asked.

'Oh, I knew him for several months. We used to meet. We understand each other. He used to say, "It looks like a cinch from now on."'

'Then why did you call me up?'

She hesitated.

'I wanted to see you once more. Then, *too*—he was supposed to arrive to-day, but last night he wired that he'd be another week. I wanted to talk to a friend—after all, you *are* my friend.'

He wanted her very much now, but one part of his mind was cold and kept saying: She wants to see if I'm in love with her, if I want to marry her. Then she'd consider whether or not to throw this man over. She won't consider it till I've committed myself.

'Are you in love with The American?' he asked.

'Oh, yes. It's absolutely arranged. He saved my life and my reason. He's moving half-way around the world for me. I insisted on that.'

'But are you in love with him?'

'Oh, yes. I'm in love with him.'

The 'Oh, yes' told him she was not—told him to speak for himself—that she would see. He took her in his arms and kissed her deliberately on the mouth and held her for a long time. It was so warm.

'Not to-night,' she whispered.

'All right.'

They passed over suicide bridge with the high new wire.

'I know what it is,' she said, 'but how stupid. English people don't kill themselves when they don't get what they want.'

They turned around in the driveway of an hotel and started back. It was a dark night with no moon. The wave of desire had passed and neither spoke for a while. Her talk of kings had carried him oddly back in flashes to the pearly White Way of Main Street in Erie, Pennsylvania, when he was fifteen. There was a restaurant with lobsters in the window and green weeds and bright lights on a shell cavern, and beyond behind a red curtain the terribly strange brooding mystery of people and violin music. That was just before he left for New York. This girl reminded him of the fresh iced fish and lobsters in the window. She was Beautiful Doll. Minna had never been Beautiful Doll.

They looked at each other and her eyes asked, 'Shall I marry The American?' He did not answer. After a while he said:

'Let's go somewhere for the week-end.'

She considered.

'Are you talking about to-morrow?'

'I'm afraid I am.'

'Well, I'll tell you to-morrow,' she said.

'Tell me to-night. I'd be afraid——'

'—find a note in the car?' she laughed. 'No there's no note in the car. You know almost everything now.'

'Almost everything.'

'Yes—almost. A few little things.'

He would have to know what they were. She would tell him to-morrow. He doubted—he wanted to doubt—if there had been a maze of philandering: a fixation had held her to The Man, the king, firmly and long. Three years of a highly anomalous position—one foot in the palace and one in the background. 'You had to laugh a lot,' she said. 'I learned to laugh a lot.'

'He could have married you—like Mrs. Simpson,' Stahr said in protest.

'Oh, he was married. And he wasn't a romantic.' She stopped herself.

'Am I?'

'Yes,' she said unwillingly, as if she were laying down a trump. 'Part of you is. You're three or four different men but each of them out in the open. Like all Americans.'

'Don't start trusting Americans too implicitly,' he said smiling. 'They may be out in the open, but they change very fast.'

She looked concerned.

'Do they?'

'Very fast and all at once,' he said, 'and nothing ever changes them back.'

'You frighten me. I always had a great sense of security with Americans.'

She seemed suddenly so alone that he took her hand.

'Where will we go to-morrow?' he said. 'Maybe up in the mountains. I've got everything to do to-morrow, but I won't do any of it. We can start at four and get there by afternoon.'

'I'm not sure. I seem to be a little mixed up. This doesn't seem to be quite the girl who came out to California for a new life.'

He could have said it then, said, 'It *is* a new life,' for he knew it was, he knew he could not let her go now; but something else said to sleep on it as an adult, no romantic. And not to tell her till to-morrow. Still she was looking at him, her eyes wandering from his forehead to his chin and back again, and then up and down once more, with that odd slowly-waving motion of her head.

. . . It is your chance, Stahr. Better take it now. This is your girl. She can save you, she can worry you back to life. She will take looking after and you will grow strong to do it. But take her now—tell her and take her away. Neither of you knows it, but far away over the night The American has changed his plans. At this moment his train is speeding through Albuquerque; the schedule is accurate. The engineer is on time. In the morning he will be here.

. . . The chauffeur turned up the hill to Kathleen's house. It seemed warm even in darkness—wherever he had been near here was by way of being an enchanted place for Stahr : this limousine, the rising house at the beach, the very distances they had already covered together over the sprawled city. The hill they climbed now gave forth a sort of glow, a sustained sound that struck his soul alert with delight.

As he said good-bye he felt again that it was impossible to leave her, even for a few hours. There were only ten years between them, but he felt that madness about it akin to the love of an ageing man for a young girl. It was a deep and desperate time-need, a clock ticking with his heart, and it urged him, against the whole logic of his life, to walk past her into the house now and say, 'This is forever.'

Kathleen waited, irresolute herself—pink and silver frost waiting to melt with spring. She was a European, humble in the face of power, but there was a fierce self-respect that would only let her go so far. She had no illusions about the considerations that swayed princes.

'We'll go to the mountains to-morrow,' said Stahr. Many thousands of people depended on his balanced judgment—you can suddenly blunt a quality you have lived by for twenty years.

He was very busy the next morning, Saturday. At two o'clock, when he came from luncheon, there was a stack of telegrams—a company ship was lost in the Arctic; a star was in disgrace; a writer was suing for one million dollars. Jews were dead miserably beyond the sea. The last telegram stared up at him:

I was married at noon to-day. Good-bye; and on a sticker attached, *Send your answer by Western Union Telegram.*

CHAPTER VI

I KNEW NOTHING about any of this. I went up to Lake Louise, and when I came back didn't go near the studio. I think I would have started East in mid-August—if Stahr hadn't called me up one day at home.

'I want you to arrange something, Cecilia—I want to meet a Communist Party member.'

'Which one?' I asked, somewhat startled.

'Any one.'

'Haven't you got plenty out there?'

'I mean one of their organizers—from New York.'

The summer before I had been all politics—I could probably have arranged a meeting with Harry Bridges. But

my boy had been killed in an auto accident after I went back
to college, and I was out of touch with such things. I had
heard there was a man from *The New Masses* around somewhere.

'Will you promise him immunity?' I asked, joking.

'Oh, yes,' Stahr answered seriously. 'I won't hurt him.
Get one that can talk—tell him to bring one of his books
along.'

He spoke as if he wanted to meet a member of the 'I am'
cult.

'Do you want a blonde or a brunette?'

'Oh, get a man,' he said hastily.

Hearing Stahr's voice cheered me up—since I had barged
in on Father it had all seemed a paddling about in thin
spittle. Stahr changed everything about it—changed the
angle from which I saw it, changed the very air.

'I don't think your father ought to know,' he said. 'Can
we pretend the man is a Bulgarian musician or something?'

'Oh, they don't dress up any more,' I said.

It was harder to arrange than I thought—Stahr's
negotiations with the Writers' Guild, which had continued
over a year, were approaching a dead end. Perhaps they
were afraid of being corrupted, and I was asked what Stahr's
'proposition' was. Afterwards Stahr told me that he pre-
pared for the meeting by running off the Russian Revolu-
tionary films that he had in his film library at home. He also
ran off *Doctor Caligari* and Salvator Dali's *Le Chien Andalou*,
possibly suspecting that they had a bearing on the matter.
He had been startled by the Russian films back in the
twenties, and on Wylie White's suggestion he had had the
script department get him up a two-page 'treatment' of
the *Communist Manifesto*.

But his mind was closed on the subject. He was a
rationalist who did his own reasoning without benefit of
books—and he had just managed to climb out of a thousand
years of Jewry into the late eighteenth century. He could
not bear to see it melt away—he cherished the parvenu's
passionate loyalty to an imaginary past.

The meeting took place in what I called the 'processed leather room'—it was one of six done for us by a decorator from Sloane's years ago, and the term stuck in my head. It was *the* most decorator's room: an angora wool carpet the colour of dawn, the most delicate grey imaginable—you hardly dared walk on it; and the silver panelling and leather tables and creamy pictures and slim fragilities looked so easy to stain that we could not breathe hard in there, though it was wonderful to look into from the door when the windows were open and the curtains whimpered querulously against the breeze. It was a lineal descendant of the old American parlour that used to be closed except on Sunday. But it was exactly the room for the occasion, and I hoped that whatever happened would give it character and make it henceforth part of our house.

Stahr arrived first. He was white and nervous and troubled—except for his voice, which was always quiet and full of consideration. There was a brave personal quality in the way he would meet you—he would walk right up to you and put aside something that was in the way, and grow to know you all over as if he couldn't help himself. I kissed him for some reason, and took him into the processed leather room.

'When do you go back to college?' he asked.

We had been over this fascinating ground before.

'Would you like me if I were a little shorter?' I asked, 'I could wear low heels and plaster down my hair.'

'Let's have dinner to-night,' he suggested. 'People will think I'm your father but I don't mind.'

'I *love* old men,' I assured him. 'Unless the man has a crutch, I feel it's just a boy and girl affair.'

'Have you had many of those?'

'Enough.'

'People fall in and out of love all the time, don't they?'

'Every three years or so, Fanny Brice says. I just read it in the paper.'

'I wonder how they manage it,' he said. 'I know it's true because I see them. But they look so con*vinced* every time.

And then suddenly they don't look convinced. But they get convinced all over.'

'You've been making too many movies.'

'I wonder if they're as convinced the second time or the third time or the fourth time,' he persisted.

'More each time,' I said. 'Most of all the last time.'

He thought this over and seemed to agree.

'I suppose so. Most of all the last time.'

I didn't like the way he said this, and I suddenly saw that under the surface he was miserable.

'It's a great nuisance,' he said. 'It'll be better when it's over.'

'Wait a *min*ute! Perhaps pictures are in the wrong hands.'

Brimmer, the Party Member, was announced, and going to meet him I slid over to the door on one of those gossamer throw-rugs and practically into his arms.

He was a nice-looking man, this Brimmer—a little on the order of Spencer Tracy, but with a stronger face and a wider range of reactions written up in it. I couldn't help thinking as he and Stahr smiled and shook hands and squared off, that they were two of the most alert men I had ever seen. They were very conscious of each other immediately—both as polite to me as you please, but with a softening of the ends of their sentences when they turned in my direction.

'What are you people trying to do?' demanded Stahr. 'You've got my young men all upset.'

'That keeps them awake, doesn't it?' said Brimmer.

'First we let half a dozen Russians study the plant,' said Stahr. 'As a model plant, you understand. And then you try to break up the unity that makes it a model plant.'

'The unity?' Brimmer repeated. 'Do you mean what's known as The Company Spirit?'

'Oh, not that,' said Stahr, impatiently. 'It seems to be *me* you're after. Last week a writer came into my office—a drunk—a man who's been floating around for years just two steps out of the bughouse—and began telling me my business.'

Brimmer smiled.

'You don't look to me like a man who could be told his business, Mr. Stahr.'

They would both have tea. When I came back, Stahr was telling a story about the Warner Brothers and Brimmer was laughing with him.

'I'll tell you another one,' Stahr said. 'Balanchine the Russian Dancer had them mixed up with the Ritz Brothers. He didn't know which ones he was training and which ones he was working for. He used to go around saying, "I cannot train these Warner Brothers to dance."'

It looked like a quiet afternoon. Brimmer asked him why the producers didn't back the anti-Nazi League.

'Because of you people,' said Stahr. 'It's your way of getting at the writers. In the long view you're wasting your time. Writers are children—even in normal times they can't keep their minds on their work.'

'They're the farmers in this business,' said Brimmer pleasantly. 'They grow the grain but they're not in at the feast. Their feeling towards the producer is like the farmers' resentment of the city fellow.'

I was wondering about Stahr's girl—whether it was all over between them. Later, when I heard the whole thing from Kathleen, standing in the rain in a wretched road called Goldwyn Avenue, I figured out that this must have been a week after she sent him the telegram. She couldn't help the telegram. The man got off the train unexpectedly and walked her to the registry office without a flicker of doubt that this was what she wanted. It was eight in the morning, and Kathleen was in such a daze that she was chiefly concerned about how to get the telegram to Stahr. In theory you could stop and say, 'Listen, I forgot to tell you but I met a man.' But this track had been laid down so thoroughly, with such confidence, such struggle, such relief, that when it came along, suddenly cutting across the other, she found herself on it like a car on a closed switch. He watched her write the telegram, looking directly at it across the table, and she hoped he couldn't read upside down. . . .

When my mind came back into the room, they had

destroyed the poor writers—Brimmer had gone so far as
to admit they were 'unstable.'

'They are not equipped for authority,' said Stahr. 'There
is no substitute for will. Sometimes you have to fake will
when you don't feel it at all.'

'I've had that experience.'

'You have to say, "It's got to be like this—no other way"
—even if you're not sure. A dozen times a week that happens
to me. Situations where there is no real reason for anything.
You pretend there is.'

'All leaders have felt that,' said Brimmer. 'Labour
leaders, and certainly military leaders.'

'So I've had to take an attitude in this Guild matter. It
looks to me like a try for power, and all I am going to give
the writers is money.'

'You give some of them very little money. Thirty dollars
a week.'

'Who gets that?' asked Stahr, surprised.

'The ones that are commodities and easy to replace.'

'Not on my lot,' said Stahr.

'Oh, yes,' said Brimmer. 'Two men in your shorts department get thirty dollars a week.'

'Who?'

'Man named Ransome—man named O'Brien.'

Stahr and I smiled together.

'Those are not writers,' said Stahr. 'Those are cousins of
Cecilia's father.'

'There are some in other studios,' said Brimmer.

Stahr took his teaspoon and poured himself some
medicine from a little bottle.

'What's a fink?' he asked suddenly.

'A fink? That's a strike-breaker or a company tec.'

'I thought so,' said Stahr. 'I've got a fifteen hundred
dollar writer that every time he walks through the commissary keeps saying "Fink!" behind other writers' chairs.
If he didn't scare hell out of them, it'd be funny.'

Brimmer laughed.

'I'd like to see that,' he said.

'You wouldn't like to spend a day with me over there?'
suggested Stahr.

Brimmer laughed with genuine amusement.

'No, Mr. Stahr. But I don't doubt but that I'd be impressed. I've heard you're one of the hardest working and most efficient men in the entire West. It'd be a privilege to watch you, but I'm afraid I'll have to deny myself.'

Stahr looked at me.

'I like your friend,' he said. 'He's crazy, but I like him.' He looked closely at Brimmer: 'Born on this side?'

'Oh, yes. Several generations.'

'Many of them like you?'

'My father was a Baptist minister.'

'I mean are many of them Reds. I'd like to meet this big Jew that tried to blow over the Ford factory. What's his name—'

'Frankensteen?'

'That's the man. I guess some of you believe in it.'

'Quite a few,' said Brimmer dryly.

'Not you,' said Stahr.

A shade of annoyance floated across Brimmer's face.

'Oh, yes,' he said.

'Oh, no,' said Stahr. 'Maybe you did once.'

Brimmer shrugged his shoulders.

'Perhaps the boot's on the other foot,' he said. 'At the bottom of your heart, Mr. Stahr, you know I'm right.'

'No,' said Stahr, 'I think it's a bunch of tripe.'

'—you think to yourself, "He's right," but you think the system will last out your time.'

'You don't really think you're going to overthrow the government.'

'No, Mr. Stahr. But we think perhaps you are.'

They were nicking at each other—little pricking strokes like men do sometimes. Women do it, too; but it is a joined battle then with no quarter. But it is not pleasant to watch men do it, because you never know what's next. Certainly it wasn't improving the tonal associations of the room for me, and I moved them out the French window into our golden-yellow California garden.

It was midsummer, but fresh water from the gasping sprinklers made the lawn glitter like spring. I could see Brimmer look at it with a sigh in his glance—a way they have. He opened up big outside—inches taller than I thought and broad-shouldered. He reminded me a little of Superman when he takes off his spectacles. I thought he was as attractive as men can be who don't really care about women as such. We played a round robin game of ping-pong, and he handled his bat well. I heard Father come into the house singing that damn *Little Girl, You've Had a Busy Day*, and then breaking off, as if he remembered we weren't speaking any more. It was half past six—my car was standing in the drive, and I suggested we go down to the Trocadero for dinner.

Brimmer had that look that Father O'Ney had that time in New York when he turned his collar around and went with father and me to the Russian Ballet. He hadn't quite ought to be here. When Bernie, the photographer, who was waiting there for some big game or other, came up to our table, he looked trapped—Stahr made Bernie go away, and I would like to have had the picture.

Then, to my astonishment, Stahr had three cocktails, one after the other.

'Now I know you've been disappointed in love,' I said

'What makes you think that, Cecilia?'

'Cocktails.'

'Oh, I never drink, Cecilia. I get dyspepsia—I've never been tight.'

I counted them: '—two—*three*.'

'I didn't realize. I couldn't taste them. I thought there was something the matter.'

A silly glassy look darted into his eye—then passed away.

'This is my first drink in a week,' said Brimmer. 'I did my drinking in the Navy.'

The look was back in Stahr's eye—he winked fatuously at me and said:

'This soap-box son-of-a-bitch has been working on the Navy.'

Brimmer didn't know quite how to take this. Evidently he decided to include it with the evening, for he smiled faintly, and I saw Stahr was smiling, too. I was relieved when I saw it was safely in the great American tradition, and I tried to take hold of the conversation, but Stahr seemed suddenly all right.

'Here's my typical experience,' he said very succinctly and clearly to Brimmer. 'The best director in Hollywood— a man I never interfere with—has some streak in him that wants to slip a pansy into every picture, or something on that order. Something offensive. He stamps it in deep like a watermark so I can't get it out. Every time he does it the Legion of Decency moves a step forward, and something has to be sacrificed out of some honest film.'

'Typical organization trouble,' agreed Brimmer.

'Typical,' said Stahr. 'It's an endless battle. So now this director tells me it's all right because he's got a Director's Guild and I can't oppress the poor. That's how you add to my troubles.'

'It's a little remote from us,' said Brimmer smiling. 'I don't think we'd make much headway with the directors.'

'The directors used to be my pals,' said Stahr proudly.

It was like Edward the Seventh's boast that he had moved in the best society in Europe.

'But some of them have never forgiven me,' he continued, 'for bringing out stage directors when sound came in. It put them on their toes and made them learn their jobs all over, but they never did really forgive me. That time we imported a whole new hogshead full of writers, and I thought they were great fellows till they all went red.'

Gary Cooper came in and sat down in a corner with a bunch of men who breathed whenever he did and looked as if they lived off him and weren't budging. A woman across the room looked around and turned out to be Carole Lombard—I was glad that Brimmer was at least getting an eyeful.

Stahr ordered a whiskey and soda and, almost immediately, another. He ate nothing but a few spoonfuls of soup and he said all the awful things about everybody being lazy so-and-so's and none of it mattered to *him* because he had lots of money—it was the kind of talk you heard whenever Father and his friends were together. I think Stahr realized that it sounded pretty ugly outside of the proper company—maybe he had never heard how it sounded before. Anyhow he shut up and drank off a cup of black coffee. I loved him, and what he said didn't change that, but I hated Brimmer to carry off this impression. I wanted him to see Stahr as a sort of technological virtuoso, and here Stahr had been playing the wicked overseer to a point he would have called trash if he had watched it on the screen.

'I'm a production man,' he said, as if to modify his previous attitude. 'I like writers—I think I understand them. I don't want to kick anybody out if they do their work.'

'We don't want you to,' said Brimmer pleasantly. 'We'd like to take you over as a going concern.'

Stahr nodded grimly.

'I'd like to put you in a roomful of my partners. They've all got a dozen reasons for having Fitts run you fellows out of town.'

'We appreciate your protection,' said Brimmer with a certain irony. 'Frankly we *do* find you difficult, Mr. Stahr —precisely because you are a paternalistic employer and your influence is very great.'

Stahr was only half listening.

'I never thought,' he said, 'that I had more brains than a writer has. But I always thought that his brains *belonged* to me—because I knew how to use them. Like the Romans— I've heard that they never invented things but they knew what to do with them. Do you see? I don't say it's right. But it's the way I've always felt—since I was a boy.'

This interested Brimmer—the first thing that had interested him for an hour.

'You know yourself very well, Mr. Stahr,' he said.

I think he wanted to get away. He had been curious to see what kind of man Stahr was, and now he thought he knew. Still hoping things would be different, I rashly urged him to ride home with us, but when Stahr stopped by the bar for another drink I knew I'd made a mistake.

It was a gentle, harmless, motionless evening with a lot of Saturday cars. Stahr's hand lay along the back of the seat touching my hair. Suddenly I wished it had been about ten years ago—I would have been nine. Brimmer about eighteen and working his way through some mid-western college, and Stahr twenty-five, just having inherited the world and full of confidence and joy. We would both have looked up to Stahr so, without question. And here we were in an adult conflict, to which there was no peaceable solution, complicated now with exhaustion and drink.

We turned in at our drive, and I drove around to the garden again.

'I must go along now,' said Brimmer. 'I've got to meet some people.'

'No, stay,' said Stahr. 'I never have said what I wanted. We'll play ping-pong and have another drink, and then we'll tear into each other.'

Brimmer hesitated. Stahr turned on the floodlight and picked up his ping-pong bat, and I went into the house for some whiskey—I wouldn't have dared disobey him.

When I came back, they were not playing, but Stahr was batting a whole box of new balls across to Brimmer, who turned them aside. When I arrived, he quit and took the bottle and retired to a chair just out of the floodlight, watching in dark dangerous majesty. He was pale—he was so transparent that you could almost watch the alcohol mingle with the poison of his exhaustion.

'Time to relax on Saturday night,' he said.

'You're not relaxing,' I said.

He was carrying on a losing battle with his instinct towards schizophrenia.

'I'm going to beat up Brimmer,' he announced after a moment. 'I'm going to handle this thing personally.'

'Can't you pay somebody to do it?' asked Brimmer.

I signalled him to keep quiet.

'I do my own dirty work,' said Stahr. 'I'm going to beat hell out of you and put you on a train.'

He got up and came forward, and I put my arms around him, gripping him.

'Please *stop* this!' I said. 'Oh, you're being so bad.'

'This fellow has an influence over you,' he said darkly. 'Over all you young people. You don't know what you're doing.'

'Please go home,' I said to Brimmer.

Stahr's suit was made of slippery cloth and suddenly he slipped away from me and went for Brimmer. Brimmer retreated backwards around the table. There was an odd expression in his face, and afterwards I thought it looked as if he were saying, 'Is *this* all? This frail half-sick person holding up the whole thing.'

Then Stahr came close, his hands going up. It seemed to me that Brimmer held him off with his left arm a minute, and then I looked away—I couldn't bear to watch.

When I looked back, Stahr was out of sight below the level of the table, and Brimmer was looking down at him.

'Please go home,' I said to Brimmer.

'All right.' He stood looking down at Stahr as I came around the table. 'I always wanted to hit ten million dollars, but I didn't know it would be like this.'

Stahr lay motionless.

'Please go,' I said.

'I'm sorry. Can I help——'

'No. Please go. I understand.'

He looked again, a little awed at the depths of Stahr's repose, which he had created in a split second. Then he went quickly away over the grass, and I knelt down and shook Stahr. After a moment he came awake with a terrific convulsion and bounced up on his feet.

'Where is he?' he shouted.

'Who?' I asked innocently.

'That American. Why in hell did you have to marry him, you damn fool?'

'Monroe—he's gone. I didn't marry anybody.'

I pushed him down in a chair.

'He's been gone half an hour,' I lied.

The ping-pong balls lay around in the grass like a constellation of stars. I turned on a sprinkler and came back with a wet handkerchief, but there was no mark on Stahr—he must have been hit in the side of the head. He went off behind some trees and was sick, and I heard him kicking up some earth over it. After that he seemed all right, but he wouldn't go into the house till I got him some mouthwash, so I took back the whiskey bottle and got a mouthwash bottle. His wretched essay at getting drunk was over. I've been out with college freshmen, but for sheer ineptitude and absence of the Bacchic spirit it unquestionably took the cake. Every bad thing happened to him, but that was all.

We went in the house; the cook said Father and Mr. Marcus and Fleishacker were on the veranda, so we stayed in the 'processed leather room.' We both sat down in a couple of places and seemed to slide off, and finally I sat on a fur rug and Stahr on a footstool beside me.

'Did I hit him?' he asked.

'Oh, yes,' I said. 'Quite badly.'

'I don't believe it.' After a minute he added: 'I didn't want to hurt him. I just wanted to chase him out. I guess he got scared and hit me.'

If this was his interpretation of what had happened, it was all right with me.

'Do you hold it against him?'

'Oh, no,' he said. 'I was drunk.' He looked around. 'I've never been in here before—who did this room?—somebody from the studio?'

'Well, I'll have to get out of here,' he said in his old

pleasant way. 'How would you like to go out to Doug
Fairbanks' ranch and spend the night?' he asked me. 'I
know he'd love to have you.'

That's how the two weeks started that he and I went
around together. It only took one of them for Louella to
have us married.

*The manuscript stops at this point. The following synopsis of
the rest of the story has been put together from Fitzgerald's
notes and outlines and from the reports of persons with whom
he discussed his work:*

Soon after his interview with Brimmer, Stahr makes a
trip East. A wage-cut has been threatened in the studio, and
Stahr has gone to talk to the stockholders—presumably
with the idea of inducing them to retrench in some other
way. He and Brady have long been working at cross-
purposes, and the struggle between them for the control of
the company is rapidly coming to a climax. We do not know
about the results of this trip from the business point of view,
but, whether or not on a business errand, Stahr for the first
time visits Washington with the intention of seeing the city;
and it is to be presumed that the author had meant to return
here to the motif introduced in the first chapter with the
visit of the Hollywood people to the home of Andrew Jackson and their failure to gain admittance or even to see the
place clearly: the relation of the moving-picture industry to
the American ideals and tradition. It is mid-summer;
Washington is stifling; Stahr comes down with summer
grippe and goes around the city in a daze of fever and heat.
He never succeeds in becoming acquainted with it as he had
hoped to.

When he recovers and gets back to Hollywood, he finds
that Brady has taken advantage of his absence to put
through a fifty per cent pay-cut. Brady had called a meeting
of writers and told them in a tearful speech that he and the
other executives would take a cut themselves if the writers

would consent to take one. If they would agree, it would not be necessary to reduce the salaries of the stenographers and the other low-paid employees. The writers had accepted this arrangement, but had then been double-crossed by Brady, who had proceeded to slash the stenographers just the same. Stahr is revolted by this; and he and Brady have a violent falling-out. Stahr, though opposed to the unions, believing that any enterprising office-boy can make his way to the top as he has done, is an old-fashioned paternalistic employer, who likes to feel that the people who work for him are contented, and that he and they are on friendly terms. On the other hand, he quarrels also with Wylie White, who he finds has become truculently hostile to him, in spite of the fact that Stahr was not personally responsible for the pay-cut. Stahr has been patient in the past with White's drinking and his practical jokes, and he is hurt that the writer should not feel towards him the same kind of personal loyalty—which is the only solidarity that Stahr understands in the field of business relations. 'The Reds see him now as a conservative —Wall Street as a Red.' But he finds himself driven by the logic of the situation to fall in with the idea which has been proposed and is heartily approved by Brady, of setting up a company union.

As for his own position in the studio, he had in Washington already thought of quitting; but, intimately involved in the struggle, ill, unhappy and embittered though he is, it is difficult for him to surrender to Brady. In the meantime, he has been going around with Cecilia. The girl in a conversation with her father about the attentions Stahr has apparently been paying her, has carelessly let Brady know that Stahr is in love with someone else. Brady finds out about Kathleen, whom Stahr has been seeing again, and attempts to blackmail Stahr. Stahr in disgust with the Bradys abruptly drops Cecilia. He on his side has known for years—having learned it by way of his wife's trained nurse—that Brady had had a hand in the death of the husband of a woman with whom he (Brady) had been in love. The two men threaten one another with no really conclusive evidence on either side.

But Brady has an instrument ready to his hand. The man whom Kathleen has married—whose name is W. Bronson Smith—is a technician working in the studios, who has been taking an active part in his union. It is impossible to tell precisely how Scott Fitzgerald imagined the labour situation in Hollywood for the purposes of his story. At the time of which he is writing, the various kinds of technicians had already been organized in the International Alliance of Theatrical Stage Employees; and it is obvious that he intended to exploit the element of racketeering and gangsterism revealed in this organization by the case of William Bioff. Brady was to go to Kathleen's husband and play upon his jealousy of his wife. We do not know what Fitzgerald intended that these two should try to do to Stahr. Robinson, the cutter (there are notes on this character), was originally to have undertaken to murder him; but it seems more probable from the author's outline that Stahr was to be caught in some trap which would supply Kathleen's husband with grounds for bringing a suit against Stahr for alienation of his wife's affection. In Fitzgerald's story outline, the theme of Chapter VIII is indicated by the words, 'The suit and the price.' This is evidently partly explained by the following note of material which Fitzgerald intended to make use of, though it is impossible to tell how it was to be modified to meet the demands of the story : 'One of the —— brothers is accused by an employee of seducing his wife. Sued for alienation. They try to settle it out of court, but the man bringing suit is a labour leader and won't be bought. Neither will he divorce his wife. He considers rougher measures. His price is that —— shall go away for a year. ——'s instinct is to stay and fight it, but the other brothers get to a doctor and pronounce death sentence on him and retire him. He tries to get the girl to go with him, but is afraid of the Mann Act. She is to follow him and they'll go abroad.'

In any case, Stahr is to be saved by the intervention of the camera man, Pete Zavras, whom he has befriended at the beginning of the story, when Zavras had lost his standing with the studios.

In the meantime, Stahr is now seriously ill. He and Kathleen have been 'taking breathless chances.' They have succeeded in having 'one last fling,' which has taken place during an overpowering heat wave in the early part of September. But their meetings have proved unsatisfactory. The author has indicated in an early sketch that Kathleen was to 'come of very humble parents'—her father was to have been the captain of a Newfoundland fishing smack; and in another place he says that Stahr has found it difficult to accept her as a permanent part of his life because she is 'poor, unfortunate, and tagged with a middle-class exterior which doesn't fit in with the grandeur Stahr demands of life.' It is possible that the labour conflict in which her husband has become involved was intended to alienate her and Stahr. Stahr is now being pushed into the past by Brady and by the unions alike. The split between the controllers of the movie industry, on the one hand, and the various groups of employees, on the other, is widening and leaving no place for real individualists of business like Stahr, whose successes are personal achievements and whose career has always been invested with a certain personal glamour. He has held himself directly responsible to everyone with whom he has worked; he has even wanted to beat up his enemies himself. In Hollywood he is 'the last tycoon.'

Stahr has not been afraid, as we have seen in the conference in Chapter III, to risk money on unpopular films which would afford him some artistic satisfaction. He has had a craftsman's interest in the pictures, and it has been natural for him to want to make them better. But he has been 'lying low' since the wage-cut and has ceased to make pictures altogether. There was to have been a second series of scenes showing him at a story conference, at the rushes and on the sets, which was to have contrasted with the similar series in Chapters III and IV, and to have shown the change that has taken place in his attitude and status.

He must, however, stand up to Brady, who he knows will stop at nothing. He evidently fears Brady will murder him, for he now decides to resort to Brady's own methods and get his partner murdered. For this he apparently goes straight to the gangsters. It is not clear how the murder is to be accomplished; but in order to be away at the time, Stahr arranges a trip to New York. He sees Kathleen for the last time at the airport, and also meets Cecilia, who is going back to college on a different plane. On the plane he has a reaction of disgust against the course he has taken; he realizes that he has let himself be degraded to the same plane of brutality as Brady. He decides to call off the murder and intends to wire orders as soon as the plane descends at the next airport. But the plane has an accident and crashes before they reach the next stop. Stahr is killed, and the murder goes through. The ominous suicide of Schwartz in the opening chapter of the story is thus balanced by the death of Stahr. In the note that Schwartz had sent him, he had been trying to warn him against Brady, who had long wanted to get Stahr out of the company.

Stahr's funeral, which was to have been described in detail, is an orgy of Hollywood servility and hypocrisy. Everybody is weeping copiously or conspicuously stifling emotion with an eye on the right people. Cecilia imagines Stahr present and can hear him saying 'Trash!' The old cowboy actor, Johnny Swanson, who has been mentioned at the beginning of Chapter II and for whom in his forlorn situation Cecilia has later had the idea of trying to do something at the time of her visit to her father's office, has been invited to the funeral by mistake—through the confusion of his name with someone else's—and asked to officiate as pall-bearer along with the most intimate and important of the dead producer's friends. Johnny goes through with the ceremony, rather dazed; and then finds out, to his astonishment, that his fortunes have been gloriously restored. From this time on, he is deluged with offers of jobs.

In the meantime, a final glimpse of Fleishacker, the ambitious company lawyer, a man totally without conscience or creative brains, was to have shown him as prefiguring the immediate future of the moving-picture business. There was also to have been a passage towards the end between Fleishacker and Cecilia, in which the former, who has been to New York University and who was perhaps to have tried to marry Cecilia, was to have attempted a conversation with her on an 'intellectual' plane.

Cecilia, on the rebound from Stahr, has had an affair with a man she does not love—probably Wylie White, who has been after her from the first and who represents the opposition to Stahr. As a result of the death of Stahr and the murder of her father, she now breaks down completely. She develops tuberculosis, and we were to learn for the first time at the end that she has been putting together her story in a tuberculosis sanatorium.

We were to have had a final picture of Kathleen standing outside the studio. She has presumably separated from her husband as a result of the plot against Stahr. It had been one of her chief attractions for Stahr that she did not belong to the Hollywood world; and now she knows that she is never to be part of it. She is always to remain on the outside of things—a situation which also has its tragedy.